The Sands Motel
Sheila Kindellan-Sheehan

Library and Archives Canada Cataloguing in Publication

Sheehan, Sheila Kindellan, 19 -
        The Sands Motel / Sheila Margaret Kindellan-
Sheehan.

ISBN 1-896881-47-5

        I. Title.

PS8637.H44S36 2004   C813'.6   C2004-906094-5

Cover from a design by Glen Graham
Production design: Studio Melrose/Ted Sancton

Printed in Canada

Price-Patterson Ltd.
Canadian Publishers, Montreal, Quebec, Canada
www.pricepatterson.com

For Gina
A true believer

LIST OF CHARACTERS

The Sands Motel Guests

Larry Stormer (37) – an occasional dumpster worker at Publix

Steve Granger (28) – an occasional sweeper at Dunkin' Donuts

The C's

Caitlin Donovan (31) – English-speaking, recently widowed author and part-time professor from Westmount, Quebec, Canada (a suburb of Montreal, Canada's second largest city)

Carmen (28) – Caitlin's best friend, English-speaking, sales rep from Laval, Quebec (another suburb of Montreal)

The Other Club One Regulars

Morty (77) – retired businessman, former owner of a small hosiery store in New Jersey

Sarah (81) – his wife and the candy lady

Michel (56) – French-speaking, retired policeman from Quebec & his wife

Yvette (59) and her husband Pierre – French-speaking, wealthy couple from Quebec

Raoul – the handyman

And the others

The Miami-Dade Police (MDPD)

The Uniforms
Sergeant Tully
Officer Ruiz

The Suits
Detective First Class Maria Garderella
Detective Michael Dunn
Detective Ramirez

The Bad Boys
Harris Chalmer (24) – the leader, the "captain"
Bobby "Number Boy" Wells (21) – second-in-
    command, the bagman
Ian "Nipples" Johnson (19) – the insecure and
    perennial scapegoat
And the rest

The Other Memorable Characters:
Hilda (70) – the mall lady, and her animal entourage
Toothbrush (62) – Larry's friend, owner of The Bar

Nota bene: All temperatures in Fahrenheit.
                      100°F = 38°C
                       80°F = 27°C
                       60°F = 16°C
                       40°F = 4°C
                       32°F = 0°C

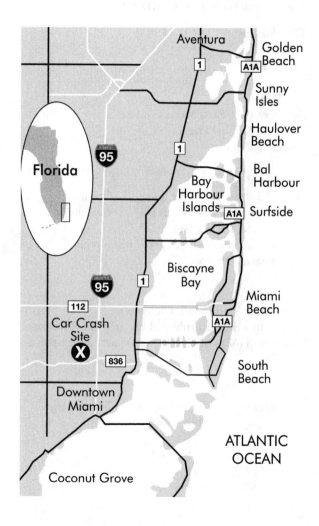

'Money is a more democratic medium than blood.'
– Martin Amis in *Money, A Suicide Note*

CHAPTER ONE

STREET TRASH NEVER made it to Sunny Isles. For the most part, veterans stayed around 70th Avenue, drinking what they could scrounge outside cheap dives on Collins Avenue and huddling in the park on Harding at night. Younger guys roamed the streets of South Beach. By day, they walked and begged on Washington Avenue guzzling from bottles they found in dumpsters. By night, the wary crashed in alleys near the trash. Men who had lost their focus to booze stumbled across Ocean Drive to the beach. Groping their way through the darkness, zigzagging across the coarse rippled sand, the men collapsed or fell beside the white wooden legs of the lifeguard stands built at measured intervals along the beach. But this meagre shelter had proven to be unsafe, even fatal.

Any of the men who had spent the last year around the beach knew the story. For more than a month, it was all the media and the tourists talked about. The lingering presence of the tragedy hung around the beach with the aftertaste of a nightmare. One bright February morning, when the streets were already shimmering with the heat, two young sisters from France walked the block and a half from their hotel to the beach. The sand was already an ocean of brightly coloured swimsuits with pale yellow, green and blue umbrellas dotting the landscape around the bathers. Carrying beach towels and lotion above their shoulders, the women tiptoed around and sometimes over sunbathers looking for free space. When they saw a spot near the lifeguard stand, they headed that way. Once there, the sisters spread the towels, applied lotion and lay down in the sun like everyone else around them. Smiling at one another, the sisters stretched languidly on the hot sand beneath them, relishing that soft buzz all tourists feel the first day on the beach – *'C'est magnifique!'* – *'Le paradis!'*

On Washington Avenue, two officers on bikes were chasing down a pickpocket as he ran recklessly through the crowds, knocking some people to the sidewalk and others onto the road. He flew down a side street and dashed between screeching cars on Ocean Drive. He made it to the beach, well ahead of the bike patrol. The officers radioed for assistance. A patrol SUV raced to the scene, leapt the sidewalk onto the beach, spraying sand in its wake. As the officer sped across the sand in pursuit, his vehicle narrowly missed scrambling sun-bathers. 'What the hell,' they shouted after him. 'Are you out of your mind?' Still, the officer did not use his siren. Bathers stood shaking their fists at the van, 'Can you believe that guy?' 'Thank God we're O.K.' The officer continued to speed with his head out the window as he swerved back and forth across the sand. He never saw the sisters, not even as he drove over them length-wise.

'Stop!' 'Stop!' tourists nearby shouted and hollered as they jumped to their feet. A crowd ran to the vehicle that had come to a halt on top of the women. They banged on the side doors, shouting in angry hysteria, 'Jesus, you've just driven over two people!' 'They're under your truck, for Christ's sake!' 'We've gotta move the truck off these people,' yelled a tourist through the open window, making a grab for the officer who seemed frozen to his seat. 'Leave me alone,' he shouted back at his wife who was trying to pull him away. 'That could be you and me down there!' His tirade stopped abruptly when he heard the horrified screams of one sister beneath the SUV. 'We need some help over here!' he shouted with new dread to the tourists behind him. He stepped back quickly when he saw her hand clawing at the sand. For a second or two, no one said anything.

On either side of the vehicle, brown blood began to seep into the white sand. The same man who had reached into the SUV now took the lead. 'We've gotta move. You can't drive forward. Do you hear me asshole? You'll crush their heads. You'll have to drive back over them.' One sister continued to scream horribly in pain and desperation. 'All right guys, get up here and help me lift the van as he drives backwards. Some of you get on the other side and lift when I give you the signal. Now back up slowly, slowly, I said!' Tourists stood with one arm around their stomachs, the other covering their mouths, as the SUV moved back over the sisters. 'Holy Jesus,' he whispered when he saw them. One was writhing on the sand. The other lay as still as a rag doll. People began to sob and clutch one another. Medics called to the scene worked furiously to save the lives of the women. Tourists continued to hurl insults at the officer who stood slumping in the sand a few feet away. 'Bastard!' 'Asshole!' 'Look at what you've done!' Other patrols that had made it to the scene grabbed the cop under his armpits to support him and quickly led him to a patrol car for his own safety.

One sister died on the brown sand – the other would face months of rehabilitation. It was their first visit to Miami. The officer later told his commander he felt he had driven over a refuse basket. That was the reason he had stopped his vehicle. In a single sentence, *The Herald* reported that the pickpocket was never apprehended.

Homeless men knew the beach was dangerous. Earlier in the day, when they could think almost clearly, they understood that if high-paying tourists weren't safe from beach patrols, what chance did they have late at night when officers rode the same vehicles across the sand expecting only to meet up with men nobody cared about? But there wasn't much of a choice. South Beach had become a tougher place for homeless men, to say nothing of the women who slept in doorways in full sight of passers-by to protect themselves. New money and the younger hordes it brought with it had crowded these men out. Cops turned sour overnight and arrested the vagrants instead of moving them along. Crashing in lanes was not any safer. Danger there came from the lead pipes wielded by guys these men might have drunk with earlier that night. To survive, they often travelled in pairs. Or a few smarter men moved on.

🌴

Sunny Isles, in North Miami Beach, was a safe place, free of vermin. It comprised about thirty blocks that began at Haulover Park and stretched its way to Golden Beach. Twenty-five years ago, motels spread their arms across the sand. The Castaways and the Marco Polo were the most prestigious. Today, Sunny Isles was feverishly caught up in a rash of multi-million dollar high-rise construction. When Trump moved into the Isles, ordinary tourists could see the end of an era. They sometimes stood and watched as places they had enjoyed for years were razed in an afternoon. The days were numbered for the remaining motels and condos that stood defiantly against these rising giants.

The beaches in this area were sparsely populated with die-hard Jews from New York and New Jersey, and 'Snowbirds' from Quebec who came in the winter to escape the cold northern climates. The owners of the million dollar condos were either absentee owners or they worked in the city. However, two rituals remained steadfast in the eye of the construction storm. The first was the Jewish septuagenarians who rode the trolley from the Winston Towers and stood in interminable lines that snaked around Rascal House. They went for the talk, the bags of sweet rolls they carried home and the opportunity to wave and call friends forward to stand with them in line. Hapless Gentiles found themselves further back in the line forty-five minutes after joining it. It was not a rarity to see one of them, beaten down by the Jewish humour and the staying power of people thirty years their senior, surrender to age and call it a day.

The second ritual defied time and fashion. Some men from Quebec still sported Speedos and beer bellies. Courtesy of Labatt, they rode those fat suckers proudly across the sand. With a wide smile and a row of gleaming false teeth, these sunburned men walked across the sand immune to snickers and disgust. They were happy guys and their *joie de vivre* was contagious.

One night early in January, a lone figure stood at the ocean's edge silhouetted against the strong beam of a full moon. The man was tall and wore only a pair of faded red shorts. He looked first to his left, then to his right, stretched, raised his arms high above his head and urinated into the ocean. He shook his member, turned and began a slow walk back to the wooden deck. Instantly, he heard the drone of a police dune buggy, the ATV that patrolled the beach. 'Jesus,' he cursed, diving, then crawling, scrambling under the outer deck of The Desert Inn that gave him only a foot and a half margin, scraping his bare chest across the coarse sand and bumping his elbow into the ribs of his sleeping friend. 'What the …,' Larry moaned, before Steve jammed his hand over his mouth.

'Cop,' he whispered. 'He probably saw me pissing into the ocean.' They both lay still.

Officer Ruiz cut the engine, slid off the dune buggy, raised his flashlight above his shoulder and walked back and forth at the foot of the deck, directing the spike of light along the poolside and at the empty chairs against the far wall. He could pick up no movement. Ruiz was puzzled. The two men below the deck swallowed shallow breaths. The officer ambled over to the next condo, but saw quickly that it was fenced and its gate was locked. He stood for a few moments, wondering where the asshole had gotten to so quickly. Then he thought of the paperwork involved if he knocked on doors and had to write up a report. In seconds, he was revving his engine and off down the beach. Ruiz did not think to look under the deck. In his second year of beach patrol, he had never once come upon street trash this far north along the ocean.

'Jesus, you bruised my rib,' Larry said, his breath stale enough that he himself turned his head when he smelled it. 'If you'd piss against the fence like I do, you wouldn't be running from cops.'

'Don't be such a pussy,' Steve laughed, bumping his head on the deck above him and cursing in pain.

They were wedged under the deck like sardines, even though Larry had dug out the sand, handful by handful, a year earlier. Leaning against the palm tree a few feet from the deck, Steve had watched the work and offered direction. That night they had crawled on their bellies and then turned very slowly onto their backs. Off to the side, they had stashed a bar of soap, three disposable razor blades caked with hair and sand, a comb they shared, two shirts, a pair of shorts and jeans. No jackets. No one would ever suspect men actually *lived* under the wooden structure. It was no wonder Officer Ruiz had missed them. Most guests at The Desert Inn, who generally stayed only a few days, mistook them for fellow tourists, because no one ever looked closely at the men.

Like most motels that were still in business, The Desert Inn did not attract the clientele it once had. Its owners waited greedily for a purchase offer and made no repairs. Rates fell, attracting a rougher trade, mostly weekenders. At this motel, it was not unusual for cops to arrest rowdies and bring their drug-sniffing dogs with them. Teenagers from Kendall drove down, rented a single room and partied all night, or at least until the police were called.

Larry and Steve blended in easily. They sat on the sand beside the deck, out of the sun. At six two, with shoulder length bleached-blond hair, a solid tan and a full mouth of good American white teeth, Steve was almost awesome. Young girls often passed him beer and hung over the railing, coming on to this twenty-eight year old. Steve ate up the attention. Both men also worked part-time. Three mornings a week, Larry lugged garbage to the steel dumpsters at the back of Publix, one of Florida's large supermarket chains. Steve mopped the floor at Dunkin' Donuts a couple of days a week. Larry got his hands on fruit and bread – Steve brought home the doughnuts.

The guys worried more about the condo next door, the one Officer Ruiz had found fenced in and locked. It did not take them long to recognize the Snowbirds who came every year. So these people were repeats and they stayed for a couple of months. They felt somewhat secure when they realized the ones who sat fairly close to their deck were French-speaking. There was a kind of security in their foreignness. But the men soon heard all of them speaking English and learned they were

French-speaking Canadians from Quebec. One day, one of their group gave the men bagels and cream cheese and wine and struck up a conversation with them. Steve knew they knew. Hell, they were neighbours. It was the French woman who dubbed their place 'The Sands Motel'.

The guys felt at home here. One day, Steve's father flew to Miami, rented a car and spent a whole day with Steve and Larry beside their 'motel'. He brought money and food and clothes – and left Steve with a chair as a present. While the Snowbirds wondered how his father could sit all day on the sand laughing and talking as though everything was normal, the 'motel' guys were laughing at the Quebec men who sat in the shade playing Hearts all day. Before the day came to an end, Steve had assured his dad he had plans for better things and even came close to believing so himself.

Steve was a guy who hated details. He hated planning things. He liked to think of himself as a drifter. But there was one detail that began to bother him as much as sand in his shorts. He needed a place of his own. He was tired of bunking with Larry. The guy was old. He must be in his forties for God's sake. Steve had no intention of moving, so he was forced now to do the very thing he hated. He thought hard as he mopped the floor of Dunkin' Donuts. Eviction was not an easy prospect even in the most normal of times. Lead pipes and thrashing were not the way he liked to go. Larry would just have to understand a younger guy needed his own space. He would tell Larry to leave, as simple as that. Threats could follow. Steve was a peaceful guy at heart. When Pat handed him ten bucks and a bag of day-olds, Steve saw that today was as good as any to approach this ticklish subject. Larry arrived at Dunkin' Donuts to pick Steve up and Steve waved him to the back of the store. Better to deal with this stuff away from home.

Larry was walking his bike home and wheeled it to where Steve pointed. Larry never talked about the bike or how he had come by it. One day he just had it. After work, back at the beach, Larry walked it across the sand and wedged most of it under the deck at the back. He kept his eye on that bike. Seeing the way Larry babied that thing, Steve knew enough not to go near it.

'Hey,' Steve said, and nothing more.

'What's up?' Larry asked.

'I need more space, man. A place of my own.' He hoped Larry would get the message from those few words. Paying close attention to the older man firmed up his desire to have him gone. Even with his shirt on he could see that his chest was gaunt. Steve was disgusted.

'You're movin'?'

'Not me man, I want you to go. I need the place for myself.'

'When I found it and dug it out? Shit!' Larry snorted.

'It doesn't matter who the hell found it or set it up. I need the deck for myself. I want you to move out and find yourself another place. I don't want trouble here. If I had to, man, you know I could rip you apart. But that's not what I want to do.' Steve, feeling things were settled, turned away and took a step.

'Find your own place,' Larry shot back and began to follow Steve back to The Desert Inn.

'That's it man. You need to learn the hard way.' Steve whirled around and lunged at Larry. He intended to push the older man hard against a dumpster, to knock some sense into him.

With a sweet move, Larry just turned his hip and

shoulder aside. The feint was instinctive, something he had learned as a tight end back in high school. Propelled by his own force, Steve crashed head first into the dumpster, sharply striking his temple against the side of the steel container. He crumpled to the ground like a sheet. The fall occurred so quickly it took a few seconds for it to register with Larry. He walked cautiously over to his friend and knelt down beside him. A puff of air escaped from Steve's mouth. His eyes opened slightly, staring ahead with vacant surprise. Larry rose, shaking his head. He knew immediately he should not stay around.

He picked up the fruit he had dropped at the side of the dumpster, left the doughnuts scattered on the ground near Steve, walked over to his bike that rested against a tree, rode home and never looked back. He sat on the sand, looking out at the lapping waves, rocking back and forth across the shoreline. For two days, he lay on the side of the deck, afraid Steve would come home in a rage. He had no work until Monday. He could not go back and ask about Steve. He dug a *Herald* out of a garbage bin, but there was nothing. He did not expect anything. People like Steve and him never merited black ink. On the third night, lying alone under the deck, he stretched his arm tentatively over to Steve's side. Larry had to admit Steve had a point about extra space.

The next few weeks transformed Larry. Even after he began sleeping under the deck again, he stayed alert. He had learned from a guy he knew at Dunkin' Donuts that Steve had been taken to Mount Sinai. Whether his heart was still beating remained uncertain. He figured Steve might still show up in one ugly mood if he found his way back to the deck. Some nights, he lay on the sand under the deck, and he felt like a mouse in a trap. Those nights,

Larry's heart began to leap and he shivered often in the night. He was forced to take precautions.

For one thing, he stopped drinking beer. He needed his wits about him. He dug out more sand, affording him additional room. He found some work at the Dollar Store and spent ten bucks on shampoo, shaving foam, blades, scissors and a towel. That afternoon, he walked over to Gilbert Samson Park, a block or so away from The Desert Inn. There he showered, shaved and cut his hair in the washroom. Mornings, without the usual hangover, the cry of gulls woke him early, and he began swimming in the ocean before the condo guests appeared. Each day he swam for a longer period. He even found a few hours work at McDonald's. Larry was on a roll. A maintenance worker he recognized from the condo, Club One, offered him a painting job. All together he was pulling in a hundred and fourteen bucks a week.

Larry himself was changing. With free hamburgers and fruit, he took on a few pounds and muscles from swimming. His clean hair was suddenly thick and the bleached-blond strands shone in the sun. He had plans to purchase new sneakers. He bought himself a chair and he sat in it after work, enjoying himself. He could have passed as Steve's brother. He looked even younger than his thirty-seven years. At least once a week, women from The Desert Inn noticed him and a few even came down and stood on the sand in front of him.

Larry was up. He saved his money, wrapping it in napkins from McDonald's and burying it in the sand beside a wooden plank. He guarded his wheels and hid Steve's chair under the deck every night. He heard a bunch of guys rented a motel room and seven of them shared the cost, eights bucks apiece. Larry intended to look into that kind of plan, but for the present, the deck was fine. He saw that the first of the repeats had arrived at the condo. He hoped the two women friends were back this year – he liked them especially. Finally, something good was about to come his way. He could smell it in the salt air. This time Larry intended to be ready.

CHAPTER TWO

THE WOMEN WERE indeed coming back to Club One in February. In fact, the first departure was minutes away. But at this moment, Caitlin stood by her front window on Wood Avenue in Westmount and opened the verticals. She ran her fingers across the cold glass panes and sighed. Across the street sat the Mother House, at least that is what her mother still called the long, rectangular, pale yellow building that rested sedately over an entire block of prime real estate on Sherbrooke Street and Atwater Avenue. It was a monument to the Congregation of Notre Dame nuns who had served the English-speaking Catholics of Quebec and dedicated most of their lives to teaching. Now it was Dawson College. Caitlin was a graduate of Marianopolis College and McGill. For the past three years, since the accident, Caitlin hated leaving the city she loved because she had learned that loss is irrevocable, and random. She'd miss the cozy Double Hook bookshop on Greene Avenue where she often passed an easy hour with the works of David Adams Richards and Alice Munro. Her own book launch would be held there in May. She'd long for Schwartz's smoked meat and St-Viateur bagels. The whole city, especially Westmount and downtown, was in her heart and veins. In the summer, Caitlin walked downtown from home and back. Montreal was such an accessible city. Even during such a short trip, she'd miss the weekly trek up the hill to her parents' house on The Boulevard. The Nine-Forty weather report broke into her reverie with the forecast of freezing rain beginning sometime in the afternoon. *That I won't miss!*

Her two suitcases and knapsack stood a few feet from the front door. She wore a white polo shirt and navy blue silk slacks with a matching Ralph Lauren jacket. The Nike sneakers were new. Making her last rounds, she checked the fridge, the stove, the windows and the taps in the bathroom. She walked to the knapsack and checked once more for her passport, her cards, cash and keys. With twenty minutes to spare before the cab arrived at the front door, she stepped out onto her back patio, hugging herself against an early February morning in Montreal. It was a few minutes past six. So far it had been a winter of thaws. The ground below her was only dappled with snow.

She stood directly above the place where Derek had fallen three years ago. But there was no use. Drawn like a mariner to search every day for drinkable water, Caitlin looked down for answers at the few square feet of pavement. She could still see Derek and herself standing beside one another on their roller blades. She was clutching the helmets. Three years had bleached the moments leading up to the accident, but not the accident itself. Derek was trying to decide if he would wear the helmet. He was classically handsome, but there was no way he wanted to flatten his Kennedy hair with a helmet. He hated hats of all kinds. He felt he looked like an idiot in any hat, let alone a helmet. Caitlin's vanity was almost as strong. 'Well?' Caitlin asked.

'Well what?' he had responded jokingly.

'Should I ditch these things in the bushes or are we going to wear them?'

Even on skates, he tended to lean on one side with both hands on his hips, like a kid. 'Your call,' he said. Then Derek made a sudden jerky move. In a parody of coordination, he lost his footing. One leg flew out in front of him and his left hand reached out vainly for her. Caitlin felt a nervous twitch in her stomach. She was about to laugh because she thought he was fooling around. This was Derek, for God's sake, who had played Triple A hockey. Then she saw the terror in his eyes as he fell backwards. There was no chance for her to steady him – he fell that quickly. His head struck the concrete walk with such force that it bounced. Instantly, he fell into a coma. Two days later, he died, four days shy of his thirty-fifth birthday.

The phone had rung three times before Caitlin heard it. Dashing back inside, she picked up the receiver, knowing full well it could only be Carmen. 'You're all set for the big day?' a sleepy voice said.

'Hi, I think so,' Caitlin answered quietly, listlessly. 'I spoke to my publisher last night and, barring any last minute copy-editing, the book will be out in March. That's a huge relief, but I've left my Florida number with her for any eventuality. I can set things up for the launch when we get back.'

Carmen knew Caitlin too well. 'Don't tell me you've been out on the balcony this morning,' she said more in a statement than in a question because she recognized the tone. When Caitlin said nothing, Carmen continued, 'Derek would want you to enjoy this vacation. Both of us have worked a whole year for it. I'm sorry we didn't manage to snag the same flight out and that I'll only be there for ten days this year, but I'll be in Miami Beach with you in twenty-four hours. We'll celebrate at Tony Roma's tomorrow night. You can gorge on their baked beans.'

'It says a lot about my life when a plate of beans should cheer me up.'

'It says you're a quirky person. If molasses and beans

still do it for you, you're the kind of friend I want!' quipped Carmen.

'All right, I'll snap out of it,' Caitlin laughed. 'I can taste those beans already. I hate that I'm such a wimp since Derek died. I'm afraid of everything. I used to be impulsive, even a little wild – I wish I could have my old life back.'

'Are you worried about flying?'

'Who isn't since 9/11?'

'I'm scared too, Caitlin, but we'll be OK. Think of what's ahead: ocean, sand, sleep-ins, good food and plenty of laughs.'

'I'm looking forward to all of that too. Self-pity demands too much of my attention. I have to let go, I know. Geez, I have two minutes to get the bags and myself downstairs. See you soon!'

'All right, get going. Keep your chin up. Think of beans and call me at the office as soon as you reach Club One.'

'I will, and thanks for the boost. I'll leave poor Derek behind. Gotta go.'

The cab was waiting for her, and the drive to Trudeau International Airport was a short one. Passing through U.S. Customs took longer than usual. Caitlin checked both bags, carried her knapsack to Gate 22 and selected a seat near a window. Only a few people had arrived before her. With an hour and a half wait time, Caitlin reached into her sack for Robert Parker's latest, *Widow's Walk*. *Appropriate*, Caitlin thought. She was in the mood for a Parker man who cut down his adversaries with great quips and good sense. Sometimes the idea of being invisible appealed to Caitlin and she lost herself to the widow's problems.

Some time later, when she looked up, Caitlin saw the place was crawling with fellow passengers. Flight 928 would be full. She put the book back in her sack and began to study the people around her, something she had begun to do after 9/11. Most people seemed to be travelling in families, a good omen. An uneasy tickle crossed her chest when she spotted a twenty-something man of Arab descent sitting all alone in a corner. What drew her attention as well was the trench coat he was wearing and pulling around him. All others, including Caitlin, had taken off their jackets. She could see no carry-on either. When their eyes met, Caitlin felt the muscles in her throat constrict. The hairs on her arms rose. The man looked away first. Caitlin checked the corridor where she saw armed patrols, a new addition to most airports.

What's the harm? Caitlin thought. *What's the harm in wanting to be safe?* Leaving her jacket on the seat, Caitlin walked up to one of the patrolmen. 'You'll probably think I'm nuts, and I feel like an idiot standing here, but there's a guy at the gate who has me worried. Is there any way you could frisk him or something before he boards our flight?' The guard was not about to turn away from this pretty woman who had the darkest green eyes he had ever seen. But he did not need his training to see the fear banked behind them.

'Of course, I can be of help. What I want you to do is to walk slowly back into the area, circle around and stop behind his chair, so I'll make the connection. Then go back to your seat. I will scan him just before he boards. You're on holiday, are you?' he asked, wanting to keep her talking.

'Yes, I've waited all year for this vacation in Miami Beach.'

'Lucky you. I'll see to it you get there safely.'

'Thanks for being great about this. It's probably nothing.' *A Robert Parker man*, Caitlin thought. Half an hour later, Caitlin passed the guard as she boarded her flight, and he gave her a thumbs up. She left him her best smile. The knapsack was stuffed in the seat in front of her, but not before she grabbed *Widow's Walk*. Holding the book on her knees, Caitlin closed her eyes, expelling a deep sigh of relief. After all, she had gotten up at five this morning. Unable to sleep on planes, Caitlin soon opened her eyes and gasped. 'Mohammed', the mystery Arab, was sitting in the aisle seat across from her. The 'widow' was shoved back into the knapsack. Mohammed was sleeping, making it easy for Caitlin to be on guard. For the next two and a half hours, Caitlin white-knuckled both armrests. Mohammed slept on. Some time into her watch, Caitlin still took deep breaths but felt brave enough to hunt down the oatmeal cookies she had brought with her. When Mohammed rose to use the bathroom directly behind him, Caitlin's mouth was full of oatmeal. *God, maybe he's stored a box cutter or a bomb in the washroom,* Caitlin worried and panicked. She wanted to know what Mohammed was doing in the washroom! Caitlin crumpled the piece of cookie that was in her hand and spat the rest into a Kleenex. There was no way she wanted her body found with a mouth full of oatmeal. She sat and waited for the explosion. When Mohammed finally walked the few feet back to his seat, all Caitlin could pick up was the scent of airline soap. *I can't go on like this. I'm two bagels short of a dozen.* It was to Mohammed's credit that Caitlin made a firm decision to break free of the web of nerves that had held her close for three years.

Thanks to her overactive imagination, every muscle ached as Caitlin made her way down to baggage claims in Fort Lauderdale-Hollywood International Airport. From here, Club One was only twenty minutes away. She spotted one of her bags within minutes and Caitlin snagged it quickly from the conveyer belt. Then she watched as lucky passengers grabbed their bags and headed for the doors. While she stood near the only other passenger, her second bag snaked its way around to her. There was no getting around it, Caitlin was tired. *I've probably just missed the shuttle too,* she moaned. As she began to roll her luggage to the door, an older man suddenly swooped down like a seagull in front of her. He smiled a familiar Quebec smile and handed her his card – *Georges – Mon chauffeur en Floride.* Georges spoke in French, telling her he could drive her to the beach for a mere twenty-two dollars. Much less than a taxi, he pointed out to her. 'I was thinking of the shuttle,' Caitlin told Monsieur Georges. '*Mais pauvre fille, les délais, les arrêts!*' he said. While he was doing his shtick, Caitlin was betting that, at thirty-one, she could take Georges out with an elbow. At this moment, reclamation claimed the day. '*Oui, Georges, je profite de votre offre.*'

And off she and Georges went in his Buick Century. He recounted his sad tale of losing his wife, but Caitlin had made a promise to leave Derek behind and she kept it. Georges was a retired postman, and Caitlin was pretty sure she could trust a postman. She kept her elbow braced, just in case she needed to deck the old fart. *At least with the older crowd, I'm not such a wimp!* She even made a reservation for Carmen the next day. 'How will my friend know you?' she asked Georges. '*Je porterais une casquette rouge.*' *Carm will get a charge out of this,* Caitlin thought.

Caitlin felt the thrill of arrival when she saw Club One. She gave Georges a better tip than the two dollars he had suggested. Like the gallant he was, he lifted the heavy bags from the trunk, bowed to her and left. This moment belonged to Caitlin. Standing beside her luggage, she threw her head back into the sun, spread her arms wide, closed her eyes and breathed in the blanket of warm air. For one moment, for one instant in this day, care fell away, her soul slumped into a calm as feathery as a white cloud, a world that endured for only a moment. Through circumstance, Mohammed had swelled this moment even further. This small space of time was unknown to native Floridians. It was a marvel that only Snowbirds knew – today this quiet whoosh was Caitlin's. When the moment had fled, Caitlin bent down to lug her bags into the front office.

CHAPTER THREE

CAITLIN QUICKLY SETTLED the rent with a money order. For five bucks, Raoul the handyman carried her luggage up to the second floor condo. Caitlin followed Raoul carrying two sets of keys for C-4. Club One was, without a doubt, the smallest condo complex on North Miami Beach. The individual units were privately owned and rented out weekly or monthly by the owners to American and Canadian Snowbirds. A manager (and owner himself of twenty-four units) ran the complex. Renters who were lucky enough to discover the place always returned, so people knew one another at Club One. It comprised only two floors for its forty-eight units. The building was private and secure. Indoor entrances cut down the noise of Collins Avenue. The pool out back was fenced in as Officer Ruiz had discovered well over a month ago. The women's apartment fronted Collins Avenue, but the large wrap-around balcony afforded a good view of the ocean several hundred feet away. Each year, there was talk that Club One would be sold and knocked down, but each year it survived.

The newly renovated one-room condo was large and bright. The mirrored walls conveyed the impression of additional space. All the appliances, a glass kitchen table with padded white chairs and the wickerwork furniture were spanking new. A plastic chandelier hung in the center of the room above glistening white tiles. Nothing in life is perfect – there was one drawback. It was the Murphy bed, a box spring and mattress you had to pull down from a side wall and hoist back up every night. Both women were light and restless sleepers – there was no way they could share a bed. Last year they had purchased a good air mattress that Caitlin hoped was still safely stored in the basement with her bike. She would have Raoul haul the mattress up tomorrow and pay him to inflate it for her. When Carmen arrived, they'd flip for the bed.

As soon as Raoul had left, Caitlin drew the blinds, got a chair from the kitchen nook and carried it to the wall in front of the Murphy bed. Standing on it, and stretching, she hid her cash on the stationary ledge above the bed, pushing the money back a few inches. Hopping down, she walked to the other side of the room, assuring herself that the cash was not visible from the floor. She made a quick call to Carmen, saying she'd relate the details of her flight that night. Her two large bags lay on the floor. After Derek's death, Caitlin had become a neat freak. She was more comfortable when everything was in place. Then she felt that she couldn't be caught off guard. Mohammed had brought about a change in Caitlin. 'These bags can wait. So can food shopping,' she said to herself, opening both bags. Rifling through each of them, she found her swimsuit and flip-flops. Grabbing a towel from one of the recessed cupboards and one of the keys, she headed for the ocean.

Caitlin had no misgivings about what she looked like in a swimsuit. All her life, she had been a tomboy. Tennis, swimming, cycling, hiking, walking, sit-ups and weights were part of her daily life. The seasons deter-mined her sports. She hoped that she could get to the surf without bumping into her Florida friends. Clearing the deck, she was already standing in the sand in front of the second gate when a small, happy chorus broke

out behind her. '*Bonjour*, Caitlin!' 'Hello everybody,'
she called back, waving as well to Morty and Sarah from
New Jersey who had left their seats and were leaning
over the deck smiling down at her. Carmen and she
would share an umbrella with this older couple they
both liked. 'See you all after my swim!' she called back
as she swung the gate open. Side-stepping a tourist who
had put his chair very close to the gate, Caitlin felt there
was something familiar about him, but she could not
place him. Larry watched her as she walked across the
sand.

A few feet from the surf, Caitlin dropped her towel,
kicked off her flip-flops and hid the key under one of
them. For a minute, she threw her head back and took
a few deep breaths of the salty whiff of high tide, her
eyes closed in the face of the sun. Everything around
her was muffled in the pounding surf. Without a
moment's hesitation, Caitlin ran through the slop of the
first wave, and the second. Then she dove under the
collapsing crest of the next wave. With the wind, the
surf was white-capped, almost angry. The shock of the
cold, sandy water caused Caitlin to shiver violently. She
began to swim hard out beyond the breakers to where
the water was clearer. Out by herself, she bobbed and
kicked, pushed back and forth by the power of the
ocean. Then, as she always did for better exercise, she
swam with steady, strong strokes toward shore and
turned and faced the cresting waves head-on. Carried
aloft and sunk like a cork, she rode the water back to the
edge of the ocean. Sinking in the sand as she walked to
shore, she shook her head and water drops fell all
around her in a halo. She stopped ankle-deep in the
surf, threw out her arms, and the sun and wind swept
over her. Larry had watched her every movement.

As she weaved between bathers back across the sand,

the fatigue of her early morning in Montreal and the air travel began to settle on Caitlin's shoulders with the pressing intensity of the Miami sun. Making the rounds quickly, she explained to her friends that she hadn't unpacked or shopped and she had better attend to both. Up in the room, she tossed her towel and suit onto the glass table. After showering, she found her favourite ice green t-shirt and white shorts. With the spending money she'd left on a side table, Caitlin ran across Collins Avenue. It was actually safer to jaywalk in this area, or run between cars as Caitlin did. Crossing with the signal lights meant your life was at the mercy of Quebec motorists and Florida's elderly drivers.

After two trips to Milam's grocery store across the street, she had carried back bottled water, Cokes, milk, Apple Jacks, Granny Smith apples, bananas, raisins and fresh strawberries. On her third trek, Caitlin decided on her dinner – two toasted bagels with cream cheese and a salad. She remembered then that half an oatmeal cookie was all the food she had eaten since last night. The groceries and luggage lay on the floor all around her. After the bagels, Caitlin ate Apple Jacks from the box. She leaned back on the sofa, sipping her Coke. She waited for the first small burp before she got up and began to tackle the work in front of her.

A little after six, she called Carmen, telling her about Mohammed and *la casquette rouge*.

'Holy shit,' was Carmen's first reaction. 'Are you for real?'

'You better believe it. For the whole flight I was scared shitless.'

'You're scaring me – I have to fly tomorrow.'

'He was harmless, Carmen. My imagination created the monster. Well, that and 9/11.'

'All right. Then you're telling me, after Mohammed,

you got into the car of a perfect stranger? You need your head examined.'

'You think? Georges is at least seventy years old, a retired postman from Montreal; his wife died of cancer last year. He's a cute little French guy. The truth is that I was feeling lucky after surviving the flight and I was too tired to wait for the shuttle. And I felt brave.'

'Do you hear what you're saying?'

'You'll love my next move. I told Georges that he could meet your flight tomorrow. You'll recognize him because he'll be wearing his *casquette rouge*.'

'I'm not that crazy.'

'Wait till you see him in the hat. He drives a white Buick and he can have you at Club One in no time. Just ignore him tomorrow if you still feel the same way.'

'I have to think about all this.'

'See you tomorrow – with *la casquette rouge*.'

'Yeah, yeah. Goodnight.'

Before locking up for the night, Caitlin made two more grocery trips. By nine-thirty, she was tripping over herself. When everything was put away, she lay on the Murphy bed dozing off with Parker's 'widow'. For someone like Caitlin who struggled to find sleep, to let go of the day – and Derek, the first night in Miami was a small miracle. With two hours of sleep last night and with today's travelling, Caitlin's head felt like an anchor on one of the yachts in Biscayne Bay. It began to sink heavily into the pillow. Within a minute, the 'widow' slid across her chest, and she and her problems were stuck in chapter four for another day. A heavy sleep wrapped itself around her and held her down.

Within minutes, Caitlin was far away from Miami. *She was cycling alone on Route 28 in Dennisport on Cape Cod. In her hand she was carrying two cold Cokes and a quarter pound of penuche fudge. Turning right at the post office, she headed to Lower County Road. Her face was flushed from the heat; drops of perspiration fell from the tip of her chin. Something wasn't right about the Keegan house where she and Derek rented the back room. The grey-shingled house with blue hydrangeas was three stories high with a wooden balcony. Up on the balcony, she recognized her mother who was sitting at the end closest to her. The scene unsettled her. Then something up there moved.*

At first Caitlin was not certain what. It was nothing the eye could see, but it had the feel of a tremor. The Cokes and fudge fell to the road, and Caitlin didn't notice them. Her eyes were locked on her mother, and the balcony. She jumped from the bike and began running toward her mother. Terror kept her from calling out to her. Caitlin kept running. Her mother saw her tearing across the grass up the hill and waved. As she stood, the wooden beam supporting the balcony collapsed. The wood fell first. Her mother fell backward then, alone into the air. Caitlin screamed as she ran to her mother. To break her fall, she'd catch her mother or let her fall on top of her body. The ground was uneven and twice Caitlin almost fell. Caitlin's arms were extended as she ran. Her heart was cracking. Her mother hit the ground four feet in front of Caitlin, and bounced. The scream, deep in her throat, woke Caitlin in an instant. Her face was wet with tears and she was shivering because she had fallen asleep on top of the sheet. She got up and stumbled to the bathroom in the darkness. Back in bed, she curled up in the fetal position and stayed that way under the sheet until the sun came up.

CHAPTER FOUR

THE SUN ROSE early, laying the palm of its hand first across the ocean that shimmered with its touch. The light crept across the sand, even a few inches under Larry's deck. It felt its way around the south wall of the condo, and fingers of light cast long beams through the cracks in the verticals in Caitlin's room. At about the same time, the traffic on Collins began to create more noise than the air conditioner.

Caitlin stirred from the shallow sleep she had allowed herself after the nightmare, her mind undercut still with the horrid image of her mother's fall. The sheets were twisted around her legs and she kicked at them now. With a deep breath, she stretched both arms and legs. Caitlin rose slowly from the bed. The tiles were cold under her feet as she walked over to the a/c and turned it off. Sun flooded the room as soon as Caitlin opened the blinds. She was met with a squeal of gulls and wide rushes of warm, humid Miami air when she slid open the patio door.

Before splashing water on her face, Caitlin headed for the phone and called her mother back home. 'Hi Mom,' she said with a whiff of relief as soon as she heard her mother's voice. 'Just wanted to check in and tell you I arrived safely.'

'Hi to you too! Isn't it something that I hear from both my children this morning. I worry till I hear your voice – you know me. I can relax now that I know you've arrived and you're safe. Chris called and wanted to know if you were intending to come with us to his

graduation in April. It's not every day your only brother graduates from Harvard.'

Her mother's voice and the impending good news
buoyed Caitlin's spirits. 'Of course, I'll go with you and
Dad. I'm proud of Chris too.'

'You take care down there. Miami can be a dangerous place. I'm glad that Carmen will be with you. Call
me at least once more to let me know that all is well,
Caitlin.'

'I will, Mom. Say 'hi' to Dad for me. And, I love you,
you know.'

'It's always nice to hear you say so. Goodbye, daughter of mine.'

'Bye, Mom.' Caitlin walked back to the patio door
and looked over at the ocean. She leaned across her balcony, stretching to her left and found herself caught up
in the panorama of cresting waves and in the air that
glistened with warmth. Editing and preparation for the
classes she'd teach both seemed far away. The railing
was warm against her stomach. Work was back in
Montreal, and she really didn't mind that Derek was
down here with her. Sometimes she felt a real pain in
her heart, knowing that one day soon he wouldn't be in
her thoughts. She inhaled the warm air, enjoying one
last stretch before heading for the shower. After the
necessary chores, she'd run across the sand to the
ocean.

She hadn't noticed Larry, hadn't realized he was
walking just below her balcony. He had seen Caitlin
though, had stopped to watch her hair ruffled by the
morning breeze. Larry was smiling to himself, remembering Caitlin's toned buns twitching against the con-
straints of her navy blue one-piece. He was heading for
the park to shower and shave. Today he would wear the
new dusty blue t-shirt he had bought at Marshalls. It

was safely tucked away with his stash under the deck. His day was full of promise. Early this morning, Raoul had hired him to paint the back patio and railing. Of course, he'd be very careful with his new shirt. He wanted Caitlin to see him at his best. He wondered if the other woman was coming to Miami.

In a pair of white biking shorts and a white t-shirt from Banana Republic, Caitlin stepped into her flip-flops and headed for the basement. As soon as she stepped out the front door and felt the breeze of warm air against her legs, her spirits rose. The coats, the boots, the sweaters and all things heavy were back in Montreal. The stairs leading to the basement of the complex were steep, and Caitlin curled her toes in the flops to keep from losing one or both. At the bottom of the stairs, washers and dryers hummed directly in front of her. Caitlin turned to her right, into a dusty, dark room littered with old mattresses, lamps, chairs and odd pieces of plywood stacked carelessly on top of one another. As pre-arranged, Raoul was waiting for her at the end of the room where a single bulb lit the room.

Raoul bowed to her as she approached him. When he had first done this, Caitlin had wanted to pull his head up and tell him obsequiousness was not the American way. But he was a happy little man with a ready smile, a full three inches shorter than Caitlin's five-six. When she learned he had a wife and a son, she knew she had nothing to tell him. He was a cute little guy and she liked and trusted him. He unlocked the door and flipped another switch. Caitlin could see her stash at the end of the linens that were stacked on wooden shelves. 'All right!' she cried. 'Everything's here.' Raoul left her for a second and returned with an air pump for the bike. 'Wow! You've saved me a trip to the Shell station.' Once the tires were inflated, Raoul carried the bike up the stairs and wheeled it to the back deck. 'You'll come up with the mattress right after this? Same deal as last year?' Caitlin called after him. '*Sí*,' he waved.

In no time, Raoul was in her room pumping up the mattress. When the work was finished, they lifted the air mattress slowly to avoid hitting the chandelier and rested it against the wall with the Murphy bed. Caitlin was glad to pay Raoul for his services, and he walked out bowing a third time. With an hour and a half to spare, Caitlin decided to cycle to Haulover Beach. She changed into sneakers and took her sunglasses.

As she walked out to the back deck to pick up the bike, Caitlin felt a little guilty that she had not yet sat down with her Florida friends. 'We'll both be down later this afternoon to catch up on all the news!' she called over to them. Larry was painting the fence just to her right, wearing his new shirt. He looked over at her and flashed her his best smile. Caitlin had not even taken note of him. She was already wheeling the bike out the back gate. Once she was out of sight, he whipped off his good shirt and kicked the sand. *What the hell is wrong with her?* he wondered. It looked like he would have to make the first move.

It had been two months since Caitlin had cycled, and bikes were her passion. The bike was a second-hand job from a shop up on 163rd Street. The seat was wide enough for two of her and Caitlin loved it. It had mountain bike wheels, no gears and weighed as much as a dirty white horse. Back home she could lift her Gary Fisher Sugar 2 with three fingers. Yet she loved this bike best because it was a no-nonsense set of wheels. For a few seconds, coasting down the small hill that led to the road, Caitlin was a kid again, her mind carried with the motion of wheels.

She woke quickly from her brief reverie as soon as she hit Collins Avenue and turned left along the sidewalk. She had realized last year that cycling on the road was suicide. Collins was a cacophony of blaring horns, screeching brakes, squealing ambulances and police sirens, the noise and allure of Miami. She was not able to pick up any real speed until she passed the Newport Pier at the corner of 163rd Street. Up to this point, construction trucks and a heavy flow of cautious tourists often blocked the sidewalk. Once she was past Oceania, one of two high-rise condominiums, Caitlin rode quickly until she turned down the path that led to the ocean walk at Haulover Beach.

At the end of this path, a small opening in the trees surrendered a quiet but spectacular view of the ocean. On one side, trees were bounded by white sand, on the other, a faded wooden staircase with sandy steps was silhouetted against a wide canvas of blue sky. In the middle of the path, a yellow lifeguard station with a red cross painted on its back and a shingled roof stood solitary before an ocean of turquoise water capped with white cresting waves. Calm emotion settled on Caitlin, and she knew why she loved Miami.

As she rode past the nude beach, dense foliage pretty much kept the area from view. She stood high on the pedals for a peek. *I'll drag Carmen down here for our annual belly laugh*, Caitlin planned. She and Derek had come across this beach about seven years ago. Because Derek was almost six feet, he saw what little there was to see before Caitlin. 'Have a look,' he told her.

Caitlin stood on tiptoes and made only one comment, 'Why are all those men wearing brown thongs?'

'They're not. They're nude.'

Caitlin began to bob up and down for a better view.

'And they're gay,' he added.

The news failed to quell her interest. Caitlin laughed and kept on bobbing.

Today, she smiled at the memory, even as she passed the monument to the Barefoot Mailman, approaching the main lifeguard clubhouse on her right that was built mid-way along the ocean walk.

'Hey there Canadian!' a voice shot out over the railing on the second floor.

'Hi Jason,' Caitlin called up, stopping once again. 'I didn't expect to see you this year. I thought you'd be at South Beach.'

'So did I. Found out in December that thirty-four is too old for the trendy crowd. They want twenty year olds.'

'Their loss – you're the All-American!' Caitlin told the six-foot, sandy-haired, broad-shouldered guy who still had the legs of Michelangelo's David.

'There's a reason I like you, Canadian. Gotta run, I'm guarding the pink station in two minutes. And don't give me a hard time with the colour. Drop by – don't be shy. Take care.'

'You too,' she agreed. From here to the Haulover Bridge, she flew on her bike, cycled up and down the hill, halfway across the bridge to Harbour House, five or six times before turning and pedalling home without a stop. Forty minutes later, Caitlin carried Carmen's deck chair downstairs to the front of the condo to catch a few rays before she arrived.

Caitlin let her head fall back on the chair and closed her eyes. With a few minutes to relax and think, Caitlin thanked the fates for a friend like Carm. She had been the bedrock of her life for the last three years. Ironically, their friendship had begun on the back of losses. What they had in common were broken hearts – what they shared was support and understanding. Carmen was coming to terms with a broken engagement, a death of sorts. Caitlin had gone into an office supplies store twice in one week and had bumped into Carmen both times. She was purchasing a cartridge for her printer; Carmen was showing a new line of 3M products to the buyer standing at the front cash when they met one another. 'You look sad,' Caitlin said. This wasn't the first time she had spoken to a perfect stranger since Derek's death. Caitlin found herself looking for that emotion in others. She had no interest in happy people.

'That's because I am. You don't look like hot shit yourself,' Carmen countered, striking a chord with Caitlin.

That's how it began. They went out for coffee on the second day. They went on talking for another three years. Carmen had never once interrupted or appeared tired as the story of Derek slowly tumbled out. Caitlin talked hour after hour that first night they had dinner together. She returned the gesture when Carmen began talking about herself. Caitlin had searched for a space where she could hide from her grief and she had found it in the tears she cried for her new friend.

Who would not have shed a tear for this intelligent, young woman who bore herself with confidence and a beautiful smile? She had prefaced her tale of woe with a rush of loud sobs, followed by a simple sentence that was almost unintelligible when it came out from the heaving sobs. 'I loved that jerk. I really loved him!' Then she laughed, long and hard. 'We broke up over poached salmon and roast beef! Can anybody believe that?' Ten Kleenex left her nose red and Carmen slammed her fist down on the table. 'I don't drink because I come down with God-awful headaches. But what the hell! Let's order a pitcher of sangria.' That was

something else they shared. Caitlin felt a buzz on half a
glass of Bud Light. They made a good pair. The young
waiter brought the sangria and gave the women a worried smile as he set it down on the table.

After the first glass, Carmen had added a laugh to
her sobs.

'You want to hear the best part? I converted to
Judaism for him! I'm a decent God-fearing, non-
church-going Catholic Italian. Was I stupid or what?'
Carmen asked, wiping her eyes with the back of her
hand. The women began to laugh so hard they grabbed
one another to keep from falling from their chairs.
They waved off the waiter who appeared ready to catch
them if they fell. 'Two weeks before the wedding, I'm
with his mother going over the menu that had already
been set. She had to be involved in everything. The
entrée was simple – poached salmon for the Gentiles,
roast beef for the Orthodox. Then this bitch, God
knows why I was ever taken in by her, decides to drop
the salmon and have only Kosher roast beef. At an extra
fifty dollars a plate, for three hundred people! She suggested not telling my parents. We were the ones paying
for the wedding.

"You're nuts if you think I can fork out an extra fifty
dollars," I shouted at her. "You're all hypocrites! I've
watched the whole family eat ham and cheese sandwiches." Then she turns on the faucets. Jake, whom I'd
dated for four years, gets up from his chair and walks
over to his mother and hugs her. I think he'd completely forgotten she'd decided to wear black for the wedding. Can you picture the scene, a witch walking down
the aisle in black? I ran from the room, expecting Jake
to follow me. Well, he didn't. Everything fell apart that
night. Two days later, Jake broke up with me on the
phone. On the phone! His mother had serious reserva-

tions, he told me. She thought that I was manipulative. And that was it. Four years sacrificed on the altar of mother's reservations.'

For a few seconds, there was no laughter. Then there was, and another pitcher of sangria. 'Then I did something really stupid. I took off with a friend to the Bahamas. I can't believe that I'm going to tell you this. The friend who went with me doesn't even know. Just so you don't think I'm a tramp, I had one sexual partner before Jake. I'm a good Italian girl. But down there, I had sex with a local. I was hurting, I was angry and I guess I was lonely too. He was beautiful, dark and creamy. He followed me around like a shadow. He opened doors for me and brought me extra towels. One afternoon he knocked at my door, and I answered not knowing who it was. He leaned in and kissed me with a sudden urgency, and I pulled him into the room. To this day, I don't know how he managed to get my clothes off so quickly. He entered me like a snake, in a moving wave. It was like nothing I had ever experienced. His body slithered above me, and I arched my back in response into an explosion of flesh. I came quickly again and again. Then he collapsed on top of me.'

Caitlin's eyes grew wide.

'I panicked. I rolled him off me. I slapped him on the cheeks, I tried to shake him, but he didn't seem to be breathing. I got dressed as fast as I could. I thought about dressing him. But what if he was dying, and the hotel people knew I had wasted time dressing him when I should have been calling for help? What would my parents say? The story would probably make the papers back home. The bitch would have her revenge. My room was on the first floor and there was a window with a hedge. For a few seconds, I thought of dragging him to the window and throwing him out. I ran to the telephone instead, and Jonas, that was his name, woke up before I finished dialing. He explained that he suffered from 'fits' when he became too excited. Ten minutes after he left the room, I was still shaking.'

Caitlin dropped her head into her hands and began rocking back and forth.

'You think I'm really awful, don't you?' Carmen whispered.

'No, no, I don't Carmen. I might have thought of the same thing in your situation. I'm thinking about something I almost did, something I've never told anyone, not even my brother and I tell him everything. It's a secret that pinches my heart in the night. You've got to promise me that you will never tell anyone.'

'You have my friendship on it. You also have Jonas in safekeeping as well.'

'I always liked the fact that Derek was such a clotheshorse. He ironed his polo shirts! Who does that? He was my GQ guy.' Before Caitlin could go on, she began to cry. 'The day Derek fell, the way he fell backwards, was so unlike him. His hair flew up, his arms flailed awkwardly at the air, one leg leapt up before the other. I felt the wiggle of a laugh. It was almost like that terrible smug little smile I get when an Olympic skater falls on the ice. I guess it's something about the best-laid plans. Anyway, before I saw his eyes, I had begun to laugh inside. The laughter never got out because he fell so quickly.' Caitlin began to laugh and cry simultaneously, still rocking back and forth. 'If Derek had fallen on the grass, the first thing he would have done would have been to look around to see who had caught his fall. But that's not the point, damn it. The point is that I was laughing inside when Derek fell. I'll never forgive myself.'

Carmen got up and hugged her. 'We make a good

team, you and I. I'm ready to throw an unconscious lover out a window, and you're laughing seconds before your husband dies.' Then they both started laughing uncontrollably, nasal snorts and all. They were bound together now by secrets and laughter.

CHAPTER FIVE

LARRY TOOK HIS lunch break around one-thirty. He had cheese and bread tucked away in the tool shed, a cabana really. Raoul had told him he could sleep there as long as he was painting and on condition he stored his things in a corner when he got up in the morning. His money was still safely hidden under the deck. Larry kept a close eye on the hideout as he worked. Two cold Cokes would taste good right now, he thought to himself as he walked to the front of the complex.

Larry stopped dead in his tracks when he came upon Caitlin sitting in a chair. Her green eyes were closed, her body relaxed under the warm insistent hand of the sun. He had Caitlin alone to himself. But Larry made no move toward her. Under the weight of his pinching nerves, his bones began to shrink. He felt like a man who had stepped onto a stage dressed inappropriately. His arms were smeared with white paint, his nails were caked with it, his shirt was stained – Larry could smell himself. He began to back away, almost crawling like a spider in reverse. He would drink the water he had out by the deck.

When the Buick pulled into Club One, Caitlin was still adrift and never heard the car. 'Is someone using my chair?' a familiar voice said from an open car window.

Caitlin jumped in surprise. 'You're here! Hello, hello there Carm! You made good time,' Caitlin said, hugging her friend.

'Thanks to M. Georges,' Carmen said. Georges,

wearing a broad smile, came over to shake Caitlin's hand. 'I've booked M. Georges for our return flight.' M. Georges beamed.

'That's great. I'll help you with your bags. See you in ten days, *monsieur*.' There was no problem with the bags because Carmen travelled a lot and she knew how to pack only essentials.

'I'm here! I'm here! Hello Miami. Let the games begin!' Carmen ran to the fridge and grabbed her Dr. Pepper. 'Boy, am I thirsty. Are those glazed twists for me?'

'No, they're for M. Georges,' Caitlin joked.

'Just give me a second to wolf these down. I'll un-pack tonight after Tony Roma's. I want that sun – bring me to the sun! I've gotta tell you this. At the airport, I'm still undecided about Georges, but you were right, I was dead tired. I was in Chicago two days ago. I am jet-lagged out. Anyway, I see this man with a sign that says 'Georges'. No hat, I'm thinking to myself. What the heck, Caitlin said he was safe. I go up to this guy, and he's not M. Georges. I feel like an idiot, until I spot *la casquette rouge* a few feet behind this Georges. Go fig-ure.' Ten minutes later, both women were on the back deck pulling up a couple of lounge chairs. Carm could not have exposed more of her body to the sun without being downright indiscreet. Like seagulls to bread crumbs, their friends began to converge upon them.

Larry moved as far away from the women as possi-ble. He began to jab his paintbrush into the side of the deck. With each jab, a fine spray of paint flew back at him. Within a few minutes the top of his hand and fore-arm were white with paint, but he did not seem to notice.

Morty was seventy-seven years old. Every morning of his month's vacation, he walked barefoot alone for an hour along the beach long before the rest of Club One was even awake. He was tall and slim. A healthy diet that never included a condiment of any kind, not even salt or pepper, had kept him in good shape. Morty was a listener, a pensive man who wisely left the talking to Sarah, a task she took up with relish. She was the first to speak to the women. Sarah did not want anyone to know she was eighty-one. She looked like the grand-mother that everyone wanted – roundly plump and sturdy, the twinkle of a twelve year old in her eye and candies in the purse she carried everywhere. 'Well, hello,' she said loudly in her New Jersey accent, 'you two girls from Canada get younger every year!' There was a reason Caitlin and Carmen liked Sarah.

'Now Sarah, you know that's not true, but it's nice to hear,' Carmen smiled, shielding her eyes against the sun with the back of her hand. 'You're looking pretty good yourselves.'

'She's always busy. You should have seen her list before we left home,' Morty added, feeling he wanted to give a reason for Sarah's perkiness. 'She's making that list three months before we even leave for Miami.'

'I don't want to worry about forgetting anything, Morty. I know I'm a worrier, but I'm not about to change at this late date. I have a caramel for you, Caitlin – I know Carmen doesn't want one. She doesn't know what she's missing.'

As Sarah began rummaging through her capacious bag for her candies, Yvette spoke up. '*Bonjour les filles*! Have you noticed our new handyman painter?' Yvette was just shy of her sixtieth birthday and the most stylish of the group. She never left her condo without make-up, or appeared by the pool in the same bathing suit two days in a row. When the women looked over to see the painter, he was nowhere in sight. 'He'll be back. He's one of the guys from The Sands Motel. Only Larry, the older one, is still here – we didn't ask about Steve. Larry sleeps in the cabana now.'

Michel, a retired cop from Montreal, jumped into the conversation before Yvette and Caitlin launched into an extended talk. '*Bonjour* Caitlin, *bonjour* Carmen. Now, the whole gang is here. Is it still the same pact between you pretty women – no dating here in Miami?'

Had it been anyone but Michel, both women would have taken umbrage at such an intrusion, but that was Michel, and he was sort of voted and accepted as the Club snoop. People were O.K. with Michel's snooping because a good measure of protection accompanied it.

'Yes, Michel, we come down here for rest and a friends' time out,' the women answered in unison. 'No change in our agenda,' Carm added.

'Such a pity,' Michel sighed, although he was happily married. He was lucky his wife, who was standing behind him, took all his kidding in good spirits. 'I ask only because I know Larry, our painter, has a crush on you, Caitlin. He watches you with longing, every chance he gets. You have a boyfriend if you want one.'

'Give me a break, Michel.' Caitlin was somewhat taken aback because she knew Michel, for all his teasing, was a hawk who never missed a thing at Club One. For a second, she wanted to tell him she knew he himself had a crush on Carmen. But Caitlin opted for an apple instead, leaving the group and running up to the room.

🌴

Larry was standing across the street with two Cokes, waiting for a break in the traffic. As he looked to his left, he was unnerved and began breathing deeply to steady himself. The man, who had drawn his undivided attention, was a few hundred feet away from him, walking in the other direction, but Larry felt he recognized the strut, the easy amble, of Steve. Larry swallowed hard, his eyes trained on the stranger until he was lost among a group of tourists. *It can't be him – it's gotta be someone else. His eyes were glazed for Christ's sake!* Larry thought. He immediately remembered the three hundred and seventy-two dollars under the deck and he decided to sleep in his old haunt that night to protect his hard-earned stash.

He loathed the thought of going back to sleeping on damp sand, crawling under the deck like a sand crab. In the cabana, he slept on a lounge chair, covering himself with old towels one of the maids had given him. She had even found him a pillow. He had a roof over his head now and a toilet and sink that the tourists used during the day at the pool. He did not want to be reduced again to that shallow grave. A blank, stale existence of a non-person. This job was important and he had to keep it, extend it even beyond the high season. Yet Larry would not think of moving his cash – it was safer under the deck. Any number of people had access to the cabana during the day. He struck a bargain with himself. He'd stay at the 'motel' for two nights. If Steve did not show up, he would move back inside. That could not have been Steve, he told himself again, no way. Yet he felt a hum of nerves around his heart. He focused on the traffic once more, and when he saw his chance, Larry ran more slowly than usual back across Collins.

🌴

Caitlin had already finished half her apple when she opened the side door that led to the pool area and almost bumped into Larry. Caitlin was the first to break the awkward silence. 'Hi,' she smiled guardedly, remembering what Michel had said, 'I wondered if you guys were back.'

Larry's words did not come out with the assurance he had felt a half hour ago. 'Hi, I'm back. Steve took off a while ago.' Larry wanted to say more, open up a connection, but his tongue was heavy. Easy broad rhetoric was nowhere around his vocal cords. He had forgotten the density and power of a young woman's scent. He could smell Caitlin, the lightness and the dazzle of her. It felt like a warm current of water you discover in the ocean, a soft embrace you try to gather around yourself. Larry wanted to reach out and touch her, pull her inside of him, but at that moment, he did nothing. A drop of salty sweat streaked down his back – his knees felt loose. Neither one of them spoke. Larry's shoulders bunched with tension. He felt naked standing there in front of Caitlin, with nothing but the weight of wasted years and empty hopes.

'Good luck with the paint job,' Caitlin said, walking past Larry, unaware of the commotion in him, making certain that her remarks were conclusive.

'Yeah, thanks,' Larry managed to get out, not even bothering to turn and watch her walk away. He knuckled his eyes, seeing that three hundred bucks and one new shirt did not seem like much now, not to a woman like Caitlin anyway, not even to a guy like himself. He walked back to work, with slumping shoulders, taking the long way around so the women would not take notice of him. He settled back into his painting because he had to get out of the hole he had dug for himself four and a half years ago. He had to be ready for Steve if he showed up. With the idea of Steve's appearance yanking his chain, Larry was edgy, a contagion he had suffered from for at least seven years.

When his wife Linda had kicked him out of the apartment, keeping their son with her, he had gone to his father for a roof over his head. 'I'm not taking you in. Think of this time as a learning experience. Otherwise you won't amount to shit.' His father was a cold bastard – always had been. A few months later, his father was laid off. Then he too was without a roof and no savings. Before his mother had died of cancer, Larry learned his father had broken her arm one afternoon for not getting him a beer. For as long as he could remember it was his mother who had worked and supported the family. His mother had not told him the truth about the fracture until well after the cast was off her arm. She knew the beating Larry would have given his father if he had known. When you came right down to things, his father had not really amounted to shit either. It had been a bittersweet revenge watching his father now have to contend with the crap he had dished out to him all his life. One night they had both ended up at the same shelter. He had heard his father snoring and coughing well into the night. He wanted to walk over and smother him. In the morning, with his eyes stained red from a sleepless night, Larry decided to get as far from his father as possible. He left without a word to him. What was there to say? From Buffalo, he hitched rides to Miami to cut his ties with his father and to get out of the cold.

A few hours later, Carmen roused herself from the lounge chair, slippery with suntan lotion and announced, pulling on her t-shirt, 'I think I've had enough sun for my first day. It could even be a Noxzema night for me.' New sun blocks on the market could not prevent burns for Canadians who were drawn, like moths, to the heat of the ultra-violet rays. Noxzema remained a Canadian staple. 'Lucky I brought some with me this year. I'm ready to head up for the shower, Caitlin, if you are.'

'You're incorrigible where the sun is concerned.' Caitlin put down the 'widow' again and accepted the fact that Parker's troubled woman would have to walk the walk alone. Now that Carmen was here, there would be little time for reading.

After showering, dressing and some of Carmen's unpacking, the two "C's" headed for Tony Roma's early bird. The manager, a tall, slim, thirty-something remembered them from last year and told them to choose their own table. They waited for their meals with non-alcoholic Margaritas. 'This is what it's all about,' said Carmen. 'This is what I work for eleven months a year. Montreal and hard-selling mounting tape to tough prospects seem a world away. I love the taste of these strawberries!' A few minutes later, Carmen was finger-deep in ribs and Tony's Carolina Honeys with extra sauce. Working on her beans and salad, Caitlin waited for the appropriate moment before speaking. 'I have a favour to ask of you.'

'Shoot, but I'm not promising anything.'

'Once we get settled, would you walk with me to Mitch's restaurant around 70th Avenue?'

'I know where Mitch's is, but I can't walk one hundred blocks the way you and Derek did.'

'I'll shorten the trek. How about we walk to Bal Harbour and take a bus from there. I know the place is closed, but I want to see if it's still standing. There are so many memories of that restaurant. In its day, Mitch's was quite a place. It served the best Kansas City steak and garlic bread I've ever eaten. The line-ups used to snake all the way around the block to the old Broadmoor Hotel. After eating, many diners would wait in line for ice cream at The Sweet Spot. A family from New York owns the Spot. They've been trying to sell the place for a few years now. Overnight, the movie theatres shut down, and the Cubans moved into the neighbourhood. They opened their own pastry shops and food stores. Mitch's and The Sweet Spot lost their clientele. The transplanted New Yorkers moved farther north along the beach. They filmed some scenes from *Scarface* at the Broadmoor. Now, it's just an apartment for older people. A couple of blocks south of Mitch's, the old open-air dance floor is still standing. Anyway, once I see Mitch's, we'll bus it back to the shops, and you can scout the Banana Republic. From there we can walk home. If you do this for me, I'll go to the dogs with you, for five races.'

'You've got a deal! You must really want to see Mitch's to go to the dogs with me!'

'I do. Great!'

Caitlin never gambled, never even bought lotto tickets, but she was another kind of risk taker. She thought nothing of running at night; she rode the most dangerous rides at La Ronde, an amusement park in Montreal. Derek used to stand on the ground watching her go on ride after ride on the roller coaster. Sometimes he was envious of her, but he decided he liked living too much. She was a speeder and was sometimes rewarded with tickets. Carmen, on the other hand, was raised to love pinball in Hampton Beach – the slots in Montreal and Atlantic City answered a passion when she became an adult. She worked hard for her money, as the song goes. Carmen was always hoping for the big jackpot that would change her life. She didn't have Caitlin's trust fund from her grandmother or the insurance money from Derek's policy. She was an unlucky gambler who lost a hundred bucks every five weeks or so. Seven years of losses had not taught her anything. She was right in there with most gamblers, people with a thin layer of desperation who could not recognize losing because they had substituted words like 'ahead' and 'little bit' and 'don't ask' for the bottom line.

CHAPTER SIX

TWO DAYS LATER, just after four o'clock, on a warm February afternoon, Carmen's face was still pinching from the sunburn when she and Caitlin left on their trek, carrying sun block, money and water bottles.

In twenty minutes, they were on the ocean walk on Haulover Beach. 'I'm not stopping for the thongs,' Carmen said as they approached the nude beach. 'You have a week to get me down here again.'

'All right. The nudes aren't going anywhere, and I don't want to be greedy today. I'm just happy for the company.' Where the beach opened up, because there were no trees on the ocean side of the walk, a two-foot cement wall that tourists used as a bench protected the sand from being blown onto the path. Nevertheless, it still spilled over the wall like salt and found its way first into cement cracks, and then lay on the walk like confetti. Erosion was a continuing problem for the beach. Twice a year, sand was hauled in by the truck load and dumped and spread across it. The women stopped and sat on the wall and drank some water. The vivid mix of white sand, pale green water and a blue and white sky, was so true and so uncomplicated that they lost themselves for a few minutes in this artist's palate. When Carmen turned to her friend, she noticed Caitlin's eyes were glued to the plaque of the Barefoot Mailman. The bronze plaque depicted a postman in shorts with a mailbag, his story printed underneath. 'What's so special about him?' she asked.

'As you can read on the plaque, in the 1880's mail

was often carried between the coastal communities of
South Florida by barefoot mailmen. These carriers
walked most of the route barefoot on the firm sand near
the water's edge. The usual route was from Hypoluxo
Island, past the Orange Grove and Ft. Lauderdale
House of Refuge and Baker's Haulover, then to Miami
by small boat and back again. That was a distance of 120
miles which the barefoot mailmen covered in six days.
They walked barefoot twenty miles, six days a week, to
deliver the mail, trudging along the sand. Think of it,
twenty miles on uneven sand! Derek and I used to walk
ten miles a day – the postmen doubled that.

Every year, in March, boy scouts from all over the
States retrace their route. I've come upon the scouts
when I was out walking. One year I followed them back
to Haulover Beach. Every size of teenage boy, from
really heavy to unbelievably slight, from truly beautiful
to pimply plain, from giants to the size of little people,
hike their way along Collins Avenue in a single day and
end up at Haulover where they spend the night. These
teenagers have energy to waste, but you should see what
this hike takes out of them. The boys walk, stumbling,
some limping badly, along the sidewalk like little old
men, long socks fallen around their ankles, laces dragging alongside their shoes, shirts pulled out from their
khaki shorts, stained with sweat and food they've spilled
along the way. Their faces, beet-red from sunburn and
exertion, stretch out from their necks, pulling the rest
of their weary bodies with them like fledglings that drag
the shells around behind themselves once they have
broken through. Some of the boys pour the last of their
water on their heads, discarding the empties – others
gulp what they have left, spilling much of it down their
necks. Curses and sighs hang on the humid air. Once
they stumble onto the beach, the kids drop their gear

and fall to the ground with a thud that makes anyone with a bad back wince. And these are kids, for God's sake! Their scout leaders don't look any better. So yes, I think men who walked this route, because there was more than one, deserve the memorial plaque. What they accomplished was memorable. Today, in our Thorlo double-sole socks, our Nike Airs, we run or walk along Haulover Beach for a mile and a quarter and we feel we've accomplished something. All runners should stop here by the plaque, humbled by what they've read. It puts things in perspective.'

'Well, as least I feel I'm doing my bit today, Caitlin.'

'The mailmen would salute you today, Carm. Jason is right down there, but I see he's not having any trouble attracting women.' Jason was leaning over the wooden railing from his pink hut, built on stilts. All six stations or huts were newly painted this year in pink or yellow embodying the spirit and fun of Miami. These lonesome structures replicated to a degree the fishermen's bungalows that were once quite a community on the southernmost tip of Key Biscayne. 'I'll shout down at him and hope he hears me, because we should really be on our way. Well, he's seen us.'

'Come on down, Canadians!' he shouted back, waving them over. Caitlin pointed to her watch in a signal Jason understood. 'Catch you later.'

The women walked more briskly now along the dune-backed beach walk that lay on the eastern side of the park. They came to a section heavily bordered by thick, stocky trees. A siren began to blare in the near distance, but the C's paid it no heed. They simply spoke louder to one another. This distinctive, blaring cacophony was as indigenous to Miami as sun and sand. Danger in Miami was a fear but also a magnet. The tourist who would admit the truth confessed to being both titillated and aghast at the violence that was reported daily in *The Herald* and on network television. There was a buzz to the city and the beach that one did not have in other parts of Florida, particularly on the gulf side.

Caitlin and Carmen were no exception. Yet they did use many of the violent events as springboards to ethical questions. Caitlin usually began these late-night conversations, and Carmen was a willing joiner. It was of great interest to her to read and discuss the skewed perceptions that seemed to be an epidemic everywhere. Last year, a banner in *The Herald* read – *Tragic Death on Christmas Eve*. The story was uncomplicated, but horrific. On December 24, after eating dinner with his brother and their respective wives, one of the brothers followed his sister-in-law, eight and a half months pregnant, up to the bathroom where he raped her. Hearing his wife's screams, her husband ran upstairs, discovered what his brother had done, ran for the ever-available gun and shot and killed him. *The Herald* played up the death of the twenty-something brother. Caitlin saw the tragedy not in him, but in the destruction he had left behind. His brother would certainly face a second-degree manslaughter charge; his wife, the rape victim, would lose her husband to prison along with the livelihood he had been providing; the unborn child would lose a father for a period of time; the rapist's wife was suddenly a young widow; and lastly, but certainly not the most important thing, the rapist had lost his life. Everyone, *but* the rapist, was a victim here. Caitlin's banner would have read – *Tragic Aftermath*.

The siren's high pitch, ever closer, still did not get their attention. The friends stopped talking out of habit, as one does when a plane is passing overhead. Neither heard the sound, because of the siren's squeal, of a Hummer's eighteen-inch Pirelli tires jumping the cement curb, smearing the road to the ocean walk with burned rubber. What they did see was a yellow blur with a heavy spray of sand behind it. The women stood transfixed. The driver of the Hummer, twenty-four year old Harris Chalmer, did not see them either because both women were camouflaged by the trees on their right. As his SUV sped furiously towards them, Harris was busy grabbing two backpacks from the front seat. Before Detective Garderella had made the turn onto the ocean walk, Harris, buzzed on adrenalin, threw the first bag, then the second, into the thick trees on his left. The very instant, the very second, the second pack left his hand, he saw Caitlin and Carmen, silhouetted ghostlike against the trees. One of the flying straps from the bag whipped the side of Caitlin's cheek. When their eyes met, all six of them, they were each branded with one another's image. Harris battled the roiling emotion of a jumper who has let go of the railing, of a man who has relinquished control to the thin air.

He had begun to shout into his cell phone. 'Bobby, Jesus fuck! I've ditched the cash. I had no choice. There is no way I'm going down with drug money on me. Fuck the drugs! I never saw them and I threw the bags right in front of two bitches on the ocean walk. Things happened too fast. If I had just waited one second longer, I would have seen them. You've gotta get down here now! The cash is somewhere on the ground in the trees, on the left hand side of the ocean walk, immediately after the first turn onto the walk. You can't miss the bags – they're both banana yellow. The bitches saw them, man! I threw the bags right past both of them. Get your ass down there. Now! You've gotta go get those bags. Even if the bitches take the cash, they won't be heading in my direction. They'll have to make a run for it back over the bridge. If you get your ass here fast enough, you'll see them.'

'We are screwed, Harris. You got rid of the money? That's two million bucks! Literally out the window.'

'What the fuck was I supposed to do? I was made the minute I pulled out of the parking lot of The Tiffany. Before I even made it to Collins! The cop was in the parking lot waiting for me, for Christ's sake.'

'All right, shut up for a second. The rest of the guys are here at the mall waiting to celebrate with you after the exchange. I'll get everybody out on the road. They won't get far if they were stupid enough to take the money. There are seven of us, eight with you. What did these bitches look like?'

'Lookers! One's Italian. She has layered dark brown hair and she's wearing a neon green t-shirt and white biker's shorts. The other has sandy-blonde hair in a light blue t-shirt with loose white shorts. About five-six, both of them. Both are wearing Killer Loop blue shades. I know because I wear them too.'

'I'm on my way. Do you think they'll take the money?'

'Who the fuck wouldn't? Money dropping at your feet like that – it's everybody's dream.' Harris had thought of cutting out to Collins on the entrance beside the lifeguard station, but with the money back there, he wanted to be as close as possible to it. As he sped down the half mile, bathers dove into the bushes or trees, screaming for others to get out of the way. 'Idiot!' they shouted after him. Harris' wheels tore up beach towels, split lotion tubes and mashed books that had fallen to the ground as their owners dove for cover. Moses parting the Red Sea. 'There are two Beach Patrol cars ahead; I'm stopping. All they can pin on me is 'reckless', right?' The Hummer skidded, sliding a few feet side-

ways, before it came to a complete stop, neatly avoiding
the two police cars that had been set up as a road block
on the walk. 'They can't screw up my whole life over
'reckless'. Get that money – get those women, you
hear!'

'Of course, we'll find them. It's our cash, too.'

Detective Garderella never saw Caitlin or Carmen.
They had ducked into the trees for cover as she sped
past, listening to Sergeant Tully from Beach Patrol.
Curious heads peaked out from the bushes along the
way as Garderella tore down the path. 'The suspect has
stopped without incident, almost in front of the main
station here. He's just sitting in the vehicle. Do we make
the arrest, over?' Tully radioed her.

'I'll be there within seconds. Do not approach, over.'

'You've got it, over.'

Harris' mind was whirling with disbelief. White-
knuckled, he sat with both hands clearly visible on the
steering wheel. He wanted to make certain that the cops
saw he was not resisting. In his head, he began ranting
in tortured dialogue. *How the fuck was I made that soon?
It was like the bitch was waiting for me. If it's Nipples, if it's
that scumfuck, he's dead meat. What a worm! He's a dead
man, he's a walking dead man. Gotta get that money. I
worked too hard to lose it now.*

Once the tip was received at the precinct, Detective
First Class Maria Garderella, was assigned three days of
surveillance on Chalmer. If he were about to make the
exchange, he might move early. Metro-Dade Police
Department wanted to know more about this All-
American rich boy; more importantly, the MDPD
wanted the bust. Garderella had chewed her sugarless
Dubble Bubble until her mouth cankered. She never
drank coffee – blessed or cursed like her mother with
energy to spare. Sleep had not come easily after Peter

walked out on her and the two kids. He couldn't deal with the stress of a family. At least, that's what he had told her. That's how he had packaged eight years of marriage. He had not called once in four months. She was lucky her mother took the kids during her shifts. It was the waste that got to Maria, and a sense of failure. Peter's father had done the same thing to him as a kid. She had dealt with the abandonment dry-eyed. Kids did not give you the luxury of sighs and tears. Two nights a week she worked at a strip mall on 74th Street. Maria was wired, too tired to sleep. The surplus energy and her anger were now levelled at Chalmer.

As she had promised, Garderella pulled up within seconds. Tully was keeping an eye on the Hummer while Officer Ruiz kept the beach crowd behind the cement wall. He was happy to be in a car, out of the dune buggy during the day. Unlike Tully, Garderella, while not drawing her weapon, unfastened the leather sheath tucked neatly on her right hip and held her hand very clearly on the standard issue, 9 mm semiautomatic Walther P99. LAPD might have equipped each radio car with nonlethal weapons that fired beanbag bullets, but Miami had not yet moved in that direction. Garderella had had no problem with any of the mandatory courses teaching female survival techniques, especially street survival. She was a natural.

College kids were sometimes difficult felons to deal with, unpredictable. If the anonymous tip was correct, this kid was part of an ecstasy ring, the leader. What made them dangerous was their ruthlessness. Just a few years ago, one college buddy had murdered his best friend because he had skimmed from the pot. And most of them knew the law; they were not easily intimidated. Like this smart-ass in the Hummer. These rich kids already had money behind them and powerful parents who sought out the best lawyers when their kids got into trouble. They were not afraid of anything. Entitlement, that's what all this was about, that and the juice they got from breaking the law. They were greedy kids who wanted more and they took it. Garderella could understand dead-end kids who had nothing and were going nowhere. But these rich kids who tore lives apart for sport left her with a rage that rose in her throat.

Harris' sighting of Garderella had made it necessary for her to move in immediately for the arrest. At least with the tip and her visual of the bags had come probable cause for a vehicle search. She already knew Harris was carrying two million bucks for a buy. Joe Public is instrumental in police work. This anonymous information had come into the station two days ago. The wet fear in the caller's voice gave credence to its import. 'I can't give my name, but I've got information for you. I've gotta draw the line somewhere. They don't care who they hurt now. It's all about money. In the beginning, we sold only to zoned-out ravers. I mean these guys were out to buy, why not from us? Now, Harris is going after kids, young kids, sixth and seventh graders. He says they'll go for the cartoon figures stamped on the pills. I can't be part of this. In the next four days there'll be a two million dollar drop. The mule is our 'captain', Harris Chalmer. That's what he says we have to call him. He lives with his father at The Tiffany, suite 311, at Bal Harbour. I can't come forward, I can never testify. But I have to draw the line somewhere. The buy is MDA. I'm only ratting him out now because I have a younger sister and brother. Enough said.'

Enough said, all right. That Chalmer was a resident of Bal Harbour was saying a mouthful. Mainly posh, elegant residential areas occupy the Barrier Islands located north of Miami. Flashy hotels, moneyed condos and one of the most stylish and chic malls anywhere make up this exclusive community with its own private police force. Bal Harbour is said to have more million-aires per capita than any other city in the U.S. It's a snobbish place with a tropical setting. High fashion, old money, new money, dog walkers and security staff in neo-colonial uniforms and pith helmets set the tone here. Though the sidewalks are wide enough for cars, no bikes are permitted in this privileged sanctuary. Old men and women in wheelchairs were dressed to the nines and pushed along the walks slowly by private nurses. Up 96th Street one finds galleries and a swarm of plastic surgeons. Even if these residents couldn't walk on water, they could easily cross the ocean on a bridge of money.

With her right hand inside her jacket, Garderella walked slowly to the vehicle. She could not afford to make any mistakes with the likes of Harris Chalmer. The windows of the Hummer were down. 'Get out of your vehicle, sir. Get out now! Lay your hands across the hood and spread your legs.' Tully had walked over to stand beside her. Ruiz was forced to turn his back on the action to keep the bathers from standing on the cement wall for a better view. Jason could not leave his lifeguard station, but standing on its wooden platform, he had a pretty good view of the events unfolding on the walk.

'All right, officer, I'm coming out. Relax.' Harris took his sweet time.

'Move, sir. Stand up against the car as I just said.'

Harris winked at the crowd, gave Garderella a mock salute, turned very slowly and complied with her instructions.

She frisked him, taking his wallet from the back pocket of his surfer shorts and looking at his ID.

'I'm not carrying, officer.'

'It's Detective Garderella, Mr. Chalmer. Sergeant Tully, search the vehicle.'

'You're searching the vehicle for a moving violation, detective?' Harris moaned, dragging out the word 'detective'.

'I have probable cause, sir.'

Harris' heart froze. *That snitch.* He knew for certain now that someone had ratted. Nipples was the only one of the eight guys he could think of. His forehead knotted in anger, but he knew enough to keep his mouth shut. He would settle things with Nipples in his own way.

Tully opened all four doors with their dark-tinted windows and gave the vehicle a thorough search. Though the Hummer was large, its square shape really did not offer great hiding places. Garderella and Harris watched the search in silence. 'Nothing here but a couple of empties,' Tully said, climbing out of the Hummer with three empty Bud Light cans.

Garderella was perplexed for a minute. She had seen him toss the bags into the Hummer, and he had not been out of her sight. Until… until he had made that turn onto the ocean walk. He must have gotten rid of them then and they must be unguarded now. *For who so firm that cannot be seduced?* Shakespeare said that. Harris was looking intently at Garderella now. He knew exactly what she was thinking. Things could be so easy for her. What could he report? The temptation, wet and appealingly close to Garderella, slithered away. Her resolve was firm. She liked things simple, liked the structure she had built around her family in these long four months. She couldn't let loose the furies now. She knew a great deal of the damage they left in their wake.

'Have you lost anything, Mr. Chalmer?' she asked.

'Only my good sense, detective.' His eyes were blue, but very pale, anemic, ice-cold. They bore into her own, daring them, or mocking them for a missed opportunity.

'What about the two yellow back packs I saw you toss into the vehicle?' Before Harris decided to answer, she called for backup and told the officers where to search, told them what they were looking for.

'What are you talking about?' Harris' facial features tightened, but he tried to aim a boyish grin at Garderella, and failed.

'Two bags, sir. Bags I saw you toss into this vehicle.' Garderella noted that Harris was gnawing his lower lip.

'You're mixing me up with the guy who got into his Jag back at The Tiffany. Check him out. I have nothing as you can see – I tossed nothing into the Hummer.' For the first time in the last half hour, Harris thought of the mess he'd be in if he hadn't tossed the cash. Smug is what he felt. Smug and still pissed.

'Sergeant Tully, please administer a breathalyzer test to Mr. Chalmer.'

'Give me a break, detective, I'm as sober as you are. You're going to test me for month-old empties?' He could not afford to waste any more time because he had to join the others in their search for the cash. 'All right,' he acquiesced, 'this won't take long. What do you want me to do? I can blow into the breathalyzer all day. This is a waste of time.' Harris made small work of the test. 'I'm sorry I was speeding. I didn't know who you were, detective. You're driving an unmarked car. You can buy a cherry anywhere these days. I was scared – that's why I didn't stop. Most kids speed, right? No damage, right? Nobody got hurt. I'm willing to pay for the speeding violation. I know I was wrong.' His tone was compliant now because Harris wanted the money back. He had to get out of there. He was the only one who knew exactly where he had tossed their cash.

'Sir, I'm afraid that the charge is reckless endangerment.' Garderella could sweet-talk as well as this jerk any day of the week. Forewarned and alarmed about this young adult who couldn't wait a year for his trust fund, she wrote out the citation and handed it to him. 'Sergeant Tully will escort you back to The Tiffany. Vehicles are not permitted on the ocean walk, so please follow the sergeant out to Collins and back to Bal Harbour.'

'I can find my own way home, detective. I don't require directions. I live five minutes from here.'

'Then you'll be home in no time, sir.' Garderella turned away and headed back to her unmarked car. She had a short conversation with Sergeant Tully that he could not hear. Harris watched Garderella drive back in the direction of the cash. There was nothing he could do about things for at least five minutes.

CHAPTER SEVEN

CAITLIN'S HAND ROSE to her cheek seconds after the bag strap slashed into it, before she and Carm dove into the trees off the walk. Carmen fell on top of the second bag. With all the commotion a half-mile down the walk, there was an uncanny silence here in the trees. The friends looked at one another, smothered in the roll and shock of being caught inside the action. 'There's a welt on your cheek,' was all Carm said. Then she looked hard at the bag she had tripped over. 'Omigod! Do you think this is cash?'

'I think we should get out of here.'

'Just let's see what's in the bags. If it's drugs, we're gone.' Carmen drew the zipper back from the first bag. 'Caitlin, look! Have you ever seen this much money in one place?' She moved a few feet forward and grabbed and opened the other bag. Like the first, it was stuffed with bills, hundreds and fifties. Old bills that could not be traced. 'Oh God,' Carmen whispered, staring down at the money. 'My jackpot! Caitlin, do you know how many times I've dreamed of something like this happening to me? My whole life!' Then Carmen shut her friend out and spoke so slowly, she unnerved Caitlin. 'I am not walking away from money that was thrown at my feet. I'd be nuts. I can't walk away from this. I can't.'

Caitlin said nothing, battling to control her churning emotions. Then she herself stepped closer to one of the bags, bent down and took a closer look. When she spoke, it was with another voice. 'Do you know that Derek and I used to have this fantasy that we'd find a bag of money? We used to hope it would fall from a Wells Fargo truck that was travelling so quickly we couldn't catch its licence number. Then we'd tell ourselves that the money should be ours.' There was no resolve in her voice, just the echo of disbelief.

'Well, Caitlin, here's your fantasy – only this is real.'

'This is probably drug money. We should just get out of here.'

'Are you crazy? This is our chance. This motherlode will never fall in our path again. Whoever threw these bags from the Hummer is being arrested down there. Do you think he's about to admit anything about this money? He's not an idiot. Caitlin, don't tell me you couldn't use some of this cash. Think of all the time you can take off for your writing. You wouldn't have to go back to full-time work. I could kiss my clients good-bye forever. Please do this with me. At the first sign of real trouble, I promise we can ditch this stuff ourselves and walk away.'

'It's not that easy, Carmen.'

'Why not? Let's just go for it! Let's take this chance together, please.'

'He saw us – he saw both of us. Are you forgetting that?'

'We saw him. Do you remember what *he* looked like?'

'Yeah, I do. He had Hugh Grant hair, pale blue eyes, chiselled, tanned cheeks and a lantern chin.'

'For shit's sake, you're a writer. You see details that most of us miss. Anyway, what are we worrying about, he's already arrested down there.' There was desperation in Carmen's voice that Caitlin had never heard before.

'We don't know that for sure. And this money doesn't belong to us.'

'I know the money doesn't belong to us. But Caitlin, I don't have wealthy parents and I work my butt off, and you know what I make. Apart from three sick days, which come out of my salary, I have no other benefits. That means no pension – I'll be working till I drop. This money is a chance to change my life. I know this is hard for you to understand because money has never been a real problem for you.'

'Right. I only had to lose my grandmother and Derek to acquire it.'

'You know that's not what I meant, Caitlin. I don't mean to sound so mercenary. This money is my break. Try to understand. Put yourself in my place. If we don't take the cash, someone else will. Please Caitlin, just take a chance with me. We'll run at the first sign of trouble. Please, Caitlin.'

'Do you promise, on your word of honour, that we'll throw the money away at the first sign of trouble?'

'You have my word.'

'All right, I have a very bad feeling about this whole thing, but I'll help you out. Let's grab the stuff and get out of here. We'll go to the Bal Harbour Shops. I think there are lockers there. We can figure out what we're going to do from there.'

'Let's get a move on. The cops are bound to come back along this way. Here's to us, Caitlin! We're rich!' Carmen whispered, hoisting her yellow bag in the air. There was a hollowness to her bravado.

The bags were heavier than either of them had imagined, and they walked as quickly as they could from the trees to Collins. They ran, with a little difficulty, across the street and began the short hike up to the bridge.

'Don't walk so fast, Caitlin. As slight as it is, I have asthma, remember.'

'I know, but we have to get to the other side of the bridge as quickly as possible. We're out in the open here. Easily spotted by anyone.' Caitlin could feel worms in her calves.

'You're right,' Carm agreed and picked up her pace.

Today, Caitlin was oblivious to her surroundings. But a few days ago, she had stopped cycling on the bridge for a breathtaking view of Sunny Isles, Aventura's sister city on the coast. In the past few years, the transformation from a sleepy little stretch of Collins, that quiet Quebecers had made their own, was emerging as a hip and trendy place in Northeast Dade. Looking back, Caitlin could clearly see the assault of the high-rise castles. Old style 50's hotels were giving way to these massive self-contained resort-style condominiums. But the ocean was changing and unchanged, its rhythms impervious to capricious whims and greenbacks. Out there, the surf was splashed with white sails and cargo ships in the far distance. Below Haulover Bridge, the drone of waverunners, probably the best, high performance Yamahas, criss-crossed the choppy water under and around the bridge and out the narrow waterway to the ocean. On the west side, blue, yellow and green kites, in all shapes, even in the contour of a man, flopped and soared in the wind. Everywhere there was colour and movement. It wasn't only the warm weather that Canadians sought here in Florida, it was also the colour they lost to the many days of leaden skies back home.

At this moment, what Caitlin heard was Carmen's wheezing behind her on the bridge. What she felt was a puddle of perspiration around her breastbone where she held the bag of money close to her chest. Sweaty droplets snaked their way around her breasts and then fell quickly into the waistband of her shorts. Caitlin wiped her face across the top of her bag. 'Wrap your arms around your bag, Carmen. Try to hide its colour as much as you can. Keep your face from view. We are very exposed on the bridge.'

'I will. Geez, this money is heavier than anyone would expect. I hope you're right about those lockers at the Bal Harbour Shops.'

'I remember seeing them mid-way down the mall a long time ago. Holy God, I hope I remember the right place.'

'Holy shit, Caitlin! You mean you might not even know where we're going?'

'I'm pretty sure I saw them in this shopping centre. But I'm realizing as we walk, I wouldn't bet my life on my assumption.'

'Let's just make it there safely and we can work things out once we're inside the mall. Are you scared?'

'Shitless! We're almost at the end of the bridge.'

'Thank you, God,' Carmen wheezed, her relief obvious.

🌴

Harris got back into the Hummer quickly, trying to hurry Sergeant Tully along. He revved the engine a few times to get his attention, but Tully took his time. He was following Garderella's orders, but there was just so much time he could waste. In a few minutes, both men, in separate vehicles, drove back onto Collins Avenue heading south to Bal Harbour. With Tully behind him, Harris stayed off his cell, but he was on the lookout for the rest of the guys, and more importantly, the women. As the cars drove to the bridge, Harris looked over quickly to the ocean walk. It was difficult to manage a view because traffic was heavy as usual on both sides of Collins. MDPD was on the scene. He could make out the flashing lights of the patrol cars. He hoped that somehow Bobby had been able to get there first.

On the bridge, Harris saw nothing. At the end of the bridge, bordered by the ocean on one side, trees and canals on the other, Collins levelled out once more. His heart began to leap. Already, he was damp around his mouth and forehead, and his hands began to knuckle with the tension of a hunter. Coming off the bridge, he spotted the two women, and his bags. If only he had been alone! With Tully behind him, Harris was forced to drive past his money and had to be very careful not to alert the cop behind him. 'Jesus fucking Christ! You stupid bitches. I'll cut off both your hands when I catch up with you.' *Waitaminute, the cops haven't got the cash. We can still get it back. All right!* 'Maybe you bitches did me a favour!'

Since Carmen was still behind Caitlin, she was the first to see the Hummer. 'Oh no, oh God no! There's the Hummer and the driver has seen us.'

Caitlin stopped dead in her tracks and Carmen almost bumped into her. 'Now what do we do? Let me think. Maybe the guy lives a good distance away. Then we're safe!'

Up ahead, the Hummer made a left turn into the circular driveway of The Tiffany. The patrol car followed behind the Hummer.

Caitlin wiped the sweat from her forehead with her forearm. Carmen did not move. 'Quick, follow me,' Caitlin said, as she ran from the sidewalk, up the private driveway of an older apartment building. Carmen ran after her, wheezing. The west side of Collins, from the bridge to the Bal Harbour Shops, was populated by stately two-storey apartments and a few semi-detached dwellings that had refused to be torn down and sacrificed on the altar of greed. The lawns were manicured.

The green shrubs were neatly squared. Of the eight to ten buildings, one was generally under renovation at any given time. The owners and their children, who were rarely seen, were referred to as the real gentry of Bal Harbour. All of these quiet, old money people had lost their spectacular view of the ocean to progress and the giants on the east side of the street. The same side the Hummer had just entered.

Once she and Carmen were safely behind the apartment building, they dropped the bags and doubled over, panting. Carmen used her inhaler. 'We have to keep moving. We have at least a good five minutes. He can't make any move against us with the police escort. If we keep behind these buildings and keep running, we can make it to the mall before he has the chance to come out looking for us.'

Carmen began to mumble something. 'I'm…'

'There's no time for that now, Carmen. Just keep up with me. We can't be separated from one another. He's probably not alone. I've never read of anyone working alone with this kind of money. We have to keep running! The money is slowing us down; we should try to spot a safe place to hide it before we get to the mall. If someone else finds it, so be it. It's our lives I'm worried about. I'm not certain of anything right now– even less sure of the lockers I think I remember.'

They both ran together behind the condos. Carmen was dragging air into her lungs as best she could. Each time they came to a new driveway, they stopped, looked out at the sidewalk, and seeing no one suspicious, ran across the driveway to the next building. A few handymen saw the women, but said nothing as the two friends ran on to the next property.

Behind the second-to-last apartment building, they came across debris from renovation: boards, bricks, stones, smaller pieces of wood and collapsed cardboard boxes. The stuff appeared to have been there for a while. Beside the heap was an old drainage sewer with the grate partially twisted off its moorings. 'Here,' Carmen wheezed. The women dropped the bags a second time and dragged the grate farther away from the hole. They threw the smaller pieces of wood into the hole and then a few bricks. What they had thrown into the sewer hadn't fallen more than five feet. The drain had probably been blocked up for years. The women dropped the money into the hole. 'Just a second,' whispered Carmen. 'I have only forty dollars in cash and my cards. I think we should take some of this cash for emergencies.' Caitlin agreed. Carmen unzipped one of the bags and grabbed a good handful of hundred dollar bills. She gave Caitlin her share. She closed the bag, and both women covered the money with cardboard and bricks and wood. Then they dragged the grate back across, securing it. For additional safety, they dragged larger boards across the grate.

For a few seconds, before they began to run once more, the friends sat on the grass, each of them thinking her own thoughts, each looking away from the other. At the core, each of them felt very much alone.

CHAPTER EIGHT

ROBERT WELLS, 'BOBBY' to his friends, made the mistake of altering Harris' frantic orders. When the two met much later that night, that miscue flew back and hit him squarely on the jaw, with Harris' right fist on the other end of the punch. Bobby was second-in-command, a position he wanted and enjoyed over the other guys. He secretly craved the power hat, but he knew enough not to think of himself as Harris' sparring partner. In a physical ring, Bobby did not stand a chance.

He was, however, the cerebral power craft of the group, the accountant and bookkeeper. It was largely due to his efforts that the guys had amassed two million dollars in the first place. Bobby doled out the spending money and banked their savings like Scrooge. He had set the goal of four million dollars. Today's drop and pick-up of the 'peace and love' drug was their chance to move up from low-level dealers to million-dollar buyers. The guys' plan was to retire from dealing within the next four months once they had made the pick-up and walked away with enough ecstasy to see them to the finish line, a cool four mil.

This illicit drug had achieved such popularity in Miami that it was now the narcotic most often seized at the city's major airport. The methamphetamine represented eighty percent of the estimated value of the drugs seized so far this year. Coke was making a comeback in South Beach, but colleges, high schools and now grade schools, if things had worked out, preferred ecstasy. The kids still did not perceive the drug as dangerous.

Bobby's father was a senior architect who had moved him and his mother down to Miami for a three-year contract. He was designing new luxury dwellings on the Intracoastal. The view for the buyers promised passing yachts from their balcony, the Turnberry golf course a few steps from their gates and the Aventura Mall on the other side of the lake. The company his father designed for had set the family up at the Sheraton Bal Harbour Resort, across from the mall. Bobby lived in a tropical paradise. His window overlooked a garden with a mystic rope bridge suspended over a lagoon. This swanky place had drawn the likes of Bill Clinton and Bill Gates. He might have liked to meet Bill Gates who was into awesome work, but he had no interest in Clinton. His time was over, yesterday's news.

Bobby liked to create his own entertainment. When he was away from his computer, he strategized in his head and he was rarely off his BlackBerry, first cousin to the Palm Pilot. He was the fact finder – he was the source of any important information the group needed to know and remember. Their business figures were carefully encrypted in his PC, and only he and Harris had the entry code. Everything about Bobby was planned and meticulous.

He selected his clothes with the same care. The other six guys dressed to impress Harris. None of the team had come from the great unwashed. Each of the guys had no trouble with purchasing power. But Bobby didn't want to be a clone. He envied and hated that gift that Harris had of looking 'there', 'in the moment' with whatever he threw on. His apparent carelessness attracted the chicks and set the bar for the guys who were his friends. Bobby definitely looked as though he had worked on his clothes. His only extravagance and miscue was his fondness for gel. His black hair was combed back from his forehead and temples and heavily gelled. His hair glistened. He wore a yellow polo shirt and black shorts from Ralph Lauren. Black-lensed shades, black Nike Air Max's with no socks, a black titanium band on his Rolex all helped seal the package he was selling. When Bobby was nervous, he rotated his shoulders, and this nervous tick at times unravelled this hard sell.

Bobby changed Harris' plans because he felt his were superior and finding the cash under his direction could only enhance his prestige within the group. He moved with alacrity after Harris' frantic call. 'Settle the bill, Ted, and take two of the guys with you. The rest of you come out with me to the Navigator. Come on guys, get a move on! Finish up here as quickly as you can, Ted. But don't do anything to attract anyone's attention.' Bobby's group left the restaurant quickly and jumped into his Lincoln Navigator. 'Here's the problem. Harris had to dump the money.' Waiting for Ted, Bobby explained the situation. 'He wants some of you guys to be on the lookout at the bottom of the bridge on the south side. I think we all should get to the beach as quickly as possible and find the cash. The captain says a detective will be there in a matter of minutes, probably with backup. We have to get there first. We can't afford to leave some of you here on lookout. That money belongs to all of us, and I think it's still where Harris threw it. Searching together is the best way to find it. Call Ted on his cell and tell him what we're doing. All right. Let's get going!'

Getting out of the Bal Harbour Shops parking lot, which was always filled to capacity, was a bummer. The place was a showcase of the finest late-model automobiles: Bentleys, Jags, Mercedes, BMWs, Hummers, Corvettes and SUVs. Seniors who moved like slugs and were as old as Miami drove most of these cars. They were rich and cantankerous and did not give a hoot's ass about speed anymore. It was a cardinal rule in Bal Harbour for anyone younger than fifty to settle fender benders with seniors as quickly as possible. The dyed-heads reigned supreme in word-fests. They enjoyed confrontations, used them for dinner talk. That's why Bobby stayed a polite four feet behind a little old woman, a dandelion gone to seed, in a white Jag. He would have preferred to crowd her, but Bobby was a quick study. Two traffic lights later, a white helmeted attendant in a red uniform and white sash, a perfect replica of a British guard, finally directed him onto Collins. Five o'clock traffic is heavy and slow on the avenue. Your average Joes and Marys, who work at the mall and in the luxury condos, are filing out onto the sidewalk like a colony of ants and running for buses. The traffic moves as slowly as a senior.

Immediately, the soot grey Navigator with vanity plates and Racing Dynamic steel wheels was snarled in traffic and forced to the right-hand lane; behind him, Ted fared no better. Finally, Bobby drove through the second light and was approaching the bridge. If the women had been walking down this side of the walk, the SUV was moving so slowly that any one of the guys could have reached out and grabbed the cash. As they began to drive over the bridge, still hemmed in the right lane, two 'S' buses, one following the other in the middle lane, drove up beside their vehicle. 'What luck,' Bobby hissed. 'Anyway, keep your eyes open on this side. James, be ready to jump to the sidewalk if you see them. As soon as we can park at the beach, run with me. We have no time to waste. The bags were thrown into the trees on the left side at the beginning of the walk. We have to find them.' The guys had no trouble taking orders from Bobby.

'James, you stand as lookout. As soon as you see the cops, whistle twice. We have to clear the area before anyone of the cops can spot us. With James' signal, get out of the area. Head back to the SUV's or walk onto the beach. Don't be caught standing around. The last thing we need to do is to cause further suspicion. Once a crowd gathers, we can join it. In a crowd, we'll be unremarkable. If we find the cash, whoever does, carry it quickly back to the Lincoln. I left the trunk unlocked. Then honk once. That'll be our signal to get back to my SUV. Am I clear on all this? Tell Ted's guys.'

Heads nodded with tension.

Once Bobby and Ted had parked, the guys ran into the trees with the stealth and speed of stray cats along the ocean walk. They heard James' whistle one minute later, but they had had no time for any kind of search. They scrambled out of the trees and bushes seconds before Garderella's car came to a stop. Backup was there in a flash of lights. Bobby stepped into the bushes that led to the ocean, cursing every god he didn't believe in. His arthritic knees began to ache, a gift from his mother and today's humidity. More than once he had wished he could blame his bad knees on a sport's injury. There could have been some redemption in that. This was hardly the time for stretching and squats. Even in the best of times, Bobby abstained from these things. He stood quietly and let his knees do their aching. While he stood there, rotating his shoulders, a curious crowd began to gather around the patrol cars. Bobby walked out of the bushes and joined it. The other guys did too.

Bobby's cell rang. With the cover from a motley collection of bathers standing around him, answering it was no problem. 'Where the fuck are the guys?' Harris shouted. 'I told you to have them on the south side of the bridge. There was nothing I could do. I have a police escort. What the fuck happened?'

'Harris, I thought we'd have a better chance of finding the items if we looked together,' Bobby answered, conscious of a sickening blend of suntan lotion coming from the crowd. 'But the cops are already here and we never had a chance to search for the lost items.'

'Well, you fuck-up, we could have had the cash back in our hands if you had listened to my orders.'

Orders! Orders! Who the fuck do you think you are? 'I'm sorry, Harris.'

'You will be.'

'What happened?'

'The bitches got the money just like I said they would. I saw them at the end of the bridge! Where our guys should have been! I can't talk any more – I just drove into my parking lot, and the cop is getting out of his car. Get back to Bal Harbour. That's where they're heading, just like I fucking said. Get your asses back here and find them. I'll meet you at Neiman Marcus as soon as I lose the cop. Did you hear me this time, Bobby? Are we clear on this?'

'We're on our way. I'm really sorry. I just thought…'

'Fuck it!'

It took another few minutes to round up the guys, time they did not have to waste. Bobby snuck a peek at Garderella before he hightailed it to the SUV. She was the only cop in plainclothes. She was rubbing the side of her cheek.

I know what I saw, she was thinking. *Either Harris had backup himself to retrieve the cash, or someone on the beach found it and ran off with it. But there was no one in sight*

when I drove onto the walk. What the hell happened here?
She called Tully.

'I'm just explaining to Mr. Chalmer that I would like
to accompany him to his door.'

'We can't force him to do anything, so don't push
things, sergeant. Frivolous lawsuits are not the way we
want to go. But I want you to idle at the exit of the parking lot – I want to see where our Mr. Chalmer is heading. I don't think he'll stay put very long.'

'No problem.'

CHAPTER NINE

ON THE ROUTE back across the bridge, Bobby checked the rear-view mirror to see if they were being followed. There was too much traffic to catch much of anything. He did notice Nipples gnawing on his lower lip. It took only a second or two to recall Harris' words; *I was made before I even left the parking lot.* The snitch had to have come from the inside, one of their own. *It has to be Nipples.* He made a quick scan of the other faces. All he saw was anger and frustration. On Nipples' face he saw fear.

Nipples was tall and narrow-shouldered, with narrower hips. He was built like a carrot, or a scarecrow. Nipples had been unlucky enough to inherit his grandfather's breasts. It was unusual, to see small, hard breasts on a man. Of course, older guys had breasts, and men with prostate cancer who were forced to take steroids had them too. But a nineteen year old? Tits were depressing for a guy. Nipples wore loose fitting shirts, never t-shirts, and stood stooped-shouldered to hide them. But these guys had a nose for weakness, and his breasts had been unceremoniously uncovered in a friendly shoving match. From that day on, Nipples had been assigned pothole duty.

Bobby and Ted pulled over to the side of Collins soon after they had crossed the bridge. Bobby took command. 'All right, check behind these apartments, look everywhere. Under balconies, behind bushes, in doorways, anywhere you can think of. You have their descriptions. We'll meet at the shops, outside, around

Neiman Marcus. If you find the women, grab the cash and run. The Navigator will be in the lot with the trunk unlocked again. Harris may have different ideas, but I don't think it's wise to beat up on the women. We just want our money. No one has ever been arrested – we don't want to break with tradition. Nipples stay with me. Harris and I need you at the mall. The rest of you get out and start searching. You all have cells; use them.'

It took minutes he did not have to find a parking place back at the mall, but Bobby did find one close to the red zone, Neiman Marcus. He felt their luck might be changing for the good. He took command and gave an order to Nipples. 'Circle around to the back of the store to scout out the number of employee entrance/exits they have. I'll wait here for Harris. Get back here in five.'

'See you in five.' There was no way he'd use his cell and call the cops again. He did not even know where the money was, and the last thing he wanted was to be implicated in all this bullshit. His father wasn't as understanding as Harris and Bobby pretended their fathers were. His would probably kill him, or close to it. It was up to the cops now. He had done all he could. He had to worry about himself. That was the problem with gangs – once you joined, even collegians like Harris' group, you could not walk away. There was an unwritten rule about AWOLs. He had been better off as a loner, a kid who ate alone in the cafeteria. He had been trying to remember what had been so rotten about that. At least, he wasn't 'Nipples' then. In the beginning, he had not really minded being the gopher, but he had hoped to move up in the ranks. That hadn't happened. Now he wasn't a loner; he was a felon. Since his call to the cops a few days ago, Nipples had not really slept. He had heavy pouches under his eyes like someone with

allergies, and the whites were streaked with red. He had
money enough to be noshing on stone crab-stuffed por-
tobello mushrooms, alligator tail nuggets or simple fare
at Quizno's. Instead he was freaked about his life and
frightened of his father. He knew that Bobby had kept
him close today for a reason. He found two exits and
walked back to the front of the store to meet Bobby.

Once inside the suite, Harris changed clothes and
threw on his father's floppy sun hat. He flew out the
door, raced to the condo next door and crossed to the
shops from there. He did not see Tully and he hoped
Tully had not seen him either.

Who does he think he's kidding? Tully smiled. Although
he had parked his vehicle on the grounds of The
Tiffany, he was standing out on the front sidewalk with
a good view of Collins. When Harris bounded across
the street, Tully made a call to Garderella.

Harris easily spotted Bobby and Nipples and waved
them both around to the side of the store, pretty much
out of sight. 'Anything?' he asked Bobby.

'Not yet, but we're looking.'

Harris' left jab caught Bobby flush on the chin, split-
ting his lower lip. He fell back into the concrete wall,
smacking his head. Harris caught him before he fell to
the ground. 'That's for not following my orders,
Number Boy! That's the end of it. Take this like a man
– we have a lot of work to do and I need you.'

Bobby's face morphed into a deflated soccer ball and
he mumbled something that might have been 'sorry'.
His cranial skin tightened and Bobby offered Harris a
thin smile. A thing ugly, vengeful, bitter. Harris saw the
threat, but its effect did not last longer than a pack of
chips. Nipples could not quash a quiet smirk. He began

to breathe a little easier. Maybe no one suspected him.
That's what he was hoping. 'We can settle the accounts
another time. Right now, we have to find the bitches
who have our money. Have you heard anything from
the other guys?'

'They've found nothing. They will hook up with us
in a few minutes. I told them the Armani shop.'

'Fuck. Call them again. I just remembered that one
of the bitches was sunburned. That screams tourist.
That's why I'm more certain than ever that they're
headed to the mall. There's better cover. I want all the
guys here. This is where we'll start looking.'

'Done,' Bobby said, making the call.

Garderella was disappointed, but not surprised not
to have found the cash. If Chalmer was carrying two
million bucks for a huge buy, he had backup. But why
hadn't she made the other car as well? Tourists were a
possibility, but she was certain she had not seen a single
one on the walk where he had to have thrown the cash.
She wanted another crack at him before she called it a
day and drove back to the precinct on NW 25th Street.
Garderella picked up Tully's call. 'All right, their backup has picked up the cash, or they've lost it altogether.
I'll drive out to the mall. Keep your distance. I don't
want to spook him. I'm certain Harris Chalmer's making some connection there, but we have no grounds for
an arrest.'

'10-4.'

Garderella hoped she could have an additional day
for surveillance. Budgets were tight, and she might not
manage it. However, all cops were well aware of the
mayhem that usually resulted from a pick-up or a drop
gone bad. Chalmer was a college kid from a prominent

family, lured by the drug's enormous profit potential. He was too cocky to realize the violence of the international crime groups who had staked claims to the ecstasy market.

Chalmer might not realize the retribution exacted from competing organized crime groups. Though the violence linked to ecstasy had not risen to the level of other drugs, it had risen from infancy to the childhood stage, and it was definitely on the increase.

Recent reports suggest Russian and Israeli crime groups are the big players in the ecstasy trade; Columbian and Dominican groups are gaining ground. Last year, a lab was uncovered in Ottawa, Canada. It was a massive drug operation that stretched overseas. Connections to this lab were discovered in Toronto, Vancouver and Hong Kong. That buyer was never found.

Though Garderella had taken a dislike to Chalmer, she did not want him to meet the same fate of a college student and part-time floral deliveryman who was gunned down near his townhouse on a quiet *cul-de-sac* in Prince William County, Virginia. Another ecstasy dealer, a twenty-three year old from Mineola, a New York suburb, was stomped to death because his supplier felt he was shortchanging him. She did not want Chalmer Senior to discover a son he did not know lying face down on some side street on Miami Beach. Garderella had good instincts and a decent heart, despite the hard times she was struggling through.

Before Harris and Nipples began to walk briskly around to the front of the store, Harris' cell rang. When he saw the caller ID, he took a few deep breaths before answering. 'Yes, sir.'

'We have a C.O.D. delivery, Mr. Chalmer, that should have been picked up a good while ago.'

'I've had car trouble,' Harris said, fighting his tightening vocal cords. His lips were as stiff as cement.

'Has it been resolved? Have you been able to get your hands on another vehicle?'

'I haven't, but my car will be out of the dealer's shop in a couple of days.'

'I'm afraid the warehouse does not have the storage space, sir. You will have to borrow another car and pick up the merchandise.'

Harris lost it. 'Look, I can't pick up the merchandise today. I have to wait to get the Hummer back. I can't work without it.'

'I urge you to consider another form of transport. Our creditors have to be paid.'

'I've always picked up all my orders on time. Can I take the item on consignment?'

'That's not the way we work, sir. We also don't feel such a move would be wise on your part.'

Harris shook his neck from side to side, trying to loosen the tension that was as tight as a wire. It was fine when he was causing such tension in his own crew. It kept them in line. When he found himself on the other end of clenching fists, he felt quite differently. 'I can't pick anything up for at least three days. Just give me that time.'

'I have to put you on hold, sir.'

Harris began rocking back and forth on his heels, never taking the receiver from his ear.

'Sir, are you there?'

'Yes.'

'You have three days.'

CHAPTER TEN

CAITLIN AND CARMEN ran faster now, without the weight of the money. After seeing the Hummer, their throats were dry and both friends coughed as they ran. Carmen added a few asthmatic wheezes. 'We have to stop for a minute, Carm. My shorts are dirty from the debris we hoisted on top of the money – yours are too. Let me think. We have to think of something. That guy is out there, and he's seen us. He knows what direction we're taking.'

Carmen took this break to use her inhaler again.

'Don't use too much of that stuff, Carm.'

'I know, I know.'

'We have to get a change of clothes. I think our best bet is Neiman Marcus. It's right at our end of the mall. We'll buy some new clothes there and get rid of these,' pointing to the ones they were wearing. 'Then, we'll get out of the mall as quickly as we can and hightail it to Sheldon's. I don't think we should head back from the mall. At Sheldon's, we'll wait till it's dark, after six. It's already after five now. It's dark by six-twenty. We'll grab a cab home from the drug store. Let's get going.'

Carmen added nothing and fell in behind Caitlin. When they reached the mall, the women thought of trying to get through the hedge, but it was too thick and wouldn't budge when they tried to pry the branches apart. Sprinting to the main driveway, they ran to their right, stayed in the parking lot and used the cars for cover as they hurried to the department store. They carefully scanned the area when they were in sight of the front entrance.

Harris was busy finishing his call at the side of the store and never saw the women sprint up to the front door and into the store. He missed seeing them by a second or two. By the time he and Nipples rounded the corner, the two C's were searching the first floor for leisure wear. Harris had stationed Nipples at the front door beside the parking lot. He himself walked into Neiman Marcus, every muscle alert, his manner vulpine. Caitlin and Carmen had figured out that the women's wear was located on the second floor.

The friends stepped onto the escalator, bristling with fear. Exposed, they couldn't crouch behind the customers in front or behind them. They were compelled to search the first floor to assure themselves they were not being followed and cornered up there on the second floor. Carmen was about to take another drag of deep breath when her eyes locked with Harris'. It was the sunburned legs that he had first spotted. 'Caitlin,' Carmen whispered, 'he's down there and he's seen me!'

Harris was so surprised at his good luck that he didn't make any move for a second or two. The friends used those seconds to bully their way to the second floor. Still Harris did not make a move. He called Nipples on his cell. 'They're here! I just saw them. They're headed up to the second floor. Get your butt up there. Stand by the escalators – I'll search the floor. Don't move from that position. Call Bobby. Tell him to have the rest of the guys guarding the exits of the mall. Tell him to rush the guys to their posts! We have them. Holy fuck, we have them!'

Within minutes, Bobby had spoken to the other guys. There was soon a human noose around the mall. He ached to be the one who tightened it. He took up

what he felt was the best position, leaving the rear to
the lesser guys. He was sure the asshole had loosened
one of his teeth. He had no time to plot his revenge –
first he wanted the spotlight on himself. He knew one
thing. Numbers were not ever going to do it for him. It
was a pity, he thought, that guys in general sneered at
everything but action. Revered it, in fact.

It took Nipples time to take up his position. Neiman
Marcus is a large department store. Shoppers were
everywhere, hungry for sales. It was not always easy getting around older customers, some amiable, some not.
Nurses, pushing wheelchairs around the store, accompanied several old women, all seasoned shoppers.
Others had maids lugging a load of parcels. The older
folks, proprietary in nature, sometimes moved slowly
on purpose to clear the way. The young ones frequent-
ed the boutiques. Nipples moved, but not as quickly as
Harris would have liked. He did not know what he
wanted. Either way, Harris would eventually probe for
the snitch angle. Nipples also knew that Harris would
be in a hellish state if he lost the money. He ran the rest
of the way to the second floor, stepping around customers as he walked and tried to run up the escalator.
Until he could figure something out, he had to play
according to Harris' rules. Once he was close to the
descending escalator, he began to search the floor himself.

Tully had crossed Collins but had lost sight of Harris
when he had walked around the side of Neiman
Marcus. When he spoke with Garderella, she told him
to get back out on the sidewalk. She was coming to the
mall, but she too would monitor the situation from a
distance. She wanted to discover what friends he was
hooking up with.

Both Caitlin and Carmen were in a wild state of

panic when they reached the second floor. Caitlin's face was slippery with perspiration as she sought a hiding place. There were no exit doors she could see. She ran instinctively, with Carmen close behind her, to a women's changing room on her far left. Caitlin remembered something odd that gave her hope. Back in Montreal, she had gotten off her bike one day beside a small park. A young boy had just taken the leashes off of both his dogs to allow them to run free. The dogs spotted a squirrel and they raced out after it. One dog ran on either side of the squirrel, leaving the small animal no means of escape. The hunt was mean and frantic. The dogs' demeanour was ferocious. The young boy was visibly afraid to call them off for fear they would turn on him. The three raced up and down in a relatively small space. Caitlin turned away three or four times when it appeared the dogs would tear the little animal to pieces. When she looked back, the beleaguered little guy was still running for his life. In total disbelief, Caitlin watched as the squirrel made a sudden leap and escaped with his life. The dogs returned to the boy's side snarling and beaten. If this little guy escaped when he was outnumbered, maybe she and Carmen would too.

When they reached the dressing room, the friends encountered Hilda. She was a tall woman of some bulk, her grey hair tied in a bun. She wore a resigned look that came from strength and durability, or just a jaded weariness from waiting on the ungrateful rich.

'We need your help!' Caitlin cried.

Hilda was a woman who never wasted a word, but she could see Caitlin's terror and Carmen's tears.

'Is there an exit in the changing rooms?'

'There is, but it's locked by management.' Hilda sat down at a small table covered with clothes people had dumped on her after trying them on and deciding they wouldn't do.

'Is there another exit?' Caitlin was speaking so quickly she was tripping over her words.

'At the far end.'

'Jesus, that's too far.' Then Caitlin spotted the lockers, five of them. Four fitted with locks. She read Hilda's nametag. Caitlin made her decision quickly. 'Hilda, my name is Caitlin. There are some men chasing us, and we'll be badly beaten or worse if they find us. My friend will hide in the locker here. Do you have a lock for it?'

'Yes, but…'

'Please Hilda help us – you have to help us.' Caitlin pushed Carmen into the locker and closed it before Hilda had a chance to stop her. 'I'm going to hide under this table. Please sit down and give me some protection. Our lives are at risk. If those men find us here, you won't be safe either. They won't leave witnesses behind. I'm really sorry Hilda,' Caitlin said as she dove under the table, pulling clothes down the side of the table to keep herself hidden. Then she said not another word.

Hilda was seventy years old and she did not want to die. She had seen panic in the eyes of her grandson who had succumbed to cancer at the age of thirty-two three months ago. 'I don't want to die, Gran,' he had wept, rolling back and forth across his bed two days before his death. Hilda recognized the same panic in Caitlin's eyes. Hilda was a tough broad who had outlived two husbands and one of her five sons. Hilda had made up her mind long ago that she'd meet her maker on her own terms. These did not include being written up in *The Herald* as a helpless victim, an innocent bystander, who just happened to be at the wrong place at the wrong time. She had no interest in ciphers and foot-

notes. Besides, a golden retriever and a tabby cat waited for her at home and wanted dinner. It was that simple for her.

Hilda was on the lookout for Harris and she saw him
before he was aware of her. Once he was on the second
floor, he ran to the first changing room, pushed his way
past the hapless attendant and checked each cubicle of
the changing room. He slammed his fist into the side-
wall for good measure. Back on the floor, he stood
motionless, scanning everything he could see, waiting
for Nipples to take up his guard post. Once his sentry
had arrived, Harris ran to Hilda's station, but she pretended to ignore him.

'Hey,' Harris said gruffly. 'Two of my friends are
playing hide-and-seek on me. One is blonde – the other
is dark. I saw them on the escalator. Have you seen
them?'

Harris reminded Hilda of a red-lighted burner, hot
and dangerous. 'Sir, we've been pretty busy here all day.
I haven't had the time to notice anyone.'

'Are you blind? They just got to the second floor.
I'm sure they were running. You must have seen something.'

'No, sir, I can assure you I am not blind, and I didn't
notice anyone.' Hilda drew her knees more tightly
together.

Crouched like a mouse in a corner, Caitlin could just
make out the tips of Harris' Sperry boat shoes, rocking
angrily back and forth. Her palms were red as they
shouldered her weight. The small joints ached and
strained. As quiet as a mime, Caitlin dared take only
shallow breaths. She could smell Hilda, the heavy, sweet
odour of older people who applied perfume with a
heavy hand. Would Hilda betray them? Caitlin hoped
not – all three lives depended on the saleswoman.

Carmen's shoulders ached from the moment Caitlin pushed her into the locker. The school-size locker was not wide enough for anyone's shoulders. With only the four slats at the top of the locker, Carmen could not see Harris, but she felt his closeness. She dared not move an inch – lockers creaked. A dry hacking cough wanted out, but Carmen kept swallowing her phlegm to keep herself quiet. Her nose began to bleed, but there was no room to tilt her head back to stop the flow. Carmen caught the blood drops in her hand. Her cheeks were red with panic. Sweat dripped from her hair, a tiny drop making its way into her ear. What if he had a knife and rammed it through one of the slats? She would never see it coming. Her nails bit into the heels of her hand. What if?

Harris pushed past Hilda and headed for the changing rooms.

'Sir, you are not allowed back there,' Hilda called after him.

He punched each of the doors open. He found only one woman older than Hilda in the last cubicle. When the door of her cubicle flew open, spider-like, she backed into a corner. Harris left the old woman in her web of fear and went to the exit. He gave a vicious kick at the door. 'Come back here and open this door for me!'

Hilda thought of making her escape while Harris was back at the exit, but thought better of it. He'd catch up to her; she knew that well enough. She took only a few steps towards the back door. 'I have no key for that door. Management has their meetings back there. Only they have keys. Your friends have not gotten through this door.'

'Fuck!' Harris ran back to the front of the dressing room and saw the lockers for the first time. They had been right behind him, but he had not noticed them. Jabbing at the first one, he sneered, 'What are these? What's your name, lady?'

'Hilda.'

'O.K., Hilda, what are these lockers for?' He could sense that this Hilda was a firewall that would take him time he didn't have to break through. He could almost admire her take-charge no-nonsense attitude. She reminded him of his grandmother.

'They contain the day's discarded clothes,' Hilda answered, unafraid of this spoiled brat. At least, that was the message she wanted to send out. Her sciatica told a truer story. 'I lock the clothes away to keep shoplifting to a minimum. I'll open the lockers if you like.' Hilda moved to the first locker closest to Harris and unlocked it. She moved to the second, unlocking it too. Then the third.

Carmen felt the scream rise in her throat. Slowly she raised her hand to her mouth to smother it, smearing her hand with blood.

Hilda unlocked the fourth locker.

Caitlin began to arch her shoulders to spring at Harris. He would never expect an attack to come from the floor.

'Fuck! Stop it, Hilda. They're not here. Where the fuck did they get to?' Harris paced quickly back and forth, forcing himself to think logically. 'Hilda, don't do anything stupid after I leave. Do you understand me? Are we both clear on the concept?'

'I have nothing to report, sir. I hope you find your friends.'

'I'm sure you do, Hilda.' He called Nipples. 'Anything?'

'Nothing.'

Harris walked a few feet away from Hilda before

speaking again. 'Is it possible they hid on the other side of the escalator and took it back down? Think, Nipples.'

'I don't know, Harris. I got here as fast as I could. I checked the other escalator, but they could have been crouching on the stairs, so I wouldn't have seen them. Did you check them when you were coming up to the second floor?' Nipples asked nervously.

'I didn't see the stairs either,' Harris had to admit. He called Bobby. 'Keep an eye out – have the guys alert at all the exits. We can't lose them now,' Harris whined, desperation in his voice.

'All the exits are accounted for, Harris. No one has gotten by us. Keep looking.'

'All right.' His nerves were fraying – he felt a fist around his heart.

Harris called Nipples again. 'Stay where you are. I'm going to check every inch of this floor. I still think those bitches are up here somewhere.' He ran to the exit at the far end of the room, noted that an alarm would be activated if anyone opened the door and began a methodical search. He stopped at each clothing display rack, frisking the garments. He got on all fours searching for legs, he checked behind cashiers' counters and he swore. They were up here – he knew they were still here. But where the hell were they? It was very difficult for Harris to believe that the 'bitches' had outwitted him. He moved around like a cat because he remembered his supplier's phone call. For the first time in his life, Harris was scared. But he told himself to keep focused; that was the only chance he had of ever seeing his cash again.

Hilda walked to the dressing room and took the eighty-something customer's arm and led her back out on the floor. 'You're all right now. There is nothing to worry about. Do you need any help to get down the escalator?'

'What kind of place are you running here?' she scolded. 'I am quite capable of getting downstairs on my own. I made it up here didn't I?' That rotten nature would probably keep the old woman alive a few more years. *More power to her*, thought Hilda. With speed no one might expect of Hilda, she first located Harris at the other end of the floor. Then she made a deliberate manoeuvre of her own. One thing she had learned about men was that they fed on challenge. Well, so did she.

When Harris had covered half the floor and was approaching Nipples, he began to recap all the places he had searched, counting each one off on his fingers. When he came to Hilda's dressing room, he stopped dead in his tracks. 'Lockers! There were six! And I only checked three! Jesus fucking Christ! That old broad!' Harris practically flew back to Hilda's dressing room.

She was sitting at her table sorting clothes and did not even look up when Harris came to a stop inches from her table.

'Open the other three lockers! Now! Slamming his fist down on the small table, causing the garments to jump.

'I am a little tired of this game, sir. I am beginning to think your friends don't want to be found, and I'm busy.' Hilda just did not like this smartass.

'Open the lockers,' he spoke so quietly that Hilda's stomach lurched, but she stood up as straight as a yard-stick.

Carmen's lips were cracking at the corners because she had been breathing through her mouth since the nose bleed. Her nose was blocked with dried blood.

Caitlin's fists were clenched – her eyes were closed tightly.

'Fuck, just give me the keys,' Harris roared. He opened the fourth locker and found only clothes. He slammed the door shut. He unlocked the fifth, found more clothes. Swore. Unlocked the sixth, discovered even more garments.

Hilda had stuffed number six with garments to hide the blood on the floor.

Harris kicked the sixth door shut, turned and saw the table, seemingly for the first time. With one swipe, he threw the clothes to the floor. There was no one under the table. He had been so certain.

'I told you, sir, your friends never came to this dressing room. If you haven't found them, they must have run back downstairs.'

'Shut the fuck up. Just shut the fuck up,' but there wasn't much heat in the second curse. 'We checked the first three lockers, right? Maybe I should look at them again.'

'You have the keys, sir.' Hilda's little smirk was not lost on Harris.

Harris knew he was coming apart and drew the line at making a fool of himself in front of this old bag. He tossed the keys back on the table. 'Get back to your clothes, Hilda. Remember, don't think of calling anyone,' he warned her as he walked away.

'I'm repeating myself, sir, but I hope you find your friends.' *Men are so predictable*, Hilda thought. *Chump.*

He ran to the escalator, spoke with Nipples, who was no help and continued his methodical search of the other side of the floor.

Hilda whispered into the first locker. 'You can't come out. The two young men are still looking for you on this floor. I also heard the angry one who searched this area speaking to others who appear to be on the lookout downstairs. What are your names?'

'Caitlin and Carmen,' Caitlin's very frightened voice whispered through the slats. 'You saved our lives. How can we ever thank you?'

'I don't know about that, but I do know real trouble when I see it. I'll pass a wet handkerchief to you to wipe some of the blood from your face, but I can't do anything until those scoundrels leave my floor,' Hilda whispered to the second locker. 'I know that young man doesn't trust me, so both of you had better not move a muscle while they're still on the floor. I'm betting he won't come back to check your lockers. Don't make any noise to attract attention. I have to go to the racks now to hang some of these clothes. I'll be back in a few minutes.'

The silence around the lockers was a shield, but it was also ominous. Neither woman dared whisper anything to the other. If Harris had returned to the lockers, he would not even have heard the women breathing. They had been standing perfectly still or crouching for almost an hour and a half. Sharp, stabbing pain ran up their thighs. Caitlin's right foot began to cramp, the arch curling inside her Nike. She raised the foot, clinging to the sides of the locker with her fingers and tried to straighten it. Her calf began to spasm. Caitlin covered her mouth to keep from screaming. Gently, she lowered her foot and pressed it to the floor of the locker. The spasm began to break up. It was easier for her to breathe.

There was the sound of someone approaching. 'Hello! Hello! You can never find an attendant when you need one.' 'Hello, is anyone serving this section? Oh, there you are,' said a customer.

'Yes, madam, here I am. I'll take you to number two.'

Hilda led the way. 'Call me if you need assistance,' she told the prospective buyer.

In a few minutes, the customer came waltzing out from number two. 'Are they making size fourteen smaller today, trying to save money? I know I'm a size fourteen, sometimes a twelve.'

'You might have a point there,' Hilda smiled.

'Anyway, I really don't need a thing today and I'm not about to give my good money to a company scrimping to save a few dollars.'

'I agree with you completely,' Hilda smiled a second time. 'I know for a fact that Sacks carries this line. You might want to give it a try.'

'Well, thank you. Maybe I will.'

'She's gone,' Hilda whispered. 'Your nemesis is still on the floor. I have to get back to work. I'll be back in a short time. Stay very quiet.'

When Caitlin and Carmen were alone again, Carmen had a sickening thought. She had always been afraid of small places. What if Hilda never came back? She did not owe them anything. What if she was stuck in this locker for the whole night? *What have I done to myself? What have I done to my best friend? If only we could go back and start the day over...*

CHAPTER ELEVEN

IT WAS ALMOST seven o'clock and once the two other changing rooms opened up again, there were no more customers for Hilda's station because hers was the farthest away from the escalator. She purposely carried clothes to the other side of the floor to hang back on the racks. Hilda wanted to keep an eye on Harris – she also wanted him to see she had nothing to hide. He looked over her way a few times when their paths almost crossed. Her presence made him feel more the fool by the minute. Harris had a hard time letting go of an idea, and Hilda was reminding him he had made a mistake believing the women were still on the floor. He knew he could not waste any more time. Jabbing at the racks, he walked over to Nipples. 'Let's get the fuck out of here. We'll go downstairs and help secure the exits of the mall. You better pull your weight. Do you hear me?' Harris screamed.

'Yeah, I will. I've been doing what you told me to,' Nipples answered, following Harris like a kid going to the principal's office.

Hilda was rather pleased with herself when Harris and his cohort left the floor. Although she was loath to admit it, Hilda was just a little bit excited. This was a lot better than looking forward to a night of reruns on network television. Her mind was as sharp as a tack and Hilda was feeling younger than she had felt in years. In fact, she began to construct a plan of escape for the two women. If she succeeded in getting them off the grounds of the mall, she would feel very good about herself. After that, Hilda knew she wanted no part in this thing, whatever it was. But an idea was hatching. Two actually. A small smile began to curl around her lips before she walked very briskly back to the lockers.

Before she spoke, she made very sure there was no one else around. 'It's me. I'll unlock the doors. But please don't step out. Both young men have gone downstairs, but they could come back. I can't be implicated in whatever this involves. I just can't. You both have to understand that.' When Hilda unlocked and opened both doors, her heart melted when she saw Caitlin and Carmen. Both women were crying, and Carmen's face was streaked with blood. Neither woman made any attempt to move – they appeared to be stuck to the lockers. Their clothes were drenched with perspiration, and there was a bad odour emanating from both the C's. There could be no doubt they were afraid for their lives. Though her own stomach was clenching, Hilda remembered Sam, her golden retriever. These two young women did not look much better than Sam had the day she had rescued him from the shelter. These women could have been her daughters, her granddaughters even.

'The only way you can leave the lockers is to leave my floor. I know you're both in a dangerous situation, but, since you told me what could easily happen to me, I can't take any chances. There are more than two of them downstairs – I know because I heard the mean one shouting into his cell phone. I have a plan.'

Hope in the young was something to see. Caitlin and Carmen's shoulders straightened; blood rose in both their cheeks. Hilda could see the energy surging through both of them.

'You can't take the chance of leaving now. But, after nine, all the employees of the mall swarm out together.

Close to a couple hundred of us. You're safer to make your escape from the front door at the centre of the mall because that's the exit that's most used. It'll be seething with activity then.'

Neither woman blinked as they listened.

'There's something else. We could simply call the police.'

Carmen's brain raced. 'No, no, Hilda. We can't do that. I've been thinking about that while I was holed up in here. What could the police do? What can we even say that guy has done to us? Nothing. The fallout might put our addresses in his hands. Then where would we be? We just want to get back to our place here. This has been a day we both want to forget.'

'All right then. But you can't leave the mall in those clothes. Those young men know what you're wearing and they'll be looking to catch sight of those clothes. I can't use your credit cards because people know who I am. I recognize the accent. You're Canadians aren't you?'

The C's nodded.

'Another thing I know about Canadians is that many of you prefer to use cash than plastic. Is that true of you two?'

'We use both,' Carmen answered.

'Well, if you give me some money, I'll get the clothes for you: shorts, a couple of tops and anything else I can think of. Do you have enough money for those things?'

'We were intending to shop here and we have emergency money,' Carmen said sheepishly. Not wanting to alarm Hilda, Carmen tried to arrange the hundred dollar bills while she spoke. Then she handed over the large bills.

'All hundreds?' Hilda asked with a hum of suspicion.

'That's our Canadian banks for you. Trying to

squeeze fifties and twenties requires advance notice. I've only been here a few days and I didn't think I'd have any trouble with large bills at this mall.'

Hilda took the cash, somewhat reassured. 'You can't leave these lockers. There is no way I can put myself in jeopardy. So you must stay hidden until nine. At nine, you can walk out with the rest of us, but I can't walk with you. I can't take that chance. I have to be here tomorrow – I need this job. There is not a whole lot out there for a seventy year old. Will you both follow my plan?'

The friends nodded again.

'I have to shut the doors and lock them,' Hilda said, her lips bent in a humourless smile. 'You have a little less than an hour and a half to wait.'

Caitlin and Carmen nodded grim-faced, as the locker doors shut on them once again. Since it was dangerous to speak to one another, they were each forced to rely on inner strength and resolve to get them through until nine o'clock. Caitlin tried to escape the physical and mental discomfort by thinking about Derek. But her thoughts were grim, bleak. She recalled that she felt herself choking on that last day at the funeral parlour when the director closed the casket on Derek. She tried to breathe for him, but she was having trouble breathing herself. When she thought of the absolute darkness closing in on Derek, her body trembled, almost violently. Caitlin rested the palms of her hands against the sides of the locker to steady herself. She knew she would escape this cage of steel tonight and, with that thought, her heart relaxed. Tension in her shoulders eased because Caitlin could see her door opening. How she wished she could have opened the casket and helped Derek from his night of darkness!

Carmen spent some of her time trying to clear her

nose, to open a decent air passage. There was no way she would use her vent in the locker. Someone might hear her drag of breath. Her lips were sore – her lip balm was back at the condo. The sunburn was not helping the situation. Carmen kept her thoughts on the present, listening attentively for any noise outside the lockers. Three times she heard women come into the dressing room and leave, complaining because Hilda was not at her desk. A sharp pain that began in her feet wiggled its way up her legs. *Even my toes are sore!* Carmen realized. It was very strange that she heard nothing coming from Caitlin's locker, nothing. She tried to think of the clothes Hilda was buying for them, wondered if they would fit. Despite her predicament, Carmen smiled. *It doesn't matter where Italians are – they want to look good.* As quickly as the smile had come, it disappeared. Carmen was well aware that getting back to the condo safely was still ahead. She had learned the hard way that there are no shortcuts.

Outside, Tully was still around because he had requested overtime and had gotten it. His stomach growled. It was quite a while since he had eaten. He could have gone for food, but he wanted to see what unfolded here. He was back in his car at The Tiffany to give his feet a break. Garderella was back at the precinct with the drug unit requesting more time from her lieutenant. He figured she'd manage it. Her arrest record was commendable – her instincts the best. She was tough and Tully liked that in a woman. Her rep was solid everywhere. Tully liked women. He had grown up with four sisters, and women had always just been people, not mysteries, just flesh and blood human beings.

At nine-fifteen, Hilda was back at her station depositing her purchases on the seats inside one of the changing rooms. She had also brought back a handful of wet paper towels. With one last look at the floor and the few remaining customers that were heading to the escalator, Hilda took out her keys. Once both locker doors were opened, Caitlin and Carmen stumbled out, tear-streaked and tired. Hilda shuffled them into the dressing room. 'Wash your faces with these wet towels before you do anything else. Get a move on. You haven't much time to join the off-duty workers heading for the buses.'

Aching in every muscle and bone, the C's grimaced, even as they washed their faces and arms. They tore off their dirty clothes and stepped into new shorts and tops. Hilda had bought a Red Sox designer cap and two hair clips. Caitlin took the cap while Carmen pulled back her dark hair, attaching the clips. The only upbeat thing about their clothes was the cap. They wore old women's shorts, black and beige, that fifty year olds might buy to hide their cellulite. Their tops were dumpy and too large. Of course, this was part of Hilda's plan to alter their appearance. Before the C's could say anything, Hilda pointed to their legs, and the women rubbed them with the towels as well.

'I have over four hundred dollars left over. I broke one of the large bills into smaller denominations and loose change. You'll probably need it,' Hilda said, handing over the money to Carmen.

Carmen took the change and smaller bills. Then she offered three hundred dollars to Hilda. 'Hilda, we can never repay you. Please take what's left of the money. You've saved our lives. Carmen threw her arms around Hilda. Caitlin's eyes teared.

'I can't take your money, girls. I didn't do this for money.'

'We put you in danger,' Caitlin spoke up. 'Do whatever you want with the money, but we'd feel better that we tried to thank you in some small way.'

'Well, there are support shoes I need...'

'There you go,' Caitlin smiled. Carmen handed Hilda the money.

'Get going now! I can't walk with you, but join the large group and walk to the bus stop with it. Don't make the mistake of getting on the bus together – walk on separately. Keep your heads down. Most of us are tired at the end of our long days and that's pretty well how we walk. Good luck! I'll be thinking about you. Now, get going.'

The women ran to the escalator and quickly stood closely behind the other three women riding down. They half-walked, half-ran to the exit in the mall and fell in with the other employees heading for the main exit in the centre of the mall, remembering what Hilda had advised. It was hard, but they kept their heads down. Caitlin walked into the midst of the group – Carmen stayed two or three people behind her.

Outside, the guys had taken up their positions.

CHAPTER TWELVE

HARRIS WAS VERY definitely in charge and he told all the guys that they had better kick ass tonight. He was convinced that the women were still in the mall and that they would make their escape at closing. Ten minutes before closing, he had run across the street for his Hummer, parking it in a no-parking zone in front of the condo. Private security wouldn't touch him because of his father. He saw Tully.

'I hope you are not giving me grounds for harassment, Officer Tully,' Harris called out to him in an exaggerated soft voice, bordering on a sneer.

Tully was tired, caught off guard. Something that did not happen very often. 'We just wanted to be certain that you calmed down before driving again. Trying to protect our tourists, sir. You have a good night now.' *Dangerous, rich, spoiled, mean brats who should be men!* Reluctantly and slowly, Tully pulled out of the driveway. He didn't pull back into another luxury condo until Harris had run back across the street.

Harris did allow Bobby to set the guys up at strategic points, but not before he gave another description of the women. Bobby worked this problem out with his usual zeal. One was standing at the main exit. One more at the entrance gate of the mall – two at the bus stop at the corner of 94th Street and Collins – two on the east side of Collins for the bus heading north over Haulover Beach. Harris stayed on the east sidewalk close to his Hummer, but on the lookout nonetheless. Nipples was sent running three stops down Collins, fairly close to the bridge. Harris was so pissed and scared, he almost wished he'd make a run for it. He could blow off some steam using Nipples as a punching bag.

But Nipples' defiance was crumbling and he regretted calling the cops. He scrambled down the sidewalk, determined to find the women. Weighing his possible losses, his life, he decided to opt once again for group conformity. He might survive as 'Nipples' if he stayed with Harris – as Ian, outside the gang, his chances were not good. Nipples did not need Bobby's brain to know that. He thought he had snitched for his brother and sister, but maybe his call to the cops had had more to do with his nickname. He wanted to live, and his best chance of doing that was to have a hand in finding the bitches who had the money. They were the ones, Nipples saw now, who had put him in such jeopardy. If the cops had found the cash, as Nipples had intended they should, Harris would have been busted, and Nipples would have been free of him. But that wasn't the way things had turned out.

Once he reached his post, Nipples came up with his own idea. He'd stop each bus in the next half hour and pretend he was getting on it. That way he could catch a good view of the passengers. Fumbling in his pocket, he'd finally tell the driver he did not have the right change and jump back off. He was pretty good on his own, he thought. He was also smart enough to know Harris wanted him to run, but Nipples was not about to do that. His mind was clear now. He'd make a mistake, but he was about to correct it.

Bobby was calculating the odds as he stood at the bus stop on 94th Street. In the bitches' place, he would have left the mall as soon as possible. He would never have waited around with the wagons circling and positioning themselves. There was a good chance Harris was wrong about them still being here at all. He was certain, if they had hidden until closing time, they would use the busiest exit for cover. Harris had figured that one correctly. Bobby told Ted to scan the line of passengers who waited for the bus – he'd stand near the front door of the buses as they arrived. No one would get by him because Bobby was a detail man. Nothing got by him, except maybe Harris' sucker punch.

While Caitlin and Carmen were in the throng making their way to the main exit, Caitlin decided on a daring plan of her own. She recalled an interesting fact from a Doris Lessing novel. In it, a woman who had left her husband and two daughters in their London home for her own vacation of one month in Portugal, came home two weeks early. A tryst, and the young lover it involved, had proven more foolish and miserable than the life she had fled. What was odd, what Caitlin remembered for eight years, was simply this. The woman had passed her husband on a wide sidewalk where there were a few other pedestrians, and he had not noticed her. The truth Lessing noted was that we do not see people we are not expecting to see. The husband thought his wife was in Portugal, and that was the reason he did not see her when she walked past him. Another variation of 'out of sight, out of mind'.

Caitlin decided to adopt Lessing's idea. 'Carmen, I'll walk four or five people behind you, but don't look back at me. Wherever they've set themselves up to find us, you can be sure they'll be craning their necks and standing on tip-toe, thinking we're hiding in the middle of the crowd. That's not what we're going to do. We're going to walk on the edge of it, and my bet is that they'll be so busy looking over our heads, they'll miss us completely.'

'What if they don't?'

'We'll make a run for it then. I'm pretty sure they'd discover us in the middle of the crowd, so we can't hide there. What choice do we have? We have to take our best chance, and I think this is it.'

'Don't make a run for it without me.'

'Goes without saying. Keep your head down a little and make no eye contact.' Employees making for this exit from the opposite end of the mall joined them as they arrived at the central exit. This was a tidal wave of humanity, or locusts on a slow swarm from each of the stores in the mall. Before they exited the mall, they were both forced to push their way to the edge of the crowd like running backs running down the field. Though her stomach gripped hard, Caitlin found new energy in this challenge. Five bodies behind her, Carmen chewed her cheek.

Small rescues come when they are least expected. Carmen was feeling light-headed and fearing she might fall when a woman jostling on her side began to talk to her. Heavy-set, in her fifties, or thereabouts, she looked as though she were carrying the heavy bags of money. Yet all she carried was her purse and fatigue. 'What a day! I hate sales. You work like a dog. I won't see any commission for another two months. That's as long as I've been here, so I don't qualify for commission yet. If you don't mind me saying so, you don't look great your-self.'

Carmen found herself answering, so glad of this camouflage; she could have hugged the woman beside her. 'I've been on my feet all day too. It's not easy.'

'Tell me about it. But you're still young – you shouldn't be tired.'

'Tell that to my feet,' she said, forcing a laugh she didn't feel.

Caitlin's heart was racing, her fingertips tingling, as

she walked out the front doors, and nothing happened. Number Boy had figured wrong. The next gauntlet was passing the guards' hut to the sidewalk. Caitlin gave her best impression of a bored, weary salesgirl. Without intending to, her eye caught a college student like Harris, his eyes intent on each passing body. She settled her nerves with the thought of a toasted bagel spread generously with strawberry jam, topped with thinly sliced cheddar cheese. Trying to imagine a slow bite, Caitlin purposely looked at her watch and sighed wearily as she passed so close to the student that their arms touched. He was bobbing up and down, and she frowned as she passed him. Carmen's camouflage was still beside her, recounting a world-weary life. They crossed at the light with a good crowd, turned left and walked to the bus shelter, choosing to stand on the sidewalk with everyone else.

Harris was busy making signals to Ted across the street when the C's passed within fifty feet of him and his Hummer. Ted was throwing his arms up, indicating he had nothing to show. Harris grabbed his cell, punched in numbers and spoke with each of his men. Nothing. His anxiety was not about to level off, not with this non-news. He was about to walk over to the long line of passengers waiting for the next 'S' or 'H' bus, but decided against it. He had two guys there after all. The light was changing again, but the line was stalled because an 'S' bus was coming up to its stop. His neck cords were taut, his stomach as tight as cement. Out of habit, he began to flex his butt muscles. Harris hated seeing men who had lost their butts – they were worse than women whose tits had fallen. Three days, three days…

As Caitlin stepped up into the bus, she spoke to the older woman in front of her. 'Watch your step now.'

Ted ignored her and began to inspect the people behind her. Six or seven people later, Carmen and her friend were actually laughing together. Carm stepped safely onto the bus too. Neither friend acknowledged the other. They both stood with their backs to the windows, smothered by the pounds of tired, lumpy flesh all around them. Caitlin and Carmen both silently thanked Hilda for the change she had remembered to get for them. Like a bloated bug, the bus pulled out without incident. The women were shoved back and forth with each lurch of a heavy foot on the gas pedal.

The 'S' bus drove past the first two stops. Both women dared to hope. Then their bus pulled into the last stop before the bridge and stopped. Nipples' plan backfired immediately as six or seven people got off the bus from the front door and he could not get near it. Weary people can be quite rude. Nipples was pushed up against the side of the bus. Beleaguered, bone tired, Carmen fell into a window seat vacated by an exiting passenger. Her act was instinctive, habit, something automatic. Like a bag of chips that has been wrapped up, shoved onto a top shelf, away from temptation, that suddenly feels fingers grabbing a handful of bad choles-terol. The fingers seem to have a will of their own, quite outside the jurisdiction of the operating grey matter. The horror of her mistake was etched on her face, in a silent scream.

That's what Nipples recognized when he stared up at the window. For a long second, Carmen and Nipples shared the bizarre chemistry of the lost. He knew Carmen – he knew her fear because it was his own. Holy shit, he had found the bitches, at least one of them! Not Harris, not Bobby, he had found them! Nipples even forgot he was the one responsible for the money getting lost in the first place. The bus was pulling away while Nipples was still in a state of euphoria. He made a mad dash to the front door and banged on it. Jenny the driver was a large woman who filled her whole seat and stuck to her schedule. Not bothering to look down at Nipples, she simply waved her large thumb, curled it, as a matter of fact, towards the bus coming up behind hers. Nipples hollered – Jenny drove on up the hill to the bridge.

Nipples grabbed his cell and punched in Harris' number. 'Harris, I found them! They're on the 'S' bus.'

'All right, Nipples, stay with them. I'll get the guys together and we'll follow in the Hummer.'

'I'm not with them.'

'What the fuck are you talking about?'

'I saw them only as the bus was pulling away – the driver wouldn't let me on.'

'Jesus, fuck. All right. Is it an 'S' or 'H'?'

'An 'S' and it's just driving very slowly onto the bridge. I can still see it. I got the plates too, Harris!'

'We can catch it. Get out on the side of the road, and we'll pick you up. Bobby's taking half the guys with him. We'll need everyone to track them. I haven't got the time for a complete stop, so you'll have to run alongside the Hummer. The doors are small. Ted will lean out and do his best to pull you inside. Be ready to jump as high as you can if you want to be in on the chase. You fucking better be sure, Nipples.'

'I am for chrissake.' Harris hung up as he ran for the Hummer and began dialing the other guys. 'We've just gotten another chance at the bitches,' he shouted through the line at Bobby. 'Round the guys up as fast as you can!'

CHAPTER THIRTEEN

CAITLIN COULD NOT believe her eyes when she saw Carmen grab the empty seat. It happened too fast for Caitlin to reach out and grab her friend. Although the bus was pulling away and Nipples never saw Caitlin, she certainly did not miss him and his surprise that turned quickly to triumph when he recognized Carmen. A prickly heat rose in her throat.

'Oh my God, I'm sorry Caitlin. I am so sorry.' Tears welled in Carmen's eyes, her face blanched with fright. 'I don't know what made me do that. What have I just done to us? I'm so sorry.'

'We haven't got time for sorry. I have to think of what to do. That guy was shouting into his cell as we pulled away. We also know the Hummer is across from the mall. They're coming after us.'

The brakes on Jenny's 'S' bus began to squeal as she pulled it into a stop at the edge of Haulover Bridge. Five people fought their way to the front of the bus and took their sweet time to exit. Harris and his guys had just earned bonus time in their pursuit.

Colour drained from Caitlin's face. 'What are we going to do?' she whispered into Carmen's ear. Carmen had risen from her seat and was hanging onto the handrail beside her friend.

'What if we jumped off the bus at the next stop?'

'That's not going to work. They must have six or seven people. If we get off in the middle of the park, we're thirty-five minutes from home. They can drop guys off at different intervals, come at us from both directions. We're not safe in the park – there's no real cover. We can't let them get ahead of us!' Carmen was clearly panicked, and her body of opinions fell far short of the mark they needed to hit.

The bus made two more stops. More time lost. The women hung their heads.

'What if we stay on the bus all the way to Aventura? We can lose ourselves there and grab a cab. We've gotta get off this bus. We're trapped in here!'

'Let me think Carm. Try to calm down a little. We can't head for Aventura because the Hummer will overtake this bus, and they'll be right behind us when we try to run from it. And that mall is out, too.' Caitlin made her way to the back of the bus and stared out the window. There were cars behind the bus, but it was too dark to make out the Hummer she knew was somewhere out there on Collins pursuing them. Carmen had not followed her.

Jenny made another stop beside what used to be The Sandy Shores, but was now a gaping field of dust and sand. When Derek and Caitlin first came to Miami, they stayed in this motel. Caitlin wished she could go back to that simple time and hide.

When Jenny stopped for another light, Caitlin made her decision, once she had walked back up the aisle and joined Carmen. 'Here's what we have to do. We're going to get off at the Newport Pier. If you need it, use your vent again. We'll be five minutes from home. I want you to run with me as fast as you can along the sand. We don't dare stay on Collins. We'll run to the pier, jump down its side to the beach and stay as close to the condos as possible. We'd be easy targets if we ran along the ocean's edge. We have a chance of making it to Club One. We'll leave by the back of the bus. Once we hit the sidewalk, break into your sprint – don't look anywhere else! Every second has to count.'

Carmen nodded her assent and took a long drag on her vent, balling the fist of her other hand.

There was road construction on Collins in front of Oceania on the east corner of 163rd Street, and traffic bottlenecked into a single line. Caitlin curled her lower lip and bit into it. The C's moved to the back of the bus, both staring out the back window. Because of the night construction and the good lighting from the luxury condominium, they saw the yellow Hummer, four or five cars back.

Carmen began to shake and Caitlin grabbed her by the shoulders. 'Listen to me Carmen. Don't lose it now! Your life depends on how quickly you can run. Don't look back! Keep your eyes on me and keep running.'

Carmen's eyes were numb, dazed.

Caitlin shook her friend, shook her hard. 'You have to stay with me now. Follow me and we'll make it. We'll make it!' When the bus stopped at the side of the pier, the friends jumped both steps to the sidewalk and ran for their lives to the wooden pier.

'Jesus fuck, do you see that? Those bitches just got off the bus!' Harris held things together for a second before speaking again. He had to think fast. That god-damn prick Tully was a single car behind them. Harris did not want to lead the cops to the money. When he finally drove through the traffic light, he pulled over at the Newport and called Bobby, 'Get your guys after those bitches and track them down. They must be heading north along the beach. Three of you run that way. Kevin should run south along the beach. If he sees nothing, he should run back and hook up with the others. I'm sure they're headed north. Haul ass!' Ted, Kevin and James leapt from the Navigator and took off with lethal speed. Nipples was pumped as he leapt from the Hummer – he might even be a hero.

Harris drove back out onto Collins, right into another red light. 'Fuck! Why don't they synchronize these goddamn lights? What kind of a dumb ass did this work? We're wasting time. I'm going to pull in beside Rascal House. That prick can't do anything if I want Reuben sandwiches for my friends and me. The rest of you guys get out there with me. If that turd follows me into the restaurant, I'll talk to him and that's your chance to get yourselves to the beach as quickly as you can. We'll get those bitches coming and going. Check everywhere,' he ordered, picking up his cell. 'Bobby, get to the beach, don't turn back, run on ahead in case they're actually faster than I think they are. Don't hurt them till I get there. Once we have the money, we can all party with them. The bitches deserve everything we give them. I'll handle Tully.'

'What if they have already run into one of the condos?' Bobby threw his thoughts into the mix.

'Then we'll know they're in this small stretch and we'll stake it out.' When the Hummer and the Navigator pulled into a small strip mall beside Wolfie Cohen's Rascal House Deli Restaurant, the operation went into full swing. It was a warm night and although many of these young Turks showered twice a day, the stench of perspiration was thick and unpleasant.

Harris and his two henchmen walked in to the take-out line at the restaurant, famous for its six-inch high deli sandwiches and home-made matzoh ball and chicken soup. This landmark was alive and well. The old mom and pop beachfront motels may have given way to places like Oceania Island; the Tahiti, Dunes, Blue Seas, Colonial and Driftwood may have been reduced to memory, but Rascal House still drew customers, even

late at night. The fossils were long gone. The Winston
Towers' trolley had driven the white-hairs back to their
dens. Harris, though his neck muscles were as tight as a
violin string, found himself eyeing stacks of five-inch
cherry pies, taller meringue pies and black and white
muffins piled high on glass shelves. A stack of fresh
challah and rye breads were piled by the cash. A sweet
odour of sugar and meat and soup pervaded the deli and
wafted out the door onto Collins Avenue. 'Eight
Reubens, fries and eight Cokes,' Harris ordered. As he
turned around, Tully was a few feet behind him.

His guys wanted to leave, but there was such a wary
curiosity in Sergeant Tully's eyes that they hung around
longer than they had intended. Tully was taking mental
notes, and the guys knew it. It was a few minutes before
the cop turned his attention to Harris, and they felt
they could leave. 'Take it slow across Collins,' Bobby
warned. 'He's seen us, can identify us, and we sure as
hell don't want to rouse his curiosity.' The traffic is
always bad on Collins, and the guys knew this was not
the time for jaywalking, so they walked to the corner
and waited for the light.

Tully felt he should say something banal to Harris
when he turned back to him at the counter. 'We all have
to eat, right sir? I guess we had the same idea about
food for tonight.'

Harris had had it with this dogged tailing, but he
lowered his voice so as not to betray his exasperation.
'You are not still following me by any chance, are you
Officer Tully? I get the feeling you are. You know, it
makes me feel uncomfortable.'

'I'm sorry you feel that way, Mr. Chalmer. Actually,
I'm not following you, sir. If I were, you would not have
noticed. I'm on my way home and I guess we like the
same deli, so we're not alone on that score. In fact, I'll

be leaving when I get my order. Will you be going back home yourself, sir?'

Though wary, Harris' mood lightened somewhat. There was a very slim hope Tully was not on his tail. 'We're young, Officer Tully, we'll probably hang out for a while on the beach before heading back.' Yet he could not let go of the bone. He was hungry and asked, 'I hope you are not dogging me, officer. You don't have that right, you know. My father wouldn't be happy knowing I was being tailed for a speeding violation. I think that would be grounds for something, right officer?'

'I certainly don't want to be causing you any undue stress, Mr. Chalmer.'

'I'm very glad to hear that, officer. Good night then. Enjoy the sandwich.'

'Good night.'

Harris rapped his fingers on the counter, waiting for his order, waiting for Tully to take his butt out of his business and on home. Tully's badge was unnerving him. From all the cop shows Harris had watched, including his favourite, *The Shield*, he knew his chances of getting his money back would fall dramatically if he and his guys did not find those bitches tonight. When his order arrived, Harris slapped two bills on the counter, grabbed the Rascal bag, punched the door open and ran to the sidewalk. Tully's car was nowhere in sight. One of his three days was drawing to a close. Harris could taste his own perspiration.

CHAPTER FOURTEEN

THAT NIGHT, THERE was no moon. When Caitlin and Carmen jumped to the sand from the steps of the pier, they ran across the beach into a dark night that shielded them. A west wind worried the sand beneath their feet as they ran. Only once did Caitlin almost trip across a wave of sand, but she righted herself before stumbling and ran on ahead. Wheezes and gasps were the only sounds that reached their ears. The rhythmic lapping of the waves with their rocking comfort made no impression on Caitlin or Carmen. Unluckily, they ran head-first into a spike of light, coming from a thirty-foot lamp abandoned by a Miami group producing a Bud Light commercial that afternoon. Careless lighting crews were legend along the beach.

The first onslaught of the guys who took off after Caitlin and Carmen were smart enough to run to the pier first. There, they had a good view of the landscape, north and south along the beach. Even with no moon, there was light enough from the ocean for a pretty good scan. Nipples might never get past the torment of his name or the humiliation of his tits, but tonight, the little gods were with him. Leaning as far as he could over the wooden railing, he detected two running figures as Caitlin and Carmen ran into the light. The gopher, the titty boy, had just seen what the jocks had missed. 'Shit! Shit!' he shouted with glee. 'I see them. I see them.' Nipples shot up in the air like one of the kites on Haulover Beach. 'Guys! They're way ahead down the beach,' he roared, pointing in the direction of his coup. 'I saw them! They're down the beach. I found them!'

'You positive, Nipples?'

'Yeah, I'm positive. Fuck they're down there,' he hollered, gesturing wildly.

Like a riptide, the guys tore themselves from the pier and ran for the side stairs. 'Bobby,' one of the guys shouted. 'Bobby, over here!' And the hunt was on.

About thirty feet from the gate of Club One, Caitlin turned to see if they were being chased, in time to catch Nipples' Broadway performance. 'Oh my God, they're back there!' She stopped dead in her tracks, and Carmen crashed into her, almost knocking her friend to the sand. Caitlin knew in an instant they could not take the chance of unlocking the gate. Their hands were shaking badly and would undoubtedly struggle too long with the lock. Even if they managed to get the door open, the noise would pinpoint their location. 'We'll hide under the deck. Larry's sleeping in the cabana.' Caitlin was grateful that she knew of The Sands Motel.

🌴

For the first time in a few months, Larry had drunk a few beers, perhaps for courage if Steve showed up, more to dull his hungry longing for Caitlin. It was well after nine. The combination of sun and suds had taken Larry from the dark world of his troubles. Before he fell asleep, he remembered how he had wanted to escape the cold, as he had by living in the cabana. Now Steve might come back and ruin everything. Tonight, he was back on wet, damp sand that never seemed to dry out, and he blamed Steve for his shivers.

But Larry did not sleep long on the wet sand. Ten minutes later, he pushed himself out from under the deck. He was softening, one might say. Larry did not

fool himself into believing that he was staying at The
Four Seasons, but the cabana was a far cry from The
Sands Motel. He had a real roof over his head, a
makeshift bed, a pillow, a blanket, a slated window he
could close at night, a door he could lock. But Larry
had no intention of vacating the 'motel'. If fact, as he
stood on the sand, he began planning renovations.
Tomorrow he'd borrow a shovel, dig out a better crawl
space, take a few plywood boards he had seen in the
basement of Club One, build a floor and bank the sand
on the far side to discourage would-be intruders. For a
temporary wall, he'd take some old phone books that
were discarded down there as well. Then he'd cover his
paper wall with sand. For a moment he forgot Caitlin's
blow-off. *What I also need is real toothpaste and more
clothes, new clothes. When Caitlin sees how well I'm doing...*

Larry left his cash hidden under the sand. *I made that
money after Steve's fall. He won't know where to look for it,
even if he does come back.* As an added precaution, he
walked over to the side of the deck, knelt and piled sand
even higher over his stash at the top of the deck. His
head was clearing, and he walked with a swagger back
to the cabana. Larry had plans again. Wiped out by the
stress of Steve's probable reappearance and the hot sun,
he was asleep on his lounge chair before the C's made
their run across the beach.

🌴

The 'motel' was vacant when a familiar figure in
stained blue Bermuda shorts and a baggy t-shirt walked
haltingly onto the beach and appeared lost. For a while,
the man stood at the ocean's edge, looking up and down
the beach, trying to remember his bearings. He still
wore a faded hospital plastic bracelet. His blond hair
was closely cropped, and a vivid red scar ran up the side

of his temple into his scalp. A day ago, Steve had walked out of the halfway house up on Biscayne Boulevard and headed for the beach. A month and a half ago, Steve's coma had persisted for three nights. 'You're one lucky man,' the lead physician had told him. 'It was touch and go for a while there.' Steve might be a lucky guy, but he often couldn't remember what happened yesterday. The piercing headaches struck without warning, leaving him with tremors and tears.

Without any thought or sense of direction, Steve followed his feet, and they led him to the deck. He crawled under it as though he had slept there the night before. The place seemed familiar, but he could not quite place it. In minutes, Steve collapsed, worn out from his long walk. He lay deep in sleep in the same dugout Larry had just vacated. He heard nothing, not the lapping of the waves nearby, nor the quiet invasion.

On their backs, squirming frantically like worms, Caitlin and Carmen bore their way under the deck. Caitlin chose the left side, Carmen the right. Above their heads were only inches of space. Larry had not dug out the whole area under the deck, only his own. Caitlin felt a wood burn on her thigh as she pushed herself sideways with her left hand and left foot, moving under the deck only inches at a time. Carmen felt her panic of small places as she too bore her way towards a sleeping Steve. It appeared that the women were attempting a slow crawl in quicksand. After much pushing and straining, the deck swallowed them.

In his disoriented state of mind, Steve could not comprehend the assault from both sides of the deck. His head shot up like a bullet, striking the wooden joint above him with such force that he shattered his nose. A piece of bone cut into his upper lip with a fierce stab of pain – blood flew up like a geyser. Steve tried to cry out, but dark, brown blood smothered his cries. There was a fire in his throat.

'Shush, shush,' Caitlin whispered. 'It's Caitlin, Larry. You're O.K. Shush, please.'

Nothing made sense to him. He tried to reach out blindly and push the voices away. Why was the hammering in his brain back again? His head was burning – he had to sit up. He had to breathe – he had to get out into the air. But arms and sand were everywhere. He could not move to his right or left. He was dying, was that it? Hands were closing the top of the casket – he could feel the wood on top of him. But he wasn't dead. The searing pain in his head told him he was still alive. Who was trying to bury him? With brute force, Steve bolted upright once again and smashed his face a second time. His moan was low and guttural.

'Shush, shush.' All Caitlin and Carmen could do was toss sand at Steve, begging him to be quiet. 'Shush, shush.' Steve could not make another attempt to rise; he was light-headed, panic breaking behind his broken nose. Opening his mouth very wide, he began to gnaw at the air, turning his head from side to side. Muscles in his neck knotted in spasm. He swallowed the first gush of blood and the second, mixed with sand. Steve began quickly and violently to smother on the cocktail of blood and sand. His head never shot up again. His jaws tried to spread unnaturally wide, his skeleton straining to break through the flesh of his face. Steve was smothered to death as quickly as one drowns in water, and almost as silently. His left leg jerked a few times, but that was all. He never knew he was lying beside Caitlin and Carmen whom he had spoken to last year. His life did not flash before his eyes. Pain flashed in his head to the right of the scar, white and red, like signal lights. His thoughts never waded above the murk of his agony.

Soon, the sand in his eyes did not bother him, or the rope of blood in his throat. Then, there was no pain at all.

Steve's life was over a good fifty seconds before Nipples and the troops got close to the deck. By that time, a deathly silence hung in the quiet air above the deck. With Bobby trailing, the guys ran like panthers after prey. When the women that Nipples had seen suddenly vanished, and the guys were chasing air, they stopped running. They formed a jagged line of young men grabbing their knees, their heads thrust forward like sprinters at the end of a race. Their gasps were loud and long. 'Well, Nipples, where are they?'

'I don't know. They were here. I know I saw them – maybe they've run ahead.'

'Or maybe, they've hid in one of these condos,' Bobby added, pointing to the buildings on their side. 'Or maybe they weren't here at all.'

Harris had crossed onto the beach at Gilbert Samson Park and could make out dark figures to his right. When he caught up with them and saw they were alone, he was edgy and angry. 'Why are you all standing around? You should be out here searching everywhere!' Harris shouted the last word so his guys would get the message. As he did, his men who had run north along the sand ran back and joined them. In his disgust, he threw the food to the ground.

'What's your problem, Harris? We're hungry,' Bobby said, stepping into his proper place as second-in-command. 'We'll search a lot better if we have something in our stomachs.'

'How do we know that Nipples even saw them?' Ted wanted to know.

Harris gave Ted a good smack on the side of his

head. 'We all saw them get off the bus and run to the beach. Nipples did not make that up, did he, asshole?'

'Jesus,' Ted swore, rubbing his head and backing out of line.

'All right, pick up the food, Nipples,' Harris ordered while pointing to the bag.

Nipples no longer felt entitled or territorial about his find. He knelt down on the sand and picked up the bag, but his eyes shimmered with rage at the rotten deal he'd gotten his whole life. He had spotted the bitches *twice*, and still he was on his knees. He could feel the cold fury in Harris. Nipples smiled to himself in the dark where no one could see him gloating. It was good to see the tables turned. When he stood up with the food, Nipples noticed Harris' cheek was twitching.

Pissed that his guys had come up empty, Harris jock-eyed from one foot to the other to contain his fury. This sure plan was imploding in front of his eyes. Colour drained from his face like wind taken from those high-flying kites. 'What the fuck happened? Were you pussies dragging your feet? If we don't get this money back, we can kiss our lives goodbye! Do you under-stand, assholes! And you're worried about food? Shitheads!'

Bobby stepped forward. 'Listen, we all worked for this money and we all want to see it again, but ragging on us is not helping the situation. We should keep searching. If we don't find them tonight, I think we should send a few guys to the ocean walk tomorrow ask-ing lifeguards if any of them know these chicks. You said they were foxes – someone must know them.'

'Are you giving up hope of finding them tonight, Number Boy?' Harris walked over to him and stabbed him with a stiff finger. 'You're a negative guy and you're useless.' Bobby stumbled but did not fall and stood his ground. He did not recoil as Harris might have hoped. *You lost the money you shithead, not me!*

The other six guys took a step towards Bobby in a show of support. Harris whirled around in their direction and took a deep drag of air and held it high in his nose. The guys backed away.

They were all standing together beside the fence of Club One, twenty to thirty feet from the deck. Harris smashed his fist into the fence. 'Here, for example has anyone looked in here?' Instantly, a light went on in a second-floor condo. The guys jumped out of view, ten feet from the deck.

'They couldn't have come in here. The gate's locked and we would have heard the noise if they had unlocked it,' Bobby spoke up again.

'Fuck! Have you looked here?' he exploded, stomping across the sand and pointing to the deck.

Bobby knelt at the front of the deck to placate the ever-so-sure-of-himself Harris. He gave it a cursory look, a mental measure, and stood back up. 'They'd have to be sand crabs to get under this deck. We'll start searching each of these condos, Harris. How long do you want us to keep looking?' Bobby asked, wisely throwing the control back to Harris.

Harris seemed to shrink as he stood there, rocked by Bobby's friendly fire. Aware he needed these guys, he got himself back under control. This was not the time to bring a weapon to bear. 'It's almost eleven,' he told them. 'Keep up the search for another couple of hours. We're in this together. If you find these bitches, grab one of them at least. Forget the other. One bitch can lead us to the money. Meet me at Rascal House at two. All right, get out there.' When he was alone, Harris' mouth slackened, 'Oh shit.' He sat on the edge of the deck, in a sad parody of The Thinker. Harris sensed the odds were beginning to stack up against him. The light in the condo had gone out again. Except for the sound of Harris kicking the sand and the lapping waves, everything was quiet. When he heard the drone of the dune buggy patrol a few minutes later, he cringed before jumping to his feet and getting the hell out of sight. Once an hour, an officer rode across the beach, scouting suspicious activity.

Officer Ruiz was not on duty. The patrol dune buggy, with its oversized rubber tires and yellow canvas roof, drove by the deck and on up the beach toward the Thunderbird Hotel where it would make a turn and retrace its ride, cruising across the sand.

CHAPTER FIFTEEN

'HE'S DEAD ISN'T he?' Carmen whispered in hushed tones after three in the morning. Her shoulders rose a little and fell as she wept, still buried beside Steve on the sand under the deck. She knew the time because of the illuminated digits on her watch. For nearly three and a half hours, not a word had passed between the women. Neither friend had dared to say anything for fear of being discovered.

Caitlin did not respond to her friend for another ten minutes. She was shivering on the sand, distracted by her own thoughts. For most of her life, she had lived in verbs: cycle, run, study, feel, love, laugh, grieve. Tonight, and maybe forever, her life was caught between the parentheses of conjunctions: if, why, but. The nouns, motionless, heavy substances, lay in wait for each of them: fear, remorse, guilt. Cries in her throat kept threatening to erupt, bone chilling sounds that would pierce the night, but for the time being, Caitlin kept them barricaded behind her thoughts. 'Yes,' was all she whispered, vomit rising in her throat. There was nothing else to say.

When Caitlin began to feel the deck collapsing on top of her, desperate needs took hold. 'We have to get out of here,' she cried in a sudden panic.

'Do you think they're gone?' came the strained voice from the other side of the deck.

'I heard the Harris guy say two o'clock, but who knows? We can't be found under the deck when the sun comes up. We have no time to wonder about things.

Wiggle out very slowly on your side, try not to make any noise, watch your head. Listen very carefully to me. As you begin to clear the deck, use your free arm to sweep across the sand. We don't want to leave the imprint of our bodies on the sand under the deck. Do you understand, Carm?'

'Yes. Then what?'

'Wait for me to come to you. Don't stand up whatever you do.'

Worming their way from under the deck, they were able only to move sideways by inches, each of which was won with effort. It was difficult not to panic and try kicking at the deck that held them tight like a coffin. First it was a leg that was free, then an arm, finally a shoulder that pried itself from the shell of the deck. Once she was free, Caitlin rolled a few feet from it before she crawled over to Carmen and helped pull her friend the last few feet. Looking cautiously around, seeing no one, they took a few moments to breathe in fresh air that did not smell of wet wood.

They were a sorry lot, under other circumstances, even funny-looking. Looking very much like two overgrown children who had waged a sand fight with one another, they sat exhausted on the beach. Because it was dark, Steve's blood was the colour of mud. Sand stuck to their arms and legs, to their necks and cheeks, caking thickly at the back of their heads. They shook themselves out like dogs, but most of the sand clung and would not let go. When Caitlin realized their next problem, fear began to percolate in her gut. 'We can't walk into the condo with all this sand because of the trail we'd leave.'

Carmen was alert, but fraying nerves had cast a sudden disinterest into her.

'Carmen, stay with me – we have to work together.'

'Yes, I know,' Carmen replied without any purpose.

'I have to think of a place we can wash this stuff off.' Their own pool was close by, but that was not an option. Michel would certainly hear them or the water. He never really slept. Once a cop, always a cop. He invariably knew when kids managed to jump the fence for a midnight swim in their heated pool. There was a shower too, but using it was akin to standing under a spotlight. The ocean lay at their feet a few hundred feet away. The danger there was clear and present. Caitlin thought then of the *Ancient Mariner.* There was water everywhere, but none they could use.

Her spirits rose somewhat when she found a solution. 'We'll go to the Florida Ocean Club. It's very private, but they have a pool that is not gated. We have to crouch; we have to look in both directions when we cross the beach to reach it. Follow me. Carmen, please don't give up. We're almost home.'

There was no response, but when Caitlin looked behind her, Carmen was following. They ran like field mice, stopping abruptly and scurrying on. When they spied the pool, they sat in the darkness of the palm trees and took off their socks and shoes. They crept to the water and slid into it. Hungry and tired, Caitlin and Carmen felt the shock of cold water and the tremors that began on their outer skin before boring and stabbing beneath it. With the cold, their limbs were sluggish, and they struggled to wash the sand from their bodies. When they dunked their heads and shook them, piercing, sharp needles of pain shot to their foreheads, very much like ice cream headaches. Crawling from the pool, over to their shoes, Caitlin's teeth chattered and she bit her tongue. Though it was not easy pulling socks onto wet feet, they managed.

'Try not to kneel in the sand when we make our run

for it. Stay crouched, but don't kneel,' Caitlin was able to whisper between her shudders. 'Stay behind me, Carmen. We'll go in the side door. Once we are inside, run as quickly and quietly as possible to our door at the front. Let's go.' When they reached the edge of the driveway, twenty feet from the side entrance, the women took special care to scan the area before running across to the door. Caitlin reached into her pocket for her keys, then the other two pockets. 'I've lost my keys!' Caitlin moaned.

'Use mine,' Carmen finally came to life, handing hers over. Once they were safely inside the building, they had no trouble reaching their door, unlocking it ever so quietly and throwing themselves inside.

'I've lost my keys,' Caitlin began to cry.

Carmen threw her arms around her friend. 'Don't worry, we'll pay the ten bucks and get another one tomorrow.'

'But where? I have my cards, why not my keys?'

'It's all right. We'll get another one tomorrow. You're just tired.'

They stood in the centre of the room holding onto one another in the darkness. But they did not speak again that night. They stripped off their clothes and left them in a pile in the middle of the room. Lowering the Murphy bed, they crawled in together under the sheets and clung to one another, shivering and cold. What was there to say? In a few minutes, they turned on their sides, away from each other. Often in the next few hours, Caitlin wanted to peek out the front window to see if the Hummer was still there, but she did not dare. Fortunately, they fell asleep until just before seven when the traffic on Collins picked up for a new day.

That first morning, once they were both awake, the friends lay on the bed, but they did not look at one another. Though they didn't yet realize it was Steve, he was still with them – he would probably never leave. 'Are we responsible for his death?' Caitlin asked her friend. Losing her keys had undone Caitlin's purpose and resolve. It did not occur to her to be grateful that she and Carmen were still alive. If there was a divinity that shaped our ways, it had brought both of them home safely. Yet Caitlin was not considering those weighty thoughts, she was thinking of a man choking to death. A man who had crawled under the deck to protect himself and find a little sleep had ended up dead because she and Carmen had invaded his space. Why had he been so frightened, frantic, delirious? Why hadn't he heard their pleas? They meant him no harm. Caitlin knew she would never have the answers because they were buried under the deck with the man who had died there.

As Caitlin's strength began to drain away from her, she seemed to pass it to Carmen. 'I'll get you a new set of keys today, Caitlin. I still can't believe we made it. We made it! I never thought I'd see the inside of this room again.'

'Carmen, did we murder him, or are we responsible for his death?'

'I'm not a bad person, Caitlin. I know we didn't help him, but I don't know if we killed him, if that's what you're asking. Larry has been sleeping in the cabana – we never expected to find him under the deck. We didn't want him to die – we were desperate to save ourselves. I don't know what happened last night, but I'm happy I'm still here.'

'Did you toss any sand at him?' It was a question with a stake in it.

'Jesus, Caitlin, how the hell should I know? Most of last night is a blur.'

'Did you toss any sand at Larry?'

'I don't know what you want from me. Once, all right! Once to keep him quiet – to keep myself alive. I don't know where it landed either. He was already choking – he probably killed himself when he hit the top of the deck. He was choking on his own blood. We both know that, right?'

'Carmen, I tossed a handful of sand, too, for the same reason. We're both guilty.'

'I'm sorry Larry is dead. I can't even believe what I'm saying. But I'm not sorry I tried to save my life. I don't think a handful of sand, tossed sideways in the dark with most of it missing its mark, is a lethal blow. If he had just listened to us and been quiet, we'd all be alive. He went ballistic. Why? We didn't attack him in any way. Why was he so violent? He should have known us when we told him who we were. I don't get it. He's responsible too, Caitlin. I'll get you those keys as soon as I can.'

'We are never going to be able to forget what happened last night, not ever.'

Carmen turned to her friend and began to weep. 'We have to try. We have to put our lives first now – try to understand that. What do you think an arrest in Florida would do to our lives, our livelihoods? Are you ready for that fallout?'

'I don't know if I can live with this, Carmen.'

Carmen walked over to her friend and laid her hands on her shoulders. 'If we identify ourselves now, before we even know if the sand contributed to his death, we're throwing our lives away. If our photos get into *The Herald*, we expose ourselves to the gang leader and his guys. What we did wasn't an act of malice; it was an act of self-preservation. Even if we somehow were partly responsible, we're guilty of an accident, nothing more. And, we might be responsible for nothing! Are you willing to throw our lives away for nothing?'

'You sound like all the stories we argue about. What about ethics, right and wrong?'

'I'm not stupid, Caitlin. I know I'm arguing from a biased point of view. But this is my life we're talking about! And yours too! We're going to have to explain why we were under the deck in the first place. What then? Do we confess about the money too? Can't we just see what happens? Please. I'm not in a hurry to throw my life away.'

This sudden rush of partial reasoning unnerved Caitlin. Wouldn't it be so much easier to follow Carmen's advice, to do nothing for the time being? She was right about one thing – life was about survival, even if some of it was self-delusional garbage.

'Stop thinking, Caitlin. You think too much some-times. If you're worrying about the sand, I threw one handful from my waist. How high could it have flown? I wasn't able to raise my arm, any more than you could. Our sand probably never reached his face. If you want to think, think about that.'

'You have a point,' Caitlin conceded.

Sensing she was winning her friend over, Carmen challenged her. 'If you want to disclose everything, you'll have to do it yourself. I won't help you destroy my life.'

Caitlin did not need her friend to know that she was not heroic or even noble. Maybe that man had killed himself – that's what she had to hope. Caitlin's nerves felt like Jell-O; her veins were not supporting very much hope. She knew she would back down from the glare of Carmen's challenge. She wanted another chance. In time, maybe she would forgive herself. 'We won't do anything for the time being. I don't want to destroy your life or mine.'

'I know you don't. I wish… You know what I wish.'

'Let's worry about that key.'

'I don't think that's going to be a problem.'

When the friends rolled off the bed, one from either side, they saw that they were naked, their bodies still caked with sand from last night. Instantly, the women felt exposed and chastened. Caitlin grabbed the sheet and wrapped it around herself – Carmen reached for a sweatshirt. Turning slowly to her friend, she said, tempering her words, 'I know I'm off centre. But as I was lying awake this morning before the sun came up, afraid to move and wake you…'

'I wasn't asleep,' Caitlin responded, pulling the sheet more tightly around herself.

'Well, I thought you were. Anyway, Caitlin, I know that I pushed you into something wrong. I still have my compass. With a different kind of life, I thought I wouldn't have to worry about every nickel, or save every day for a two-week vacation. You've never had that problem, so you can't really know what I'm talking about. That's the reason I wanted the money that literally fell at our feet. Then, there's something I haven't told you. The company numbers are down. Last Friday, my boss let our buyer go and began downsizing by changing our territories. He's assigned me to new prospects. That means I have no commission until I discover new clients.'

'You mean you have no viable accounts?'

'All I have is my base salary and I think he'll probably let me go as well. I was the last one hired. So it figures, right? None of us got a bonus this year either. I maxed out my Visa to come on this vacation. I'm not the mercenary that you might think me to be. It's true – I didn't think of the consequences. I grabbed at what I saw as a chance for me. I'm treading water, Caitlin.

When I saw that the yellow bags were full of money, I acted on impulse, something I almost couldn't control. And I'm responsible.'

Caitlin threw her arms around her friend. 'I'm sorry for you, Carm. I didn't know. I've had all night to think about my own culpability. I have a share of responsibility too. Nobody tells you that after the anger and the grief and the loss fade, what you're left with is fear. Every night I go to bed, I'm afraid. Afraid of dying. I get on a plane and I think this is the day this plane will crash. I feel death waiting for me, on my bike, even in the classroom. For the last year, I've wanted to do something to defy death. Then I fly to Miami and I'm irrationally scared shitless by a harmless Arab sitting beside me. I want my old self back. I rode with Georges because I wanted to break the cycle, but he was a powder puff. I took the money because I thought I could stop being afraid if I did something daring. And I was wrong.'

'I'm sorry for you too, Caitlin. If we stick together, we'll make it. Just this morning, I realized something that we've forgotten to consider. While we've been focusing on that poor man and regret, we've overlooked an important fact. Some kind of angel out there is protecting us. There were at least four different times that the gang could have caught up with us: on the bridge when that guy spotted us, in the department store where Hilda helped save our lives, on the 'S' bus when one of them recognized me through the window and under the deck with Larry. We might not be around this morning if luck hadn't come our way.'

'First of all, I don't know whether it's luck or dumb chance...'

'Doesn't matter what you call it – we have it!'

'What I want to say is that you did push me into this,

but you didn't twist my arm. The second truth is that I wanted to break free of Derek as well. Last night, when I ran and hid, when I fought ferociously, pushing and clawing my way under the deck, I felt alive, I felt free for the first time in three years! So I'm as guilty as you in all this. We're in this together and we have to plan our next move. Carmen, they're going to find Larry, probably today. We have to start thinking about that.'

'I wasn't thinking that far ahead. Now what do we do?'

'Well, shower first. Ouch!' Caitlin moaned when she accidentally leaned against the bed and saw the wood burn on her thigh. 'First thing is I have to keep this hidden. I'll wear my baggy shorts. If anyone asks, I got this scratch on my bike when I rode too close to the bridge. We have to get rid of these clothes and wash the floor. Being ourselves, but staying apart from one another is important. Those guys said they would be back here searching for us today. We've gotta go out to the deck – we'd arouse suspicion if we stayed in our rooms. I'll sit with Morty and Sarah and wear a hat to hide my face and hair; you can sun on the other side of the pool with Michel and the gang, but wet your hair and comb it straight back. We can't even think of going to the ocean today.'

'I'm really scared again, Caitlin.'

'Who isn't?'

'What do we do when they find Larry under the deck?'

'We have to appear as concerned as everyone else.'

'None of this seems real to me, none of it.'

'It is, Carmen. Furthermore, we have to be on the lookout ourselves for members of the gang who will be scouting the beach and the condos.'

'I wish we had never taken that walk yesterday.'

'Ditto. Polonius told his son to beware of entering a quarrel. *But, being in*, he said, *bear't that th' opposed may beware of thee!'*

'What are you talking about?'

'Polonius' advice to his son, Laertes. His take on life. It's from *Hamlet.'*

'*Hamlet*? I can't remember exact speeches from grade eleven!'

'Polonius is saying: if you're in, go in hard.'

'That's all very well, but I seem to remember that all the characters die.'

'Point taken. But not one of them followed that advice.' Caitlin smiled ruefully, 'We'll be different! I think our safety lies in being wary and tough.'

CHAPTER SIXTEEN

IT WAS WELL after two-thirty when the gang met up with Harris and his Hummer beside Rascal House. Harris was bent over slightly, tossing his keys from one hand to the other. He was sucking down deep breaths, trying to loosen the tightness in his chest. He straightened up when the gang began to gather. A definite line of pain was etched on his forehead. He noticed Nipples had saliva on his lips. *Very soon you'll have much more than that. You'll have me slicing off part of the finger you used to make your call!* Then he turned his attention to his guys. 'Fucking nothing, right!' he spat.

'We searched everywhere that wasn't locked up,' Bobby said, stepping forward, inches from Harris' chin. Bobby knew full well that Harris needed their help. 'They disappeared, much like they did when you were looking for them at the mall,' he said, scoring his point.

'Are you implying something, Number Boy?'

'Just that these amateurs have horseshoes up their butts.'

Harris disregarded his comment and turned to the rest of his boys. 'We'll take you back to the Bal Harbour Shops, you can pick up your wheels and grab a few hours of sleep. We have two days to find the money. Do you hear that everybody? Two fucking days!'

They all nodded, their shoulders hunched like old men.

'By nine tomorrow, Ted and I will be on Haulover Beach questioning the lifeguards. One of them might know those chicks. I want the rest of you on the lookout in this area by eight-thirty, on the beach and across the street. They're here somewhere. Dress like tourists tomorrow, wear lots of lotion, caps, shades and carry cameras. Bobby don't wear that black crap you've always got on; wear something bright. The bitches have to go out for food and shit. If you spot one or both of them, alert the others with your cell phone. If they're in an area where you can't grab them, follow the bitches; see where they're staying. Ted and I can be here in a matter of minutes. Don't bring the cops down on us. We want the money.'

'Some of you don't seem to be all that shook up. These suppliers we deal with would think nothing about disposing of us as a lesson to the other dealers. It's true that I am the only one they've met, but I can't promise they wouldn't get your names out of me. They have ways of making people talk that we've never even thought of,' Harris told them.

Shoulders drooped, dissenting voices were stilled, even Bobby's. Wind gusted from the ocean and sent dust from construction nearby swirling around their heads. Squinting, the guys filed into the Hummer. None of them doubted Harris would give them up to save his own ass. These young men did not come from homes with cement lawns – common in South Florida. The crab grass around their homes was lush and as thick as a carpet. Their hands were smooth, their teeth were straight, their bones strong from good diets. They were privileged brats whose only challenge was getting through their courses at the University of Miami, and, except for Bobby, the guys were not faring well at that task. But now, each one of them tasted the queasiness of fear that slum kids lived with every day, kids who had to survive the rock and shock of the city.

Nipples was sandwiched between the guys in the

back seat. He had his longing, his pangs – nothing ever worked out for him. Twice he had had the opportunity to set things right; twice he had failed to nab his prey. His call to the cops was proving to be an onerous burden, and Nipples was rankled by another baseless search for some kind of redemption. All he had ever wanted was a flat chest. Was that too much to ask for? He was glad that Harris and Bobby were at odds – his butt might be saved for another day. If only he had found the bitches and the money, Harris would never have believed he had snitched. Now he was back at square one. His life was pathetic; even he knew that. He thought a lot about running – that was all he had thought about tonight. Life with tits was better than no life at all.

'All right guys, here we are,' Harris announced wearily, with a thin grin, as he pulled into the Bal Harbour Shops parking lot. 'Nipples, I want you to stay at my place tonight. You saw one of them close up. I want you to give me a good description; that way you can help us out even better tomorrow morning.'

Nipples' mouth dropped open and his tits sagged when Harris' order registered. He was a rat in a trap. Disposable. 'I have very little to tell you, Harris. I wanna go home tonight.'

'I wanna go home tonight,' Harris mimicked. 'I want you with me. You have the best description of the bitches. You're the key to this whole thing, Nipples. Are you telling me you don't want to help us? Is that what you're telling me? Cause I'd really like to know.'

'Christ, I wanna help. I've been busting my ass all night just like the rest of the guys. I haven't got a lot to tell you, any of you, Harris.' Nipples was thinking hard and fast. 'We recognized each other. That's what was strange about it. I mean, she didn't know what I looked like, and I really didn't know what she looked like either. What we both saw was that instant flash of recognition – it was in our eyes, that and the way she jumped up from her seat. I just knew she was one of them. I couldn't see the other one, but I could see she was talking to someone when she jumped up. Then the bus pulled away, and the fat bitch of a driver refused to stop for me. That's it man – that's all I know.' Nipples then stepped back from the centre of the group, fearful of drawing attention to himself.

'I think if you really thought about all this Nipples, you could come up with more information. Maybe there's something you're blocking.' There was a threatening undercurrent in Harris' voice.

'Fuck, that's it man – that's all I know.' Nipples kept his eyes on the ground.

'Maybe you'll remember something else tonight,' Harris said, a threat in every word.

'I won't. I've helped more than any of the guys tonight. I want to sleep the few hours we have left in my own bed. I don't give a shit whether you all laugh, but I can never sleep in a strange bed.'

'Ah Nipples, you're not telling us that you never slept at a chick's apartment? Is our Nipples a virgin?'

'Fuck all of you! I did sleep over at Jen's house, but I never fell asleep the first few times. I'm beat tonight and I want to catch some Z's.' An idea, almost worthy of Bobby, surprised Nipples. 'You can sleep at my place if you want – we can talk there.'

For a second, Harris was stymied. A reckoning of accounts would have to wait. 'I don't want to be with your family. Let's just fuck off to our own places. Don't be late tomorrow, Nipples, not with all that sleep! That goes for the rest of you too. Every minute counts – our lives depend on finding the money.'

Bobby did not seem to be overly concerned. He was planning an escape. Perhaps not tomorrow, but Bobby would take care of Bobby the day after tomorrow. What he was thinking was that Harris had gotten them into this shit. He should have looked before he tossed two million dollars. He panicked, that's what this pretty-boy did. Harris was no different than any one of them. His veins were filled with shit just like theirs. *I'm the shark – none of this would have happened if I had been in charge. Where would the fuck-face be without me? If we don't find the money, Harris will deal us all away to save his own balls. What can he tell Wolf-man if we're all smart enough to clear out?*

Harris was not about to let Nipples walk away into the night as free as the rest of the guys. 'Nipples, leave your wheels here. I'll drive you home and pick you up in the morning.'

'What's the point?' Nipples felt the sweat trickle down the inside of his arms.

'I want to talk to you about strategy for tomorrow.' Bobby and the rest of them left Harris and Nipples and headed to their own wheels. 'All right, see you tomorrow!' Harris called out behind them.

Nipples began walking to his Kia as though he had not heard Harris. He needed his wheels tonight – he did not tell Harris that his parents and sister and brother were in the Keys for the weekend. He had to think alone tonight. Christ, he needed his wheels! Bobby often defied Harris and got away with it, so he kept walking.

'Are you deaf, Titty Boy?'

'I...'

'Get your ass over here, now!'

Nipples, his armpits sticky, followed Harris toward his Hummer. When they reached the door, Harris dropped his keys. 'Pick those up for me.'

Nipples knelt quickly and reached for the keys. As he did, Harris stepped on his hand and ground his sole into it. One of the keys pierced the skin of Nipples' palm. Tears streamed to his eyes. 'Jesus, get off my hand!'

Harris' foot did not budge. 'When I tell you to do something, you do it! Understand?' Harris dragged his shoe across the top of Nipples' hand.

'Give me a break,' Nipples moaned, wincing, massaging his injured knuckle that was now bloody. *What the fuck is your problem?* He wanted to cry.

'Don't forget the keys!' Harris laughed.

Nipples bent once more and picked them up with his good hand.

Harris was already angry with himself for driving Nipples home. It took almost twenty minutes before he turned into a gated, tree-lined street, a waterfront community built in a Mediterranean style that was popular today. Nipples lived in an elegant four-bedroom townhouse, but it was a townhouse nonetheless. And Nipples drove a new SUV, but it was only a Kia, a midsize sport utility, merely a decent vehicle, nothing more. Nipples had loved the car at first. But those feelings dissipated when he parked it beside Harris' Hummer or Bobby's Navigator or Ted's Cadillac Escalade EXT. His Kia was nothing to brag about. He wondered tonight why he had ever even felt he could compete with these guys. From the very beginning, Nipples had never been first rank in this group. Why had he not seen the way things would always be back then? Before he'd gotten in too deep... As Harris came to a stop in his driveway, Nipples braced himself for one of Harris' sucker punches. A cell phone rang and it belonged to Harris.

'Yeah.'

'Mr. Chalmer, we were wondering if you might be

able to collect your order today?' Harris' nose turned green around the edges. Nipples could not see the colour because the interior of the Hummer was dark, but he could feel Harris' body stiffen like a board. 'My car is in the shop for another two days. You said I could meet with you then, sir.'

'As long as you don't forget, Mr. Chalmer.'

'I won't forget, sir.'

'I'm glad to hear that.' The line went dead.

Harris did not even look over at Nipples when he said, 'Get the fuck out of the car. I've wasted my time tonight taking you home – grab a cab to my place tomorrow. I haven't got the time to pick you up.'

Nipples jumped from the high seat in the Hummer to the parking lot and ran up his front stairs. Once he was inside the townhouse, he collapsed against a wall. Then he began to pound his breasts with both fists. *Why did I make that fucking call? Why? I'm a dead man – I'm fucking dead.* He felt something sticky on his hand. He'd forgotten the cut, and his punching had reopened it. *Fuck! Fuck them all! Look at my hand! Look at what you've done to my hand, asshole!* Even Nipples knew that this cut was just an opener; the main event was still to come. *I should go and pick up my wheels – I need my wheels. I should take care of my hand first. That asshole stomped on my hand! I oughta kill Harris; I mean really whack him. That's what he's going to do to me, right? So I should do him first. Yeah, that's exactly what I should do.* Nipples spoke to himself as he paced madly from one empty room to another, shouting. What should he use? The guys, the 'Gentlemen on Campus', that's what Harris called his men, did not debase themselves with hardware. They were gentle persuaders, and, until now, that approach had worked. He raced to his bedroom, ran to his desk and found his Swiss Army knife. *It's too bulky – the blade will close back on me when I stab him. Shit! Shit! Shit! It's too bulky!* Nipples threw the knife against a wall and dropped onto his bed and began to sob, rolling back and forth across the bed. He fell asleep when his eyes began to swell.

Harris gunned the engine, and the Hummer roared back up the quiet street, past a security guard who was shaking his fist in the air as Harris sped past the guard station. His bowels began to loosen, and Harris squeezed his eyes shut and tightened his butt muscles. Hot tears ran down the side of his nose. Nipples was the least of his worries. Right now he had to worry about shitting his pants. He tried to think of a way out, get his mind off his bowels until he was home. The trust fund could not do him any good – he could not get into that for another year. His father's money was useless. His liquidity was invested all over the world. His mother was demanding half of everything in their ugly divorce. Shit, he did not even know where to look for his father's investments, even if he could gain access to them. No, he knew what he had to do – he had to find those bitches.

He slammed the front door of the suite, waking his father. Stuart Chalmer was tired, weary from work. He was a powerboat designer specializing in Poker Run boats. His company boasted the world's fastest, safest, smoothest and best handling boats. Designing was his passion – he never thought he'd be put upon by demanding clients who each wanted some customizing on something he'd designed! Dealing with these *nouveaux riches* know-nothings was usually the purview of the managers. Lately, he had been called in to confer and alter a perfectly executed design to make the sale. Everybody wanted to be involved today! Twenty-six years of marriage and too many accommodating secretaries along the way were about to take him for half of every cent he'd ever earned. The joke of it all was that with all this annoyance and pressure of late, Stuart had not found the time for women. He had even begun to think amorously of Meg again, but what had she said the last time he had spoken to her about working out their differences? 'I've outgrown you, Stuart. You've broken my heart and humiliated me too many times. All I want from you is my share of the years I've put into our marriage. I even wish you well, but not with me!'

At the unnerving sound of a steel door being slammed, Stuart struggled out of bed and padded to the front door barefoot. 'Do you know what time it is Harris? It's after three! Don't you have courses tomorrow?'

'I'm off tomorrow,' Harris mumbled, hurrying off to the bathroom.

'Just a minute, where have you been till this time?'

'I have to take a crap. I'll be right back.'

'I'll wait.'

As soon as Harris sat on the toilet seat, there was a foul explosion, and then another. Everything Harris had eaten in the past forty-eight hours whooshed out of him as though someone had pulled a plug. He sat on the seat for a minute, weak and light-headed. His breathing was shallow; blood was pounding in his ears. He got up slowly and walked to the sink and splashed his face with cold water. He did not bother to take a look at himself in the mirror. He walked back out to the front hall to his father. 'Dad, I'm twenty-four years old. Do I still need your permission or something? I mean come on. I'm not drunk, I'm not stoned, I was out with the guys.'

'I know how old you are, Harris. I have a lot on my plate right now – I can't deal with the kind of problems that you got into back home.'

'Who's asking you to?'

'What are you suggesting? Are you in trouble again?'

'It's nothing serious, nothing I can't handle.'

'Well son, see that you do. You're not a kid anymore, and I can't go cleaning up your messes anymore. I have my own problems – you know that.'

'Go back to bed, Dad, I'm fine.'

'If you say so,' Stuart said, padding his way back down the hall to bed, guilty but glad to leave whatever Harris had gotten himself into this time behind him. Tomorrow he had to meet with the divorce lawyers.

Back in his bedroom, Harris flopped down on the bed, cupped his hands behind his head and stared up at the ceiling. Thinking was not Harris' strong suit; he left that to Bobby. Harris was a man of action; at least that's what he told himself that night. What he needed was sleep and maybe a little action to bring it on. A few minutes of wrist work failed to produce the firm release he had come to rely upon. As if he did not have enough to worry about, Harris now lay across his bed with a limp dick. This assault on his manhood and the bruise to his ego were palpable. *Now I can't even get it up! What the fuck is happening?* Though he could feel his life deflating, Harris did fall asleep. Worrying was a tiresome thing and it wore him out.

🌴

Bobby was home in no time. He lay on his bed and began to plan the rest of his life. As far as he could figure, the money was history. If the chicks had a brain between them, they'd be long gone by morning. Why would they stay around? Bobby had an uncle in St. Petersburg, one he had never mentioned. That's where he'd go the day after tomorrow. He even felt like a sabbatical from his studies. With straight A's, he could easily catch up on anything he missed. He got off the bed and began meticulously to stack the clothes he wanted to take with him, along with two tubes of gel. He packed everything neatly into his Polo carrying bags and set them back into his closet.

He had no fear that Harris would get the better of him. Harris was not that smart. Take away his looks and his money, and Harris was a nobody. At his closet, Bobby took out the clothes he'd wear tomorrow, a beige polo shirt and his Armani lenses. He leaned in and grabbed two pairs of shorts and chose the black. Fuck Harris! He reached in for his Sperry boat shoes – they were fine, easy and comfortable. Forget the camera, he wanted to be able to run quickly if he had to. Then Bobby remembered the punch and he thought of revenge. There was also the question of a quarter of a million dollars, his share of what Harris had tossed out the window. The money did not matter to Bobby, but the fact that Harris had cavalierly thrown out what did not belong to him did. *If I had lost the cash, Harris would have pounded my head into the pavement.* Maybe the best revenge would be to get the guys to walk out on Harris, not tomorrow, but the following day, the third day. Maybe… Because he always planned ahead, Bobby was able to fall asleep, and he was smiling.

CHAPTER SEVENTEEN

THE SUN ROSE slowly across the surging grey-turquoise of the Atlantic Ocean, laying its long, white fingers through the prevailing winds, touching down on the cresting water. And there was light! Warm, insistent, enveloping light. One wonders whether the natives, the few Miamians who live there, appreciate this warm blanket each of them steps out into every morning. To the tourists from Canada who have left a cold winter behind, each day is a small miracle. Morty was the first person from Club One to leave his bed for his early constitutional. Raoul had not yet arrived for the day's work. Everything around the condo was quiet. Morty left his flip-flops on the deck because he liked the feel of the coarse sand under his feet. His fisherman's cap, shrunk from too many of Sarah's washings, sat on the top of his head. Morty had a good gait for an old codger – he walked deceptively quickly, stopping only for the odd shells he found on the sand. Whatever shells he brought back, turtle wings or lion's paws, he turned over to his wife, who decided their fate. Once he found a starfish. Broken shells could be thrown back onto the beach from the deck – unbroken shells were washed, wrapped in napkins Sarah had saved from Rascal House and taken home to share with the great-grandchildren.

Morty had passed the Monaco and the Golden Strand before he met up with anyone. Actually, it was two *anyones*, two men much like himself who were walking ahead of him toward the Thunderbird and the Varadero. Morty was faster than both of them and he passed them with a nod. On his way back, he spotted Officer Ruiz approaching on his dune buggy. Ruiz gave Morty a thumbs-up for his pace and Morty waved back. Bobby and James caught Morty's attention, not because they did not blend in, but because he was not accustomed to seeing young men like them up and about this early. He had four sons of his own and he could not ever recall his boys getting themselves out of bed by seven-thirty or eight when they were not in school. These young men seemed intent on something. Perhaps they had lost something valuable the night before. Bobby and James took no notice of the old man. As Morty was reaching for his key to unlock the outer gate to Club One, Michel came down the wooden steps to the sand and opened the gate for him. '*Merci*,' Morty said to Michel in his best French. Morty and Sarah were great travellers and they had twice been to Montreal.

'You're welcome,' Michel answered. Michel was an early bird too. He had opened the gate not just for Morty, but because he wanted to check the area where the guys had been standing the night before when their shouting had awakened him. When he walked out onto the beach, a few feet from the deck where Steve lay, cold and dead, he saw no beer or liquor bottles and no butts of any kind. There was no party here as he had thought – the loudmouths must have just been passing by. Michel scratched his head; he was not usually wrong about his hunches.

Raoul drove into the parking lot on the left side of the condominium and stopped a few feet from the cabana. His day began at eight-thirty, six days a week. His wife Corrada had pulled a back muscle hoisting a mattress yesterday here at Club One. Raoul did not want his wife to further injure herself and he had called the night manager Victor to tell him he would prepare #119 for an early arrival. On any other morning, Raoul began work from the cabana, first taking out the hose and spraying the chairs and the cement walkway around the pool. Next he'd clean the pool and add whatever chemicals he felt it needed. But Raoul did not go to the back of the condo until he had prepared the room, mopped the front halls and unlocked the office for the morning maid to retrieve her cart. It was almost nine-thirty when he walked to the cabana, carrying his lunch bag.

Corrada was on his mind. He loved his wife, but injuries always worried him because he had no insurance. The family needed the money she brought in from Club One to meet the rent. Raoul left the cabana before gathering his tools for the day and walked out to the very edge of the back deck. He was immediately pleased to find Larry out painting. Raoul had worked here for two years and a few days ago he had told José, the manager and owner of twenty-four units, of Larry's good work. José had even talked of other work he had in mind for Larry. Raoul hoped Larry's good work would reflect well on him. If José began to think that Raoul was a good addition to the condo, he might even be taken on as live-in caretaker with a small apartment of his own on the premises. That was Raoul's goal.

Larry was a good man, Raoul thought, dependable and hard-working. He walked back briskly to the cabana and unlocked the second door and stepped into the workroom. He threw a light switch and spotted three beer bottles stacked neatly on the floor. Beside the bottles lay Larry's new shirt, folded to perfection. *Madre de Dios*, Raoul sighed. Had Larry begun to drink again? Raoul remembered that Larry had been out of sorts yesterday, edgy. He had not acknowledged Raoul at the end of his shift. What had happened yesterday? He could not simply ignore the beer bottles.

The handyman walked back out to the deck to have few words with Larry, to be certain he was sober. Larry appeared to be hard at work, but Raoul leaned over the deck anyway to see how much work had been done this morning. He was impressed – Larry was already painting the last side of the deck. Raoul allowed himself a wrinkled smile. *Bueno.*

'It's coming along, Raoul,' Larry pointed out, happy he had buried the shovel under the sand and laid the wood on the far side out of sight. Every morning since he had begun this job, Raoul appeared for an early morning inspection. Larry had other things on his mind besides the renovations. Last night he had heard loud shouting on the beach. Gently lifting a glass slate, he had seen a huddle of dark figures, close to the deck, but not beside it. He regretted the beer that was still buzzing above his right temple. Fearful of Michel, who missed nothing, he had not gone out to check his cash. The last thing he needed was for Michel to tell Raoul he had seen him wobbly last night.

Larry dropped his brush in the pan as soon as Raoul left. He walked the few feet to the top of the deck, knelt in the sand and reached in to dig up his money. When his hand felt the McDonald's napkins, he whistled and buried the stash once more. He leaned back and dug up his shovel. Raoul would not be back for at least ten minutes. Larry walked to the other side of the deck and began to bank the left side of the deck with sand to close it off. He patted the sand down as though it were cement. That work was finished in no time. He walked around to the bottom of the deck to further hollow out that part of his home. He knelt and began to dig. On the second attempt, his shovel struck something under the deck. The bleached hair on his fingers rose. He bent closer across the sand and stuck his shovel under the deck a third time. There was a rotten odour that assaulted Larry's nostrils, and the warm soda he had drunk for breakfast began to slide up his throat.

Faster than a stray cat, he scrambled back to his cash and dug it up. He opened the napkins as soon as he had them in his hands and breathed a sigh of relief. He stuffed the cash into his only pocket and crept back to the bottom of the deck. Using his shovel, he nudged whatever was under the deck again. 'All right, come out from under there,' he called warily, smarting at this home invasion.

Michel appeared from nowhere. 'What's wrong, Larry?'

'There's something under the deck,' Larry said, looking up at Michel, and probing with his shovel yet again. This time, a sneaker lay with the sand on his shovel when he withdrew it. Larry shook the shoe and recognized it immediately. He had seen it for over a year. 'Oh my God, that's Steve's!' He bent down as low as he could and shouted. 'All right, Steve, wake up and come on out of there.' Larry reached in with his hand, braver now because Michel had joined him and he had his money. It brushed a cold foot. He took hold of the bare foot and shook it. 'Jesus Christ,' Larry whispered, 'he's not moving. His foot's cold, real cold.' He crawled away from the deck and knelt in the sand, letting his chin fall into his hands.

Michel was in his element. There was nothing he liked better than a good mystery. 'I'll have a look under the deck.' With the clinical detachment of a cop whose senses have been dulled by the misery they've encountered, Michel knelt on the sand and groped till he too found the cold foot. Actually, he found both feet. Steve still wore the other sneaker. 'The poor guy under here is dead all right.'

'It's Steve. I recognize his sneaker. What the hell could have happened to him?' Only now did Larry remember that it could easily have been him under the deck. He began to pace, running both hands through his hair. 'That could have been me under there!'

Morty and Sarah walked out very carefully onto Club One's wooden deck because parts of it were still wet from Raoul's earlier hosing. They headed for their favourite table, the one in the corner, near the steps, beside the shower. Morty leaned over the table, grabbed the wooden pole, slipped the stay free and opened the blue umbrella. It was already a hot day. Morty did not believe in intruding into other people's lives, so, at first, he paid little heed to Michel and the deck at The Desert Inn. But he sat up very quickly when he heard Michel tell Larry to get to the office and call 911. He'd stand guard at the deck. Morty had a good nose for trouble and he told Sarah that she should go back to the room. Sarah wanted to stay with him, but she began to put her things back into her bag.

In their condo, Caitlin and Carmen sat apart from one another. Anchoring themselves back into the present, they needed a plan for the day. Carmen took the lead. 'I've been thinking – we can't just pick up and leave, much as I would like to get out of here. That's the problem when everybody knows us. Morty and Sarah and the rest of them would have a lot of questions. As you said, they're going to find Larry today, and we can't suddenly disappear from our holiday.' Carmen noticed her friend was examining her thigh. 'Are you listening to me, Caitlin?'

'I just noticed that my skin is broken and my burn bled. Oh my God, what if CSI takes blood samples from under the deck? What are we going to do? We could be arrested and charged!'

'Let me think. Stop moving – I have to concentrate.'

'Oh my God, I can't believe this. What have we done?'

'Caitlin, calm down. Let me think. Larry was a homeless person. I don't think they send out CSI for poor people like him. It's awful to say, but in the grand scheme of police business, poor Larry will be less than a footnote. Anyway, when did you skin your thigh? Can you remember?'

'Oh God, I do, as we were crawling under the deck.'

'Let me see your leg.'

Caitlin walked over to Carmen and pulled up her shorts. There were the tiniest little pinpricks of dried, flecked blood as though Caitlin's leg had been punctured with needles.

'All right, it did bleed, but hardly at all. Did you skin it again when you crawled back out? Think, Caitlin.'

'No, no, I didn't.'

'Caitlin, there's no problem. It didn't bleed as soon as you scraped your leg and you didn't catch it again on your way out. There's nothing on the underside of the deck. Nothing! No blood at all! We're out of it.'

'What about skin?' Caitlin asked, rubbing her temples. 'I lost some of that on the deck. Skin and blood are both viable for DNA.'

'We're going to drive ourselves crazy. Let it go, Caitlin. The underbelly of the deck is covered with all sorts of things. What was the name of the other guy who lived there a few months ago? I think it was Steve, yeah, Steve. He must have scraped himself a few times on that wood. It would never even occur to the police to test our DNA. Get a hold of yourself. Anyway, in all probability, Larry killed himself. Let's concentrate on our plan. I'll get your key this morning.'

'What you were saying? I was only half listening.'

'We have to go to the pool today, be on the lookout for those guys, and above all else, stay apart from one another, all right. We can't be seen together. Those guys will be on the beach today too. If you want to worry, worry about them.'

'It's almost nine-thirty, Carm. Let's get going.' A hammering heart had turned her voice reedy. 'I'll go out to the deck and sit with Morty and Sarah.' Before she could make a move, there was a loud knock at the door. Both women froze. Whoever it was kept pounding.

Caitlin rose and braced for the worst as she opened the door.

Yvette was flushed. 'Come quickly. Larry has found a dead body under The Sands Motel!'

'What?' Caitlin cried.

'A dead body under the deck. The police are on their way.'

'Oh no. Who found the body?'

'Larry, the painter. You know Larry.'

'I can't believe this! Larry found a dead body?' Caitlin's voice was hoarse. Carmen never said a word. 'We'll come down, Yvette, in a few minutes.'

Once the door was closed, Carmen whispered, 'Larry? Larry? No wonder whoever was under the deck thought we were attacking him.'

🌴

On Haulover Beach, a Miami-Dade managed park, Harris and Ted had stopped at two lifeguard huts, questioned both guards, with nothing to show for their efforts. As they approached Jason's hut, they had already made up their minds to join the others further down the beach because this idea was fast becoming a waste of time. They had decided to give it one more shot.

Jason was a people person, but he also loved the early morning when the beach was quiet and almost deserted. Harris and Ted found him on two legs of his chair that Jason had tilted back against the hut. His feet stuck out from the white railing. Behind his shades, Jason's eyes were closed, but he was not asleep. He was enjoying the ocean breeze as it licked the soles of his feet. This was the kind of day ordered up by tourists.

'How ya doin'?' Harris called up to him. He and Ted began to climb the wooden stairs up to the hut.

Startled, Jason's feet fell to the ground, and his chair jumped back onto its four legs. When Jason stood, he was as tall as Harris. 'Hi ya! Guys, you're gonna hafta get back down the ladder again. The platform is off limits. I don't make the rules.'

'We'll be gone in a minute. We really need your help.'

'Uh huh.'

'Last night we met two real lookers, one dark, one blonde, up at the mall. We wanted to get together today. They gave us their number, but this idiot beside me lost it.' Harris gave a good description of the women's clothing. 'They told me they walked here often. I was hoping you knew them. I'm sure you know a lot of chicks around here, right?'

From the description of their clothing, Jason knew who the guys were talking about. He smiled.

'You know these chicks?' Harris asked, pumped.

'Yeah, I think I know who you're talking about. You said they gave you their numbers?'

'Lucky us.'

The corners of Jason's mouth turned down. He

knew the guys were lying. 'Well, I don't really know them – they pass me on their walk is all.'

'I'm sure you know their names. I'm sure you know a lot of names, a jock like you.'

Then Jason went for it, lost his caution. These dudes were pissing him off. 'Guys, the chicks I know never gave you their number. I've been trying to go out with one of them for two years, and I know she doesn't party here on vacation. They're good people. That's all I'm going to say. You probably tried to hustle them but you never got a number.'

Who is this piece of shit telling me what I did or didn't do? Harris grabbed Jason's groin and twisted. Jason fell back against the hut, striking his right shoulder, his face screwed up in pain. 'I don't want trouble. But I want their names and where they stay. Get it, prick?' Ted stood in front of the guys so a passer-by would see nothing amiss if he saw three guys up on the platform of the guard station.

'What's your problem?' Jason moaned in an unnaturally high voice. 'Let go, Jesus. You're destroying me!'

'Not till I hear what I want to know,' Harris whispered close to the shell of Jason's ear. He added a vicious twist.

'Sonofabitch!'

'I'm listening.'

'I don't know their names all right. I call them Canadians. They stay somewhere on the strip – Thunderbird, I don't know where. That's all I have to tell you. That's it, man!' Harris let go of Jason, and he crumbled to the floor of the deck, heat rushing to his face.

'You don't want to call anybody about our little get-together, do you?'

'Just get the fuck out of here,' Jason moaned, the blood drained from his face.

And Harris and Ted did just that.

Jason hugged himself and tried very hard not to think of the sharp, white pain in his groin. He knew the C's were much closer than the Thunderbird. *Score one for me, you assholes. Jesus, this is killing me!* He rocked back and forth curled up like a beach ball.

Harris looked back at Jason. *Another guy who won't get it up tonight!* He'd have some company later on if he encountered last night's problems again. Both guys began to run back to Ted's Escalade that he had parked beside the main lifeguard station where Harris had pulled over to stop for Garderella only yesterday. Harris took a quick glance at the spot and realized that things had begun to turn ugly in a matter of hours. He did not even feel as though he were running on his own legs.

Tully was on duty, but he was in his patrol car back at the entrance to the walk and never saw them. The boys were still on his mind. Tully had gotten a decent look at four of them now. He had told Ruiz about the night's events and he had also called Garderella in the morning and filled her in as well. She was more convinced than ever that someone else had gotten the money or the drugs, whatever was in the bags. The guys were out hunting, of that she was certain. 'Keep me informed, Tully. I've been assigned to another case, but if something breaks on Mr. Chalmer, I want to know.'

'You got it, detective.'

CHAPTER EIGHTEEN

CAITLIN UNLOCKED THE side gate and joined Morty and Sarah who were standing side by side at the railing. She walked over and stood with them, stealing a few glances at Larry who stood on the beach by his deck.

'Isn't this awful?' Sarah said. 'If the body is Steve's, I remember him and all the young girls who had crushes on him. You remember him, don't you, Caitlin?'

'Let's hope it's not Steve. It's so sad that anyone died under the deck.' What else was there to say? Her attention was immediately drawn to Michel who was kneeling at the side of the deck where Steve, if that's who it was, lay dead, rigour having come and gone. Poor Steve was well on his way to rotting on the sand.

Michel knew enough not to contaminate the scene but he tried once more to get his head down for a good look. A stray cat darted out from under the deck and caught him off balance. It was too dark under the deck, but there was no chance that the sweet sour smell, sharp even, that buckled his nose, was anything other than the odour of death. He stood there waiting for the police.

Back at Haulover, the beach was home to hordes of strays. Food and water mysteriously appeared for the cats along the walk each and every day. This tabby, like Larry and Steve, must have felt life would be safer further north along the beach.

Caitlin's hands began to tremble – her stomach heaved. The gate behind her was opening again, but Caitlin did not dare look back.

Carmen froze for a second, but anyone seeing her would have thought her reaction natural for the occasion. Her shoulders stiffened when she tried to turn and head for a lounge chair. She did get to the chair, but she sat down like a person with a bad back.

'Oh dear me,' Sarah said. 'I hope you're wrong, Michel. He was such a nice young fella. I used to wonder though how a young man like that could sit on the sand the whole day. That doesn't much matter now, does it?' Morty put his arm around her shoulders.

Yvette had been cleaning her windows on her second floor balcony when she spotted Raoul's frightened face as he raced to the side gate below her. Leaving her work, she called her husband and they soon joined Michel downstairs. She had left the group for only a few minutes to alert Caitlin and Carmen of the tragedy. Everybody gathered around Michel. Tourists from across the street who had come to the beach early to stake out their place near the fence around Club One smelled trouble and rose from their chairs. Though only a handful of people had heard Michel, everybody around seemed to know there was trouble of some kind.

'What a terrible way to end your life,' Caitlin said very quietly, still sitting in her chair, but Morty heard her.

'Some people are born to sad lives,' he said to Caitlin.

Carmen joined the group, but stayed away from her friend.

In minutes, there was the shrill of sirens, from the beach and from the street. Before the authorities could reach the back deck, people appeared like gulls for a bit of bread. One minute there was a single, lonely gull – in the next, the sky and sand were white clouds of flapping wings. Michel was conversing with his group at Club

One and did not notice the clusters of curious tourists that milled around the deck. A small girl held her mother's legs tightly and circled around them. Her little brother followed his dad to the side of the deck where his father had bent to one knee for a better inspection. The little boy went his father one better. In no time, he had squeezed himself under the deck and was about to squirm closer to Steve when his father saw what his son had done. He reached in and pulled the toddler from under the deck by a leg. In his efforts to get his son away from the scene, he was overly aggressive. His son slid back out across the sand but not before scraping his knee on the underside of the deck. The youngster began to howl.

'You're not to go under there,' he scolded, picking his son up in his arms. 'I told you to stay with your mother.' The child hollered even louder, pointing to his knee. Wiping away sand with his free hand, the father kissed the small scrape. 'You're a big boy and big boys don't cry.' The hollering stopped, but the boy still shuddered as he laid his head on his father's shoulders. When he noticed the size of the crowd behind him, the father threaded his way through it and joined his wife and daughter.

Michel walked back down to the lower deck and asked people to back away from it. Most of the tourists were French, and Michel spoke to them in that language. Miami-Dade PD was the first on the scene. Rescue teams were close behind. Michel took the lead and spoke to an officer, identifying himself as a former cop himself. The blue brotherhood has long arms, and Michel was allowed to stand with the police inside the yellow tape that other officers were already setting up around the scene. Michel knew more about Steve's life than anyone else around except Larry because he had befriended him. He began telling what he knew of Steve to Detective Dunn, the lead on this case. Larry was still in shock.

Ruiz saw the commotion from the Newport Pier as he was making rounds and soon found himself in the familiar role of crowd control. Bobby and Nipples and one other gang member heard the sirens all the way from the defunct Suez that still stood but was now empty and forlorn. They ran along the beach to find out what was happening, shouting into their cells as they ran. Harris got the news while he and Ted were caught at the same traffic light at 163rd Avenue for the second time in twenty-four hours and he swore. Ted never thought to look in his rear-view mirror. If he had, he might have seen the late model Accord that had been tailing them. It had parked beside them on the beach, but Harris had other things on his mind and he and Ted had missed the shadow. 'We don't need this shit. We have only two days to find the bitches. Keep your eyes open, Ted. This is your shit too.' Harris found himself entangled in the squad cars that were diverting traffic to a single lane on Collins Avenue past Club One and Rascal House across the street. 'Shit, shit, shit,' he growled, pounding the dash. Ted pulled into a parking lot in front of a small strip mall a block down the street. The Accord pulled in beside him.

Ted had known Harris for two years and, like the others, had been drawn to this cocky guy who seemed to have it all. It was hard to see their captain coming unglued. He had defined himself by a combative style, rugged good looks and a need for adventure. For all of the guys, being part of Harris' gang was equivalent to making the A-list. Ted could actually see the weight of his ways falling on top of him, and Harris was crumbling. Ted had not slept last night and from another glance at Harris, no one would sleep tonight either if they didn't find the money today. The two guys got out of the SUV, flew across the street to the beach and ran to their right, to the commotion. The men in the Accord did not bother to move for another few minutes.

The crowd was oddly silent around the deck when the crime scene techs arrived with their white rubber gloves, cameras, evidence bags, fingerprint kits and chainsaw. Two of them knelt on the sand and manoeuvred a long-armed camera under the deck. A minute later, they stood and conferred with the suits. They decided to saw the feet of the deck and, with nine of them on the scene, they felt they could lift the top of it off the body underneath. The piercing drone of the chainsaw drove the crowd back even further. Two men stood at each of the four legs to support that part of the deck once the leg had given way to the teeth of the saw. The men's cheeks turned a dark red quite visible above their tanned faces, and their necks corded as they held their side of the deck from falling on Steve. When only the men were supporting the deck, those at the foot of the wooden structure began to hoist the deck into the air, like a wall being raised by cranes. The suits did not want the underside of the deck to rest on the sand. It stood a good twenty-five feet. The men rested the face of the deck against the side of the wall at Club One.

Once he was uncovered, Steve looked like a giant bug that had hidden under a boulder of wood. The other old, dirty sneaker was still on his right foot. To those who did not know his story, and that was most of the crowd and the suits, it appeared that Steve had dug his own grave. No one but Larry knew that he was just trying to find his way home. He lay in his crypt like any corspe whose life has left it. His legs had collapsed and they lay on the sand like sticks with the green-grey pallor that betrays the dead. His fists were balled from his last spasm, as though time had stood still. One hand was slightly elevated from the sand and hung in a few inches of air. It was Steve's face that people would remember in nightmares. A dark halo of black blood pooled at the base of his head. His nose was splayed against his cheekbones, flattening his face like a disk. Only the upper bridge of his nose resembled anything like the structure it had once been. One could not make out easily that his lip was torn because his face was a mass of black, dried blood. A small part of his cheek was white where the cat had licked it. Steve's mouth was slightly open – part of a tooth lay on his lower lip. His eyes were not closed the way one sees a corpse in a film. They were open about a quarter of an inch, and there was such a fright in them that not even death could still that last terrible moment those eyes had seen.

One flat board was torn from the deck and laid across the sand until it almost touched Steve. A second was laid on the other side. Techs crawled across the boards to preserve the sand around Steve. The older of the two men reached over and gently closed Steve's eyes. He still felt pity for men who were scraped off the streets or found on the sand. Men whose bodies were exposed to the eyes of greedy onlookers... No sooner had the lids been closed than they sprang open again. Maybe Steve wanted people to remember the way he died. In his cold eyes, there was a trace of grudge and a steely level of indignation. As the techs were examining his body, a puff of wind caught a small lock of Steve's hair. For a second or two, it danced in the breeze.

Close to two hundred onlookers had gathered around the scene, and Ruiz called for backup. 'All right everybody, please give the officers enough room. Step

back a few feet, please. Let the officers do their work!'
People were still coming to the scene of Steve's death.
Ruiz was puzzled to see Harris Chalmer and a friend in
the crowd. He recognized Harris from yesterday's
events on Haulover Beach. *I'm sure Tully would like to
know about this.* Ruiz was very careful not to make eye
contact with Harris and spook him, but he kept
Chalmer in his peripherals. Harris was too intent on the
scene and combing the crowd for the women to notice
anything.

After having heard from Ruiz, Tully called the news
in to his lieutenant who was also interested to know that
a dead body had turned up near where Chalmer and his
boys had been only the night before and were now. In
all probability, the night of the death or murder... His
lieutenant relieved him of his watch on the beach and
sent Tully to Sunny Isles. En route, he radioed
Garderella and filled her in on the details. She had
already been reassigned to a case at one of the clubs on
South Beach, but she wanted very much to be kept
abreast. If anything of significance surfaced, she would
do her best to join him. Harris Chalmer was still in her
craw.

Yvette decided the scene was too gruesome and left
the deck of Club One for her second-storey balcony.
Caitlin and Sarah left Morty's table quietly and joined
her. The three women sat together on the upstairs balcony a little distance from the scene. Carmen felt she
should stay as close as possible beside Morty to learn
what she could of Steve's death. She wanted to know for
certain how he had died. Morty had no desire to join
the crowd on the beach, so Carmen sat with him under
the blue umbrella in Caitlin's vacated seat. She leaned
forward to catch everything she could.

Michel was not on the first line of the investigation

– he stood by the yellow ribbon, speaking to one of the detectives on the scene. Yet he could hear the results of the initial exam. Each tech, on either side of the body, took one of Steve's hands, examining the fingers and the nails. The fingernails were of little help because they were caked with sand and black blood. The autopsy would show if there was any skin beneath them that might indicate an altercation had taken place. 'He's wearing a hospital bracelet. The ID is smudged, but the lab will get a name from it. I can make out the first name – it's Steve.' The tech cut the bracelet from Steve's wrist and dropped it into a plastic bag. They moved to the legs. 'No obvious trauma to the hands or legs – no evidence of a weapon of any kind in these areas,' the techs called over to Detective Dunn, the officer in charge.

While one tech began to work on Steve's head, the other walked to the underside of the deck and began first with photos. He then chipped samples of blood from the wood and what appeared to be a sliver of bone, depositing his finds in separate small plastic bags and labelling them. He stood back a few feet, examined the blood spatter on the centre of the deck, walked around the sides and took specimens from there as well.

When the father saw that his son had broken the skin on his knee, he carried him forward through the crowd to the side of the deck and stood at the edge of the yellow tape. 'Officer, I have to speak to someone,' he called over.

'Yes, sir, what can I do for you?' Tully asked, walking up to the man.

'Well, I think I should tell someone that my son crawled under that deck a while ago and cut his knee. I noticed the man over there taking samples. I guess I wanted to tell you that my son's blood might be in one of the samples he's just taken.'

'Well, let me take your name and address and someone will be in touch if that becomes necessary.'

'I assume he's not the only kid who's crawled under there recently,' the father added. 'What are you gonna do? They're too fast for us catch them.'

'You're right about that, sir. Thank you and we know where to reach you if need be.'

Tully walked over to the tech and relayed the story. The tech stood back from the main spatter before saying anything. 'I have the specimens – I don't know if we'll need them. He then passed an ultraviolet light over the sand to reveal additional blood stains invisible to the naked eye. The main trauma is here,' he said, pointing out the mass of black blood in the centre of the deck. He called Dunn over for his first assessment. He also called to the tech working on Steve. 'Anything?'

'Just the damage to the face,' he called back. Now that the photos were taken, this tech turned Steve on his side. He began parting Steve's sticky hair, examining his skull for fractures and punctures. 'There's a recent scar here on the forehead that rides up into the hairline. Probably the reason for the hospital stay.' Pulling the eyelids back, he found no petechial hemorrhaging. He worked with the same diligence on Steve's neck and chest and stomach. He crawled back off the board and joined the others at the blood-spattered deck. 'I don't know much now – we'll know more after the crime lab gets through with him. But my first take on this is that this guy killed himself, broke his own nose when he was somehow disoriented and tried to sit up. The drug tox will have more for us too. We'll want to know if he was alone when he died and what he was doing here.'

Michel overheard them and walked, taking Larry with him, over to where the suits were standing, including Dunn and Tully, because he had something further to offer. Michel began to speak before Dunn got to answer the tech. 'Larry here knows the victim. I live up there in the second-floor condo on the corner. Last night, before two in the morning, I heard some shouting down here. The noise was loud enough to wake me up. I thought it was a bunch of kids, but I checked this morning and there was no garbage left around.'

'I see,' said Dunn, who turned his attention to Larry. 'Your name, sir? You found the body, I understand, and you knew the victim?'

'Yes, sir, I did. I'm Larry Stormer.'

'You knew the victim?'

Under Dunn's scrutiny, Larry felt he was a suspect and he began to tense up. 'Yeah, Steve and me hung together for over a year. His last name is Granger. We were out of work, hanging around South Beach, but we couldn't find anything there, so we moved up to Sunny Isles. We were here for over a year.'

'Where here?' Dunn asked.

'Under the deck.'

'Under this deck? Your lived under this deck for a year?'

'We only slept here; we found odd jobs during the day.'

'Did people know you guys were living here? No one asked you to move on?' Dunn was incredulous.

'The guys here knew, the ones at Club One. One of the women, a tourist, gave the place a name – The Sands Motel. They often gave us food and stuff.'

'All right, you said this man Steve lived here with you.'

'Until over a month and a half ago.'

'Then what happened? You had a row or something?'

'Nothing like that. He had work at Dunkin' Donuts three days a week – I hauled garbage at Publix. One afternoon, after work, he didn't come home.'

'And?'

'And, I don't know. For a couple of days, he'd begun complaining that this place was too small. He wanted to move in with some guys who had rented a single room in Hollywood. I walked up to Dunkin' Donuts looking for him. He was gone and I never heard from him. I couldn't call the cops. Who's going to help street people? I figured Steve just moved on like he said he was going to do.'

'You live under here now?'

'Not any more. I found work at this condo,' he said pointing to Club One, 'and I sleep on the premises.'

'So you were nowhere near this deck last night?'

Larry's knees began to shake. There was no way he could tell Dunn he thought he had seen Steve yesterday. Keep his distance, that's what he had to do. 'Haven't been under the deck for over a month, other than painting beside it.'

'How come you found the body then?'

'I still think of it as my place. I thought I could make a decent unit here with some plywood and a shovel. Well, I had both this morning and I began to work on it during my first break. That's when I discovered Steve's body, his shoe really, but I recognized it. I called Michel over immediately.'

Michel nodded his assent.

'That's it for now, Mr. Stormer. In case I have to speak further with you, you'll be around?'

'I'm not going anywhere – I have work here. I know Steve's father lives in Columbus because he came down to visit Steve last year.'

'Here, what do you mean here?'

'He sat with us on the sand beside the deck. He brought food and cash for Steve.'

Dunn scratched his temple. *People!* 'Before you go, Mr. Stormer, would you mind showing me your place at the condo? Just a formality, sir. To eliminate you as a suspect.' Dunn followed Larry to the cabana. What struck him most was the cleanliness. He looked through Larry's few clothes and he found nothing that looked even remotely like dried blood. Since the techs had found no blood except under the deck, Dunn was pretty certain that these two men had not fought under the deck because there wasn't enough room. There was barely room for one person. He believed Larry, but not before he had checked out his digs.

He finished his notes, left Larry and returned to speak to Michel. 'You definitely heard a disturbance near this deck last night around two o'clock?'

'I did, but I couldn't make out who the people arguing were, and they moved on when I turned on my light. I know the voices were male.'

'More than a couple of people?'

'Yes, a group of guys. I heard different angry voices.'

'All right, thank you.' Michael Dunn was an ambitious careerist who would have preferred not to have to deal with cases like this one. That having been said, he also wanted a good number of closed files on his resume when he applied for captain next year. He was a fact man, a detail person, a guy who dotted and crossed whatever needed either one. He was not going to solve this case on the pet theory of a tech. Without the proper facts, a hypothesis could drive an investigation right

off the rails. He would wait for the crime lab, the prelim – in the meantime, he went about his questioning
and note taking.

Tully's radar was activated. Was it possible? Could
Chalmer have something to do with this guy's death?
On balance, Tully liked his work, but at forty-two, there
were days he felt things were getting away from him,
the way they never had when he was new to the uniform. But today, he was on target and he made a mental note to take the kid Ruiz out for drinks. He left the
group to find Ruiz to have him point Chalmer out to
him because, as of yet, he had not seen him in the
crowd. Before he located the young officer, he almost
bumped into Chalmer and Ted.

Harris shifted uneasily from one foot to another, his
mood souring by the second. The stiff was wasting too
much of his second day.

'Well, Mr. Chalmer, are you back for more Reuben
sandwiches?' Tully knew enough not to do any interro-
gating before he had clearance. They knew where he
lived and could pick Mr. Chalmer up whenever they
wanted him down at the precinct for questioning.

'Out for a run, detective. Is there a problem with
that? What happened to the guy? It's a guy right?'

'We'll find out soon enough, Mr. Chalmer.' Tully
was dialing Garderella as he walked away.

Bobby and Nipples and the rest of the guys were
about to join Harris when they saw Tully. It was
Nipples who first spotted the cop. That boy had great
eyes. He alerted Bobby. Nipples wanted to stay as far
away from Harris today as he could because he was fed
up with Harris' ass-chewing and his veiled threats.
There was no way, if he could help it, that he'd find
himself alone with Harris. On its simplest level, he
wanted to continue living, nipples and all.

Bobby put two and two together from the night before. On one level, Bobby was a dweeb and he knew it. But, with his money and his clothes, and the fact that he was smarter than any of the guys around, Bobby had come through and been accepted by most other guys. The sage of the group, that's how he saw himself. Harris was the only one who demeaned him, but Harris put everybody down. Oh yes, he recalled the light going on in one of the condos during Harris' tirade. He wanted nothing to do with Tully or his questioning – he had plans for tomorrow. Let Harris take the heat, as far as Bobby was concerned, let Harris go down for all of it. He extended both his arms to prevent the guys from going ahead and hooking up with Harris. The gang stood with him, far back in the crowd.

Steve still lay on the sand although the techs appeared to have finished with his body. They had begun to rake the sand slowly and with great care all around him. Larry thanked the fates that he had thought to grab his money. Finding it now would have served up a motive for Detective Dunn. The fact that he knew Steve and knew nothing of his disappearance would not help him either. He was aware that some cops wanted cases closed quickly, and homeless guys were easy targets.

Carmen felt tears run down her cheeks, but she was not the only one teary-eyed. Morty looked like his eyes were tearing up as well. As a gambler, an unlucky one at that, Carmen wondered what the odds were of Steve showing up last night.

The tech continued raking on the other side of Steve. On the side where the sand was banked, the rake found a comb, candy wrappers and something else that the tech bent down and picked up with a pencil to preserve prints. It was a key on a short chain with a small green marker. Michel knew the key as soon as the sand was brushed off of it. He had rented the front condo the year before the C's took it over. He and his wife had given it up because they wanted to be closer to the ocean, away from the traffic on Collins.

Carmen's heart fell and she bit her tongue. Although she could not see the key clearly, she knew instinctively that it was Caitlin's. She looked up at the balcony and locked nerves with Caitlin who froze. Then her friend left the balcony and sought refuge in her room.

Michel left the cops, stepped over the tape and walked up the steps to Club One. Before he could speak, Carmen took the initiative. 'Michel, is that Caitlin's key? She lost it yesterday morning – we have been looking everywhere for it. We bought a new one from the front office. God almighty, what was it doing on the side of the deck? We've never walked over there. This is so scary.'

This was Michel's mystery and he intended to solve it. He thought for a few minutes. 'Do you know where Caitlin lost it?'

'Do you want me to go and get her? She's up there with Yvette. Just a sec, I remember. She said she had it to come down to the pool yesterday, but she didn't have it when she left the pool because I had to let her in. So, she lost it down here, sometime yesterday morning. But how could Steve have gotten the key?' Carmen felt if she stopped talking her teeth would chatter. She could hear her blood pounding in her ears.

'I think I know what happened,' Michel said, and called Dunn who left the crime scene grudgingly.

Carmen tried to lick the roof of her mouth, but her tongue was as dry as sand. She also knew that the gang members were standing somewhere in the crowd look-ing for them, so there was no way she was about to walk to the balcony and relay this news to Caitlin and so break her cover. She was safe for the moment up on the balcony with Yvette. What was Michel about to say? Unable to contain herself, Carmen said, 'We lost the key in the morning because we didn't come back down to the beach again. We had an early night.'

No one noticed that Larry was standing off to the side.

'You've found a key, detective? It belongs to this woman and her friend. I recognized the key because I rented the same place two years ago.'

'You know who owns this key?' Dunn asked, closing in on a fact.

'Yes, and I think I know how it got under the deck too. Poor Larry has a crush on her friend. He never takes his eyes off her – it's sad. Caitlin, that's her friend's name, never notices him at all. She lost the key yesterday morning, here on the deck. Larry watches Caitlin's every move, and he must have seen the key fall. He was painting our deck, so it was easy for him to step over the railing and pick it up.

'Oh my God, were we in danger?' Carmen's shock was utterly believable. 'You think he might have come into our room?'

'No, no,' Michel assured her. 'He's harmless. Larry, come over here.'

Larry's face was crimson, but he walked over to the small group when Michel motioned to him.

'Did you find Caitlin's key yesterday?'

'Yes, I did. I kept it in my pocket and I tried to return it to Caitlin yesterday around noon, but she didn't give me a chance. Here it is,' he said reaching into his pocket and not finding it. He turned his pocket inside out, but there was no key. 'I had the key this morning,' he said, puzzled.

'The techs found the key on the far side of the deck,' Michel told him.

'Well, it must have fallen out of my pocket when I was enlarging the crawlspace this morning. At least it's not lost.' Larry didn't know whether to be relieved or not.

Dunn made no comment – he was busy listening. 'Makes sense,' Dunn finally said. 'By the way, where is your friend now?' the detective casually asked.

'She was on the balcony, but I guess she's gone back to our room,' Carmen told Dunn. 'Like everyone else, she's very upset.'

'I'd like your names and numbers, in case we want to speak to the two of you again.'

Carmen gave out the information and was very glad that her nerves befitted the situation. As she was turning to go back to her room, Dunn called after her.

'On the other hand, perhaps I should speak with your friend today, follow procedure. If you would lead the way, I'll follow you.'

For a second, she looked quite through Detective Dunn, and her eyes fell on Nipples who was standing at the edge of the crowd on her left. Nipples' eyes were on someone else, someone at the other side of the crowd because he was bobbing up and down for a better look. Unlike that time in the Bahamas or even in the lockers, Carmen did not lose it. She saw that Morty was getting up from the table and she calmly took his arm. Morty did not resist, and the three of them, Morty, Carmen and Dunn walked to the side door. Carmen felt she was in some other world, the land of adrenalin. *As long as I can keep one step ahead of them all, we'll be all right. I know it. Our luck is holding! As long as Caitlin doesn't break down.*

When Dunn and Carmen reached C-4, Carmen knocked before unlocking the door. Caitlin was sitting on the couch staring into space. 'Caitlin, this is Detective Dunn – he wants to ask you a few questions.'

Caitlin stood up immediately, much like a good suspect should.

'Miss?'

'Donovan, Caitlin Donovan.'

'Another Irishman,' Dunn smiled. 'Better, a lass!'

Caitlin's eyes teared. Dunn could see that she was genuinely upset and, after years on the force, he knew what was real and what was a sham. He had only one weak spot that he would ever admit. A pretty woman on the verge of tears. That's why he paused for a second, something he never did before asking his questions.

'Was that my key they found at the side of the deck? It must have fallen out of my shorts' pocket when I had my legs on a chair.'

To help her out, Carmen jumped into the conversation. 'Larry found it yesterday.'

'I feel even worse now. Around noon yesterday, I blew Larry off.' Tears fell down Caitlin's cheeks and she used both hands to wipe them away. 'I should have been nicer to him, but I wasn't. Michel told me when I got here about his crush. When he showed up at the side door yesterday, for the second time, Larry just stood there, as though he had been waiting for me. I felt he was about to say something, but I cut him off. I thought he was going to ask me for a beer or even a date. Now I think he was only trying to tell me he had my key. I never even gave him a chance to tell me he had my key. Now the only real friend he had is dead, and I was rude to him. I wish I had acted differently.' Caitlin did not bother to wipe away the tears.

Carmen could not believe how well Caitlin had han-
dled this situation, but she also knew Caitlin was speaking from her heart and half of what she said was true.

'These things happen, Miss Donovan. We all live
with regrets. The key will be returned to Club One if
the prelim findings are accidental suicide, as the techs
seem to think it is. We will test for prints if we're looking at a homicide.'

'I understand,' Caitlin said.

'I'd like your numbers here, and I guess back home.
How long will you be in Miami?'

'Another six days, sir,' Caitlin said.

'Good, I'll know where to reach you. We'll probably
learn that this man suffered a fatal accident, but policy
is policy.' Dunn had been taking notes as Caitlin spoke
– he was still writing after she had finished. 'Well, try to
enjoy the rest of your holiday. It's a shame that things
like this happen.' Dunn was out the door before either
of the women could respond.

A few minutes later, there was a knock on the door.
Both women walked silently to the door, expecting
Detective Dunn. When Caitlin opened the door, she
immediately took a step back when she saw Larry.
Flustered, she did not ask what he wanted before she
spoke. 'I'm sorry about yesterday, Larry, and about
Steve – I know he was your friend.'

But Larry had not come for condolences. 'I think we
should get together for coffee or something, the three
of us.'

'It's been a tough day all around, Larry. We're just
going to stick around here for a while.'

'We have to get together. Your friend there,' he said,
pointing to Carmen, 'told Dunn that you were in your
room early. But you weren't – I saw you both going in
the side door after two in the morning.'

'That was something private, Larry. Anyway, we'll meet you at Starbucks in half an hour.'

Larry did not feel good about himself, but life was all about protection.

CHAPTER NINETEEN

'DO YOU STILL think our luck is holding?' Caitlin asked.

Carmen's mind was racing. 'Larry didn't say he saw us at the deck, so we can make something up. He just wants to see you. He's using this situation to his advantage. And yes, I think our luck is holding. This morning I spotted the guy who saw me on the bus, and he didn't see me. Do you realize that the key is not our problem anymore? It's Larry's. We don't have to worry about prints! They're going to rule Steve's death an accidental suicide, just like Detective Dunn said. We have to stay positive. We just have to, Caitlin.'

'You're ignoring the main issue. I know you're trying to avoid it. It doesn't really matter that we didn't kill Steve. He'd be alive if we hadn't taken that money. That's what I will never forget.' Her guilt about whether she could have reached and caught Derek before he fell would simply extend to Steve now. That's what this jump at freedom had gotten her.

'You're right. I don't want to think about Steve. If I do, I'll fall apart. We don't have the luxury of brooding over things right now. We have to worry about staying alive, and basically out of sight.'

'You know, it's funny – I don't feel very free now. For me, that's what this whole thing was all about.'

'We're still here, Caitlin. Try to focus on the present. We have to be at Starbucks in a few minutes. I've thought of something to tell Larry about last night.'

Tully heard from Garderella that he could advise Mr. Chalmer that he might be called in for questioning. She was not one who gave much credence to coincidence. Smiling appreciatively, Tully remembered that he had heard that Garderella's hunches carried the weight of the law. Harris was about to leave The Sands Motel as Tully approached him. 'Mr. Chalmer, a minute please.'

'What's your problem, officer?'

'I have been told to advise you, sir, that you and your boys may be called in for questioning.'

'What are you talking about?'

'Well, sir, as near as these techs can figure, the man died after twelve last night. We both know you were on the beach around here last night.'

'Wait a sec! What are you saying? That we had something to do with some homeless fuck?'

'Just that you and your guys were in the area last night. Perhaps there is something that you can tell us that will assist in this investigation.'

'What do you mean we were in the area? We might have passed this deck, but we ate down at the pier.'

A clean-cut, thirty-something man was standing very close to Harris and Tully, listening to every word of their conversation.

'What is it with you guys? Are you out to nail me for something? I'll come in; I'll do anything you want me to because I had nothing to do with this shit.'

'I was just told to advise you that we might be calling you in for questioning.'

'So you've advised me – now get out of my face,' Harris shouted, struggling for control, smelling the rot under his armpits. 'Let's get the fuck out of here.'

Harris' tail did not bother to follow him – he had gotten enough information. He walked across the street to a payphone at the side of Rascal House and made his call.

Knocking people out of his way, Harris crashed through the crowd. He was beginning to see he might not find a middle ground. For the moment, he was beyond anger – even his truthful denial of any part in that guy's death was damning. The bitches were eluding him – the guys were less than useless. His father had no time for anyone but himself. He had to come up with something when the next call came in – something to prove that the fault wasn't his. *To reach the level of determination is a matter of the will.* His father had quoted that to him one day about his studies and what it would take to improve them. Harris remembered the words today because they might very well save his life. Determination and will, that's exactly what he would need. He was determined to get out of this shit with his life and he willed himself to come up with a new plan of attack. He had Ted drop him off and told him to call the guys for a meeting tonight at his place. Harris' father was away fighting with his mother and her lawyers. 'Tell them to grab food on the run and be at my place by five and not to be late!'

When Bobby got Ted's call, he was not surprised, but he had other things on his mind. He'd make the meeting, of course. Once the guys had seen Harris take off, they began to wander away from the pier and towards their own wheels. After all, they were not going to put in more time than Harris had. Bobby pulled Nipples aside. 'When you saw that chick on the bus, do you remember if she pulled a bag up with her when she jumped up?'

'Jesus, I don't know. Things happened so fast.'

'Think, Nipples. Try to get that picture in your

mind. She wouldn't have jumped up and left a million bucks in a bag by her seat.'

'Let me see – I saw her – actually, we saw each other and we freaked. I jumped back a foot. She jumped up and grabbed her friend.'

'Try to concentrate, Nipples.'

'I am. All right, what did I see? Did I see a bag? Holy fuck, I didn't! There was no bag! I remember – she flew out of her seat in one motion. She couldn't have grabbed the money that fast. Impossible. Those bags were heavy.'

'That's what I thought. When Harris saw them jump from the bus and run to the pier, I saw them too. They had no bags then either. That's exactly it. They had no money with them when they ran from the mall. The chicks ditched the money.'

'All right, but where?'

'That's what I'm going to work on till the meeting tonight. Don't tell Harris about this, I want to try and figure this out without his interference. See you tonight.' Bobby was in his element. The chicks carried the money across the bridge – Harris saw them. They did not have the cash on them when they left the mall by bus later that night. *It's somewhere in the mall! Holy shit, there are lockers on the first floor. The money is probably locked away in one of them. How do I get into them? Unless they've already been back for it while we were wasting our time gawking at some homeless stiff. Well, if I head over there and palm a couple of bills into a needy security guard's hand, he'd probably open the lockers for me. Then I'll know if the babes have been back.* Bobby ran for his wheels – there wasn't a whole lot of time before five.

In the next hour, Steve's crowd had thinned considerably. WSBN-TV news had arrived late and hadn't bothered to stay long either. The photographer, dripping with perspiration, had dropped the camera from his shoulder and was impatiently kicking at the sand, waiting for the reporters to head back to their cars. There was no Pulitzer here. Steve was lifted into a body bag that a tech zippered closed in one quick motion. Fifteen minutes later, there was nothing left around the area but yellow tape, and the hole that he had lain in on the last night of his life. Steve, the drifter, was dead at twenty-eight. That night, other crimes would steal the spotlight. Steve might be talked about at Club One, remembered for a while and moved to the side to allow the people there to enjoy the remainder of their vacation. Tomorrow, no one would leave flowers or candles as they had for Versace on South Beach when he was murdered. People still left roses on the steps of his mansion, even though his sister Donatella had sold the house. For a few hours, Steve had been the centre of attention – the way he liked things. Now that his body was gone, he had not left much behind him for anyone to remember. Even the deck would be repaired.

CHAPTER TWENTY

HARRIS PACED AS he thought. His plan began to take shape. The meeting with his guys was actually just a ruse to get Nipples over to his place. Once he had reviewed the day's non-findings, Harris would assign beach duty again tomorrow, advise them to get some sleep and alert them all to the futility of running.

Bobby pulled into the parking area of Bal Harbour and was lucky to find an empty space on his first roll around. Once he was inside the mall, he saw that a solid mental plan would require outside assistance and might not be easy to execute. The mall was crowded as usual with the wealthy elite dressed to the nines, carrying multiple designer bags with items they did not need and might not even use. Bobby headed for the lockers that were located in the middle of the mall along a side corridor of a west wall. There were two rows, each with two tiers of lockers. A security guard was standing beside the Armani shop, and Bobby approached him. 'Excuse me.'

The guard was accustomed to questions and knowledge of the mall and its stores was a requirement for the job. 'Yes, sir?'

'I'm staying with friends at the Sheraton. Last night they packed all my clothes into two yellow bags and locked both of them in one of the lockers back there. It was supposed to be some kind of joke – payback. Now no one can find the key. What do I do?'

'Do they recall the locker number?'

'Some of them have a hard time remembering their names.'

'Well, I don't have the keys to the lockers – Chief of Security has them. There's an office down the same corridor at the end. You'll find him there.'

'Thanks.' When Bobby walked back that way, he found the door to the security office slightly ajar. 'Excuse me.'

'What can I do for you?' The big palooka was not any taller or heavier than Bobby. All he had on Bobby was ten years. His uniform was the same as the other security officer's, except that he wore a red cotton braid on his epaulettes where the other wore white.

Bobby noticed the neat crease in his black pants and knew he was dealing with another dweeb. *Easy pickings!* Bobby gave an abbreviated version of his story, but added he was going away for a few days and needed his clothes.

'Well sir, I can't just go into all those lockers – there's a privacy issue.'

'I know this is a great imposition, sir, but I really need my stuff.'

'Your friends don't even remember the location of the locker?'

'We were partying – what can I say? Listen, I know you'd never do this on a regular basis, but if I made it worth your while, could you help me out?' Bobby slid four fifties under his hat on the desk.

The chief raised the brim just high enough to do a visual count. 'I can't risk this job for a couple of bills.'

Bobby added two C notes, and the chief leaned back in his chair, rocking back and forth. 'Well, maybe this once. But I can't do anything for you now. Come back around nine-fifteen tonight and we'll find your bags. I'll be here in the office, closing up.'

'I'll be here at nine – don't forget!'

'I'll be at my desk.'

Bobby decided to eat at the mall before the meeting. Four hundred dollars was a small token against the two million in the lockers that would be his tonight. Harris' sucker punch was going to cost him exactly two million dollars. Once he had the money, he had to think of a way of getting in touch with the man. He'd produce the money and leave Harris to his own inadequacy. He had told Harris from the very outset that he needed backup and he had been willing to provide it. Had Harris listened to reason, the money would still be in their hands or used to purchase the ecstasy. But Harris wanted all the glory for himself, so he'd driven off alone, lost the cash and risked all their lives. Once Bobby had the money, he saw no need to run – in fact, once the switch was made, he could step into the number one slot if he wanted it. In truth, this intrigue had ceased to amuse Bobby – he was thinking very hard of just walking away from dealing. Figures were one thing – lives were another.

He found a small, secluded table, away from the main entrance, in one of the two sidewalk cafés. He ordered quiche and Caesar salad – food that would not weigh him down. Something light to balance his heavy thoughts. Bobby knew something about revenge – he knew it had little to do with physical violence and everything to do with wits and planning. Sometimes, revenge is set into motion by the victim. Harris had never once thought of the effects of an ill-timed punch. His thoughts and his actions too often fused together. Harris never thought of the aftermath. That part of Harris had appealed to Bobby in the beginning. But he soon realized Harris' act was one ugly control scene.

Tonight, Bobby was setting him up for a lesson in cause and effect. It was time he grew up.

Before his guys arrived, Harris had taken a plastic tarp from one of his father's closets and carried it to the study. His father used these sheets to cover the floor of his pricey boats when he was showing one of them to clients he felt were simply window-shopping. Harris laid the tarp on the floor in the study. He pulled the office chair into the middle of the sheet and laid his pocket recorder on the desk. He hid duct tape and a paring knife in the wastebasket. Then he walked back to the living room to wait for his men.

At precisely five o'clock, the guys stood at his front door. No one wanted to face Harris' wrath alone. Once they were seated, the guys noted that Harris was strangely calm but pumped. Harris explained to each of them where he wanted them on the beach tomorrow. He added one idea. 'Why not approach some of the condos on the strip and ask if anyone remembers two women friends staying together? They're foxes after all. We might get lucky.' Actually, the guys liked this idea. Harris surprised them a second time when he produced a sketch of Caitlin. Harris was a good man with a pencil. 'I've made copies for each of you. She's the one I recall. We have one more day, just a day to find the cash. If we don't find it tomorrow, get back to the shops – we'll wait for the call there. I think they still need us – we were money-makers for them. They'd have to be morons to get rid of us.' Harris then went over to the wet bar and took out a tray of glass flutes. 'We began as champagne buddies and we'll continue to enjoy the best stock around.' Into Nipples' glass, he first crushed powder from seconal tablets, his father's drug of choice on sleepless nights. He then opened a bottle of Mumm's, lobbed the cork over his shoulder, poured and carried the glasses to each of his men. 'To better days!' The champagne disappeared in a single swallow. 'Now, get out of here and catch some sleep. Get to the beach by eight.'

To a man, there was an uneasy sense of relief. Harris was sweating; they could clearly see perspiration on his earlobes. Yet, he wasn't bullying or blaming them. He wasn't himself tonight. The guys filed out as quickly as possible.

'Nipples, could you stay behind for a few minutes? You saw the dark one. I need you to help me to sketch her for the guys. This won't take long – I need you to be alert tomorrow too. You've been our best spotter.'

Nipples' hand was still throbbing and he wanted to get out of there. 'I've told you everything I know. You don't need me for the sketch.'

'Give me no more than five minutes – you have that much time, right? I want to get to bed as much as you do.'

'Five minutes, that's it!'

'O.K. Let's get started.'

🌴

At the last minute, Caitlin said, 'Carmen, go across the street without me. I'll follow in a minute.' After Carmen left, Caitlin took a minute to look in the mirror, sure she'd find someone she didn't know. Staring back at her was a frightened woman, the same person who had stared back at her after Derek's death. When she left, she took her time locking the door. The coffee house was directly across the street. When she walked through the door, she saw Larry and Carmen at a corner table. What was the point of this, what was the point of anything now? A woollen lethargy had fallen on her shoulders. Caitlin sat down without a word.

Larry was low key as well, his legs splayed into Carmen's space. While there was relief that Steve would not pounce on him some night, he also knew that his connection to Steve might be a problem for him, and this forced visit was not going to win him any points with Caitlin.

Carmen took the lead. 'Larry, we came over because we're very sorry about Steve. I know you guys were close last year. That's what we came here to tell you. Who cares whether you saw us last night? We didn't tell Detective Dunn because we didn't want to look like juveniles. For the past two years, Caitlin and I have dared each other to skinny dip just once in Florida. Last night, we did the deed. We just didn't want to be involved in today's sad events.'

'Why didn't you use the pool at Club One?'

'Right, with Mother Michel at the window and our pool lit up at night. We didn't want to give anyone a free show.'

Larry smiled. 'I guess I missed something then. When I saw you run to the door, you both looked frightened.'

'We were. We heard the loud shouting and prayed those guys weren't heading our way. When the coast was clear, we made a beeline for our place.'

'The shouting was what woke me too. So you guys didn't see Steve?'

Caitlin who had not spoken said, 'No, we never saw him – I don't think he would have remembered us either.'

'We both remembered you from last year.'

There was an awkward silence. 'It's been a long day

for all of us. If you want to tell Dunn anything, go ahead. I just want to go home,' Caitlin said.

'I have nothing to say to him, Caitlin. I was pissed because of yesterday.'

'You had every right to be.'

'Would you guys ever want to have a beer together?'

'We'll see,' Carmen jumped in.

Larry still wasn't sure how things had gone. The heart is kinder when someone dies. But in a day or two, the human shell is back, a hard protector for the moving parts behind the shell. The only thing Larry was sure about was that he wanted to stay as long as possible with the C's. From Caitlin, he was having a private buzz. The glints on her hair shone – the pool of her hazel eyes was soft and warm. Yet, he knew she was out of reach. Larry felt suddenly very much alone. He had to admit he was more comfortable in his role as observer. His fantasies were free flowing, but today, his words were inadequate, clipped of flesh. Larry trailed behind the C's as they walked back across Collins to Club One.

CHAPTER TWENTY-ONE

STEVE'S BODY WOULD have stayed a few days on a slab in a freezer had it not been for Detective Dunn's insistence on a speedy autopsy. Northrop, sixty-two yesterday, was a timid man who was more at ease with the dead than the living. He was thorough, though rushed by the number of crime victims he worked on every day. Northrop believed Florida's warm weather was a contributor to the crime there. 'Hot weather brings out the devil,' he'd tell Connie, his wife of forty-one years. He had the body bags to prove his point. He was already backed up with other cases and went on with his work when Dunn walked across the grey-tiled floor.

The detective was sniffing his handkerchief with its homemade concoction of vinegar and oil that he believed cut the acrid odour that seared his nostrils in this grey steel room. Most outsiders never got accustomed to the smell of death and chemicals. 'Doc, I want to know what caused this fellow's death and to see if you can find other signs of trauma. Tox screen express too! How quickly can you do that? You'll also find quite a scar on his forehead – I'm waiting for information from Mount Sinai on that.'

Faint irritation flashed across Northrop's forehead, but it morphed quickly into a nodding assent. There was no point mentioning it was close to five o'clock and that he had not yet taken his break.

Northrop might be a timid man but he had a cast-iron stomach. On a side counter he laid his cut fruit, diced watermelon, dark cherries, cantaloupe and orange slices. The fruit mixture could easily be mistaken for a plastic specimen container. Human remains, in colours not much different than his fruit, lay packaged beside it. Whenever Dunn came down to pathology, he begged Northrop not to touch his fruit till he had left the room. Dunn always wanted results in a hurry and, generally, Northrop complied. Seven years ago, his son had been arrested on a DUI and Northrop had called Dunn. The cop had taken care of the matter and independently assigned community service to the kid. To date, there was no record of the arrest. Whatever he said to his son had taken effect. This year he was finishing up engineering at Columbia. Dunn never brought the matter up again – neither did Northrop.

The pathologist rolled Steve out from the fridge and wheeled his body under strong fluorescent lights above him and trays of unnerving, cold, grey instruments on tables beside him. 'Get some coffee – come back in an hour and a half,' Northrop instructed Dunn. 'I might have some answers then.' Dunn knew who was boss here and left without a word. Northrop began to examine the body before cutting. The head wound was extensive. He found no other visible signs of trauma on the body, so the fingernails could wait. He flipped on the overhead microphone, adjusted his facemask, reached for a scalpel and went to work on Steve's neck, parting the skin under the chin to the collarbone. He used clamps to keep the skin wide and open. Northrop worked slowly around the esophageal area. Before probing deeper into the canal, he studied what was left of the nose, noting the shattered bone chips. Then he went to the mouth, cataloguing the broken teeth, bagging chips of those too. Back in the canal, he probed with the gentle delicacy of a fine surgeon. Northrop had a real knack for finding just what he expected.

He cut carefully through the esophagus and parted the walls of the canal. *Well, what do you know?* Lodged deeply on either side of the wall was a bone fragment. The bone fragment had lodged itself in the esophagus, blocking the airway and choking the young man. He gathered specimens of blood and sand around the area before he extricated the bone itself and tagged it. From Steve's face, particularly from his lips and forehead, he tweezed wood splinters. As the tech had noted, there were no other visible signs of trauma. There was no bruising on the knuckles or forearms and no trauma to the torso. He knew the cause of death. He ran the blood and scraped under the fingernails but that workup would require more than an hour. Before Dunn returned, he also probed the older head wound. This injury had cracked the skull and no doubt had caused the brain to swell. The young man had no luck at all, Northrop thought. He was not a physician who played the God role and, although he did not take his work home to Connie, he was deeply affected by the fragility of life, the suddenness of death. What his victims gave him was his gentleness, and Connie was the beneficiary.

While Steve's liver was still on the scale, Northrop began eating his fruit – he had not taken a break in the afternoon and now he was likely to miss supper as well. When Dunn walked back into the room, he kept his eyes from the fruit to keep from gagging. 'You guys are not the strong men you pretend to be,' Northrop smiled, wiping a small red trickle of juice that threatened to roll down his chin.

'What do you have there, Nor?'

'Fill me in on where you found him first. I want to see if my findings jive.'

Dunn did just that, not omitting any detail. 'So, we concluded that whatever happened occurred under the deck. There were no blood traces on the sand around the deck, no blood on his legs or under him, which should have been there had he crawled under the deck after an altercation. He sustained his injury under the deck, and I can't see two men going at it under there because there isn't enough room. I've also gotten what I need from Mount Sinai. He was transported there on January 7th, with severe head trauma and subdural hemorrhaging, apparently from a fall into a steel dumpster. That's where he was found. No witnesses. Fell into a coma for a few days, recovered slowly and was transferred to a halfway house. Principal meds were Empracet and Dilantin. He was left with severe headaches, memory loss and impaired concentration. He walked out of the halfway house without any meds and found his way to the beach, to the deck where he had lived for over a year.'

Northrop began to pace. 'Well, the time of death was between ten and midnight. Blood and hair found on the victim were his own. Blood tox showed trace amounts of both drugs you've mentioned. No alcohol. No other signs of trauma. The cause of death was a bone fragment that lodged in his esophagus. It was coated in blood and sand. While sand is not in our diets, it would have passed through him without this obstruction. He may have found his way back to the deck, but I would guess that, once there, he became disoriented and panicky. I agree with your tech. He probably sat up very quickly and with too much force and smashed his face and head against that deck more than once. There were thirty-three splinters in his face. Yet, but for the obstruction, he would have survived that injury. With each gasp for breath, and the strain on his face indicates his struggle to get air to his lungs, he helped lodge the bone more securely in the esophageal wall. Accidental death is the preliminary finding. I'll finish up tomorrow, but I don't foresee any change in the diagnosis.'

'I called his father. The usual shock. No one believes a twenty-eight year old isn't immortal. His father even said he'd found a job at home for him, but his son didn't want to leave the sun. Thanks for the work, Nor. I owe you one.'

'No, you don't.'

CHAPTER TWENTY-TWO

NIPPLES KEPT HIS eye on the door and sat on the edge of the white leather sofa. He began pulling at the bandage on his hand. Harris' calm was more threatening than his angry ranting. When Harris left for his artist's pad and pencils, Nipples thought of running, but didn't. *What can he do in five minutes? I better stay that long.*

Harris returned with more champagne and his stuff. 'Here, Nipples, have another glass. Let's get started – I know you want to get out of here.' He pulled a chair over in front of Nipples and dragged an end table to the side of them. 'All right, tell me what you remember, don't leave anything out. I really appreciate you staying. About your hand, I was in a piss of a mood and I took things out on you. I have a good hunch about tomorrow,' Harris said, leaning back and yawning. 'I'm fucking beat.'

Nipples began yawning too. He was tired, but he had to get his facts out and head for home. A woolly fatigue settled first behind his eyes and moved to the back of his head. He slumped against the back of the sofa and took a long, deep breath. His lungs were burning for oxygen. 'The champagne is getting to me because I haven't eaten since breakfast.'

'Sit back, let it wear off – I'll wait. But before you catch a few Z's, come to the den with me. I work better there – tell me a few details about the other bitch so I can get started. The sooner we get started, the sooner we finish.'

Nipples felt as though he weighed a couple hundred

pounds when he pulled himself up from the couch. His hand had the weight of a brick. He mumbled a few things as he followed Harris to the den, bumping into the walls along the hallway. He did not notice the plastic on the floor or the oddness of a chair in the centre of the room. Nipples was bone weary and slurring his words. Something did not feel right.

'Here, sit down before you fall,' Harris turned and said, helping Nipples into the chair.

He tried to stand up from the chair, but he felt his strength dissolving. He had trouble lifting his left leg. Harris was on top of him with the stealth of a coyote, pinning first his arms with the duct tape, then his legs. Harris taped his mouth as well. Nipples shook his head, with the dull awareness of the mistake he had made by staying. His vision was blurred, disoriented. He could feel perspiration falling down the side of his face. Gritting his teeth, trying to shake his body from side to side, he used all his strength against the tape. His lungs continued to strain for air – his eyes were tearing and his nose was growing stuffy. Afraid he could suffocate, he blinked hard to stop from crying.

Harris reached into the wastebasket and pulled out the knife and pocket recorder. When he turned around, he saw the hysteria in Nipples' eyes. 'Calm down, Nipples. Struggling isn't going to help you. I need your full attention. Stop moving, for Christ's sake. Stop, do you hear me? Stop this second or I'll punch you in the throat and then you'll see how hard it is to breathe.'

Nipples fell back into the chair, praying he wouldn't black out.

'That's better, Nipples. Listen very carefully to what I'm about to say. There is no point shouting when I take the tape off your mouth because this is a soundproof condo. Before I go anywhere near the tape, I want you to hear my proposals. We don't have a lot of time, one day is all we have. Now, I know you made the call to the cops. Don't shake your head – we're beyond lying. Sit still or so help me, you'll die in that chair.'

Nipples stopped moving and dropped his head. There were spots careening before his eyes. His heart was galloping, crashing into his ribs.

'I don't even care anymore why you turned me in because now I have to save my skin. I'm not dying for you. Do I make myself clear, Nipples? If there's a choice here, you're the one going down. Here are my proposals. We can go at this problem in three different ways. First, I need you to admit on tape that you called the cops and you are responsible for losing the two million. If we can't find the cash tomorrow, I'm going to offer the tape up so the man will know who's responsible. If you shake that head one more time…'

Nipples was so scared his shaking had become mechanical and hard to stop. The whites of his eyes were almost yellow.

Harris shook him hard. He couldn't take the chance of really hurting him before he spoke into the recorder. 'You are going to confess, one way or the other. I could make things easy for myself and tape your nose. You'd be gone in what, a minute? Let's see,' Harris said as he walked behind Nipples who was struggling like a wild animal in a trap. He taped his nose and jumped around to the front. Nipples' cheeks blew up against the tape, his cheeks beet red, his chest as hard as a rock. 'See, see, how easy that is?' He ripped the tape from his nose and Nipples began to convulse. 'Take some time to catch your breath, Nipples.'

Nipples was breathing hard like a horse. He was nauseated, afraid to choke on his own vomit if he gave in to his fear.

'You're O.K – calm down, Nipples. Don't be such a pussy. Now, that's one way I can go. Forget the confession. Suffocate you, drag you out in my duffel bag, dump you in the trunk and serve you up tomorrow to the man. But that's not the way I want to handle this. I don't want to throw my life away on a murder rap. So you see, I don't want to wipe you out. But I need the confession, Nipples. Have you wet your pants? Oh, shit!' Harris ran for paper towels and was back in seconds. 'You did this to yourself, you piece of shit.' Harris wiped up the urine. He had not counted on this crap when he was planning things out. He almost wished Bobby were there to help him out.

'There is another way we can go. So, relax and listen. You can give me the confession peacefully, and I won't touch you. The third way is I have to cut you to get the confession. Either way, you are going to give me a confession I can use.' Harris reached for his knife with one hand and grabbed Nipples' shirt with the other. In one motion, he slit the shirt in two.

With his tits exposed, Nipples felt his shame, sharp as the knife Harris was holding. He tried very hard to find some courage in his panic, but he could not. The breasts he had tried so hard to hide were ugly, red and exposed. Without cutting him, Harris had opened an artery of disgust and loathing, and Nipples was numb.

'Wow! You have a pair of knockers there, Nipples. Too bad the guys aren't here! I have to stick to business. If you confess easily, I won't cut you. I'll even give you a new shirt. Here's the plan. Once I have the tape, you can take off. And I mean take off. You'll have your life, your tits and one full day to get out of Florida and disappear. One day to save your sorry life.' Harris thought that by serving up the confession, he'd walk away. He had forgotten that he was the leader and responsible for the actions of his men. Bobby would have seen the flaw in his plan, but Bobby wasn't here.

'Now, even if you make things difficult for me, I'll still do you a favour. I'm going to help you get rid of these tits. That's what you've always wanted, right? But Nipples, I really don't want to cut you. I figured that out last night in bed. Those CSI units can trace anything, and I don't want your trail leading back to me. So, I'm offering you your life, and your tits. Think very hard about this, Nipples. Will you take the easy way out and help us both? Nod once, if that's the way you want to go.'

Nipples nodded once.

'You're not such an idiot after all.' Harris walked behind Nipples and shook his shoulders with both hands. Nipples' head bobbed back and forth. 'Don't fall asleep now, you dork. I need you awake.'

Nipples stretched his forehead to keep his eyes open, threw his head back and took deep breaths.

'All right. On tape, I'll ask you if you were the snitch who called the cops. You've gotta fess up, asshole.' He gave Nipples a rough shove and turned on the recorder. 'This is Harris Chalmer, sir. I've found the pigeon for you, the guy responsible for losing our money. It's your turn, Nipples.'

Harris shoved the recorder to Nipples' mouth and kicked his shin. Nipples jerked with this sudden stab of pain.

Nipples spoke as best he could, but his words were slurred. 'My name is Iaaan; I called the copsssss the day of the dropp.'

'Say it again!' Harris swiped Nipples on the back of the head. This second time, Nipples' words were clear enough to be understood. 'So it was you, Nipples, right. You lost our money!'

'Yeah, it was me. I called the cops,' Nipples sobbed.

Harris turned his back on Nipples and played the tape to be sure the recorder had done its work, pocketed it, fetched a shirt for Nipples and began to cut away the tape. 'Get out of my place and start running.' When he heard the door slam, Harris began the clean-up.

Nipples collapsed against the wall in the corridor and then stumbled down the hall. He took the elevator to the lobby and flopped in one of the easy sofas. He threw his head back against the couch and he was smiling, shaking with relief. A solitary tear rolled down his cheek. On the back of the sofa, a perspiration stain began to swell around his head. He sensed this was a turning point in his life. For the first time since he was thirteen, and his breasts had begun to grow, Nipples saw them as part of himself, not as something hideous that excluded him from other guys. In the beginning, he had wanted to make his bones with Harris and his gang because he hated himself. At first, they sold the drugs to friends – not a big operation. Before anyone realized what was happening, Harris and his boys were just a bunch of stupid rich kids in over their heads working for the Columbians in Miami. Even he could see they were being used and they were expendable. At this moment, Nipples felt whole. Maybe that's what a second chance at life was all about, some kind of acceptance. He'd begin to work on his escape as soon as his head cleared. Right now, his body was too weary from the panic that had run ragged through his blood to be afraid. He could give himself five or ten minutes to relax in the awareness that he was still alive and in one piece. Nipples did not know that euphoria was a side effect of the narcotic he had ingested with the champagne. Nipples had been exposed and he had survived. There were no more secrets to worry about.

CHAPTER TWENTY-THREE

WHILE NIPPLES WAS enjoying his siesta in the lobby, Bobby was home at the Sheraton, lying on his bed, plotting his intro for the man at nine o'clock, munching on the stalk of his intelligence. He wanted to see the look on Harris' face when he discovered that his second-in-command had not only found the money, but had turned it over to the man himself. Payback time, Harris!

Caitlin and Carmen had ordered in pizza. There was no point going out again today if they could eat at home. Caitlin had not taken a bite because her stomach was churning. 'Do you think Larry knows more than he told us today?' Caitlin asked her friend.

'I hope not. He's worried about being a suspect himself and probably wondering if Dunn believed that he never went near the deck last night. Our lost key puts him at the scene. I think Larry would have turned us in if he had seen us under the deck. He likes you too much to turn us in to Dunn, but, if his life were on the line, Larry would save himself. Stands to reason.'

Larry was sitting on the wooden steps that led to the deck of Club One. He had finally finished painting it. Maybe the meatball sub, oozing with marinara sauce, had been a poor choice, given the circumstances. Larry rolled the sub up in its waxed paper and strangled it. He was still getting over the realization that Steve had not died behind Dunkin' Donuts well over a month and a half ago. Steve's eyes had had the half-open glassy stare. Larry could see those eyes. No beer tonight, he said to himself. He took a swig of his Coke and looked over the sand where Steve had died. *I could have been under the deck – it could have been me in a body bag.* As much as he was relieved to be alive, Larry was also angry with Steve. *You could have had things so easy. You might have found work here with me, but you had to get greedy.* Steve had spoiled things at Dunkin' Donuts and even dead, he was trying to ruin everything Larry had worked to accomplish. *Piss on him!* Larry unwound the sub, pulled the mashed meatballs from the mess and ate all three. As soon as they repaired the deck, Larry intended to go to work on fixing up his old place up. He liked it here.

🌴

From home, Garderella called Dunn, excusing herself for the intrusion, concisely giving him the facts about Harris Chalmer.

'Well, the prelim on the victim under the deck is indicating accidental. You're certain you saw those bags though?'

'100% certain,' she replied.

'The vic seems to have killed himself. If you feel these guys are out looking for the money, and we know now that they were at the scene last night, call this Chalmer in for questioning and try to shake him up. Set up the interview for eleven-thirty tomorrow. I should have the rest of the results by then and I'll try to join you.'

'Sounds good.'

🌴

Hilda was hard at work at her post on the second floor of Neiman Marcus. Every time she passed the lockers, she thought of the two young women and wondered if they had gotten home safely. Hilda was a tough lady, but Harris Chalmer in his rage had unnerved her. *Up to no good those two young men! Too much free time.*

🌴

Nipples was still in the lobby when panic began to pinch his knees. The euphoria was lifting, and Nipples was aware he was sitting in his own sweat and urine.

🌴

Harris' cell rang minutes before eight. 'Yeah,' he answered.

'Get to the pay phones in the mall – we may have found a solution,' the voice was calm, as harmless as a single palm tree.

Harris had no chance to reply because the line went dead. His back ached with concern. *I have the tape, I have the tape! They'll see this whole mess was not my fault.* There was no time to consider the thing calmly because he had to make it to the mall across the street. He made sure the recorder was still in his pocket, grabbed his wallet and ran for the front door. He took the stairs – he had no time to wait for the elevator. As he ran through the lobby, he saw Nipples in the corner of his eye, but he had what he wanted from him. In fact, he could give him up right there if the idiot did not get out of the lobby and start running himself.

Nipples saw Harris in a blur and he got off the sofa and headed for the front door himself. He did not want to catch up to him and he could not have overtaken Harris. His movements were sluggish.

True to form, Harris did not run the couple hundred

feet to the traffic light. He ran across Collins with barely a perfunctory glance. In Bal Harbour, Collins has a
lovely tree-lined median. He made it to the median in
no time. Harris did not stop – he ran across the other
side of the street. A dark vehicle idled quietly, its lights
dimmed. As Harris' foot hit the street, the driver threw
on his high beams and fired up the car. It shot up
Collins like a bullet. It never occurred to Harris that he
wouldn't have the three days he had been promised. He
did not know that someone had overheard Tully at The
Sands Motel telling him he might be called in for questioning, and that was a problem for the organization.
Too late, Harris saw the car barrelling at him, catching
him wrong-footed. This loquacious young man had
time for only one word of protest for this outrage – *shit!*

The collision was almost a thing of beauty. The front
bumper caught Harris' right hip in a clean hit. The
blunt force propelled his body up into the night, but not
before his head struck the side mirror with such force
that it too flew into the Miami air. The collision of flesh
and bone and steel was sharp, loud and blunt. There
was a little too much bass in the sound to be mistaken
for the report of a handgun. For a few seconds, Harris
looked very much like the kites rented at Haulover
Park. Unfortunately, there were few people to note his
remarkable flight. The sidewalks in Bal Harbour are as
spacious as the lawns and are tended with as much care.
But, around eight o'clock, the old folks have been
wheeled home and shuffled off to bed by their harried
nurses. The younger ones are over at the mall till closing at nine, shopping and being seen. Harris had
bought and bullied attention most of his life, but he was
pretty much alone in his last, extravagant gesture. He
came to ground like a kite too, hard and pointed.

The only flaw was the awkward landing. Both his

sneakers had flown in another direction completely. Most of Harris landed on the sidewalk. His shoulders and head had come to rest on the side of the street. The mirror had snapped his neck, and his head had collapsed on his left shoulder, so completely that they appeared to be a single limb. He looked a little bit like a sleeping cockatoo whose head tucks into its shoulder when the day has been too much for him. The damage to the side of his head was hidden in his shoulder. Harris would have been pleased that onlookers saw his good side. Both his arms were extended above his shoulders as though he were about to take flight again. From the top of his torso, Harris looked like a fallen angel. From the bottom, he looked like a broken doll. His legs were crossed at unnatural angles – one foot was facing backwards.

A prince and a pauper had died within less than twenty-four hours. Steve and Harris never met one another, but their deaths were related to the same yellow bags.

The driver of the car stopped his vehicle immediately. A forty-two year old man with greying hair and blue eyes, wearing a blue button-down shirt and a pair of Dockers, reached for a small cell phone. 'There was a good reception,' was all he said. He hid that phone and reached for the cell in the glove compartment and dialed 911. He began to shake uncontrollably. 'Help me please. I just hit a man. He ran out right in front of my car. I had no chance to stop, no chance at all.' He was able to get the necessary information to the operator. Then he called his wife. 'Honey, I've been in a terrible accident, but I'm O.K. I'm in one piece! You don't have to worry – you'll never have to worry again. I promise you that.' He heard her begin to sob. He vowed never to visit the dog track again. The price was too high.

Nipples was one of the first on the scene. His eyes flashed with fear and confusion. He ran across the street to the body. He almost tripped over Harris' sneaker that he recognized immediately. He had just stared down at it for over an hour. When he reached Harris, Nipples knelt beside him and felt for a pulse, but his hand was shaking too violently for an accurate read. How was it possible that Harris was dead? Bad things did not happen to people like him. Nipples could not keep himself from running his hand along Harris' pocket but he did not find what he was looking for. He began to crawl on all fours looking for the Sony recorder. There were people running to the scene from all directions. The Bal Harbour Police controlled the crowd until the arrival of an MDPD detective. At the edge of the gathering crowd, Nipples spotted the recorder in the thick hedge that bordered the area around the mall. It had lodged halfway up the dense foliage. He rose, backing up towards it. When he reached the hedge, he turned, pretending to sneeze and grabbed the recorder. He whimpered with relief. Nipples had never felt lucky in his entire life, but on this night, fingering the Sony in his pocket, he felt like Lou Gehrig, who had felt he was the luckiest man alive. He turned from the crowd and began to walk away in the direction of his wheels. He'd call Bobby when he got home. He could sleep in his own bed tonight – he did not have to live on the run. He threw his head back and whispered, 'Thank you, God, and all you guys up there.'

Yet Nipples could not walk away. The way his life had turned around tonight had given him a smidgen of courage and a sudden regret for Harris. He turned back and pushed his way through the crowd. A paramedic, kneeling beside Harris, was shaking his head. He took the red blanket his partner had gotten from their ambulance and covered Harris with it. 'Get these people back, Tom. This isn't a show.'

'I know him,' Nipples said, pushing forward. 'He's my friend – we were hanging out together. We just wanted to go to the mall. His name is Harris Chalmer. He ran on ahead of me. I didn't even see the accident, but I heard it. He lives at The Tiffany over there. His father is a big guy in boats.' The tears were running freely down his cheeks. 'Should I call his father?' he asked, hoping to be relieved of the terrible obligation.

'Your name is?'

'Ian Johnson.'

'Ian, we'll take care of reaching his parents. Give me your address and phone number, please. You say you were together?'

'My friend ran on ahead – he liked to dash out at the last minute. He never had a problem before this.'

'Just give us the information, sir, we'll take things from here.'

After Nipples had obliged the paramedic and an officer who had been waved over, he added, 'His parents are going through a divorce. His father lives at The Tiffany with him.' Nipples simply could not use the past tense when he spoke of Harris, even as he stared at the lifeless body under the blanket. The transition had been too swift. This was the first dead person Nipples had ever seen close up. He expected Harris to yank the blanket off and jump to his feet. He stepped away from the body. 'His sneaker is over there on the median.' Nipples did not know what to do, so he stood around. The shell of his new-found courage had not hardened to the extent that Nipples did not secretly want to nudge Harris' foot, to reassure himself that he was indeed not of this world. Although Nipples felt a nip of real sadness for Harris, what he was really thinking was one life for another. And he was the last man standing!

The driver of the vehicle was sitting on the curb, his head buried in his knees, digging his fingers into his temples. He winced as he remembered the sickening thud of Harris' body against his fender. The thumping sound of the body hitting his bumper and the sight of the kid's head snapping back played non-stop in his brain. His gambling debt was cancelled, but a new terror was already staining his armpits. He was a murderer and 'they' had that on him now. None of this would ever end. The men who had chosen him for the job knew exactly what they were doing. Thomas Walsh sold cars, BMW's and he road tested them each weekend at a racing track. He knew how to accelerate without leaving rubber tracks. Kids who raced pressed the gas pedal to the floor, often stalling the vehicle or leaving rubber trails. The trick was to depress the pedal halfway down. Once the wheels were engaged, then one could go full throttle. When the cops approached him, Thomas wanted to confess, but he didn't. He had a wife and three kids.

'Officers, the kid ran out in front of my vehicle. I never had a chance to stop. I never saw him until it was too late. I've never had an accident before! What could I do? That kid ran right into the street. I feel so bad. I feel so bad. I never even had the chance to brake.'

'You saw nothing, sir?'

'Nothing. The street is not well lit here – I saw the man as my car hit him. It happened so fast, so fast!'

'I'll need the following information, sir.'

Thomas gave the cop what he wanted. Then, he paced back and forth on the sidewalk.

'We need to execute a breathalyzer too.'

'Of course, officer. No problem. If the kid had just

looked my way, he'd be alive tonight. Who runs across Collins without at least first looking? What was so important?'

'Please follow me to the patrol car, Mr. Walsh. Other officers are examining the scene. You'll be more comfortable there.'

People were looking at Thomas with condemnation, willing him to be in the wrong, finding him culpable because he'd been at the wheel. He shrank from their stares. Thomas was relieved to walk with the officer to the patrol car. He sat slumped in the back seat of the vehicle with the side window pulled down. Not only had he lost badly at the dogs for years, he had lost big time on borrowed money. After tonight, his debts were cleared, and he would never have to tell his wife he had bet their home and lost. Right now, he needed Lynn to love him because he loathed himself. He sat shivering in the car although it was seventy-six degrees.

Once the cops realized the vic was the son of Chalmer, of big money and the prestige that went with it, they took very special care with the scene of the accident. The moneyed men in Florida wielded power and any mistake on their part could very well mean, at the very least, a suspension. Chalmer might well hire his own investigators. They wanted to be sure these outsiders didn't turn up any evidence they had missed. The vic's friend had said the boy's father was out tonight. Well, Detective Ramirez would start calling right now to cover himself.

🌴

Bobby left the Sheraton a little before nine. Because his suite was ocean-side, he had heard nothing. He was taken aback by the commotion farther down on Collins. There were fire trucks, ambulances and cop cars all flashing their lights. People were milling about. Probably some old guy had gotten hit, he thought. More important things were on his mind than gawking at some old man lying on the street. He serpentined his way though the crowd, against the flow, into the mall. It was nine-twenty before the place was almost cleared. Bobby made sure the hall leading to the lockers was empty before he walked to the office. 'I'm back,' he announced to the security guard.

'So I see. I've been thinking,' the guard said.

'Dangerous activity,' Bobby laughed, palming another bill into the guard's hand.

'Follow me,' he said. Bobby did just that.

Not wanting to be seen by other employees, the guard quickly opened the lockers, not bothering to look inside. Bobby walked beside the guard reaching into each of the metal holds. There were forty in all. Around number twenty-five, Bobby felt a burp of dismay. Could he have miscalculated? Was that possible? One after another, the lockers fell open like falling palm leaves. But they were empty. All of them. 'Well, that's it! I guess you were wrong, sir. Don't even think of asking for your cash – half of it is spent already.'

Bobby stood there, his mind buzzing with electric neurons. 'Never mind about the money. Someone is playing tricks on me.' Bobby strode down the mall to the main exit. *What was her name, the woman at Neiman Marcus? Heather, Helen, something with an 'h'.* Bobby might, on a very rare occasion, run out of gel, but he never ran out of ideas.

🌴

It was after eleven when Stuart Chalmer got back home, quietly relieved. Earlier in the day, the money drain and his impending divorce weighed on his mind, but it was Meg, his wife, who was tugging at his heart. Trying to impress her, he'd worn soft Italian leather shoes, featherweight tan slacks, a yellow tab-collar shirt and a tan silk tie that blew around his left ear as soon as he stepped onto the driveway. He was already perspiring, biting his upper lip as he drove to the lawyer's office on 94th Street. In some ways, he was thinking of this meeting as a date. It had been well over a month since he had seen Meg.

As he pulled into the exclusive offices that high-jacked for hourly fees of seven hundred and fifty dollars, he saw Meg talking to her attorney. He stopped in his tracks, his stomach curling. He melted when he saw that lopsided smile that called forth only one of her dimples. Stuart had the urge to walk over to her and pucker the other one so that they'd match. Meg turned to one side with a simple sway of her left hip that still had men taking notice of her. He saw that she was tapping her foot, a sure mark of her nervousness. He wanted to run to her and spirit her away from the past twelve years. But he didn't – he stood watching, shut out by the wall around her.

From the division of spoils, Meg had surprised and saddened him by asking for only what was due to her by law. He felt her gesture signalled that she wanted out of this marriage as much as he wanted back in. Stuart remembered her favourite college poem, *The Love Song of J. Alfred Prufrock*. It was Stuart who wanted to jump up and shout, 'This is not what I meant at all!' But he was relatively certain that Meg would not have heard him.

The first thing Stuart did when he got back was to listen to his messages. It was the fourth one that caught his attention. A Detective Ramirez asked him to call the Miami-Dade precinct ASAP. His call was forwarded to the detective who was waiting for it. Ramirez had learned from past experiences to make concise notes in such circumstances, to get all the necessary information out. He knew full well that parents often went into shock and it became more difficult for them to understand anything soon after the initial blow. He calmly recited the facts to Stuart Chalmer. He wanted to add that this was another wasted life of an arrogant young person who had thrown his life away as easily as he had probably tossed a Frisbee.

Stuart did not interrupt him. His shirt was sodden. 'I want to see my son tonight,' was all he said.

'We need you for the ID, sir. Here's the address – I'll wait outside for you.'

'The man who ran my son down, was he tested for alcohol, drugs and speed?'

'Cleared on all points, sir.'

'Did Harris suffer, aside from the fact that he lost his life?'

'I understand. Things happened very quickly. We are not certain your son even saw the vehicle.'

'I hope that was the case.' Stuart's voice was reedy. He winced in pain as he felt the blow of the bumper and the wicked lash of the side mirror. He began rubbing his temple. 'I'll call my wife first.' He was glad for a second that he had a reason to call Meg. Then he felt guilty, small and selfish. He also thought of allowing her to sleep through the night – she'd need her strength for tomorrow. But his need got the better of him. He did not recognize his own voice when he spoke to her. He felt her collapsing on the other end. Their only son had been a difficult kid as soon as he became an adolescent, but at this moment, the only thing that mattered was that Harris was gone.

'They're certain it's Harris?' Meg's voice was as cold as snow.

'Yes.'

'Where is he?'

'At the city morgue.'

'I want to go with you tonight, Stuart.'

'I'll pick you up.' Stuart ran to the car and sped along the Miami streets to Meg's apartment. She was standing at the front door of her condo. Stuart saw that her eyes were already swollen. She got into the car beside him, but neither spoke. In a minute, Meg began to sob in deep, loud wounds that shook the seat. 'We made great work of our marriage, and we didn't do any better with our son.'

'I'm so sorry, Meg, for everything.'

'A little late for both, don't you think? Harris idolized you. Did you know that? But he never had your discipline or drive. He preferred shortcuts. We started out with nothing, but Harris' life began with everything. We gave him everything but our time.'

'Meg, this was an accident.'

'That could have been prevented,' she bit back.

The city morgue is depressing in the sunlight, doubly so in the darkness. A mausoleum, that's what Stuart thought as Meg and he followed Ramirez who waited for them at the front entrance. The bowels of the building stank of formaldehyde and death. He ushered them into a small room and tapped on a mirror. A young tech with a sallow complexion and acne drew the curtain aside and rolled a monitor into view. Stuart lost his control. 'I don't want to see my son on a digital camera. I said I want to see my son!' he shouted and punched the glass with a closed fist.

'I'll be right with you.' Ramirez raced to the autopsy theatre and told another tech to clean up the body for a family showing. Actually, as the son of a VIP, Harris had already been cleaned, weighed, measured and photographed in a staging room before being wheeled into the autopsy chamber. The tech led the parents into the cold room of stainless steel and a spotless tile floor.

Meg clung to Stuart and he supported her as the tech gloved up and drew back the sheet to reveal the good side of his head. Stuart stepped forward and laid his hand to rest on Harris' shoulder – Meg hid behind him. Then she too came forward and rested her fingers against his cheek. Ramirez saw that they would both break completely, so he led them from the room. 'I lost my sister to a drunk driver when I was a kid. I know what you're both feeling.'

'Some of it,' Stuart wept dryly. 'He was our only son.' Before Stuart and Meg left the building, Stuart hung back and instructed Ramirez to send Harris' remains to Stanfill Funeral Home up on Dixie. He would never tell Meg that he suspected Harris had been in trouble again. What purpose would it serve? Stuart drove Meg back to The Tiffany with him, and she offered no resistance. When she was inside the suite, Meg realized where she was. Walking around the living room in a haze of grief, she began to reacquaint herself with the space she had once called home. When she did not sit down, Stuart led her by the arm down the hall to the guest room. 'Get some rest, Meg, I'll take care of the calls.'

Meg said nothing and stared at the ceiling. Before Stuart left the room, she called out. 'Get me some of your Seconal and some brandy. I can't bear knowing that Harris is lying on a cold slab down at the morgue. Let's get him out of there as soon as possible. Did you see the side of his head?' she sobbed.

'I saw it, Meg. One Seconal will help you out, but

you shouldn't have the brandy – alcohol and meds.'

'Stuart, I could take the whole stash. I want to be knocked out. My head is breaking.'

'All right, I'll get you a couple and a little snifter of brandy.' Once Meg was quiet, Stuart called both families. When he began to think of friends he could call at that late hour, he soon saw that he really did not have any. Most people he knew were business contacts. Apart from his mother and sister, there was no one he could really count on. He hoped Meg and he would be together in this tragedy. When his phone rang, he dropped the address book.

'Sir, I have been trying to call you all night. This is Ian Johnson, one of Harris' friends. I wanted you to know that I was with Harris, behind him really, when the car hit him.'

'You saw what happened?'

'Not really, sir.'

'What do you mean then?'

'We were together, but Harris ran on ahead. I heard the crash. I'm sorry for your loss, Mr. Chalmer.'

'So he was running across Collins.'

'As fast as you know he could run.'

Stuart really didn't know much about Harris these past four years. 'Would you call his friends for me, Ian?'

'I'll start as soon as we're off the phone. Goodnight then.' Hearing his own name felt good.

Stuart took a good swig of brandy and walked into Harris' room. He might as well have been in a stranger's. He first noticed clothes tossed carelessly on the floor. He bent and picked them up and laid them neatly at the top of the unmade bed. He could still see the indentation of Harris' body from the night before. He dreaded choosing the clothes for his *son's* funeral, but he knew Meg would be in no shape for this awful task. He walked into the closet and was overwhelmed by the excess. On one side, as least thirty suits hung from thick wooden hangers; beside them as many pairs of slacks. At the far end of the closet, the shirts were neatly colour-coded. All designer garb. The other wall sported recessed drawers filled with underwear and socks. Belts dangled from a silver ring. Ties were carefully placed in organizers. So much left behind, all of it a waste. Stuart began to run his fingers along the shirts before he selected the things he would bring to Stanfill Funeral Home tomorrow.

With a slow buzz from his own Seconal and brandy, Stuart felt his way along the hall and slid into bed beside Meg. He reached over and pulled her close to him and the warmth of her body soothed him as he fell asleep. Somewhere in the last few hours of the night, Meg woke, eased herself out of the bed and spent the last two hours on the couch. In the morning, Stuart made her some strong coffee, but their only contact now was polite conversation. He saw that Meg had no intention of confiding or sharing her grief with him. In minutes, she called a cab and left. Stuart called Stanfill and made an early appointment. He stood alone in the empty luxury all around him. He knew that, like Harris, the loss of Meg was irrevocable. Self-pity engulfed him. Stuart fell back onto a sofa and wept for himself and his losses.

🌴

Earlier in the evening, Bobby was busy retracing the steps the women had taken with the money when Ian called with the news. 'Nipples, are you saying that Harris is dead?'

'That's what I'm trying to tell you. I'd appreciate it if you called me Ian. I was pretty close behind him when it came down.'

'You were there, Nipples?'

'Yeah, and it's Ian for Christ's sake.'

'Whatever. How long were you with Harris? I thought you'd have left by then.'

'Well, we worked on the sketch and we hung out.'

'You're telling me Harris hung out with you?'

Ian tried to get his story straight. 'I was around – he just wanted to finish the champagne.'

'Makes better sense. Holy shit, you were there when he died.'

'I saw nothing. He ran on ahead, but I heard the whole thing and I saw his body. I kept thinking he'd get up and laugh it off, but he didn't. Like it wasn't real.'

Bobby said nothing for a minute.

'You still there?'

'I'm here. The truth is, Nipples, Ian, whatever, Harris was a prick – now, he's one dead prick. And he's left us with one day! Do you realize that?'

'Did you check the lockers tonight?'

'Nothing.'

'Shit.'

Bobby had a beep. 'I have a call – I'll get back to you.'

'Mr. Robert Wells?'

'Yeah, who is this?'

'Listen very carefully to every word, Mr. Wells. After this conversation, lose the phone. My colleagues and I think you are a quick study. One lesson tonight, we felt, was all that this unfortunate state of affairs called for. The order is ready for pick-up tomorrow at nine sharp. Given your evident lack of funds, this will be on consignment – for now. But we have to reimburse our creditors for this account so we must be paid soon. Also, look upon the profits you will surrender to us as an aggravation tax. If this is done well, you may be allowed to keep a portion of the profits. Delivery should be undertaken in record time. Let's say three weeks, four at most. We'll leave the distributions and arrangements to you. We have every confidence in you, Mr. Wells. Good evening.'

Harris had been murdered!

🌴

At Club One, Larry had made a life-changing decision. He had even gone to Morty early the next morning before work for counsel. 'What's a good word for what I want to do, Morty?'

'Eschew, I think that's the best word for it. I think you're making the right decision here, Larry. When a man is intent on his goal, he can have no distractions.'

'Thank you, Morty. As of today, I will eschew the pursuit of women and the consumption of alcohol for sixty days. In the last five years, I haven't done much of anything, but I'm cleaning up my act. I need the time to save what cash I can. I don't want to end up like Steve.'

'Good luck to you.'

'Thanks. That means something to me.' Larry needed time for himself. No women for two whole months. There were no exceptions. The beautiful and the ordinary, the tall and the short, the ample and the slight, banished, all of them! Let other fools deal with passion, fights, longings, break-ups and make-up sex. And alcohol. It all drained a man. For sixty days, Larry was going to look out for Larry. He had seen a bumper sticker that read: *Take care of yourself – no one is better qualified.* Right on! Larry never lost at solitaire. For now, he would step back from the human commotion and observe from the sidelines. He'd be happy – he'd be safe in his observatory.

After his consultation with Morty, Larry got his

paint out and was soon hard at work painting the second balcony a banana yellow. The hair on his arm glistened with perspiration, and he felt the burn of the sun
on the back of his neck. By his calculation, he'd have
seven hundred and sixty-five dollars at the end of next
week. A man had to eat after all. Larry was planning a
bus ride on his day off to The Bar on 71st and Harding.
Twenty-seven years ago, that's what the owner,
Toothbrush, had called the dive. Toothbrush himself
was a stringy little man with a bobble head and a buzz
cut of yellowing hair. His face was all angles; his eyes
were sharp and clear, not bloodshot like most of the
bums in the place. He had the nose of an eagle and
hunching shoulders from too much bad luck. A rash of
blackheads rode his eyebrows and peppered either side
of his nostrils. His white shirts were yellow and frayed
– his nails were bitten to the quick. Larry owed this
man. For close to a year, before he had even met Steve,
he'd hung around The Bar and Toothbrush had never
chased him off late at night, not once.

The Bar's windows were slimy with sweat and years
of city grime. Every night but Sunday, twenty drunks
stumbled in, elbowing their way onto the beaten, wood-
en stools. Inside was a choking cloud of bad breath,
butts, beer and urine. Every night, Toothbrush collected beer left behind by drunks he had tossed out, filled a
dirty beer glass and handed it to Larry after last call.
Toothbrush slept at the back of his place and he often
waved Larry over and let him sleep in his doorway. Like
clockwork, Toothbrush opened his only door after one
in the afternoon and hissed at Larry when a wave of bad
air assaulted his nose. 'You stink like a skunk – get in
here and take a shower.' It gave Larry a chance to get
rid of the fungus between his toes and break down the
itchy wax in his ears that was cracking. Twenty minutes

of hot water helped Larry forget he was a Dumpster Diver. Nothing demanded in return – not even conversation. You didn't forget a guy like that. Larry wanted to treat Toothbrush to a cold one – to show him he remembered.

When Raoul tapped on his ladder to tell him he was wanted on the phone in the office, Larry grabbed the rung to keep from falling. Had Dunn figured out he had lied? He felt Steve clawing at him from the morgue. He took his time to get to the office, rehearsing. Had someone nailed him to the scene at Dunkin' Donuts, the sight of Steve's first injury? Was he now a suspect in his death? He wiped the sweat from his hand before he picked up the receiver. 'Hello,' he said, exuding a casualness he did not feel.

'This is Frank Granger, Steve's father. Are you the Larry who knew my son?'

Larry vowed to thank every saint he had ever prayed to as a kid. 'Yeah, me and Steve hung together for over a year and a half. I met you last year. Real sorry about what happened to him.'

'Me too,' Frank responded, his voice hoarse with grief. 'I made the ID this morning. Steve was such a live wire. Hard to believe that was my boy lying there so still. A Detective Dunn told me they were ruling his death accidental – there was nothing to suggest anything else.'

Larry's sigh was audible.

'Heard about his previous injury at Dunkin' Donuts – that's the reason we hadn't heard from him in a few months. You know all this, I guess.' His tone was not accusatory or vindictive – it was an empty voice dealing with sad endings.

'Yeah, I do. We were all at the deck yesterday,' Larry added to commit others to the mix.

'I'm calling because I want to see the place where he died. I want to touch base with you – you were his only friend. I'll need directions; my mind is not very clear.'

'I work here now. Club One is close to 163rd Street, across the street from Rascal House.'

'I remember now. Later this afternoon, Steve's remains will be cremated. His mother wants him home, but before I go I'd like to leave a few of his ashes around the deck. He liked it there.'

Only problem was that he wanted all of it. 'I work till four.'

'Fine, I'll be there at four-thirty.'

'All right.' After Larry had hung up the phone, he remembered the condition of the deck and the yellow police tape around it, blowing in the ocean breezes. He spotted Michel at the end of the hall and filled him in.

After three months in the sun, Michel was ready for a project. 'I'll see what I can do – you better get back to work. Losing a good friend must be hard for you.'

In a matter of minutes, Larry had gone from possible suspect to victim by extension. It was almost too much luck for Larry to handle, but he would try. He walked back outside rubbing his hands together, trying to appear grief stricken.

Michel called Dunn and related Frank Granger's intention of coming to the scene. 'We'd like to reassemble the deck. Can we remove the tape?'

'I'll send over a cruiser – when they're through, you and your group can get to work.' The tape was gone within an hour.

Michel first approached The Desert Inn, but with three working decks, fewer tourists and the wrecking ball threatening the place, the manager had no interest in repairing the deck. Determined, Michel spoke with José and Raoul. Both were keen. While José and Michel hunted out spare wood in the basement of Club One, Raoul took his rake and walked to the site. With gentleness, he combed the sand over Steve's death spot until all of it was level. Soon there was hammering and sawing. A small curious group gathered around the working men. Later that afternoon, the roof of The Sands Motel was lowered onto new supports. Once it was secured, the 'motel' had actually gained six inches in crawl space. Larry came over to see the work on his place. Roots and new beginnings, he thought.

News of Steve's impending wake spread like sand in the wind. Guilt and expiation, just the ticket! Yvette, saddened because she had never given more to Steve than an opened bottle of wine she didn't like and some bagels, threw her heart into the affair, because that's what the event became. She drove over to Publix and bought five bunches of yellow daisies. Once it was swept, she laid two on top of the deck and three at the foot. People began leaving flowers before the sun set. Soon there was a garland of flowers all around the 'motel'. This was just the beginning for Yvette, a hostess of the very first rank. She crossed the street and ordered deli sandwiches, pickles, meats, rye bread, black and white muffins, rugelach and strawberries from Milam's grocery store. Michel drove to a liquor outlet and bought Tequila, wine and beer. Morty and Sarah headed down towards South Beach, to 27th Street for two kosher chickens and coleslaw. At six dollars an hour, Raoul could not buy anything, but he put out his second-hand boom box with music he had selected in the cabana. Carmen rose to the occasion too. She bought three dozen bagels and cream cheese from Einstein Bros. and paper plates and napkins from the Dollar Store. Caitlin was quiet. She lay on the Murphy bed and began to sketch what she could remember of

Steve. She knew she was not a maven of the arts, but she could sketch a handsome face. For a long while, she looked at his likeness. The wake took on an unexpected life, an exuberance as light as the first cobweb of summer.

🌴

Long before the commotion at Club One had begun, Detective Garderella was plotting her interrogation of Harris Chalmer, until the radio news broke into her morning. *The jerk is dead!* The first thing she did at her desk was to call Dunn, who was busy with a drive-by, one dead, one clinging to life. He gave her a quick rundown of Harris' death and directed her to Ramirez. *Accidental? Bumper meets wiseass!* Her shoulders drooped with the disappointment of a hunter who sees his prey move out of range. Harris had moved out of her world. She reviewed the details: Harris mules money or drugs, tosses two yellow bags, loses both to whoever picked them up, probably hunting the stash down, where a homeless man dies, and he himself is killed one day later. The vic under the deck is out of the equation – she accepted that. She jabbed the digits of her cell and called Ramirez again. 'Have you thoroughly checked out the driver on the Harris case? I have questions.'

'With Stuart Chalmer's son lying dead in the street – you better believe it!'

'Something smells here, but I don't know what.'

'Life's too short – move on,' Ramirez suggested before he hung up.

Garderella decided she would drive out to Club One and do a little surveillance on her own.

CHAPTER TWENTY-FOUR

HARRIS CHALMER NEVER looked better. The mortician had restored and worked such wonders on his head that Stuart could not remember which side had suffered the fatal blow. Stuart had chosen a navy blue cashmere blazer, a white Armani shirt, a pale blue silk tie and grey linen slacks for his son. Harris lay comfortably in a fifteen thousand dollar bronze casket on snow white silk. Two hundred red roses lay across the bottom half of the casket. Roses that showed any sign of weakening on the job, Stuart had replaced immediately. Harris would have been pleased at being the centre of attention, lying up there between matching bronze pedestals. He looked better than most corpses. As still as death today, there was an undeniable energy Harris had brought with him into the land of the dead. No one would have flinched if Harris had raised an arm and run his fingers through his hair. In fact, it might even have been expected.

And why not? In life, Harris had made the A-list of South Beach VIPs. He had scored four of *The Herald*'s five testing categories: he was rich, he was beautiful, he was well connected and he was *über*-confident. His Platinum MasterCard had been a sure-fire ticket past the velvet ropes of the trendiest nightclubs on the Beach: the Mynt Lounge, the Opium Garden and B.E.D. But Harris' clubbing days were over now. Yet, one would have to admit, lying up on the pedestal in his designer wear – Harris was the centre of attention, still a VIP in this room.

When the mourners did arrive to pay their respects, they could not fail to note that the large room Stuart had chosen could easily contain a hundred people. On the walls were portraits of important citizens who had chosen this room for their final curtain. Tycoons, among them two Fortune 500 celebs, mayors, aldermen, even a presidential hopeful. Italian sofas and Queen Anne chairs, bordered by end tables and bunches of yellow roses, waited for the living to make their sombre appearance. The immediate family, which totalled seven, had the room to themselves until two o'clock in the afternoon. From two to five, they waited – from five to nine, they waited. Meg, her face pinched with despair, sat slumped in a chair near Harris, knuckling her eyes – her mother sat beside her.

Harris' men filed into the room, led by Bobby. Edgy as sand fleas, the guys huddled together in a mass of nerves and twitches. On the steps outside, three girlfriends arrived simultaneously, figured quickly that Harris was three-timing each of them and turned on their spiky heels and left. *The freakin' nerve!* The hoards of collegians who bought from Harris thought hard about coming, but decided to keep their distance from this pusher. He was not their friend – he was their supplier. A few even made resolutions to mend their ways. It turned out that Harris was a lot like his father – he had hundreds of business contacts, but no real friends. Each gang member extended sympathy to both parents, but it was obvious that death, even one this elegant, made them antsy. The boys approached Harris in a single file, edging Bobby forward in the line. Bobby squinted, queasy with curiosity, craning his neck to see if Harris' chest was moving up and down. When he saw that it was not, he exhaled and walked back to the side of the room. Bobby had levelled with all of the guys about Harris' murder. Jumpy and afraid, each was desperate to rabbit from this dead trust fund baby as soon as possible. Like a rash, betrayal enveloped Stuart. These young men were his son's friends and they abandoned him after fifteen minutes! Stuart was sorriest for Meg, weeping quietly as she watched them leave. The scent the flowers gave off was failure and waste. Only fourteen people had shown up for Harris' visitation – and half of them were family. Only this second half saw him being rolled into the mausoleum at Graceland Memorial Park in his very fine duds a few days later. Nothing could change the fact that Harris ended up in a box, even if it was some box.

♟

In sharp contrast, Club One was abuzz. Food and beverages began to pile up, and Larry stored all of them in the cabana. No one knew how Frank Granger would react once he got to the complex. Showers were spraying water on tanned bodies, towels were flying, hair dryers were blowing, fresh clothes were lying across beds; emotions were high. Larry showered in Raoul's bathroom. After towelling his hair, he slid on his new shirt, wishing he had thought of new shorts and sneakers as well. Carried along on the goodwill of everybody at Club One, Larry now moved from victim to host. The clique of Club One waited around the pool out back. Caitlin had seen Derek's father – she never forgot his face. She would not be taken aback by Frank Granger's palpable grief.

Larry waited in the front hall. Frank Granger pulled up in a blue compact rental. Larry stepped out into the sunshine, shook hands with him and led him to The Sands Motel. The group on the deck held back as Frank Granger walked into their midst, his eyes dulled with anguish. At fifty-two, Frank was tall, blond like Steve, rangy, fatigued, his face white with shock. His Redford moustache reminded Caitlin of *Butch Cassidy and the Sundance Kid*. He wore simple black pants and a white shirt, carrying a jacket on his arm. In the other hand, he held Steve's ashes in a large white envelope. Before Larry began to fumble with his words, Yvette stepped forward.

'Mr. Granger...'

'Frank, please.'

'Frank, all of us here want to tell you how sorry we are about Steve. We knew him – all of us here at Club One. Girls, women of all ages, were attracted by his good looks and his wonderful smile. I suppose what caught our attention was his carefree attitude. He used to sit on that chair you gave him with a single beer, content to enjoy the ocean. We'll miss him.'

Frank dropped his head and cried. 'His mother wanted to come down, but I knew this would be too hard for her. Steve was a decent man – he wasn't always homeless.' His tears drew everyone to him.

Sarah stepped forward and hugged Frank around the chest because she was not tall enough to throw her arms around his shoulders. Yvette kissed Frank on the cheek, Caitlin shook his hand, Michel patted his back, and Morty said, 'What a tragedy, a terrible loss for the family.' Everybody said something comforting to Frank, and truth took winding turns along smooth roads. Frank was led by tender hearts from the deck of Club One to The Sands Motel next door. He saw the flowers first. 'I wish Jen could see this!' Caitlin's sketch of Steve caught his life between parentheses, 1976 – 2004. It took Frank's breath away. 'Is that for me?' he whispered, stepping up to the deck and reaching for the likeness of

Steve. 'Who drew this? This is Steve,' Frank wept openly, clutching the sketch to his heart.

'I did, and of course, you can keep it,' Caitlin answered. 'I'm glad you like it.'

'Thank you.' Frank knelt in the middle of the deck, laying his hand on the wood. 'Steve died here, under the deck. I remember where he slept.'

Raoul had been quietly arranging the chairs on the 'motel' deck while Michel and Larry brought the food and liquor. Michel slipped away and mixed Margaritas and returned with a tray of drinks. He raised his glass. 'In memory of Steve!' He handed the second glass to Frank. 'To Steve,' everybody said. Down went the first round. Then the second. Food was set on tables that seemed to suddenly appear. Other Club One guests, a little shy to come forward when Frank first arrived, walked across the sand, joined the group and brought more food with them.

Old Saul from Manhattan, from room #118, joined the mourners at the 'motel'. Saul was ninety-three years old, smoked five Cuban seven-inch cigars every day, wore a silver whistle with a navy blue ribbon around his neck, swam four lengths in the pool, rain or shine, and tracked every set of breasts at Club One from behind his shades. The only thing old about Saul was his trunks, faded, thin, shiny flowered pants beaten down by the years Saul had worn them. Saul was smart enough to take a seat beside the food and tapped his foot to the music while he shuffled food under his towel when he felt no one was looking his way.

Tina, the proud owner of seventy pairs of shoes, a woman of spunk and style, led her husband by the hand and stepped up onto the deck.

Even 'Tidal Wave' heaved her three hundred pounds to the wooden deck. It trembled under her weight.

T.W. was a sad psychologist who travelled, 'travelled' is accurate because every step was a labour of agony for her feet, to each patio table every day imposing her tale of woe and reciting her academic achievements. She called out to the swimmers that the pool was not clean; she threatened the sunbathers with cancer. She told everyone Miami was a bad place. Guests recoiled, especially when T.W. wiped her armpits mid-story with her beach towel. But today, with the warmth of alcohol, the Club One ensemble felt the throb of her loneliness and pulled T.W. into their circle to share Steve's day.

Surprisingly, the Russian, a walking stereotype, a shadowy six-footer who stepped onto his ocean-side balcony twice a day in the afternoon and retreated behind the curtains within seconds, decided to join the group with his nude dancer wife and brought two bottles of Absolut. Katarina was better known by the group because she came down to the pool with her little girl every day. Eyes of men and women followed her every move. When she reclined on her lounge chair, unfastening her top, men moaned. Women sat back in awe. Bernini could not have done better work. The cast of her legs, their ivory curves, did not seem real. If her waist was twenty inches, it was no more. Only her breasts, globes of femininity, full, inviting, perfect – all words inadequate to describe them, betrayed the skillful hands of a surgeon. What was more distressing to the women was Katarina's kindness and gentleness. Life wasn't fair! However, four months to the day from Steve's memorial, Katarina and 'Absolut' (her husband never offered his real name) were arrested for a narcotics violation and deported. But today, that bad luck was far in the future. Today, Katarina kissed Frank on the cheek, and Frank needed a chair immediately. He thought he had joined Steve in heaven!

Another round of Margaritas, wine, beer and Absolut.

'Poor Steve.'

'To Steve, everybody!'

Though his nerves were flinty, and everything about him suggested low profile, Frank began to tell the group all about his son. 'My wife would be so impressed with everything you've all done here! Steve was a good boy. He finished junior college, you know. Played tennis for the team, too. His dream was to go to Del Ray Beach and teach at Nick Bolletieri's tennis camp. He saved his money and flew down to Florida, but the camp only hired pros. The night before his pro exam back home, he tore a muscle in his shoulder and never sat for it. He figured he could come to Miami and travel from one private club to another teaching tennis at fifty dollars a lesson. All he felt he needed was four students at two hours a week each to make good money. He never counted on the courts being glutted with pros, hungry as crows for greenbacks. By that time, he had fallen in love with the sun. Didn't want to come home, but couldn't find work either. Then he just drifted, and Larry over there knows the rest.' Frank's head felt light – his heart did too. 'All you nice people...'

Raoul decided it was time for the music. Larry had told him to start with Jimmy Buffett. When the music began to resonate in the warm air, dancing seemed as appropriate as breathing. Yvette asked Frank for a dance, and he obliged willingly. Katarina danced with Absolut, Michel took his wife's hand, Sarah guided Morty to the floor, Carmen danced together and separately with Caitlin, and so on, till every foot but Larry's was moving to the words and laid-back sounds of Jimmy Buffett. *'Wastin' away again in Margaritaville / Searchin' for my lost shaker of salt / Some people claim there's a woman to blame / But I know it's my own damn fault.'* Larry was true to his oath and took care of the music. Sitting at a good oblique angle, he had a terrific view of the scene on the deck. Raoul couldn't keep from dancing himself, pulling his wife up onto the deck with him. People began to sing along and shouted to Larry to play the song again and again. 'Steve would have loved this,' Frank wept as he danced with everyone. 'His mother is Irish and she lets go of treasures with a full heart and a broad smile.'

A crowd began to gather, drawn by the music. 'Didn't someone die here a few days ago?'

'Yes, isn't this display awful?'

'You'd think these people would know better.'

'Dancing on the poor guy's grave!'

When Buffett began to sing for the fifth time, the critiquing strangers caught the mood and started to sway themselves. 'We're as bad as they are!' And they were, dancing along with the mourners, accepting drinks passed down to them, singing along with the well-known lyrics. Larry turned up the music.

The sky above the mourners, far into the horizon, glowed a velvety pink, the few clouds white and docile. Between the heavens, gulls, grackles, pigeons and even a few brave sandpipers circled the gathering, hungry for the spoils, forming a halo in the sky.

As attentive as gulls, the mourners stopped dancing when Frank did. Larry turned Buffett off and waited for his cue. Frank walked over to his chair that had been moved to the side of the deck where he had left the urn, the sketch and his jacket. He reached into the pocket of his jacket and retrieved a white envelope. 'I guess it's time,' he whispered. A line formed on either side, like an honour guard. Careful of the flowers, Frank stepped off the deck and knelt at the foot of the wood structure that had sheltered his son for a time. He opened the envelope, poured some of Steve's ashes into his hand and closed his fingers around them. Larry played Cher's 'If I Could Turn Back Time' very quietly. Frank poured the ashes over the flowers as though he were tearing off his own skin. 'Part of you will always be here, Steve,' his father wept. Michel helped him back onto the deck. Remnants of a Reuben sandwich Frank had tried to eat lodged themselves above his breastbone. He was glad he couldn't swallow food on the day he left part of his son behind.

After the kisses, the good-byes, the handshakes and the pats, Frank left Club One and took most of Steve with him. 'I'll never forget your kindness, all of you. Larry, thanks for being Steve's friend.' And then, Frank was gone. People pitched in with the cleanup – nobody stepped near the ashes. A natural silence and a sweet sorrow fell on the guests, each lost in his own thoughts. Caitlin was the exception. The wake had left her fractured and alone with regret.

When the cleanup began, Caitlin sat on the sand near the flowers, drew her knees into her chin and began to rub her neck to get rid of the knot of nerves that was settling on its left side. When Michel told Larry that the Club One guests would take care of things, he accepted the gesture because he had a full day's work behind him. When he noticed Caitlin, saw her sadness, he thought the truth might help her. He felt guilty himself because Steve's departure had made his nights easier. Helping someone was not against the oath he had made to himself. He sat down beside Caitlin, but she did not notice him at first.

'You're down about Steve,' he said to her, scooping up sand in his hand, allowing it to slip through his fingers. He waited for Caitlin to answer.

At first, she did not stir, but sat in motionless pain. When the reply came, the words were heavy with guilt. 'Yeah, I am. Someone died here and his death was probably preventable.'

'I guess it was.'

Caitlin felt a fist around her heart – the deck began to close in on her. She jumped up from the sand and doubled over trying to catch her breath. Did Larry know something of that night's events?

Caitlin's distress unsettled Larry and he stood too, taking a step back from her. 'Are you all right? You don't look good.'

'You think Steve's death was preventable?' Caitlin asked, squeamish and dizzy. Had Larry seen them that night at the deck?

Larry's eye began to twitch. What had he just said? Had he implied that he had a hand in Steve's death? His instinct was to recoil, but Caitlin's distress lured him to disclosure. 'Can I trust you with something, Caitlin?'

Caitlin fought her need to confess everything, and she had no idea what Larry was talking about. Trust was generally a dangerous bargain; it often entailed a give-and-take. 'Yeah, you can,' she answered quietly, uncertainly. She began to breathe in shallow gasps. Caitlin could not hope for closure, or trust that Larry could deliver it. After Derek's death, she knew there was no such thing.

'Steve didn't have to die. I mean, everybody is feeling so bad for him, but he brought this accident on himself.'

What was Larry talking about?

Once Larry began, there was no stopping him. 'We were O.K. for a year. Then he decides a few months ago, he wants the whole deck – and me out! Jesus, I found this place; I dug it out. I wasn't about to move.'

Larry began to kick at the sand. 'He attacked me up at Dunkin' Donuts to get the deck for himself. I slipped his punch, and he crashed into a steel dumpster. I thought he was dead and I ran. I mean, what did I do? Why the fuck do I feel guilty? Steve would be alive today if he hadn't gotten greedy. He wasn't a bad guy, but he sure as hell wasn't a saint either. And now he's dead, and I feel like shit. I don't know why you're so down – you really didn't know him.'

'Larry, you have nothing to feel badly about. You've done nothing wrong. I'll never tell anyone about this – you can trust me.' Larry was confessing his and Steve's story, and he'd done nothing wrong. Caitlin was too wired to be grateful, but gratitude would come on its own.

'I'm not coming on to you, Caitlin. You don't have to worry about that anymore. I want you to know you can trust me too. I've gotta tell you something. I never found your key. I don't know how it got under the deck and I don't care. Just remember, Steve's death was an accident; that's what the cops said. Feel better. I need my job here; I've gotta get my life back. The key doesn't matter anymore.' Larry patted Caitlin on the shoulder and walked back to the cabana. He felt the best he'd felt in a long time. A man begins with friends, he thought.

Caitlin made a beeline for her room. The Margaritas began to swirl high in her stomach. Her heart did a puddle jump.

🌴

Today, Detective Garderella chose to do a little detecting in the Club One area. At Rascal House, she thought to ask around to see if Harris Chalmer had told Tully the truth about being a regular. If he was, there

was no ulterior motive for him and his gang to be in the
area. The manager told her to talk to the Rascal's
greeter because he knew everybody, especially the
repeaters. Harold was one colourful guy. He wore thick,
black-framed glasses, a green neon tie, high-water
pants, clunky shoes and a top hat. A fellow waiter said,
'He'll be real easy to spot. He dresses like a character in
a Fellini movie.' Today, he was lugging around
Dostoyevsky's portentous tome, *Crime and Punishment*.
He reigned over his kingdom of stools and booths and
shocked people with good manners and a smile that was
as wide as the ocean. He reached for Garderella's photos with a flourish and moved away to stand under better lighting. 'Rude and obnoxious with his band of bad
boys, yes, sad to say, I know him. A repeat offender
unfortunately. What's he done? Tell me – you won't
surprise me,' Harold sighed, bringing the back of his
hand to his forehead, *à la* Meryl Streep.

'Against policy, sir.'

'You want my help, but you can't tell me anything?'

'Fraid so. I can tell you he was killed a few nights
ago.'

'Oh dear, speaking ill of the dead! Not part of my
philosophy. Bless his mean little soul.' Four nights later,
Harold himself was run down by a bus as he hurried
across the street to catch his own bus near NE 163rd
Street. 'His presence made a difference between a day
that was clouded and a day he filled with sunshine,' a
regular had told *The Herald*. He was so highly thought
of at the deli that a memorial note was printed up in
lights on the Rascal House billboard beneath the figure
of a smiling little rascal holding a trident. A week later
to the day, before Harold had settled into his new digs,
the deli took down the memorial quote and got back to
the more urgent minutiae with – *Ah, the smell of pickles,*

brewed in brine – and cabbage soup that smells like wine!
Poor Harold, a beloved friend and employee, a legend,
became the past and joined Harris and Steve, the new
kids on the block.

Garderella left the deli scratching her head. The
homeless vic had died accidentally, ditto for Chalmer
and now he and his gang were regulars at Rascal House.
That left her with two yellow bags and the mystery person or persons who picked them up and ran. She wondered if there was any chance she had *not* seen the bags.
Could she unintentionally be fabricating fodder for a
case? *No, I'd swear in court I saw them when Chalmer
tossed them into his vehicle. What the hell happened?* Had
she walked across the street, she would have come upon
the happy wake, but Garderella sat in her vehicle with
both hands on the wheel and punched the steering column before she was called to an 'abc' homicide. No
mystery here. Club One would have to wait. Up on
NW 56th Avenue, a seventy-eight year old senior citi-
zen had clubbed his wife of fifty-three years with a cast-
iron frying pan because she had refused to cook him
another mushroom omelette, the second of the day, at
three in the afternoon.

CHAPTER TWENTY-FIVE

'WHAT'S WRONG?' CARMEN asked her friend as she came back into their condo, carrying *The Herald* she had just bought.

'Larry never found our key.'

Carmen's decent mood began to unfurl. She had sworn to stay positive. 'That doesn't matter much now. I spoke with Steve's father, you know, asking him about the death, and offering my sympathies. He told me Steve suffocated on a piece of bone from his nose that lodged in his throat. And that's what killed him, not our sand. You might feel that I don't do a whole lot of thinking, but I've thought about that night. It was an accident – that's all it was. We never planned to hide under the deck; we tried to calm Larry because that's who we thought was there. In fact, from what we knew, the deck was empty. Caitlin, you may be transferring your guilt from Derek to Steve. That's all I have to say.'

'Maybe.'

Carmen sat down to scan the paper, and there on the first page was a smiling photo of Harris Chalmer under the banner: ***Tragedy in Bal Harbour*** *– The twenty-four year old son of prominent boat designer Stuart Chalmer, a third year student at University of Miami, was struck and fatally injured by a passing vehicle as he ran across Collins Avenue. Police are still investigating the accident, but no charges have been laid...* 'Caitlin, oh my God, look at this!' Carmen shouted, running across the room with the paper. 'Isn't this the guy who's chasing us?'

Caitlin rolled off the bed and grabbed the paper. A

scorching heat ran through her veins as Harris stared back at her with piercing eyes above a confident grin. 'It's him – it's him!' Caitlin whispered, her dread of a dead Harris almost alive. Caitlin quickly laid the paper on the bed and stepped away from it. A shiver followed her across the room, jerking both shoulders. The story, almost hypnotic, drew her back. Caitlin picked the paper up again, holding it at arm's length as she read the account of Harris' accident. To the tips of her fingers, fear spread like a virus.

Watching her friend, Carmen knew where Caitlin's emotions were headed. It was time for Carmen to take control. There was no way she wanted to be pulled back into Caitlin's moral framework. Enough with the guilt and maudlin. She walked to their dresser and grabbed clean clothes for both of them. 'You know what? I'm famished and you must be too. At the wake, we could not feel right about eating any of the food. I'm taking you to Tony Roma's. Get dressed, girl! I'm going for the 'Ultimate Grill Power Combo': St. Louis style ribs with Carolina Honeys sauce, grilled shrimp and sirloin steak on a bed of fried onions topped with mushrooms and tons of sauce. And I'm going to eat all of it! We've both lost weight in the last few days, and I can't swallow another dry, stale bagel.'

Before Caitlin could decline, Carmen continued on her roll. 'For you, you health-conscious person, I will order a grilled salmon steak, corn, baked beans and salad. Don't raise your hand; I'm not finished. For desert, we are going to share apple crisp *à la mode* with caramel. We can worry about lower fat and lower carbs tomorrow.'

The apple crisp was Caitlin's undoing. A little smile began to curl its way to both corners of her lips. 'I can't say no to apple crisp. It's a deal. But, I still think we should walk there separately, for safety. And Carmen, I want to pay my own way.'

'No you won't; this is my treat. And we will go there separately. Now get changed and let's get out of here.'

Larry missed Carmen's exit, but he saw Caitlin leave the condo. He stopped sweeping up the mess from the painting, and his eyes followed her until she was out of sight.

The single phone call concerning the reason for Harris' death and the instructions about the sale of the shipment kept Bobby's shoulders stiff for the next two days. Seeing Harris in a box had jellied his bones, but the only alternative was to meet the man's expectations of him. It was a little surprising after the disaster of losing the money, but the drop-off of the 'consignment' drugs was uneventful. Since the drop-off, Bobby had worked at a frantic pace. Since he was back in class, the work had to be done at night. For the last two nights, Bobby had been glued to the phone recruiting seven new connections on campus, clean-cut college students who could push the drugs without arousing suspicion. He had discovered he was not merely a numbers geek: he was also a great salesman. He had convinced all seven to peddle the drugs for nothing but the promise of money as high as ten grand a month on their next assignment. The vulnerability and blockhead stupidity of these young men astounded him. When he thought about himself, he did not feel much better about things.

Once he had the names, he began with his charts. Data poured onto the pages, and he quickly stored it all, memorized, in his head. He destroyed the electronic trail as soon as he had the facts down. With thirteen mules, he would make the deadline. At four in the morning, Bobby was still counting. Ian had quietly become his second-in-command. There was a calm, even a resignation in him, that Bobby had never seen before. Ian was not slouching or whining – he was offering decent suggestions. The guys were calling him Ian now. Bobby did not have the time to figure this change out; his head ached with charts and numbers. He would make time for Hilda, however. Ian had remembered her name. Bobby would see her tonight.

🌴

Earlier that morning, Hilda lay in bed keenly aware of the dull ache in her fifth lumbar vertebra. It would be one of those days when she'd feel that she was carrying a sand bag around in her lower back. She rubbed it as best she could before she eased herself out of bed, remembering if she moved too quickly she'd pay with a knife-sharp pain in the same area. Once she was standing, Hilda massaged both sides of her back with her fingers. Sandy, her golden retriever, was waiting at the foot of her bed. At six and a half, his arthritis had settled in his knees and jumping up on Hilda's bed was a thing of the past. Tabs was meowing by the food dish in the kitchen. Hilda began work at one o'clock and she had the time to take Sandy out for a good walk that just might loosen up her back in the bargain.

The day was already hot, too hot for this time of year, Hilda thought. It was seventy-four degrees on a cloudless, windless day. By mid-afternoon, the temperature would reach the high eighties, and flying ants would bother bathers. Hilda set the paper aside and reached for the leash, but Sandy shied away from it, preferring to stay with the air conditioning inside the apartment. 'No, you don't, Sandy. You need this exercise as much as I do,' scolded Hilda, as she attached the leash to his collar. Once they were on the sidewalk, breathing hard, Sandy walked on the crab grass as much as he could. Hilda made a mental note to buy herself a small umbrella against the sun. Hiding from the sun was back in vogue among the natives.

Twenty minutes later, after the stoop and scoop, Hilda was in better shape than poor Sandy as they climbed the steps into the apartment building. 'Now you can relax, Sandy. I want two good cups of coffee and toast with marmalade.' Hilda sat in her favourite chair, set the coffee cup down on a dishtowel with the hot toast beside it and picked up the morning paper. The bile of a few nights ago rose immediately when Hilda recognized Harris' photo. Her pulse rose. 'Good God!' was all Hilda managed to get out as she read every word of the account of the accident. Her eyelids burned. Just as she had thought, this careless young man had come from the privileged ranks, where balls and benefits defined their society. 'You were determined to cause trouble, young man. I could see that in your every move. Look where you've ended up! In my day, we would have called you a bad apple. How did all this come about?' Hilda noticed that her hands were shaking, and not from age. She did not believe in coincidence any more than Detective Garderella did. 'What's become of those Canadian women? Is there someone I should call? What do I really know?'

When the phone rang, Hilda froze, and Hilda did not freeze very often. She reached for the receiver tentatively. 'Hello.'

'Hi Mom, it's Ryan.'

A warmth and sense of security rushed through her. 'What a wonderful surprise! Is the family all right?'

'Everybody's fine, Mom. Lindsay's working in the library again, and Meagan and Emma are back in school after the break. I'm calling to invite you to dinner because I'm in town for the day on business.'

'Wouldn't you know, I work till nine tonight.'

'Don't worry, Ma. I'll meet you at the store then, and we can enjoy a late dinner. Eat light – won't be bad for either one of us. I don't want to miss seeing you.'

'You have a date, son. I'll close my stand up a little before nine and be ready for you. There's something I need your opinion about.'

'Are you all right, Ma?'

'I'm fine, but I could use some good advice.'

'You've got it. Later then.'

It was safest, Bobby felt, to meet with Hilda around eight-thirty. The shopping crowd would be thinning out by then, and he needed time for the questions he had carefully prepared. Trying to appear as casual and harmless as possible, Bobby wore stone-washed blue jeans and a pale blue short sleeved button-down shirt with brown loafers. He decided against the silver buckled belt. Heavy, he thought. Against his preference, he went lighter on the gel as well. He had no intention of goose-stepping the old woman – the gentlemanly approach was the best to employ in this situation.

Before Bobby appeared, Hilda was grateful to see a relatively quiet night on the floor and spent her time cleaning her station and observing the clientele. It was easy to recognize the usuals – they shopped two or three times a week. What was this obsession to purchase greedily, to dress expensive clothes on old bodies whose features had long ago lost their definition? *That woman over there is a walking skeleton*, Hilda thought. *Any day, those cheekbones will tear the papery skin that clings to them like a cheap tent.* The octogenarian followed her

Cuban maid who lugged more clothes to Hilda's stand. Hilda was aghast when she saw the old woman's fingers offering her MasterCard, all bones and veins weighted down with shiny diamond rings that highlighted the grotesque attrition of age. *Have they no mirrors?* Hilda wondered. *What a pitiful waste!* It was easy for Hilda to maintain a healthy disdain of the wealthy.

When Bobby walked over to Hilda's station, she had an armful of clothes the old witch had decided not to buy. If he had hoped for a timid woman, Bobby was disappointed. No matter – he'd handle a simple saleswoman. 'Hi,' he waved. 'I'll wait till you get rid of those.'

Hilda wondered what this young man wanted in mature women's wear. Whatever it was, she hoped she could be rid of him so she could get ready for Ryan. Hilda hurried back to her station. 'May I help you, sir?'

'Yes, ma'am, you can. First off, I'd like to apologize for my friend the other night. I'm sure you remember him – he was looking for two girls he felt were hiding somewhere up here. He told me he'd been quite rude to you. I guess you've seen the papers, and you recognized his photo. His father is devastated over his death. He was my best friend, but I know he was a jerk too. He was just angry that night up here because somebody got the better of him. I know you told him you didn't see the two women he was looking for that night, but I was wondering if you said that because Harris was being obnoxious, perhaps intimidating.'

Hilda's knees were rubbery – she wanted to sit down, but she stood her ground. The fallout of living alone was generally too much TV, but *Law and Order* had taught Hilda a few things. She easily recognized the 'good cop, bad cop' routine. And she preferred Harris. He was a recognizable pit bull. Behind this young man, there lured a calm menace. His manner was too controlled, even remote. 'I remember your friend, but...'

'Before you say anything, I want to give you the background. Harris was kind of a boor with these girls, came on hard. When they ignored him, he was pissed, if you know what I mean. He pushed one of the girls off her chair, and then he danced around laughing on the dance floor. Girls never 'dissed' Harris. To get back at him, one of them grabbed his yellow knapsack and ran from the club. I know he deserved to lose it. But that bag contained his Rolex watch, a gift from his father. I'm hoping you can help me get it back for him.'

'I tried to tell your friend the other night that I didn't...'

Bobby jumped back in. 'I know what you told him, but I think you must have seen something. Please help me, Hilda.' Bobby countered, fighting his control, trying hard to hide his scowl, but was unable to hide his flaring red cheeks or his feral eyes as shiny as his gel.

While Bobby smouldered, Hilda, sensing his desperation, grew calmer. Her sons had taught her about pissing contests and how to win them. 'I wish I could help, but I saw nothing. They might have hidden it up on this floor, but not in my station. Your friend looked everywhere, even in these lockers. I might have been with a customer.' Hilda grew bolder with unexpected finesse. 'As an example, since we've been talking, how many people have you noticed on the floor?'

Bobby's eyes went to slits. The old bag had a point. He bit off his impatience and gave Hilda a grudging nod. Like Harris, Bobby felt she might know something, but she was harder to crack than Fort Knox. Worse, Bobby felt the old bag could read him perfectly. 'Thanks for nothing,' Bobby hissed.

'I'm sorry I couldn't help you,' Hilda called after him, shaking and smiling.

CHAPTER TWENTY-SIX

JUST BEFORE NINE, as Ryan approached his mother's station on the second floor in Neiman Marcus, she turned to greet him. He knew immediately that she was agitated. Her cheeks were chalky, and she appeared both pale and flushed. Her blood pressure most assuredly was topping. 'Mom, are you all right?' Ryan asked, his voice pitch much too high, the way it always was when he was suddenly frightened. A childhood trait he'd never lost, and always wished he had.

'Oh Ryan, it's so good to see you,' Hilda said, hugging him with such joy and relief that she almost wept. 'Let's get out of here.'

'I know just the place for privacy, Mom. Lucciano's, a little place that's so new we won't have to worry about strangers overhearing our conversation. Their hand-made *cappelletti* are delicious, and the salads are always fresh.'

'Sounds just right. I'm so glad you're here. I took a bus to work today, so we won't have to worry about two cars.'

'That's my Mom, always on the ball.'

'Damn straight, as the kids would say.' Hilda got a kick out of shocking her conservative son every now and then, though inside her heart was shaking.

Once they reached the restaurant, Ryan directed Hilda to a side table and ordered a decently priced Chablis, his mother's favourite. Except for one other couple, they were alone in the small restaurant that housed only thirty-six patrons. Fresh white daisies gave the little table a gentle look and white wicker chairs gave the place a homey feel. It was an intimate little corner, just right for good conversation. The wife cooked out back, and the husband approached the table only when he was taking orders or carrying food. Ryan disliked the intrusion of waiters coming often to the table to ask if everything was all right. Bullying for a better tip, he always thought.

Hilda's son took after her in that he was a good listener, and she launched into the entire story and got it out of the way before the hot food arrived. 'This whole episode has unnerved me, Ryan. I saw absolute fear in those young women's eyes. Since this second young man approached me tonight, I'm doubly anxious because I know they're still looking for the Canadians. As I've just told you, the fellow who appeared to be their leader is dead, but I just can't believe that his death was an accident. Doesn't sit right with me. The one who questioned me tonight is more worrisome because he's more calculating. I feel I should do something. What do you think?'

Ryan, who had been expecting a health problem, was taken aback by his mother's story. He cupped a hand over his mouth and said nothing for a full minute. 'My gut reaction, Mom, is to stay out of this. I don't want to have to worry about you. I'm thinking as I speak. You have four children and three grandchildren who don't want you to put yourself in jeopardy. These guys are dangerous, Mom – they're used to getting what they're after from the way you're describing them. I don't want you anywhere near this mess. I assume you'd be called into a precinct with the information you have. How would you enjoy a chance meeting with one of the guys? You'd be setting yourself up as a target.'

'That's why I'm confiding in you, Ryan. I'm troubled. The thin and intense young man who just approached me was angry and full of resolve. Excess, that's what first struck me about both of the gang members who questioned me.'

'I know your first inclination is to help out in any way you can, but this situation is dangerous and volatile, and I don't want you in the middle of it. You're a tough old broad, Ma, but this is over your head and mine too. Maybe I'm being selfish, but I want you around for a long time. It's bad enough we lost Dad and Sean. I'm sure the other kids would feel the same way.'

'But...'

'There are no buts, Mom. You said the women were here on vacation. What time remaining does that give them? We have no way of knowing. With the fright they've already had, they might be back in Canada for all you know. Also, what you know is supposition – what can you really offer the cops? This dead guy was chasing women whose names you don't know, whose address you don't know, for what reason you don't know. Most important, Mom, is that, till now, those guys only think you might know something, and in that sense, you're still safe. The minute you come forward, you're not. Have you thought about that? Have you thought about us? If you call the cops, they'll use you for your information, but they don't have the manpower to protect you. You live alone – how safe would you be if one of these guys got hold of your address?'

'You're right, of course,' Hilda admitted, but the ideas knocking around in her head were still there.

'Are these women worth the personal risk to you? From what you've told me, they've done something to have warranted this frantic search.'

'I'm in the business of knowing people, and they only wanted to get away with their lives. They had nothing with them but some cash for shopping. They weren't carrying anything else, so this second young man is lying. Yet, these women are being hunted down – that's what frightens me.'

Ryan was never surprised at his mother's perspicacity to hidden secrets, but this was hardly the time to marvel at her intuitive prowess. 'My point is that you don't know the whole story. You may think I'm awful, but I think it might be somewhat selfish of you to put yourself in jeopardy. Our family has had its share of grief for a good while.' Ryan reached across the small table and gathered his mother's hands into his own. 'Let me treat you to a snifter of cognac, Mom. Please let this go, for all our sakes.'

'I'll try, son, but I'm a stubborn, old woman and I'll have to make up my own mind, even on this thing.'

'You always have, Mom. I know because I'm your son and I'm as stubborn as a mule myself. But, this isn't one of your crosswords – most mysteries are never solved.' They shared friendly banter for the remainder of their evening.

🌴

While Hilda was hoping the cognac would loosen the knot in her stomach, Bobby was seething in his wrath and disappointment, marching up and down outside the mall, trying to chart his next option. 'Stupid bitch! What the hell is her problem? The old crow knows something – I can feel it.' Yet Bobby knew a dead end when he saw it. Reluctantly, he began to plan his canvass of the condos around The Newport, even though that work would have to wait until tomorrow. Tonight, as every night, until the 'E' was sold and delivered, he met with his mules. He had to put his faith in the belief that somebody along the old motel strip might remember the women. He couldn't afford to send any of his men to Sunny Isles because they were busy with deliveries. If he found the cash, there was no way Bobby would divulge the news to anyone. After all, he was doing all the legwork.

🌴

At ten o'clock on the night of Steve's funeral, the C's had hiked to Old Navy up 163rd Street to walk off the ribs and crisp and were halfway home when Carmen laid out her agenda for the following days. 'Remember we said we'd rent a car on this trip? Let's take a day off, lie low and then rent one. I was thinking I'd walk to Alamo, pick up the car and take a short drive to the dogs. Don't worry – I won't gamble – I just want to see my greyhounds for an hour or so. You don't have to come. I'll be back around three, and we can head to South Beach. Let's try to enjoy our last days here.'

'Sounds like a plan. You don't mind going to the track alone?'

'Not at all. Doesn't it seem strange to be out on the street right now and not running from those guys?'

'I'm trying not to think of them, Carmen.'

'Understood.'

🌴

For the first time in a long while, Hilda had trouble falling asleep. Ryan's advice was sound. Though Hilda could not at first articulate her inherent need to help the young women, she discovered the truth around four in the morning. The kindness of strangers, a connection sealed in the palm of the heart. Perhaps, it was more than that. Hilda had no daughters or the consummation of kindred spirits that they bring with them. She had felt the pain of that void all her married life, and beyond. The women's desperate need had stirred Hilda's heart. Sometimes, though not often, a crisis proved to be a rewarding chapter. That's when she remembered the phones at the back of Sheldon's Pharmacy, two booths, secluded, away from listening ears. If she called the Detective Ramirez listed in *The Herald* from one of those phones, she could remain anonymous, safe and still perhaps help those young women. What if she talked too long and the call was traced? Hilda's eyes popped open with the start of a caffeine buzz, and the thought of a target crept back into her frontal lobe just above her left eye.

🌴

The food, the long walk and fresh air had a lot to do with Caitlin falling asleep quickly, but Carmen had things to ponder. She had no intention of driving to the dog track in two days time. She began planning her strategy for a high stakes gamble and, the next two nights, she fell asleep grinding her teeth, something she hadn't done since she was a child. The day of the car rental, she woke early and massaged her sore jaws.

🌴

Larry was in great spirits as dawn shot arrows of light though the slated windows of the cabana and assaulted him with its brightness. He dressed quickly, ran to Gilbert Samson Park a half block away, showered and shaved and was back cleaning his room in no time. He'd scouted out the basement of Club One a second time after the wake and found much that he felt Raoul would let him take. Old furniture lay around the dusty rooms: mattresses, chairs, dressers, even a small end table, missing one leg that he knew he could repair. Morty had stopped to talk to him as he was heading to the basement for a good ten minutes before Michel joined them. It felt damn good being part of something – Larry was energized, happy, full of plans.

Caitlin and Carmen were lying on their lounge chairs when Sarah joined them, sitting under the umbrella. 'You're up early, you two!' she called over to them, rustling in her purse.

'No candies this early in the morning, Sarah. I can hear you looking for them,' Carmen called back, never opening her eyes. 'We're renting a car today and we don't want to lose what tans we still have.'

The rustling stopped.

At eleven-thirty, Carmen left the condo to pick up the rental and drove not towards Hollywood, but up 163rd Street to what was left of the mall there. Running from the car, she scanned the shops of cheap jewellery, sneakers and jock trunks until she found one that sold duffel bags and backpacks. A few minutes later, she loaded two tan backpacks into the trunk. Sitting ramrod straight as she drove, she headed back to Collins Avenue and Bal Harbour. Once across Haulover Bridge, she double-checked her rear-view mirror to assure herself that she had not been followed, turning right up the side street she and Caitlin had walked a few days ago. Everything was so clear in the sunlight, but exposed. Saturday was perfect for her plan because there were no workmen around as she took her next left and drove slowly toward the stash that squatted anonymously under a pile of discarded boards.

The element of fun that Carmen had felt last night evaporated the nearer she got to the money. Her shoulders narrowed and arched; her nose began to run. Into the mouth of her plan crept a worm of self-doubt. *I can do this – I know I can. I mean, who in God's name would walk away from money like this?* It took all her resolve to pull her gaze from staring fixedly ahead to turn to her left, to the hole where the money lay buried. Carmen punched her left knee a few times before she bolted from the car and ran over to the hideaway.

Carmen had only her greed to sustain her. In the next minutes it swelled to a fierce passion. Down on all fours, she scurried like a rat above the hole. Focused and flushed, she grabbed the loose boards and quickly flung them aside with frantic energy. Panting, she dug deeper for the wood within the hole, her head a good foot into the earthen maw. In seconds, she felt a shadow move across the sun and pulled out of the hole, hitting her head in the process. No one was around, but Carmen scanned the lawns for any movement. Her jaw was tight – her teeth clamped down. She dropped again into the hole with a committed lunge. Reaching down into the pit as far as she could extend her right arm, Carmen yelped in pain as a jagged piece of wood splintered her palm in six or seven places. Doggedly, she reached farther down till her hand found the first bag.

Yanking, tugging, straining, she pulled the money to the top of the hole, laid it aside and plunged back down. Her hand was bleeding and throbbing, but Carmen dug deeper. She breathed in ragged, desperate gasps, got her shoulder into the hole and reached still farther into the blackness. Her finger grazed the second bag, but could not get a hold of it. Carmen slid farther down again and grabbed the bag. Too deep into the hole to manage any leverage, like a worm, she wiggled her body away from the opening, dragging the bag, inch by inch, up to the surface of the grass. With both hands she lifted the second bag out of the hole. For a few seconds, she lay exhausted on the grass. But her precarious situation quickly struck home, and Carmen scrambled to her feet, dragging the bags to her car. She pitched them into the open trunk and locked it.

Cupping her bleeding hand, Carmen opened it slowly to see the damage. Like the left side of her face and shoulder, the injured hand was smeared with dirt, but Carmen could see blood oozing from six or more welts. Running her fingers across the bloodied palm, she found a good sized splinter that she pulled from under the skin. A line of blood followed it. The other splinters, more deeply embedded, would require tweezers, hopefully nothing more. Starting up the car with her good hand, Carmen drove back the way she had come, heading back up to 163rd Street, searching for a fast food restaurant in which to clean herself up before heading home.

She turned into a Burger King, locked the car door and ran to the bathroom. While running her hand under hot water, Carmen also used paper towels to wipe the dirt from her face. A wave of panic swept through her stomach when she realized the money was lying unprotected in the trunk. With water dripping from both hands, Carmen raced to the car, opening the trunk and checking to see if the cash was still there. It was. Just once in her life, Carmen wanted the chance to deal with larger issues than the rent or grocery bills, and the security of knowing she'd have the time to look around, to see into the depth of things. Working from paycheque to paycheque, she was drowning in the minutiae of life. Carmen wanted to let go of herself without panic. Was that too much to ask? This sell-out was worth the price. She also knew that Caitlin would never forgive her for this rashness or the chronicle of her mistakes, but she hoped, in time, she would.

As she pulled into the front driveway of Club One, Larry was on the roof bending down over it, painting the yellow trim. 'Living it up?' he called down to Carmen.

Larry's friendly comment jump-started Carmen's pulse. She had never even thought of Larry sniffing around, burrowing into her affairs. Carmen began that very moment to look for threats under soft appearances. Now that she had brought the secret home with her, she began to smell invasions everywhere, in Michel, in Morty, in Raoul. All eyes grew suspicious. She waved back at Larry, purposely not calling back to him from the open window of the car as she manoeuvred the vehicle under their top balcony where she would protect it from the innocent. The money bags would have to stay in the car – it was far too dangerous to hide the cash in their room. Before revealing everything to Caitlin, Carmen would try to enjoin her in this great venture!

CHAPTER TWENTY-SEVEN

AS SHE BOUNDED up the stairs, Carmen prayed that Caitlin was still out somewhere else, and luck stayed with her. Stripping off her filthy clothes, she dropped them into the washer in the kitchen and ran for a shower. The steaming hot water, pulsating gently against her head, comforted Carmen and conspired to erase the signs of her daring escapade. Raising her sore hand to the shower nozzle, the full force of the hot water flushed the earth from the remaining splinters, soothing the aching, throbbing hand. Soaping and scrubbing with a vengeance, her skin was turning pink when she remembered the unprotected stash outside in the car. What if the car were stolen? Just a few weeks before they had arrived at Club One, a car *had* been stolen and it was a rental! Carmen leapt from the shower, threw a towel around herself, ran across the room leaving wet footprints on the clean white tile, pulled the patio door aside and stepped out onto the balcony. The car was still there.

'It's pretty decent for a rental,' Larry called down to her from the roof. 'Don't worry about it – I'll keep an eye on it for you.'

Carmen came close to dropping her towel. *Damn it!* 'Jesus, Larry, you scared the hell out of me.'

'Sorry about that. Just trying to help out.' *What's spooked her?*

'Yeah, I know, sorry.' Carmen walked back into the condo as Caitlin was opening the front door.

'Geez, what are you doing out there with only a towel to hide your goodies?'

Carmen's nerves were in knots. 'Just checking the car, making certain no one had scratched it. What can I say, I'm obsessive.'

'You were so right about getting out. What a ride! I rode into the wind, into the sun, up Haulover, over and over again. I felt released from the worries of the last week, as though I had a new start. Maybe, we can really leave all of this misery behind us. You were so right, Carmen, we have been lucky. But enough about me, as they say, how were the dogs?'

With three days left of their holiday, Carmen had no time to spend on evasion. 'I didn't go to the dogs.'

'Why not? I thought that was the main reason you wanted the car.'

'I ah…'

'Please no! Tell me you didn't go back for the money. You could not have done that to both of us.'

'It's downstairs in the trunk of the car.' Carmen's voice was flat and she began to feel adrift, slipping away from her better self.

Caitlin sat down, rocking her body back and forth, her head falling into her hands. In a voice ravaged and hoarse, she said, 'I can't believe you did this. You thought so little of our safety that you'd put us at risk again. Look at what you've become,' she said, confronting her friend.

'What I've become? Where do you come off suggesting the worst? What I've become? You're afraid of your own shadow since Derek died. I know who I am; can you say the same? I'm somebody who's made it through the last week, who couldn't find a good reason to leave all that money behind to be found by construction workers or nobody at all. I risked my life to get this money, and now, when we're pretty much in the clear, I'm not about to pack it in and leave it in a hole.'

'Risk is a good word to use, Carmen. That's exactly what you've brought back into our lives. There is no way that money is coming up into this condo as long as I'm here.'

'Don't you even want to hear about my plan for the cash?'

'No, I don't.'

'We've been friends for almost three years, and during that time, I have always been there for you. You have no idea how many times I thought of walking away when you began another story of you and Derek, but I didn't. You were my friend and you needed me. You never even stopped to realize you had more good years with him than I've had with any man. You were lucky and you were still feeling sorry for yourself. And now you're sanctimonious and self-righteous. Give me a break!'

'I care about you, Carmen, but I can't support you with this. With all we've been through, I've discovered I want to live, and you're asking me to risk my life again.'

'I need your help now. All you have to do is help me hide the money in safety deposit boxes, in four different banks. How risky is that?'

'Just having the cash in our rental is a risk. Do you even know where to find at least four banks?'

Carmen shivered when she thought of Larry and the way he was looking at the car, but put him out of her thoughts. 'I can locate two immediately. Do you want me to tell you how close they are?'

'Have you even thought of the paper trail?'

'Who cares about a trail? The banks won't know what we're leaving in the boxes. Don't go ballistic again, but I've rented the car for three days, enough time to find banks and hide the cash. To pay for the rental, I'm using some of the cash. I grabbed a handful before I came back here. I also plan on taking ninety-five hundred home with me. I think you should do the same. Anything under ten thousand, you can take through customs.'

'If you have this thing so well planned, why do you need me?'

Carmen proffered her palm – even after the shower, small red welts were everywhere.

'You hurt yourself digging for the money, right?'

'Can't get anything by you,' Carmen smiled. 'Would you help me to get the splinters out?'

'I have just the thing. My mother gave me a little sewing kit for emergencies. This qualifies.'

'Before we start, I just want to check the car.'

'You're going to drive yourself nuts. Put some clothes on first.'

The second Carmen pulled at the patio door, Larry called down from another side of the roof. 'Not to worry, little lady, I've kept an eye on it for you.'

This guy is becoming another Michel. I preferred him as a stalker. 'Thanks. I just don't want the construction guy with the red truck who lives downstairs to back up and dent the car like he's done to five others. At least, that's what Michel has told me.'

'Your worries are over – he left three days ago for another job site.'

'All right then, thanks.' When she walked back into the room, Caitlin was sitting on the couch with a wet facecloth, needle in hand. 'Be gentle with me.'

'You don't deserve it,' Caitlin said, smiling just a little. 'Let's get these splinters out!'

Carmen offered her hand, and Caitlin went to work

with her needle. 'I'll have to break the skin in most of them because they're lodged deep under it. I'll need my small scissors and tweezers.'

'Go easy.'

'Yeah, yeah.' Caitlin cut small tucks of skin which bled. She daubed the blood with the facecloth and dug with her needle for each of the eleven splinters, telling Carm to take a deep breath each time she cut or dug. The work took almost an hour, but at the end of it, Carmen could close her fist without jabbing pain. 'Go run water over the palm and clean off the blood. You'll live, and I don't know if that's a good thing.'

'Listen,' Carm said, 'a little excitement is good – it'll clean out the heart valves.'

'I wish it had wiped the money from your memory.'

'In your dreams!'

During the night, Carmen's hand pulled and twitched. The money bags pulled at the back of her brain. Six or seven times, she rose from her bed and drew the verticals aside to peek out at the car. When she couldn't see it from the front window, the air in her lungs blocked. Tip-toeing to the patio door, she pushed it open as slowly and as quietly as she could, just enough to squeeze her head out the window.

'I can't take this anymore,' Caitlin groaned. 'You're up every goddamn hour! Why don't you sleep in the car? Get back to bed and stay there. If you get up one more time, I'm kicking you out of the room! Keep the car keys by your bed.'

Carmen lay on the bed for the last few hours of the night, but her bones and her hand ached from lack of sleep. *If only I were alone, I'd have the cash up here with me!* Carmen began to sigh to relieve her knotted nerves.

'Sigh one more time and you're out of here too. Let me get some sleep, please!'

'I'm trying.'

'Try harder.'

The next morning, which in fact was only a few hours later, the C's lay exhausted on their beds. In the wakeful hours, Caitlin had come to a decision. 'Before you rush out to check the car, I have something I want to say.'

'Shoot.'

'I will drive the car for you when you deposit the money at different banks, but I don't want any of it. It's all yours. I also have some conditions. Today, I want you to leave the car here and bus it alone looking for banks because I don't want to worry about you and the money from minute to minute. I'll stay here with the car. I have a safety deposit box back home and I just remembered you have to have an account in the bank to allow them to debit the account for the price of the box. I don't know if you can pay up front without an account. You also have to furnish two pieces of ID, one a photo ID. Whether you like it or not, you'll be leaving quite a paper trail. This isn't Switzerland. I'm not babysitting the car either, Carmen – I'll check it from time to time. That's the extent of my help on this front.'

'Sounds fair enough. If this works out, you can always change your mind about the money. You might feel differently a few months from now.'

'I won't.'

CHAPTER TWENTY-EIGHT

THE MORNING WAS overcast. Banks of fog swept in from the ocean and met northerly gusts strong enough to blow lounge chairs across wooden decks and threaten banners on storefronts. The surf was dull and dark, dotted with whitecaps. Hilda's apartment was three miles west of the ocean, and she peered out at the morning through verticals onto wet grey pavement and a small patch of crab grass. Despite its distance from the surf, gulls had landed on nearby balconies. They eyed Hilda suspiciously as she looked out and flew from their perches with derisive squawks when she stepped onto her balcony.

Hilda knew the sun was nestling quietly behind the bad weather and, with the sway it held in this state, could burst through the clouds at any moment. She decided on her white Converse tennis shoes – comfort was the order of the day. A brown linen skirt and white blouse would do just fine. Hilda tied her long grey hair into a single knot that she accomplished in one fluid, familiar motion, before securing it with a silver clasp. Once her pets were taken care of, Hilda drove her Toyota to Sheldon's Pharmacy because she had decided on breakfast there. Over the years, she and some friends who worked at the store would meet at the pharmacy for Sheldon's special, poached eggs on toast with Canadian bacon, Sheldon's home fries, a slice of fresh pineapple and coffee. Old man Sheldon had worked his own place until he was eighty-seven. Hilda knew him well, but that was a few years back. A young Cuban family had bought the place, but had kept the special and done well with it. Today, Hilda knew that it wasn't only the thought of breakfast that drew her here.

Because she was alone, a booth was out of the question. She chose a counter seat as close to the phones as possible. Hilda wanted to see how many customers or workers walked to the back of the store and how often. Not many, she discovered. She needed her privacy. Ordering the special, she tried to relax, but could not. Her impending phone call upset the inner tenor of the life she had worked so hard to maintain. When her food arrived, she could manage only the slice of pineapple and one piece of bacon. Her son's advice rang in her ears, accusatorily. She was one of those remarkable people: a principled individual. Her reward over the years was no regret. She wondered now if she was about to enter the common sandlot of self-questioning and doubt.

In the next few minutes, if she made her call, Hilda would cross a line. Humans tended to clutter, like tourists on the beach – that's why Hilda had always been best on her own. Emotional decisions were trouble with a capital 'T'. Ten minutes later, when Hilda looked at her poached eggs, they were deflated and soggy. Both had lost the innocence Hilda felt she saw in them. The other piece of bacon had shrivelled. Pushing her plate away, Hilda reached into her purse for a white, plastic change bag and the phone number she had found this morning. Outside, the overcast sky was thickening. With one hand on the counter, Hilda pushed herself slowly off the stool. Quickly, she grabbed the counter with both hands, beset with a bone-weary fatigue. Yet, she straightened up, turned and walked to the back of the store. The plight of the women had caught Hilda on their very first cast. *Help us please!* The booth was empty, and she walked towards it on feet she could not really feel.

'Metro-Dade Precinct, how can I be of assistance?'

Hilda's eyes were hooded, her voice controlled. 'I'd like to speak to Detective Ramirez who was in charge of the auto accident that took the life of Harris Chalmer.'

'Today is Sunday, ma'am. He's not working. May I take your number – I'll have him call you first thing tomorrow morning.'

'I'd rather not leave my number. Is there no way you can reach him? It's important that I speak with him today.'

'Please hold, ma'am. I'll see if I can reach him at home.'

Hilda's fingers tapped the window of the booth, and from deep in her throat, she emitted a small growl. What was she doing here? It certainly was not curiosity – it was something much more dangerous. Personal involvement at personal risk.

'I have Detective Ramirez on the line. Please hold.'

'Ramirez.' The voice was gruff and all-business or simply a man disturbed on his day off.

Hilda did not recognize her own voice when she heard it. 'Detective, I may have pertinent information surrounding the death of Harris Chalmer...' Hilda described the two young women whom she had hidden, Harris and his crony's frantic search for them, Bobby's approach and the mention of a yellow bag after Harris Chalmer's death and her fear for the women and for herself. She did not pause for questions – she spoke looking at her watch. She had less than two minutes before the call was traced. Perspiration dripped onto the under-sleeves of her blouse.

'Is there any way you can come into the precinct? I can send a car for you.'

She could see the spectre of her son now, just beyond the door, telling her to cut the conversation. 'No, I can't, detective. You have the information now; that's all I dare contribute.'

'Ma'am, I know a Detective Garderella who would be very interested to hear what you have to say. Please don't hang up. I'll give you her number. Please think about calling.' As soon as he had given the woman the number, the line went dead.

Hilda made a beeline for the front door of the pharmacy and collapsed against the cement wall outside, breathing deeply, inhaling the stench of her own perspiration. *Ryan was right. Nothing is simple.* Hilda crushed Garderella's number in her fist and dropped it into her purse, looked up and down Harding Avenue for patrol cars and walked quickly past the Rolling Pin Bakery without even a nod. When she got into her car, she folded herself into the front seat and sat. She was far too rattled to drive. Once she had begun to talk, nerves had blocked out what she was saying. Sitting alone, she tried to remember if she had said anything that would lead the police to Neiman Marcus or worse.

When Hilda was safely back in her apartment, she did something she scolded her two best friends for doing. She got into her bed and pulled up the covers. Tabs and Sandy, who whined with the effort, managed to climb up onto the bed with her, but Hilda nudged her loved ones off. *It's close in here.* She began to kick at the blankets and fuss with her pillows. Her throat was suddenly constricted and she began a dry hack that would not let up. Hilda reached for water she kept by the side of her bed, but the cough continued unabated. Garderella's number, crumpled in her purse, might as well have been a pea under her mattress or a stone in her sneaker. Rain fell outside with such force, that

Hilda could feel its fingers drumming on her window panes.

🌴

After the call from the pharmacy, Ramirez wasted no time reaching Garderella. News of a yellow bag was the fire starter she had been looking for.

When her cell rang, she was in a Payless shoe store, trying to convince her eight year old that good sneakers didn't use labels. 'Yes?'

'Ramirez here. Heard you caught the frying pan case.'

'A real tough one. When I got to the scene, the old man was blubbering. "None of this had to happen. She should have made me the omelette. I'm still hungry." Not a flicker of guilt.'

'I have news of one of your phantom yellow bags. Thought you'd want to hear.'

'You have my right ear. I have to save the other one for my son Jamie who looks about ready to have it out with his sister. He's not a happy camper in his no-name sneakers.' Once she heard the story, Garderella sighed with a measure of relief. 'I was beginning to wonder about those bags myself. Think she'll call me?'

'Hard to say. What she told me was well ordered and rehearsed. Hasn't much to add I don't feel. Spooked as well. Didn't sound like a young woman, so she has more reason for concern. At least, that's my take on it.'

'Where was she calling from?'

'A phone booth at a Sheldon's Pharmacy – located on Harding Avenue, one block south of the Bal Harbour Shops. Don't know if the store she works at is on the Harding strip or at the mall. I'm off to visit family. The only thought I can offer is to get down to the pharmacy to see if anyone remembers a woman in the booth this morning. Good luck!'

'Thanks for the call.' Garderella looked over at her kids. Jamie was trying to stomp on his sister's foot – she was running around the salesman to avoid her brother. Garderella knew she could not dump the kids on her mother. Sunday was her day off. Checking her purse, she saw that she had money enough for ice cream to distract them while she questioned the staff at Sheldon's. 'All right you two, we're out of here!'

'Mom, this isn't the way home. Are we lost?'

'No, we're not. I thought you both might like ice cream or something.'

'Cool.'

Unfortunately, the drive to Sheldon's took almost half an hour, and it led nowhere. No one remembered anyone in the phone booth, middle aged or older. Garderella did manage three cones from the lunch counter, but the young Cuban behind the counter said breakfast was a busy time. Serving and clearing dishes, she had no time to be bothered with faces. Sorry.

Garderella thought of the seven files on her desk, of Jamie and Ashley, of her mother and herself. She saw now that she might have to close this case not knowing if the yellow bag or bags existed. It wasn't much, but the pie was only so big. She fought her disappointment as she drove home, glancing in the rear-view mirror from time to time at two sticky little faces.

🌴

Although Hilda was safely in her bed, she was beset with a grinding anxiety. Throwing her blankets aside, she got out of bed. Her skin ruffled with a chill she felt deep in her core although it was above seventy in the apartment. Tabs and Sandy, still smarting from her rebuke, sat together in the doorway. For the moment, Hilda was blank on the issue of calling Garderella, but not for long. *Who will take care of you two if something happens to me? Ryan and Peter often joke that they chose children over pets, a decision they question on a daily basis. You two over there could be orphans.* Home was her sanctuary; now that too was off-balance. Tabs and Sandy were family, sources of continuing comfort. Hilda could not put their lives at risk. This sudden caution forced her to confront the situation and reach a decision. *I can't call this Garderella. The fact is that I've told Detective Ramirez all I know. Another call is foolhardy, as dangerous as a stroke. I'll get back to the hiccups and burps and leave the more serious stuff to the police.* Hilda could not work against the grain of common sense, especially when it came packaged with a wagging tail and a quiet purr!

CHAPTER TWENTY-NINE

FROM THE ROOF, Larry followed Caitlin as she walked to the car trying both doors before she headed for the beach. He was pretty much finished with the front trim. He was gathering the towel he kneeled on and his other stuff, ready to move to the right side of the condo when he saw her. He thought it best not to call down. Carmen had not appreciated the attention. 'Relax,' he wanted to call down. 'It's only a sub-compact. Chill out! The car's not gold-plated.'

When he remembered he did not even own a car, Larry reined himself in and thought of Toothbrush. There was no easy word for it; Larry felt sad for his friend. Nothing in Miami ever stayed the way it was for long. The Bar had withstood two modifications over its twenty-five years but it might not survive the third. In its heyday, it was still a joint, but The Bar fit in well with Mitch's Steak House, the corner fruit store, the Jewish bakery, the Sweet Spot and the Chinese restaurant. All brought business its way. When Mitch's closed down, the neighbourhood collapsed with it. Somehow, the drunks hung on like spiders. On his visit back a couple of days ago, Larry saw that the 'hood was turning trendy, with a capital 'T'. An arts festival had taken up four blocks the day he visited Toothbrush. The familiar drinking hole had been reduced to a wart on the unblemished face of a new block. No one had even offered to buy Toothbrush out – they were hoping the old man would disappear. But Toothbrush was tough.

Larry got back to his work because feeling sad never helped anyone.

Carmen had walked the two or three blocks to 163rd Street where she stood waiting for the 'H' bus. Forty minutes later, she was still standing at the bus stop. *I should have realized it's Sunday – I could be here another forty minutes! It would have been so much easier with the car. I shouldn't have given in to Caitlin. What was the point? She's not even sitting on the car.* Forty-four minutes to the second, an 'H' made a left turn off Collins to 163rd and picked her up. She planned to look for banks along either side of this street and get off on Biscayne on her way back. It was safest to find banks some distance from Club One. *Damn it, they're closed today; all I'll be able to do today is copy addresses. I'll have to call each of the banks tomorrow morning to see if I can pay up front for a year. Holidays destroy my sense of time.*

Finding three banks was easy, but it entailed more walking than Carmen wanted to do. Her feet began to perspire and her sneakers began to pinch. She should have worn socks; she'd have blisters for sure. Carmen had to get off the bus to copy each address. Locating the last one on Biscayne Boulevard took well over an hour because she decided to walk north along the boulevard. One mile later, past the long block of boat sales, she came upon a swanky mall with a bank. The bus back along Biscayne was just as slow to appear as the 'H' had been on 163rd. A surge of panic erupted in her stomach when she thought of the bags unprotected in the rental car. Her need to get back and watch over the money itched like a flea bite.

Once she reached Collins, she ran the rest of the way home and was disappointed to find that Caitlin was nowhere in sight. Carmen thought greed was conta-gious, but, apparently, Caitlin was immune to it. The car was still where she had left it. Caitlin had the keys. Carmen took the stairs two at a time, unlocked the front door and rushed into the room looking to see if she had left them in the room. Caitlin had not even hidden the keys. Carmen grabbed them from the kitchen table and ran back down the stairs. Once she was back outside, Carm tried to walk casually to the car. Both doors were still locked – she did not dare try the trunk, but she tugged at it with her hand as she walked by. It was secure. She did not want anyone to spot the bags. Tomorrow morning, they'd turn down a quiet road and transfer the bags to the back seat. You couldn't very well drive up to a bank, open your trunk and unload huge hunks of cash. Yet, she could duck into the back seat and unload some of it into the bags she had bought on 163rd Street. That was the plan. In the meantime, Carmen went back upstairs and sat in the sun on the balcony, guarding the money bags.

An hour later, Caitlin came back to the room and saw her friend on the balcony. 'Hi. I walked to Publix and brought you back two challah rolls. You aren't going to stay out there all day, are you? The car is locked – nothing will happen to it.'

'I want to make sure nothing does. Thanks for the rolls. Would you butter them for me and give me my banana drink? I don't care if you think I'm an idiot. I can't relax until the money is safely stored in banks.'

'This is your show, Carm. Apart from driving you around tomorrow, I want nothing to do with the car or what's in it.'

'Got it! How are the buns coming along? I'm starving! I have the addresses and I'll make the calls tomorrow morning.'

'What time do you want to leave here?'

'Is ten-thirty or eleven all right with you?'

'It's fine. Here's your lunch with a coconut donut. See you later,' Caitlin waved as she left the room.

Carmen wished that Caitlin was with her in this vigil, but she realized she had made the decision to go for the money without including her. Caitlin was not a person one could easily finesse. It was after two already. In twenty hours from now, the money would be safe. Carmen inhaled her lunch and had just settled back when a vicious cramp knotted her right calf with such pain that she shrieked. Jumping to her feet, she forced her body weight to her right foot, while bending and massaging the calf. 'Christ, it has to be nerves!' She worked at the calf with both hands and saw raw blisters on both heels.'

'Is that you, Carmen? Are you all right?' Larry called down.

'It's nothing, a cramp.' Despite her flippancy, her voice was tight.

'Grab a pinch of salt and you'll be fine.'

'Thanks.' *Get out of my face and concentrate on painting! Get your own life!* What was left of the afternoon passed slowly. Carmen counted cars and randomly chose ones she'd like to own. With the money, she planned to buy herself a yellow Beemer, if everything worked out. Before the BMW, she'd pay off her credit cards.

Caitlin was angry and disappointed with her. Carmen knew those emotions had kept her friend from coming up to the balcony to keep her company. But she consoled herself by remembering that half the people with money did not come by all of it honestly. Look at what bootlegging supposedly did for the Kennedys of Massachusetts! The Bronfmans of Montreal made them rich. Despite her rationalization, Carmen felt as lonely as Midas, and as wealthy.

Caitlin joined her around five. 'What are you considering for supper?' she called through the screen.

'Pizza Hut.'

'Fine by me. I'll pick up a Caesar salad at the same
time. I'm hungry – I'll go after I shower. I gather you're
glued to the balcony.'

'Till bedtime. This time tomorrow...'

'You hope.'

Bobby had decided to take a chance himself concerning the meeting with his men at seven. He called
Ian, who answered immediately. 'Hi, I'm really sick,
man. Something I ate in the caf at lunch, probably the
grouper.' Bobby put a tired strain in his voice and began
to whisper. 'I can't even think of getting up off the
damn couch – I feel I have snakes in my stomach.'

'Call a doctor.'

'If it gets worse, I will.' Bobby pulled a fake wretch.
'Jesus, just a sec. Oh man, this is bad. There is no way I
can make that meeting tonight. I'm sweating like a pig.'

'What do you need? I can come over.'

Bobby coughed loudly. 'I need you to take care of
things for me tonight. I trust you, Ian. You're the one
guy I feel I can rely on. The call to the cops is a thing
of the past. What Harris thought is of no significance
now. I need you – can you cover for me? We have to
keep that shit moving.'

Ian did not waste his second chance on life – in the
past, he would have folded in on himself. 'Bobby, I'll
take care of things tonight, but as soon as the shipment
is sold though, I'm out. We're not making a cent out of
this sell-off and taking all the chances. We're risking
our lives, and for what? To end up like Harris? He was

wiped out in seconds and, except for his parents, none of us gave a shit. I want something more for my life.'

Bobby's performance was suddenly not quite such a fake. 'Don't think you're the only one with that idea. But, if we don't get the drug money earned and back fast, we might as well choose our own boxes! We're on this job to save our tails. Let's take care of first things first. At the meeting, take down sales numbers – set goals for the week. Don't bother me tonight, let me die in peace here. Call me in the morning before class.'

'Done. Feel better.'

Strange how things turned out, Bobby thought. Ian had gone from probable snitch to second-in-command. He had noticed Ian was not slouching any longer. Most of all, he was trustworthy. Harris' death had given Ian a backbone. Twists and turns – that's what life was about. Bobby snagged a bag of Doritos from the pantry, Snapple from the fridge, flopped down in the family room and ate quickly. Before he left, he changed, added gel and grabbed two water bottles. As he rode along Collins, he recalled the night they had chased the women. *We were so close. Where the hell did they get to?* He parked in front of the Einstein Bros. bagel shop, not far from Club One. He had charted his route and began his search at the Newport Hotel because the women had run down to the beach that night by the Newport pier. His spiel, prepared and well articulated, had no effect on the Cuban receptionist. In fact, the only noise in the lobby came from the loud, bright, yellow and green lovebirds caged in the middle of the large room.

As soon as the receptionist realized Bobby was not looking for accommodation, he lost interest. 'Sir, we have charters and small groups mostly. Tonight, we have seven hundred and forty-one guests. Who would remember two women?' This Cuban stud, whose black hair was slicked down so hard on his head it resembled shoe polish, saw the rich brat in Bobby and could not have cared less what he was after.

When a couple of fifties appeared in Bobby's hand, there were no takers.

'I cannot help you, sir. Excuse me now, there are people behind you.' The stud might have gone for the cash, but not when the manager was looking over at the front desk from her side office.

Idiots! No wonder this is the best they can do. Bobby did not hold out much hope for the exclusive condominium next door. There, he was lectured on the privacy code. Next door was a vacant lot. Beside it, Club One. Normally, when there were vacancies, the receptionist worked until eight. When there were none, Kathy locked up at six. Tonight, the place was locked. Depression and anger began to weigh uncomfortably on Bobby's gut. His calculations had proffered a simple plan – his money for information. Rejection had never been part of his self-contained little world.

Bobby held out hope for The Desert Inn, much of it showing signs of disrepair. These women probably did not have money for the Newport or Sandy Point; The Desert Inn was more in keeping with their profile. Bobby figured the night receptionist correctly and had his fifties out as he questioned the fifty-something male.

Inching his fingers across the desk towards the money, he tried his best to earn the cash. 'What did they look like again? Are they French?'

'What does that matter?'

'Just about everybody here is. I could ask around for you. I know a few of the guys who work around here.'

'What you're saying is they're not here, right?'

'Not now, yeah, that's right. But they might register today, who knows?'

When Bobby folded his bills, needy eyes followed the money into his slacks' pocket. The Monaco was a bust. Bobby didn't bother with Trump's new place. Another condo was locked. What if the women had run along the beach and then dashed across the street? Theory and practice! Why was there so little correlation? He went as far north as the Thunderbird before turning back. Bobby viciously kicked a few stones along the sidewalk. Maybe he should not have skipped tonight's meeting. Just below his rib cage, a sudden tightness caused him to swallow quickly.

Raoul opened the front door of Club One as Bobby was about to pass the condo. *Give him a try!* Raoul greeted Bobby, thinking he was a possible renter. José would be pleased if he brought in a new customer after hours. Bobby knew some Spanish and took full advantage. '*Estoy aqui para buscar dos amigas que conocí en South Beach. Las dos son muy bonitas, una es Italiana y tiene el pelo negro. Me pregunto si ellas viven aquí para invitarlas a tomar un trago.*'

A spark of recognition flashed across Raoul's eyes when he mentioned how pretty the women were. Indecision worried his eye pouches before he told Bobby he couldn't help him. But that did not matter a whit. Bobby's heart was hammering. *Gotcha! And it didn't cost me a cent!*

CHAPTER THIRTY

HE HAD FOUND the women and they were still at Club One. Bobby sailed through the air back to his Navigator, jumped into it, slapping his thighs and singing Ricky Martin's '*She bangs, she bangs…*' off key. Club One was a small place; he would have no trouble staking it out. 'Wow!' he shouted, thumping on the steering wheel. Easing his vehicle out of the parking lot, he drove the single block it took to find another place beside Rascal House that gave him a clear vantage point of all goings-on at the condo. Just as quickly as he had burst into celebration, Bobby settled down. He hated waiting and he wished he could boast to the gang, but that was out of the question. He thought of calling the boss but nixed the idea, because the money rightfully belonged to him and the boys. Furthermore, Bobby had no intention of sharing any of it with anyone. He began his stake-out a little after eight with his water bottles on the seat beside him. On his BlackBerry, he began to calculate the odds of the women going out again tonight; they were slim to none.

The C's had finished with the 'hut' and soft drinks. Reluctantly, Carmen had agreed to walk along the beach to the Newport and back. She hated to leave the car, but Caitlin was helping her out tomorrow and she could not easily refuse to go for a walk. Both women were back at their condo and ready for *The Sopranos* by nine. Carmen looked out the front window – the car was still there. She failed to notice the grey Navigator or Bobby's eyes that were glued to the front door. Bobby did not see them. A guy, even a smart one, could not catch everything. Carmen would have gone out on the balcony but she was leery of Caitlin reneging on tomorrow's work, so she settled for a window check. Bobby and the women were less than three hundred feet apart.

Bobby counted eleven people in and out of the condo, but his odds were proving true. The women were a no-show. Most of the people here were old, he noted, but he saw a family, two girls and a boy, run ahead of their parents to the front door. Bobby wished he could follow this young group into the condo and ask around. The door closed quickly behind the family, and he abandoned that idea. What if he had misunderstood Raoul's reaction? Had he read something that wasn't there? Maybe he should call Ian and see how things had gone. 'It's me. Just checking in,' he said in a sickly voice.

'The meeting went pretty well. We didn't reach our quota, but I had to admit myself it was a slow week. I emphasized what you told them at the last meeting. Next assignment, if they worked well with this one, they could each make five grand a week. Keeners, all of them, and they said they'd double their efforts in the next seven days. How are you feeling?'

'Not bad enough for a doctor, not good enough to get off the couch.'

'Feel better. I want to crunch some numbers tonight and be rid of this stuff as quickly as I can.'

'I'll try for the afternoon class tomorrow – see you then. Ian, remember to destroy any hard copy. No paper trails.'

'Got it.'

Somewhere after ten, Bobby was antsy and hungry. Should he take a chance and run to Rascal House for take-out and perhaps miss the women? He wished there was someone he could have trusted, really trusted. He had better not leave his post, not when he was so close. At least he had water – fasting was good for the waistline.

Caitlin remembered that she had not double-checked to see that Raoul had locked her bike up in the cabana with Larry. 'I won't be long,' she called back to Carmen.

Long enough for Carmen to go out on the balcony to have a good long look at the car. Long enough to cause a major celebration on the other side of Collins.

'Holy Shit! That's one of them! HOLY SHIT!!!' From Ian's description, Bobby recognized the dark one, standing *as pretty as you please* up there on that balcony. He jumped so high on his bucket seat that he hit his head on the roof of the vehicle, but he was too happy to curse. 'I did it, I DID IT! If only Harris were here! That very first night we all walked right by that condo – we were so close.' It wasn't really Harris that Bobby missed. It was his approval.

Bobby forgot about the salt that lay in his gut like a stone, forgot about his dry throat. He'd save the second water bottle. When the lights went out in the corner condo, Bobby squinted up at the window, riveted. The distance between them lay like a live grenade. As the hours passed, some of that high voltage faded into fatigue. Should he sleep? That was not a good idea. *I can't lose sight of them, not now. Not 'till I have the money. Shit, it's only two o'clock.* A little after three, Bobby noticed the parking sign. *No Overnight Parking – Cars will be towed at the owner's expense.* Underneath the printing was the number of the towing service. His was the only vehicle in the parking lot. Around that time, his back began to ache; his buttocks felt like sand. Now, what should he do? He could not run the risk of a tow truck or a ticket.

Bobby showered twice a day, but at this moment, his body was grimy, and the gel on his hair felt like a clamp on his head. He jumped from the SUV and ran the few feet to the street, looking back at the darkened room on the corner of the condo twice as he ran. There was no overnight parking on the street either. Well, he couldn't stay where he was. He ran across the street to scout out the parking at The Desert Inn and Club One. In both places there were prominently placed white signs – *Private parking – Unauthorized cars will be towed at the owner's expense*. Why was everything complicated? He was not about to leave the women; that was out of the question.

He ran back across the street, started up the car, drove out of the lot, turned left on Collins for a couple hundred feet, made a U-turn north on Collins and eased his car into the parking lot of The Desert Inn, beside Club One. He was less than a hundred feet from the condo – he could almost reach up and touch the second-storey balcony. Harris would have climbed up onto the balcony, broken the patio window or at least part of it and rushed the women. Bobby wasn't Harris. What if the money wasn't there? He knew he would have vetoed that assault plan. Should he try to catch a few hours sleep? Not a good move. He reclined the front seat as far back as it would go, but that seemed to concentrate all his weight on his aching bum. He brought the seat back up and began to shift his weight from one hip to the other. Then he leaned over and rested his head on the leather steering wheel. A knock on the driver's window and a white beam of light sent Bobby's leg into the dash and he swore with pain and fright.

'Excuse me, you can't park here.' The watchman was about Bobby's age. He wore faded blue jeans, a white shirt rolled at the sleeves to the elbows and a gold badge. He held his flashlight for effect like a cop, above his right shoulder.

Bobby lowered his electric window. 'Sorry,' he said. 'I know I shouldn't be here, but I had a fight with my girlfriend and she threw me out. My stuff is still in her room; I don't want to wake her up because I'm still hung-up on her. You know what I'm talking about, right? Here's a twenty. Just let me stay for three or four hours, and I'll move the vehicle in the morning before anyone at the Inn is even up.'

'I don't know.'

'Here are two twenties. Gimme a break. No one will even know I was here.'

'You've gotta be out by seven or I call the tow.'

'That's fair. Thanks.' Bobby took deep breaths. At seven, he'd drive back to Rascal House across the street. Any thought of sleep was over. He crawled into the back seat and tried to lie across it to relieve his back. There were two separate seats back there, and a gap between them, so the lie was uneven. Twenty minutes later, mumbling, Bobby crawled back to the front seat, reclined it once again, rubbing his temples. In his weary, tangled thoughts, he squirmed. That he was alone, that there was no one he could really trust for backup, settled on Bobby like a dull ache. He began to stamp his feet because both feet had fallen asleep. He stretched, cleaned the crystal dirt from the corner of his eyes and tried to keep from yawning.

He had a plan for some of the money and he focused on that to stay awake. With his father's formidable connections, and this money, he easily saw himself gnashing on a thirty dollar burger at Prime 112 Steakhouse on lower Ocean Drive where scoring a table could take as long as a month. There was one other place he'd visit before leaving Miami for good. Facts and history were as important as numbers to Bobby. With all his money and looks, Harris had been nothing more than a 'smash and grab' lughead. In a few weeks, South Beach would launch The Club at Casa Casuarina. He wanted membership to this rococo mansion, formerly owned by Versace. That place had history – history and tragedy. Versace had set the fashion world on fire. He had been shot down on the steps of his mansion, not much different than Julius Caesar cut down at the foot of Pompey's statue. Both murdered by people once close to them! He could see himself chilling out at the designer's mosaic pool and dining in private quarters, savouring the heady scene. What could be hipper in the hip-hop scene? P. Diddy in a wing chair beside him, that's what. There was a negative pop-up to this daydream – Bobby was now hungrier and thirstier.

He would have been pleased to know that Carmen was not faring any better in the sleep department. Her mattress was firm and the sheets were clean, but she tossed and punched her pillows at every turn. She longed to get up and stretch and step out onto the balcony, but Caitlin would wake up and walk away from tomorrow's work. She groaned, happy for the white noise of the AC, and reached for her watch. It was only twenty after three. The AC itself was pinching her nerves. Every few minutes, the machine emitted the groan of a small engine starting up. With each strain of that engine, Carmen jumped a little, even with the cover over her head. Chinese torture, Florida style, that's what it was!

For two nights now, her money had lain in the trunk unprotected. Her mind was a muddle of possibilities and apprehension. Thoughts about her moneyed future sprang at her like pop-up menus on her computer. If all went according to plan, should she stay in Miami or go home and come back a few months later? Was there a point in going back to work at all? What would she tell her friends back home? How much money did the bags hold? Could she pay for everything in cash? The new car could wait. Her debts came first. Depositing all that cash was bound to be a problem. Laundering money was something she heard about from gangsters on TV. When she thought of the work involved in 'cleaning' the cash, she was overwhelmed. To calm herself, she began to count the shadows that floated across the ceiling, slim shafts of light darting around like white stilettos, driven by the current of wind from the AC. Something else occurred to her, and she rubbed her palms together. If Caitlin stuck to her word, all that money was hers!

Sometime after five, the pains eased, and Bobby's body felt light, his breathing faint. His head came to rest on his left shoulder. Tense thoughts of Club One faded until there were no thoughts of it at all. Inside the condo, with her legs drawn up into a tent, Carmen succumbed to the spell of Morpheus and forgot about the trunk and the money.

Just before seven, the watchman rapped angrily on Bobby's window. 'You said you'd be out of here. I could lose my job.'

'What the …? All right, all right, I'm gone.' Bobby looked at his watch. 'I have five minutes.'

'The day patrol will call for a tow as soon as he comes across your Navigator. He knows every tenant's car on sight. I'm trying to save you the hassle.'

Bobby shook his head, dropped his face into his hands and rubbed his eyes and his stubble. Bringing the seat to its upright position, he started up the vehicle and drove off the lot, back to his old spot at Rascal House. He had to take a leak, God, did he need to take a leak. He looked up at the room. The verticals were drawn. Bobby jumped from his Navigator and ran to the deli. At the counter he passed thirty dollars to the Cuban behind the glass at the take-out. 'Get me a double toast with peanut butter, double coffee, bottled water, napkins and bring the order out to the grey Navigator in the parking lot. The change is yours.' He made a bee-line to the washroom. In seconds, he was back out on the street. No way would he lose sight of the women at this stage. He waved the young cashier over and grabbed his order. Once he had wolfed down the toast, gagging on the peanut butter, he took his time with the coffee. Dipping the napkins in his water, he tried to clean himself up. His stubble shredded the tissues and Bobby swore, picking small white pieces of paper from his face.

Carmen was wide-eyed by seven as well, jolted into consciousness by the surge of early morning traffic on Collins. The money bags tugged at her nerves. Caitlin was awake, she was sure, but she did not want to take a chance of disturbing her if she was still sleeping. Carmen lay on her mattress, drumming her fingers on its sides. Carmen sighed loudly.

'Relax over there; I'm not moving 'till eight-thirty or later. Don't even think of going out to check the car. I'm sure it's fine. You can't call the banks before ten anyways.'

'I'll leave you in peace.'

'Good.'

CHAPTER THIRTY-ONE

WHEN IAN CALLED, Bobby was gathering the remains of his breakfast, twisting the brown bag into a ball. He jerked, spilling what was left of his coffee on his jeans, leaving them with a brown stain across both legs. *Son of a bitch!* He grabbed his cell. 'What's the problem, Ian?'

'Nothing; you told me to call you in the morning. Are you going to classes today?'

'Had a rotten night. I might show up for the three o'clock like I said yesterday. I'll be at the meeting tonight. See what's what.'

'Today's Monday; it's the one day we don't have one.'

'Right. This goddamn food poisoning has knocked everything out of whack. Thanks for the help yesterday. I gotta let you go – I think I can actually fall asleep.'

'*De nada.*'

Caitlin forced herself to stay in bed until just before nine. They both needed the rest, although Carmen would never admit that fact. As soon as she could, Carm was back on the balcony, guarding her rental and catching the rays. Caitlin opted instead for an early swim; Carmen could make her calls on her own.

When Caitlin reached the edge of the surf, she stood still for a few minutes, allowing curling, rushing waves to wash sand over her feet, splashing her thighs. The ocean was a sea of golden light. Gulls screeched high above, as Caitlin's feet sank into the warm sand and she surrendered to the consolation of its cool embrace. Under the pull of the ocean and the winking horizon, she walked into the surf until white-capped waves crashed against her shoulders. Raising her arms above her head, she dove head-long into it. With sure, power-ful strokes, Caitlin swam to the marker, floated on her back a few feet farther out for a clear view of the sky. Her reprieve was shallow; soon she began to kick fierce-ly until there was a spray of water bursting above her body. She kicked at the water until she was out of breath. Grabbing the marker and breathing hard, she glanced back over her shoulder at Club One. *Can you swim away from a promise?* Reluctantly, and with small knots that began in her calves, Caitlin swam toward shore. Her feet sank once more into the rolling sand at the water's edge as she left the ocean behind. On shore, she stood on sand curled by the tide, staring out at a tanker, silent and quiet. The southeast wind and the early morning sun dried the signs of her brief escape before she headed back up to the room. Her word was important and she rarely broke it.

Already dressed, Carmen was on the phone, sitting at the kitchen table, taking notes. 'I understand. I'll see you this morning, Mr. Hughes. Thank you.' She turned quickly when she heard the door opening. 'Hi! Glad you're back. Great news! I can pay up front for the box. A hundred and fifty a pop. Not cheap, but can one put a price on security? Take a quick shower, and we can begin the final leg of this caper. My fingers are crossed. I am so buzzed! I can't wait to get going. I can't wait to have the money safely stowed away.'

'Have you thought about the danger involved in this?'

'What danger? Have you seen anything of the guys?'

'The fact that we haven't seen them doesn't mean they're not still looking for us.'

'In two days, we're home. All this will be behind us.

Unfortunately, I have to leave the money behind too. But, life isn't perfect, is it?'

'Not if we keep screwing up.'

'I don't want to hear anything negative today. I need to feel positive vibes.'

'I'll go and get changed.'

'Good. I want to get the money out of the car.'

Caitlin showered quickly, dressed and put her cards and cash into the left pocket of her shorts and zippered it. Carmen wore a pale yellow t-shirt, green cotton shorts, sandals and the give-away tourist pouch around her waist. Caitlin stuck to her red shorts and white polo shirt. Neither woman wore a watch in Florida or any jewellery. A flawless tan was important. The sun was strong today, and they grabbed their shades from the wicker table beside the sofa. Carmen's heart was bouncing like a rubber ball as they approached the car. Her temples were wet with perspiration.

'Settle down, Carmen. You're wound tighter than a watch. Last night, I figured out that I'll drive around back of the cycle shop on 163rd Street. I was at the shop the day I was alone at Club One. I noticed there were no second-hand bikes at the back of the store. The place is quiet, and the street behind it is secluded. You can switch the bags safely to the back seat of the car and fill your backpack with bills for your first bank visit. Once you have that money deposited, we'll search for another quiet street and repeat the manoeuvre.'

'Here I thought you were uninvolved.'

'I want this whole thing over with as quickly as possible.'

'You and me both. Oh no! I have to run back to the bathroom.'

From seven to ten, Bobby slouched and smacked his steering wheel with the palm of his hand until there were red welts. He was depressed, and Bobby was never depressed. When he wanted something, he got it. When he planned something, the thing worked. He hated having to depend on others to make the first move. Today, though he was excited he was also pissed, sitting here in his own stench, in wet jeans, waiting for the women to make their first move. He swore often this morning, and his voice rose an octave.

When he spied the women walking out the front door and towards a nondescript car, Bobby was close to an attack of tachycardia. *HOLY SHIT! This is it!* He quickly started up the SUV and the AC. He noted that they were not carrying anything. *Take me to the MONEY!* He'd tail their car; dog them for as long as it took. He was pleased that his gas gauge registered half full and he began to marshal his strategy. Follow them; see what happens. Simple, by the numbers, that's what he wanted. When he saw Carmen run back up to the room, he gasped. *Get back to the car!* As if at his command, Carmen did just that in short order. *All right!*

'You all set?' Caitlin asked nervously, standing beside the driver's front door.

'Believe it!' Carmen was holding the remote. Before depressing it, she purposely walked to the trunk and tried to open it. When the trunk door unlatched, Carmen gasped audibly. 'Caitlin, the trunk's not locked! Oh, my God! Are the doors to the car locked?'

Caitlin tried hers. 'It's locked.' She peered across to the passenger door. 'From here, that one looks locked as well. See if the bags are still there,' Caitlin whispered, walking to the back of the car.

Carmen raised the trunk door about a foot, bent and peered in. 'Oh man, they're still here!' Carmen whistled. 'Thank you, God!' Closing the trunk, her hands stiffened with nervous strain. She pressed the remote,

and the car doors unlocked. She used the remote a second time; the doors locked and she tried the trunk a
second time. It wasn't locked. 'I took for granted the
remote locked everything. The trunk has to be locked
manually.'

'Didn't you check it over the last day and a half?'

'I can't believe this. And, no I didn't. With Larry
perched on the roof like a hawk, I didn't dare go near
the trunk and give him a hint of what was inside.
Doesn't your remote lock your trunk? Mine does.'
Carmen's face was crimson.

'Let it go, Carm. The bags are safe. We have to get
moving.'

Caitlin got into the driver's seat and reached over
and opened the passenger door for Carmen.

'Get that air on! It's an oven in here! Watch out you
don't burn your hands on the wheel. I feel like I'm sitting on a barbecue. I should have moved the car to the
shade. I can't believe I never thought to check the
trunk!' Carmen moaned, shaking her head. 'Thank you,
God, for not letting anyone else find the money. I owe
you big time.'

'All right, already. Concentrate on what you have to
do at the banks.'

Across the street, Bobby wailed, 'The money was in
the trunk! I spent the night beside the cash!' He pounded the steering column so hard he yelped. *She was on the
balcony watching that damn car! I should have figured that
out.*

Caitlin pulled out of the parking lot onto Collins and
repeated the U-turn that Bobby had made a few hours
earlier. Bobby was waiting for them; he pulled in barely four feet behind the tan Neon. Speeders never bothered Caitlin; she was one herself. Tailgaters did. A
touch of anger crossed her shoulders as she saw the soot

grey Navigator on her bumper, its size a menace. From the moment Caitlin looked back at the SUV, she was unnerved. She hoped it would not follow her up 163rd Street. Trying to untie the knots in her stomach, she did not look back at the SUV until she had turned the corner. Had she, she would have noticed that Bobby, sensing his error, had pulled back, permitting another car to elbow in front of his, behind Caitlin.

Hoping for the best, Caitlin did not look back until she stopped at the lights on Biscayne Boulevard. Glancing first across at Carmen, she felt she could smell the greed in her friend. When she looked in her rear-view mirror, she could make out the roof of the Navigator and her hands froze on the wheel.

'Caitlin, the light just turned.'

'O.K.' No way would she alert Carm now, when she wasn't certain of the danger herself. After all, the driver might very well have business unrelated to the bags in their car. When she spotted the auto-parts store on the corner, she knew the cycle shop was in the next small block and she slowed to make her right turn. The silence between the friends was brittle. Caitlin pulled in behind the shop and stopped, but left the car running. 'Get the bags into the back of the car as quickly as you can.'

'You don't have to tell me. I want this over as much if not more than you do.' Carmen opened the back door of the car, ran back, flipped open the trunk, dragged out the first yellow bag and lugged it into the back seat. She worked even faster with the second bag. Caitlin screamed before she so much as touched the brown bags she had bought at the mall.

The grey nose of the Navigator was sniffing around the corner. 'We're being followed! GET BACK IN THE CAR!'

CHAPTER THIRTY-TWO

CAITLIN'S SCREAM PIERCED the air, causing Carmen to hit her knee on the open door before she jumped back into the car. She howled as she pulled the door shut.

Bobby gunned his SUV and it roared straight for their car, sending sand and dirt flying behind it. *I have you now!* Bobby never counted on the C's having the nerve to challenge him. *Jesus, what the hell are you doing?*

Instinctively, Caitlin floored the gas pedal and the Neon jumped like a rabbit off the curb onto the road. Caitlin headed back to 163rd and drove west, adrenalin surging through her body.

Bobby came very close to crashing into the back of the shop. He slammed on his brakes, leaving rubber on the driveway for thirty feet. Two repairmen ran out to see what was happening. 'What the fuck are you doing?' shouted a repairman, enraged when he saw that the SUV was inches from the back wall. He had been working on a Specialized Stumpjumper M4 when he heard the noise. With his only protection an aging cement wall, he knew he might have been killed if Bobby had not stopped in time. He gave Bobby his middle finger and pumped his forearm, too.

Bobby threw the car into reverse, roared backwards, slammed on his breaks once again and sped out of the lot, back to 163rd. *God damn it! That's my money. We spent two years busting our asses for it. You're both going to pay for all this.* He hollered when he saw their car stopped at the next traffic light on 163rd. *Here I come!* He made a right turn and was only two cars behind the

Neon when the light turned. Before the C's could do much of anything but take the light, Bobby had bullied his way in behind them.

'He's right there!' Caitlin shrieked, pointing out the back window. 'I don't even know where I'm going,' she shouted over to Carmen, tears rolling down her cheeks. 'But I know one thing for sure. I'm not stopping for him. He could have a gun or God knows what.' Caitlin sped up and continued west on the Sunny Isles Causeway. Carmen knew enough to say nothing.

With a screech of rubber, Bobby pulled up beside them. His window was down and he was gesturing wildly, pointing like a cop. 'Pull over!'

But Caitlin had no intention of complying. The Neon hopped down a side block, and the Navigator roared after it, a mouse scampering away from a lion. The vehicles hopped and roared up and down main streets and side streets in and around I-95 to the Palmetto Expressway and off it, past roads and directions Caitlin did not recognize. What was strange about the chase was the speed, or rather the lack of it. Bobby and Caitlin both feared being pulled over by the state police. If the Neon were nabbed, the C's ran the risk of a car search, and Bobby knew he would never see his money. If Bobby were stopped, the women escaped with the bags. The cartoon chase went on.

Gas was another problem for both cars. The Neon, it seemed, could hop on indefinitely; the SUV could not. It drank fuel every foot it travelled. As pesky as a chipmunk, the Neon would hop off with all the cash. With cops and gas consumption on their minds, the chase was controlled but jerky, a parody of an 'all or nothing' pursuit. Of course, neither combatant was in a position to see the humour. Bobby was as tight as a steel rod, Caitlin was losing water, what with all those tears, and Carmen was shut up like a clam. With a deadly earnestness, they raced west and south and back east like rats across the maze that is Miami, like bumper cars at an amusement park. All three caught up in a rush of high tension.

Then Bobby made a mistake. As the vehicles drove west in the right lane of State Road 836 approaching a curve near the southbound turnpike ramp, Bobby accelerated, pulled up beside the Neon and feigned broadsiding the car. Caitlin instinctively pulled the car further right. The passenger wheel caught the soft shoulder and snared the other three. In a hail of sand and pebbles, the car was dragged off the state road, spinning three times around one hundred and eighty degrees on the grassy embankment. When the spin stopped, the car slid another ninety feet sideways.

No one had time to suspect that the shoulder was only eight feet wide, half road, half grass – not nearly wide enough for a fast-moving car to suddenly pull onto. There were no guardrails or barriers either. The Neon kept sliding down the hill. Caitlin remembered that in a skid on ice back home, the rule was to pump your brakes. With Carmen's shrill scream filling the small car and Caitlin's foot frozen on the brake pedal, there was no chance to pump anything. Unfortunately, under state standards, when the outside lane is more than thirty-six feet from a water hazard and the slope beside the road is not steep enough, guardrails are not required. The Neon slid approximately ninety feet, past a clump of trees into the lake in front of them where it sank into twenty-six feet of water. The lake had strong currents.

But the car did not sink immediately.

Bobby shouted obscenities as he drove by. Caitlin had often asked Carmen if she thought there were any roads in South Florida that were not crowded. Unhappily for the C's, they had come across just such a road. Apart from Bobby's SUV and a distant car behind him, they were alone on this stretch and curve in the road. But for Bobby, their plunge had gone unnoticed. As soon as he could, he brought his vehicle to a stop, drove slowly off the road, approaching the shoulder with great care. He manoeuvred his vehicle carefully across the embankment and drove back to the clump of trees where he hid his vehicle. But this task took him almost ten full minutes.

A huge splash of water erupted and enveloped the Neon as it dove into the lake. At first, the car gave the impression it was amphibious and it floated like the Love Bug. Under the pressure of the lake's current, it made a few turns, like a coloured top or a young dancer, floating behind the trees and out of sight, but there'd be no applause for the Neon's final, wonderful pirouettes on this watery stage. The seconds seemed long and stretched, buoyant and circular. Then the little car began to sink. Water pushed hard against the windows, crashing back and forth against them, devouring the car with the gnawing determination of a 'gator.

Inside the car, the women froze in a hypnotic lethargy, staring out the window as the water rose to meet it. The car sank, not as quickly as a stone, but more subtly, like a falling leaf in autumn. Caitlin snapped back into the present when she realized the car had electric windows. To give her an idea of the depth, she began to count the seconds it would take for the car to come to rest on the bottom of the lake. For a long minute, water slapped at the windows, but Carmen was as limp as a laundry bag. Caitlin gasped audibly, counted and elbowed her friend. 'We've gotta get out of here if we don't want to drown. Do you hear me, Carmen?' She elbowed Carmen more sharply, and Carm cried out.

Tears streamed down her cheeks into the side of her mouth. 'We're going to die. I've killed us both.' She began to rock back and forth in a wet panic.

The car dropped another four feet.

'Carmen, listen to me. We're not dead yet. I'm not going to drown in this lake, and neither are you. Please listen to me; stop crying. We have to wait 'till the car settles before we can open the doors. The windows are electric, so there's no hope of opening them. We can't try either door before the car is completely submerged. It's something to do with water pressure. Remember we saw that show on TV last year, telling you what to do in case you found yourself in a car in a canal? Are you listening?' Carmen nodded dumbly.

The car fell another two feet.

'When the car hits the bottom of the lake, we have to work together. Lose your sandals. Take off your seatbelt. When the water rises above the windows, we'll be in darkness. Grab the door handle and don't let go. Turn towards the door right now. When I give the signal, take the deepest breath you've ever taken. Gently, push the door open. The water will pour into the car. Using the door handle as a guide, push yourself out of the car. If you can remember, use the door for leverage. Swim towards the light.'

The car fell seven feet more.

'What the hell are you doing, Carmen?'

She was trying to lift a money bag from the back seat.

'You're willing to die for a bag of money? Jesus Christ!'

The car fell another five feet. Water flowed into the car to the level of their seats.

'You'll drown for sure, Carmen, if you try to take the

money with you. You won't have enough oxygen or strength to haul the money from the car and drag it to the surface. It's over! Do you hear me?'

The car bounced onto the muddy bottom of the lake and a grey cloud rose around the little Neon. Darkness entombed the car and the C's.

'This is it, Carmen. We have to go! Let go of the bag, please. Take a few practice breaths.'

Bracing cold water rose to their breasts.

'On the count of three, open your door and swim like hell. I love you, Carmen.'

Caitlin took her last breath, pushed her side door and it opened slowly but easily. Using the door, she pulled herself from the car, raised her arms to her sides and kicked furiously.

Thrashing and kicking, Caitlin burst through the surface of the lake. Gasping, she expelled the air that had saved her and greedily breathed in more. She kicked, keeping afloat, waiting for Carmen. Seconds ticked by. 'That idiot, that God damn idiot!' She threw her head back, took a deep breath and dove back into the lake. Of its own accord, the air expelled from her lungs and she swam back to the surface. She took practice breaths and dove back down. The bright taupe Neon was winking with water currents.

Caitlin swam to the passenger door, eased it open and reached in for Carmen. Like Derek had three years ago, Carmen floated back away from her hand. Caitlin's lungs were burning, bursting. She reached in one more time and caught Carmen's arm. Using the side of the car for leverage, she pulled Carmen from the front seat. Turning her around, Caitlin grabbed her friend under the arms and began the rescue struggle. Tendrils of Carmen's hair floated around her mouth, teasing the air so safely guarded. Small amounts of water found their

way into her lungs. A surge of weariness overtook
Caitlin's legs. Carmen felt rigid. Beset by a torrent of
emotions, Caitlin kicked and flailed her way to the air
above them. Hacking and swimming hard, Caitlin
pulled Carmen to the edge of the lake. Her feet sank in
the rocky, muddy embankment as she dragged Carmen
a few feet out of the water.

There was no time to lose. She turned Carmen onto
her back, pinched her nose shut and began mouth-to-
mouth resuscitation. One breath, two breaths... ten
breaths, eleven breaths, twelve... Then she began CPR,
thankful for the course she'd taken at school. Within a
minute, bone weary, Caitlin fell onto the mud and bits
of grass beside Carmen, exhausted, still panicked,
wheezing loudly.

Carmen's head jerked up and she began to choke,
water spurted from her mouth and she choked again.
Caitlin rose quickly, lifted by adrenalin and hope. She
turned Carmen on her side and patted her back with
force. Carmen choked again, but she was breathing!
She was breathing!

Personally, Bobby did not care whether Carmen
died. But, tactically he did. He'd fare better one-on-one
with Caitlin. When he heard Carmen cough and choke,
he walked out from the cover of the trees, down to the
shore to meet the women who had caused Harris and
him all this trouble. What he saw were not the amazons
he thought he'd encounter. Sprawled against the raw
edge of the lake, wet and muddied from the knees
down, the C's lay like miners rescued from a pit, deflated clay figures. *Half dead* is what Bobby thought and he
was angry. He needed the blonde to go back into the
water for his money. Sure as hell, he himself was not
about to dive into the lake!

Lying on her side, her arm resting across a smooth

rock, Carmen was breathing easier now, coughing only sporadically. Caitlin lay on her back – her eyes were closed. Even miles from the ocean, the air was full of salt. The day had become a scorcher. Back on the highway, the road shimmered with the heat. From a distance, cars seemed to be floating on water. For now, the C's lay quietly, enjoying the cool balm rising from the lake. Caitlin was unusually calm, her breaths now deep and slow. In the eye of this moment, only Derek knew the reason. The scab of guilt had fallen off in the lake as Caitlin pulled her friend to safety. Underneath the scar, the skin was pink, new and as loose as a Miami ocean breeze. *You can let go now, Cait. You can forgive yourself.* Caitlin's body grew light, the grass and mud under her soft as the mercy of redemption.

Bobby was uncertain about his grand entrance. He wanted to sound cold, vindictive, cruel. He wished he had the Glock 9mm that Harris boasted his father owned. But he had nothing but himself, and he did not look much better than the C's. He walked to within a foot of the women, but neither of them stirred. 'Get up both of you! Did you hear me? Get the fuck up!' Bobby shouted louder than he had intended. Little reaction. He stepped into the mud and gave Caitlin's shoulder a rough shove with his foot to get her moving. 'Both of you, get up, for Christ's sake!' His voice, high with fishwife, nasal pitch, had no muscle at all in it.

Caitlin rose and faced Bobby, but not before she had reached for a good-sized rock. Her left foot sank in the mud and she had to steady herself. 'Your money is in the back seat of the car at the bottom of the lake. If you stand at the edge of the right tree, and swim out in a straight line for about twenty feet, you'll find the car directly underneath you under about twenty feet of water.' She added nothing else.

'That's not good enough. You take what doesn't belong to you and you think you're just going to walk away! You think I'm nuts? Dive back into the lake and get it for me. I want my money here, on land. I wanted it a week ago! Do you understand? You have no idea all the trouble you've both caused. But you will if you don't get back into the lake and start diving.'

'Or you'll what?' Caitlin asked. Unafraid, she took one step toward Bobby, and he flinched. 'My friend is not going anywhere near the lake. She's lucky to be alive. I'm not going back in either.' Caitlin turned away and helped Carmen to her feet.

'Don't turn away from me! I'm talking to you.' Bobby's eyes were shiny, and his throat was dry with anger. *Who the hell did these bitches think they were?* Yet, without Harris, he did not know what to do. He had not figured on this. Before he could plan his strategy, the blonde spoke again.

Carmen stood leaning against Caitlin. 'I'm taking my friend out of here,' Caitlin said. 'You can try to stop me, but I'll use this rock if I have to. You have a gang; get them out here to help retrieve the bags. You'd better get it done quickly because I have to report the car. As of now, we're through with this whole thing.'

Bobby's cheeks ballooned with rage that was left hanging in the air as the C's walked away from him. He had a tough time identifying the posture of the woman who had defied him. Cowards and bullies rarely dialogue with courage. Without Harris' muscle, and the gang's numbers behind him, Bobby was not terribly brave or tough. In the end, it did not matter who the women were; the important thing was the money. Bobby was a strong swimmer – he liked solitary sports where he did not have to worry about rating against other guys. In fact, he didn't need the women. Yet, he was not about to let them walk away without it being his idea. 'Get the fuck out of here, fast, or I'll change my mind,' he shouted shrilly, the words shooting from his mouth.

The women did not move fast enough for Bobby. He ran behind and shoved Caitlin to the ground. She got up, without bothering to look back at him, and kept walking away from the lake. Bobby cursed them both. He hated people and their unpredictability. He bent and picked up some stones and threw one hard at Caitlin. It missed her by a couple of feet. Bobby did not want to humiliate himself further so he dropped the others. He needed to start retrieving the bags. He walked over to the edge of the lake on the right side of the trees where Caitlin had directed him. He swore again when he saw the mud. Stripping down to his shorts, he folded his clothes and left them in a small pile on the grass. Slithering through the mud, his arms spread wide for support, almost falling twice, Bobby began to wade into the lake.

CHAPTER THIRTY-THREE

'THROW YOUR ARM across my shoulder,' Caitlin told Carm as she struggled to the highway. 'Can you make it?' Caitlin held her friend at the waist and guided her forward up the incline.

'I'm O.K.,' Carmen answered weakly. 'I didn't sleep last night so I'm tired, but don't worry, I'm up to the walk.' Then she began to cough once more, and Caitlin waited with her until she had stopped.

Since it was no time for a lecture on stupidity, Caitlin made no comment on Carmen's last point. 'Geez, it's easy to lose control and end up in a lake or a ravine. The wet grass might as well have been snow. There was no traction at all on it. I always thought 'losing control' was a major error on the driver's part, but it's only a slight miscalculation. Things happened so fast. We're really lucky to have gotten out of the lake alive! Imagine poor people who can't swim! It's life over for them. Just a little farther, Carm, we're almost at the highway.'

'I don't think I can walk too much more.'

Once they reached the shoulder of the 836, Caitlin told Carmen to sit on the grass while she'd try to flag down a car. Enticing anyone to pick them up wasn't going to be an easy task. The C's resembled two giant, muddy cockroaches or to be kinder, two women who had come out at the wrong end of a mud-wrestling contest. For what seemed longer, though it was only five minutes, seven cars passed them by. The mud on their bodies was drying, and Caitlin dusted herself and peeled off the wetter pieces. Carmen was quiet and nearly asleep sitting cross-legged on the grass like a Native American.

Caitlin decided her thumb was the wrong way to go. For the next vehicle, she stood on the road, waving both arms. Panic was nipping again at the edges of her new-found serenity when the driver of an old, dirty white Ford pick-up slowed down for a better look. The driver pulled onto the shoulder of the road a good ways in front of them. Caitlin and Carmen stayed put when they saw the driver's door open. Caitlin stood in front of Carmen shielding her as a displaced Texan ambled towards them.

His cowboy boots were as muddy as their feet, his jeans as stained, his fingernails caked with dirt. A yellow perspiration stain snaked around his Stetson. His striped shirt was open and blew behind him as he walked. The only thing he was missing was a cigarette hanging from the side of his mouth. Caitlin backed up a few steps as he approached them. Sensing their fear, Zack flashed them one of his Miami smiles. Though he was under forty, his face broke into a harvest of lines and crags, the history of a working past.

'I'd hate to see the other guys,' he laughed. 'What are ya'll doin' up here alone?'

'We're the other guys,' Caitlin admitted. 'We're trying to get back to Collins. Our car went off the road and into the lake, but we were able to make it to safety. We had no cell.'

'Are you hurt?' he asked, a genuine concern opening crow's feet at the corners of his eyes.

'Just tired and dirty and in need of a shower.'

'What about your friend? The quiet one.'

'Almost didn't make it. Took in some water.'

'No kidding! Well, I'm heading for I-95, I can take you to that point.'

'That'd be great.' Carmen unzipped the pocket of her shorts and pulled out two wet bills. 'I have thirty dollars left. If I give you twenty for the gas, is there any chance you'd take us back to Collins?'

Caitlin's hair was almost dry and she was blushing and vulnerable, and Zack wasn't a strong man where women were concerned. 'I can't take your last twenty.'

'Yes, you can. I saw the gas prices, and you'd be saving us a bus wait. That's more than worth a twenty. We can sit in the back of your pick-up. That way we won't wreck your seats.'

'What're your names?'

'I'm Caitlin; Carmen's behind me.' Carmen gave a little wave.

'Zack,' he said, extending a hand. 'My father read his Bible a lot and he liked the name Zechariah. When you see what's left of my seats, you'll know a little mud is the least of their problems. Let me help your friend.' He walked around Caitlin and before she could say anything, scooped Carmen up in his arms. He carried her back to his pick-up.

Zack was right about his seats. Stuffing from both was bursting through torn covers. Pieces of the vinyl on the steering wheel had worn away and were hanging in shreds. The shift had no knob – their door had no inside handles for the windows or for the door itself. 'This baby's been to hell and back, but I can take any engine apart, and nasty as she is, my baby's still got heart with kick. Don't worry,' Zack said as Caitlin saw the door. 'They don't lock. Reach out the window and use the escape handle for quick exits. But you won't need one,' he laughed, and Caitlin thought he appeared boyish. 'I'm harmless. Always was.'

When they set out, Carmen sat between them, and Caitlin sat with her arm out the window on the handle.

🌴

Wading along the muddy bottom of the lake, Bobby walked out in a straight line. *How the hell can this water be so cold when it's eighty-five degrees?* The hair on his arms rose up like small nails and he hugged himself, massaging both arms because he was cold. The lake was live and fed into a river before the water found its way to the ocean. Bobby worked hard to keep his balance against the currents. He swam out in the direction Caitlin had advised, took two deep breaths and dove. Keeping one arm straight for protection he swam strongly toward the bottom. His left hand hit the back bumper before he saw the car. Using the handle, he pulled himself around to the side, opened the passenger door and felt his way inside the car. He yanked the first bag to the front seat, then the second. *Damn it, the bags are heavy! They've both taken water.* He swam back to the surface.

He floated for a full minute before breathing deeply and diving a second time. He knew it was sixty seconds of rest because he checked his Rolex; Bobby checked everything. The watch, a twenty thousand dollar job, had been a gift for his twenty-first birthday. He never took it off, not even in the shower. On this dive, he came down on the roof of the car, swam to the side and opened the door slowly once more. Reaching in for the first bag, he lugged it out of the car and began a more fervid swim with wicked kicks to the surface, every sinew of hairless chest rapt with anticipation. He shivered with excitement and with the cold water. With the weight of the bag, he did not burst through the water, but he reached the surface, writhing and straining.

With the first yellow bag on his stomach, he back-stroked to the edge of the lake. God, he was tired! He

swayed and stumbled through the five or six feet of
stones and mud to the embankment, heaving the bag
another four feet above the waterline. He would have
sat and rested, but with wet mud and slippery grass all
around him, there was no place for respite. He turned
back and waded into the lake. Lining himself up, after
inhaling a deep breath, he dove again for the second
bag. His legs protested and began to knot with cramps.
He was not going to end up with jack shit, that much he
knew, so he began kicking furiously, ignoring the sharp,
shooting pains. The door had closed again. That's what
Bobby had intended because he feared the bag might
float loose and he'd lose it. His chest began to burn and
he thought of swimming to the surface again, but he
didn't. With the buzz of adrenalin, he pulled the door
open, grabbed the bag and kicked and muscled his way
back to the surface. He lost some precious air and urinated in panic. The small rush of warm water against
his legs was soothing.

He coughed as soon as he broke from the water, and
coughed some more. Repeating the same backstroke to
the edge of the lake, he half cried out in pain as he
kicked his sore legs to shore. Greed drove him on; pain
slowed him down. His heart galloped against the con-
straint of his ribs. Twice, he mistakenly splashed water
into his mouth, and his head sprang up choking. *Concentrate on the money; don't think of anything else! I'm
almost there.* And he was! Again he turned, cradling the
bag, ready to drag it to shore. When he looked up at the
embankment, he squinted; he closed his eyes quickly
and opened them. Bobby hadn't figured on this.

That was his first thought. *I never figured on this!
Don't panic, don't panic!*

Four solid legs stood beside the first bag. Above the
legs, tall, heavyweight, burly, brawny men. Men dress-

ed in silk shirts and grey slacks, both of them. Men who
followed orders. On one of the faces, a smile broke out,
the deep-set brown eyes softened. 'Were you going to
tell us about the money?' the lips asked, the voice
almost a whisper.

Bobby waded in five feet of water clutching his bag.
Like everything else, there are degrees of panic. Bobby's
rose until it pulsed, punched and thundered. He could
hear his answer, but the sound seemed far away. 'Of
course, I was going to tell the boss. I didn't want to
make Harris' mistake of telling him he had the money
before he had the cash in his possession.' Gnawing on
his lips, Bobby waded, leery of coming to shore. He
could hear the blood pulsing in his neck.

Both men nodded and smiled, and they seemed to
relax.

Bobby kept wading, but the bag was heavy, and he
was tiring. They seemed to be enjoying his plight. But
he caught his breath and he wanted to know something.
'How did you know where I was?'

The same lips smiled and spoke again. 'That was
easy. We put a tracker under your SUV. Once you
stopped moving last night, we drove to my brother's
and caught some shuteye. We picked you up again this
morning as you made the turn up 163rd. We have to be
pretty tight on surveillance in our business. We felt you
might lead us to the money, and you did.'

For a second, before panic gripped his windpipe,
Bobby wanted to shout, 'For Christ's sake, it's our
money, not yours. We busted our asses for two years to
save it, and I was the one responsible for stockpiling it.'
But his brave thoughts never made it to the short distance between them. His legs felt as heavy as the bag. If
he dropped it, what then?

'All right,' said Lips, 'Pass Rico the bag, and he'll give you a hand back in.'

The black-stubbled quiet menace, a man in his late thirties, moved towards Bobby like an ocean liner, blocking out the sun. He waded into the muddy water and, for a second, Bobby thought it was a shame he had ruined good shoes and slacks. Although the whole lake was behind him, he was too tired to try that means of escape. He was not about to leave his cash behind either. Muddy Shoes took the bag with his right hand and flung its heavy weight through the air as though the bag were a Frisbee. Then he turned back to Bobby, extending his arm.

Bobby needed time to work this out, but there was no time. Bobby was caught in the limbo of a grey, wet world. Flinchingly, he held out his arm. Up on shore, Lips had turned away and was dragging the money bags up the bank to the trees. Muddy Shoes did not take Bobby's hand. He stepped deeper into the water and clamped his hand on Bobby's shoulder. Before he could protest, the other, meaty hand came down on his head in a vice grip, hooking his small finger into Bobby's left eye. A sharp, piercing shaft of pain exploded behind his eyeball. There would be no pocket of mercy for Bobby. Muddy Shoes pushed his head under the water. Confusion morphed with panic and a torrent of emotions.

Bobby kicked out at Muddy Shoes. He connected with one knee, but it didn't budge. He raked both arms with his nails, but they held on. It wasn't fair, Bobby thought, trying to cogitate around the knife in his eye, as a wave of weariness flooded his lungs. Then he did figure something out. *They purposely kept me in the water, letting me tire myself out. Making it easier for them.* Bobby had an idea. Rather than struggle against the vice grip, why not try to swim down and out from under the clamps? His lungs were stinging, white-hot, even in cold water. The hands held firm, boring deeper into his flesh and, in three feet of water, there was no squirm space to escape the vice. Bobby's struggle began to fade. His body went rigid when water entered his lungs and began to flood his pulmonary tissue. The rigours lasted only five or six seconds. Bobby needed time to think, to straighten things out. To accept that he would never get out of this lake alive, that he'd die younger than Harris. He managed one last thought before his body levitated and went as limp as a bundle of laundry. It was not a grammatically articulated thought because it was all over for Bobby. Something about grazing the edges of life.

Lips had walked back to the scene where he bent and picked up Bobby's clothes. 'Take his watch,' he called down. 'Get him under the trees.' As Rico dragged Bobby by his arm along the bank, blood from his eye mingled with the mud and whatever gel was left in his hair. 'That's far enough.' Lips came down to the body. 'I'll grab his legs, you take his arms and, on the count of three, toss him as far into the lake as possible. No one from the road can see us from here.'

Bobby flew through the air a good six feet into the lake, a lesser arc than the magnificent flight Harris had taken. A domestic flight, let's say. He would not have been happy – always a second to Harris, even in death. The afternoon was bright with sun and heat as the lake drained the last vestiges of life from Bobby. In his chest, the pump had broken down, and the tiniest water waves nipped at his heart. Not a single eye watched him splash down on water that was fresh and clear. Not a bad place to swim with the fishes.

Rico and Carlos walked back to the SUVs, Bobby's

and their own. Carlos threw Bobby's clothes into the trunk of the BMW X5, and they landed on top of the bags. Both men eyed the bags, a whiff of greed passed from one to the other. Carlos looked back at the lake and noticed that Bobby had not left so much as a ripple behind him. He slammed the trunk closed. He wanted to keep his hands and feet. He turned to his muscle. 'Listen carefully, Rico. Follow me. I'll drive his SUV to Bal Harbour and leave it there. With any luck, Number Boy will float downstream into the ocean. Follow me into the Bal Harbour Shops and pick me up after I stash his wheels. The boss will be pleased when we get to his place.'

'Can I go home to change before we head out to the Grove?'

'No, Rico, you can't. I want the boss to see we had to work to get this money for him. More in this for us if he sees you all muddied up.'

Rico mumbled his discontent, but he knew better then to contradict Carlos.

From the back seat of his own SUV, Carlos pulled out a brown satchel. He lifted out black gloves, a wig and a baseball cap. The wig slipped on easily over his close-cropped hair. The hat was large enough to hide his forehead. He slipped on his shades and gloves to prevent any of his DNA from showing up in Bobby's vehicle. When both men were at the wheel, they waited for the traffic to thin out before they drove back to the highway.

They still had some time before four o'clock and they might be able to head for the Grove ahead of the snag of five o'clock traffic. Disposing of the SUV at the mall went without a hitch. The attendant was on the phone and never even looked at Carlos as he drove past him into the parking lot. Of course, Lips and Muddy

Shoes had made trips similar to this one. Part of the job.
They headed west on 94th Street and turned left on
Biscayne Boulevard and set out for the Grove.

The boss had three homes in Miami, but now did
business only from his loft at the Mayfair, a spectacular
space designed by Reinaldo Borges. Located on
Virginia Street near Cocowalk, it was nestled in the
heart of the Grove. When Carlos called him on his cell,
the boss had been at the Coral Reef Yacht Club, showing off his Beneteau 373 sailboat with its patented rotating helm that turned 90 degrees. The coded news
pleased him and he drove over to his business address
and waited. He sent Ramon down to the parking area
with white towels and a steel cart. Ramon did not know
what the towels were for, but he'd soon learn from
Carlos and Rico. He waved them over to one of the
three parking spaces as soon as he spotted them.
Without wasting time on talk, they loaded the wet bags
into the cart on top of the white towels, and Rico covered the bags with another towel. The boss saw to it
that he never raised cause for alarm. As they rode the
elevator, Carlos knew one thing for certain – he wanted
a place like this. 'Sophisticated living' they called it in
the brochure downstairs, a place with nine-foot ceil-
ings, sliding glass doors, walk-in closets, marble floors,
a full bathtub in each of the three bedrooms and gran-
ite counters. Luxury, that's what life was all about.
Finding this money was a step closer, or at least a move
up from head muscle. Carlos had his plans like everybody else.

As they rode the semi-private elevator to the loft,
Carlos eyed Ramon with envy and checked his watch. It
was well after five. As 'executive assistant', the title
given to him by the boss, Ramon lived outside the
threat of muddy embankments and murder charges.

The story went that Ramon had saved the boss' life at undeniable risk to himself. The right place, at the right time, that's all it was. Carlos risked his life every week and he was still paired with Rico, the heavy. This money and the neat disposal of Bobby Wells should change the pecking order. Carlos was not thinking those exact words – he was thinking he'd like to meet Ramon on a dark corner some night. But with any vocabulary, it came down to the same thing. Carlos wanted a promotion, and these bags brought down the checkered flag.

CHAPTER THIRTY-FOUR

'I SEE YOU'VE got your arm back inside the car,' Zack said, smiling and sun-wrinkly again.

'It was falling asleep,' Caitlin confessed.

'It was there for an emergency exit, I know. So the change is not trust then.'

'Need.'

'That's what everything comes down to I guess. Are you guys hungry?'

'We just want to get home. It's been a long day.'

Carmen had not said a word. Actually, she had fallen asleep, leaning on Caitlin's shoulder. She'd be fine – exhaustion is treatable. Caitlin was busy planning their escape from Miami. As soon as they got back to the condo, she'd help Carmen into the shower and then take one herself. But first, she'd call Air Canada to see if they could fly out tonight on stand-by. They dared not spend another night at Club One. What would that gang member do once he had the money? He knew where they lived. Carmen and she would not be around to find out. What if he couldn't drag the bags from the car? He'd be royally pissed, that's what. The next thing for Caitlin was a visit to Alamo car rental. Carmen had used Caitlin's insurance because they were both going to drive the car, and Caitlin's was more comprehensive. As soon as she was cleaned up, she'd set out. When Carmen was feeling a little stronger, she could start the packing.

Against Carmen's ribbing, Caitlin kept the condo spotless each and every day. Today, that was a bonus –

there'd be little or no cleaning for them to do. Lastly, she planned to talk to Yvette and ask her to spread the word that none of their friends were to disclose that the C's lived in Montreal. Guys might come asking for them, she'd tell Yvette, because they had given them the brush-off a week ago. If they could just make a clean get-away! Order, that's what Caitlin needed to impose to work their way out from between the lines.

When Caitlin saw the traffic lights at the Newport Hotel, she straightened up, newly energized. This morning was the past – in mental anguish, it happened days ago. This minute, with familiar sights, was now. Now was all she could handle. 'Zack, turn left on Collins. We're staying at The Desert Inn not too far from the corner.'

'You've got it.'

'You can pull in up ahead. You have no idea what this ride has meant to us. Thank you so much. Without your help, we might be still sitting on the shoulder of 836.'

'No problem. Naw, someone else would have picked you up.' Zack pulled into the driveway of the motel. Caitlin reached out the window for the handle and jumped to the pavement. Carmen had woken up when Caitlin gave Zack the directions on Collins. She carefully stepped from the truck.

'Take care and good luck finding work.'

'Ya all come back next year. We need the tourists.'

'Will do.'

From now on, until they lifted off, Caitlin was going to call the shots. As soon as Zack was back on Collins, the C's made a beeline for Club One. It was just before four, and no one saw them because their friends were down at the ocean this time of day. Caitlin breathed a deep sigh of relief as soon as they locked the door

322   Sheila Kindellan-Sheehan

behind them. 'Get into the shower, Carm. I want to get us out of here tonight.'

'Tonight? We're supposed to leave tomorrow at two.'

'We're going to try to get on a flight tonight, on stand-by. The eight-thirty. We can't stay here. I don't care if we have to sleep at the airport – we can't be in this room. Get into the shower. I'll wait for a few minutes to be sure you're O.K.'

There was no argument from Carmen.

'Forget my shower; I'm going to head out to Alamo. I hope I see the cop we wave to every day on his beat beside Walgreens. He'll recognize me. I'll ask him to take the police report. Here's the official story. Some black SUV pulled too closely in front of us, and my right wheel caught the shoulder just before the curve and pulled the car down the embankment. The rest of the story doesn't vary from what really happened, minus the money bags. Do you have that, Carmen? The cop might come back here to see how you are.'

'Yeah, I have it. We were forced off the road by a black SUV.'

'Good. All right, get into the shower. We have no time to lose. Could you call Monsieur Georges and ask if he can pick us up tonight? The number is in the zippered top pocket of my backpack. I have ten dollars left. Tell him I'll send a cheque as soon as I'm home. I'm sure he'll trust us for the rest.'

Carmen reached down to unhook her hip bag. It wasn't there. 'I've lost my wallet and the forty-four dollars I had!' She began to laugh hysterically. 'I have nothing. I haven't got a cent!'

'Carmen, get a hold of yourself. Are your passport and ticket still in your luggage?'

'Yes.'

'Then you have all you need.'

Carmen walked dumbly to the bathroom, shedding her clothes as she went. She was still laughing. 'I'll call old Georges – I'll promise him a fortune at the bottom of a lake.'

'Carmen!'

By the time she left the condo, her clothes were dry, but she still drew a few stares as she walked along Collins to the car rental. The cop was on his beat, sitting in his car, waiting for speeders. She ran over to his patrol car, gave him a quick rundown and asked if he'd take the police report. He drove Caitlin the rest of the way and went into the Alamo office with her. The story was plausible – her dishevelled appearance added fodder to it.

'Were you able to see the make of the other vehicle?' the cop asked.

'Everything happened so quickly. From the few seconds he was beside me, it was a *he* and young, in his twenties, I saw the SUV. It was black, new. When he pulled dead in front of me, my wheel immediately caught the shoulder. From the second I saw the SUV in front of me, I'd say it was a Cadillac or a Buick. Florida licence plates; that I remember. The next second, we were spinning around. When that stopped, we slid into the lake.'

'Was the driver alone?'

'I think so. Yes, he was.'

'How is your friend doing? You're both extremely fortunate. Most victims are not as lucky as you two. Florida leads the country in fatal water crashes.'

'She's tired, but she's O.K. She doesn't have hospital insurance. That's why we're trying to get home tonight. She's up and around and I'd take her to emergency if I felt she needed it.'

'You're sure the accident occurred on the westbound State Road 836?'

'Yes, we were approaching the southbound turnpike ramp. The good Samaritan who picked us up said to tell you we went off the road just before the sharp turn at the right side of a clump of trees, the only ones in that area. The car is submerged about forty feet from shore. It's in a direct line with the tree on the right. He also told us we were not the first car to go into the lake in that very area.' Caitlin filled out the necessary forms, signed the police report.

Since it was her insurance, Caitlin thought of something else. Turning to the agent at the counter, she asked, 'Is the car a write-off?'

'Not necessarily. While you were filling out the forms, I called vehicle rescue. They'll try to bring the vehicle up today. I'll get back to them right after you leave. It all depends on the water damage to the major components. Your insurance company will balance the price of the vehicle and its age against the cost of repairs. The Neon was new. If we get it out of the water today, we might salvage the vehicle.'

'Officer, did you want to speak to my friend?'

'I don't think that'll be necessary. You've given me what I need for the report. Take care now.'

'You better believe it. Thank you both.' Caitlin arched her back and stretched as soon as she was back on the street and ran back to the condo.

Carmen had held up her end. 'Monsieur Georges will pick us up at seven. He trusts you, so a cheque is fine by him. Did you call Air Canada while I was in the shower?'

'Yeah, but they won't know anything for sure until flight time. I'd better get into the shower myself. Let's have a pizza tonight from across the street. We've gotta pack too. I won't feel safe until we're back in Montreal.'

Both women stood stiffly when they heard a knock at the door. Carmen slumped onto the sofa and whispered, 'Do we get that?'

'Shh…'

Whoever it was knocked again.

Caitlin tiptoed to the door and brought her eye to the peephole. In a cracked whisper, the person said, 'It's Yvette.' As she opened the door, she pulled her friend inside.

'Sorry to bother you. You both look so frightened. Is there anything I can do?'

'Were you able to speak to everyone?'

'Yes, yes. Everybody will say you are from Toronto. I sent your good-byes as well. Do you need something else?'

'We hope to get out tonight and we have only an hour and fifteen minutes to shower, eat, clean and pack.'

'I won't keep you then, but you have me concerned.'

Carmen felt hot tears well up in her eyes. 'We'll be O.K., Yvette.'

'I won't ask what happened but I will feel much better when you're both home,' Yvette told them, hugging each of the women before she left. 'Call me from Montreal.'

'For sure.'

After Yvette's departure, the apartment was a blur of activity. Suitcases flew open, clothes and cosmetics were tossed into them, tickets were placed on the kitchen table with the condo's keys beside them. In a whirlwind, Caitlin cleaned the shower, sink, floor and hung the wet towels on the small line out on the balcony, ran back inside and continued packing. She rushed across the street for the pizza, and soon the room was a blend of shampoo, cleanser, pepperoni and cheese. When the eating and work were done and the fridge emptied, the C's collapsed, one on each sofa and waited for their *chauffeur en Floride.*

When Caitlin looked out the front window and saw his car pull in, she ran out to greet and thank him. Georges lifted their bags into the trunk, and the C's hopped into the car. As they left Club One, Caitlin saw Yvette standing in the driveway and she waved back at her.

Monsieur Georges handed Caitlin a copy of his name and address. Caitlin assured him she'd mail him a cheque the day after she got back to Westmount. No one spoke much on the way to the Fort Lauderdale-Hollywood Airport. Georges secretly worried about his money – the C's quietly worried about their lives. Then they fretted about time. Ubiquitous construction forced Georges to take one detour after another. When they finally reached the airport, Georges unloaded the bags, and the women grabbed them and lugged them to the Air Canada counter.

The line was long, a motley collection of tanned faces, howling children running in between waiting passengers, boulder-sized luggage pushed, shoved, yanked, even kicked forward with each new inch gained as the line snaked toward the counter. Nerves frayed, shoulders slumped with fatigue and anxiety and passengers were at the stage where they began to wonder if the vacation was worth all this bedlam. The C's sat on their bags when they were not pushing them one foot forward every five minutes.

When they finally reached the counter, Caitlin gave the ticket agent a glorious smile she did not feel in exchange for false hope. 'Well,' he said. 'There's good news and bad news. Freezing rain has delayed the eight-thirty in Montreal; the good news is that five minutes ago, a couple decided to take the early flight tomorrow morning, so I have two seats for you. The rain has stopped in Montreal, and we expect the flight to arrive at ten-thirty. You should be out of here by eleven or eleven-fifteen. That's our hope.'

'Better than we deserve,' Caitlin answered. 'I mean, arriving this late and snagging two seats.' At the inspection desk, people all around them were asked to take off their sneakers. The C's must have looked harmless because apart from totes x-rayed and bodies checked, they were left alone. Caitlin took both boarding passes, and the C's walked past a limited array of fast food, Nathan's foot-long hotdogs in particular, the duty-free counter, down the long corridor to gate twenty-two. 'Carmen, we can't sit here. Find a seat at the Houston gate across the way; I'll sit with the Detroit crowd. We can't be seen together. Try to get some sleep.' Zombie-like, Carmen found a seat, slumped into it and was soon fast asleep. On the other side of the large room, Caitlin fought the urge to sleep and kept vigil from behind her South Beach cap.

CHAPTER THIRTY-FIVE

THE ELEVATOR THE men took to the loft was semi-private and serviced only one other apartment on that floor. Ahead of the two men, Ramon pulled the cart across the palest green carpet Carlos had ever seen. The silk walls in the hall were lit by brass torch lamps. When they reached the door, Ramon called the boss from his cell. Carlos and Rico stood a few feet behind him. The phone he used today would be discarded. Inside the apartment, a walk-in closet was stacked with new cell phones. Twice a day the loft was swept for electronic bugs, as it was thirty minutes before the arrival of the three men. In fact, the boss would not do business here for more than a couple of months and then he'd put the unit on the market. He opened the blue steel door himself and motioned the men inside.

Carlos was awed by the elegance of the loft. The boss waved the men across a marble foyer to a spacious room of high-end furniture and fixtures, all the work of a renowned architect. He had designed everything from the floor to the ceiling and managed to harvest, with the assistance of an import/export company, endangered mangrove wood from Guatemala for the end tables. The sofas were rich leathers of deep blue, their armrests sculpted by hand-wrought details. The wall boasted authentic Art Deco. The living room, though very large, was a carefully utilized space, cornered by red-beaded star lamps that created the intimacy and the ambiance of old world Cuba, bathed in ocean colours. Carlos remained standing, and Rico, in his muddy shoes, had not moved from the doorway.

The first impression of the boss, 'the man' as he was also called, who inspired fear and dread in his own men, was always disbelief. Pedro Duarte looked nothing like these three 'made' men he employed. For one thing, he wasn't yet thirty. If one passed him on the street, if the stranger took notice at all, he'd feel that Pedro was a graduate student from an ivy-league college. An inch over six feet, he was as slim and as fit as the late John F. Kennedy Junior. In a short-sleeved silk shirt, linen slacks and Magli loafers, Pedro wore only two accessories. A Cartier watch with a brown alligator band and a gold signet ring with a hand-carved family crest. His small professor glasses camouflaged the eyes behind the lenses. Pedro's eyes were dark brown with flecks of black coal.

Pedro also had an annoying manner of speaking, not actually in a whisper, but so purposely low, that he forced his listeners to bend forward like old men to catch his words. Carlos and Rico were heavy-handed men who bulldozed the way for youngsters like Pedro, but they never forgot that Pedro was the one who casually muttered the order to tear the thread of a life apart as though he were asking for a weather report. He was out of their league, and the men did not enjoy his company. No one was safe, not even them. 'Sit,' Pedro gestured. 'Ramon, put a chair by the door for Rico.'

Ramon rolled the money cart beside his chair. Pedro did not touch the cash; nor did he rise to see the bags bundled in towels. Ramon would open them in a minute or two and later verify the amount. Soon after, another man would take charge of the money, depositing it in a storage locker whose address not even Ramon would know. It was a real shame that Bobby and

Pedro never met because both men shared a meticulous love of detail and figures.

'Good work, men,' Pedro said.

In an effort to impress the boss, Carlos tried to be as brief. 'All in a day's work.'

Pedro talked as though the money were not even there, ten feet away from him, as though it were an afterthought. 'I'm pleased. Effort should be rewarded.' He even spoke like a graduate student.

Carlos nodded, not knowing what to say, afraid to appear greedy. Yet, he could not resist licking his upper lip.

'I guess the next move is yours Ramon.'

For the first time, Carlos leaned back in his chair, allowing both arms to dangle from the side. Bringing both his muddy shoes together, Rico leaned forward – he wanted to see the cash.

Ramon stood, bent over, removed the top towel and spread it across the floor. With one hand, he lifted the first bag out of the cart and laid it on the towel. He did the same for the second.

Carlos sat up – his scalp tightened. *Effort should be rewarded.* That's what Pedro had said; that's what Carlos wanted. He could smell the money. He flexed his neck, and his short ponytail pulled at the back of his head. The small craters on Rico's cheeks widened.

Ramon unzipped the first bag, reached in and pulled out soggy telephone sheets, protection for the cash, he supposed. He reached in again and pulled out more of the same sheets, actually chunks of telephone books. 'Jesus!'

Pedro's expression did not change, except for a mirthless laugh.

Blood leapt from one valve to another in Carlos' heart. Rico thought the cash might all be in the second bag.

Ramon tore into the second bag, more phonebook chunks...

Pedro's left eye began to twitch, stabbed by the facts in front of him. 'We have a problem,' he said softly.

Rico stiffened against his chair. Carlos tried to focus on what went wrong and not on the penalty he and Rico might soon suffer. 'I don't know what happened, Boss.'

'Sure you do. You've come to my home with torn up telephone books instead of the merchandise. That's pretty clear, wouldn't you say?'

'Boss, we didn't want to touch the bags before you had them.'

'Was that very wise?' Pedro's eyebrow began to quiver and he took off his glasses.

'I...' Carlos wished the venom of Pedro's words were aimed at the person standing directly behind. But behind him was only a locked steel door.

Pedro brought his shoulders up tight, clasped his fingers into a steeple. His knuckles were white, and he looked like a long coiled screw. 'Well,' he hissed, 'you'll have to bring Bobby Wells to this office.'

Carlos shot a look back at Rico. Rico looked away; he could feel his bowels loosening. Carlos knew the silence in the room was a string that began with him and could be cut. He felt the knife. 'We can't bring him to the office.'

'Why is that?' Pedro asked, levelling each of his three words with a threat.

'We had the money – we thought you didn't want loose ends.'

'You thought!' Pedro spoke, barely above a whisper. 'Do I pay you to think?'

Carlos dropped his head before he made another mistake – he offered an idea. 'Wells thought he had the money. He wouldn't have gone into the lake after it if he didn't think the cash was in the car. We were sure he had the money.'

'But you were wrong, Carlos. Bring me the people he was chasing. You know where they live because you stayed on Wells' tail.'

This time Carlos' silence was as icy cold as the marble floor. He shivered, alone as any defendant. Even the air was silent. Cold sweat dripped from his eyebrows.

Giving no quarter, Pedro whispered, 'Well?'

Like a cold blast of air from an air conditioner, a fresh terror blew through him. 'We both fell asleep after three; we didn't see where the women lived; we picked Wells up on 163rd Street.'

Pedro put his glasses back on and looked with sadness on this employee. 'I like things neat, Carlos. Let's review the details. Harris lost the money, the women took it, Bobby found them and risked his life to retrieve the cash. It doesn't really matter where the women are, does it? There is only one important question.'

Carlos fought to keep his balance. The floor was moving under his feet, blurring the lines.

Pedro leaned back, crossed a leg and dropped his chin into the palm of his hand. Quite drained of passion, he asked his last question. 'What did you do with my money, Carlos?'

Carlos shrank inside his clothes, giving him the appearance of a scarecrow. A fresh strip of goosebumps rode up his arms. Grabbing his stomach with one hand, he tried to keep his guts from falling out. He had watched Rico put three men down in the four years he had worked for Pedro, had stood by impassively. Had watched without pity as panic leached into the vital organs of each of those men. It was his habit to light up a cigarette as Rico unleashed the vertical blow of death. He looked back at Rico slumping in his chair, a muddy, grieving clown.

Carlos felt strangely present in this moment; the past and the future came together with the seconds that were bleeding from his life. All these neurons collided, scalding the air to his brain. He was no one now, a cipher, like all the rest.

Ramon had moved and he stood in front of the door now with a pager palmed in his hand.

An idea found its way through the sweat pooling down his legs, though what courage he had left was fast leaking out of him. A last ditch thing, common as sun in Miami. 'Pedro, give me the same chance you gave Chalmer. Three days.'

Pedro's mouth was sad. 'There's a difference, Carlos. Chalmer was an amateur – you're a professional.'

CHAPTER THIRTY-SIX

A SOMBRE CLOUD settled over Club One. Everybody felt sorry in the place where it hurts most. After the triumph of Steve's wake, the sadness of his death lingered in the sand around the deck. Yvette always felt at loose ends at the end of the vacation when the Florida gang began to pack for home, but this year, she felt downright uneasy. Everything about this vacation was all angles. Caitlin and Carmen's sudden departure left questions and worry up and down the halls.

Raoul felt he had betrayed the C's and he walked his own self-imposed gauntlet past the guests. Morty and Sarah were packing in their rooms though they had another three days. Sarah wanted to keep busy. She looked at all the candy in her purse and realized how little she had seen of the C's. This vacation had big holes. That's what Sarah thought. Yvette knew something about the mystery of the C's, but Sarah knew enough not to approach her. Morty left his wife and decided to take a second walk along the beach. He passed Michel talking to some newcomer and did not interrupt. There was no one out back. It was past dinnertime.

Morty noticed the door to the cabana was open. He popped his head in and called out. 'Anybody home?' Strange, he thought. He pushed the door a little and took a few steps inside. It wasn't like Larry to leave his things without locking up. He called again. 'Hello Larry!' The room was silent. Morty stole farther into the room and shouted, 'Larry, are you here?' He stood and scratched his head. *Ah, he's over working on the deck!*

Pulling the door tightly shut, he left the cabana and padded over to the deck above The Sands Motel. The boards, nails and hammer Larry had taken from the basement of the condo lay on the side of the deck. 'Larry, are you under there?' But he wasn't. Within minutes, all the guests who hadn't gone out for dinner were searching for Larry. It was bad enough to lose Steve!

Sarah and Yvette led the women – Michel and Morty led the men. Ten minutes later, the search party met out back under the blue umbrella. Morty had an idea. 'Maybe Steve's death was too hard on Larry. I don't believe he would ever have gone back to The Sands Motel if he lost his work here at Club One; he could never lie on the sand where he lost his friend.'

His words were met with nods.

Sarah had a better idea. 'Morty, do you remember the homeless man we hired years ago in our garment shop?'

'Yes, yes I do. He swept up and washed walls for us – we paid him the same wages we gave our only salesgirl.'

'Go on, Morty,' coaxed Sarah.

'Well, one morning he never showed up. We heard later he'd gone out drinking. The odd thing was Sarah and I saw him sitting against a wall in a lane about ten days later, and he saw us, but he never came back to work. I guess there is an underlying reason these men are homeless, something we can't correct with work and wages. A few days ago, I had a good talk with Larry. He'd set goals for himself; maybe those goals broke him.' Morty grabbed hold of the wooden railing, looked out into the ocean and said, 'I don't think Larry will ever come back. Steve's ghost is a reminder of the way he might end up.'

Now, the Florida gang was downright numb. They headed for their rooms in silence.

🌴

At the airport, twice Caitlin fell into a slouch and her head fell back against the seat in sleep. Twice, she jerked her head back to consciousness. Yet there was no need for such vigilance. Pedro had taken his dues from Carlos and Rico. He was a man who knew when to cut his losses and move on. A few times, when Caitlin looked over at her sleeping friend, she thought of severing their ties once they got home. What did we really know of anyone? Caitlin had to admit that she herself was not the same person she'd been just ten days ago. Yet, she could not deny that a double rescue had taken place in the deep waters of the lake. She had shed a skin so tightly bound she'd only dared take shallow breaths in the past three years. Risk and gain, for both of them.

She was also forced to admit that saving Carmen's life also brought with it a cord of responsibility that could grow taut or loose in the years ahead. She doubted Carm would continue to live on the edge, but, whatever the case, Caitlin saw that she could not abandon her friend. After all, she thought, they shared a private history that bound them to one another. Who but Carmen could reminisce about the saga of The Sands Motel? Laugh and roar and weep about it. She understood now that running along the edges shakes the heart and fires the nerves, but it can also allow the runner to sit quietly in a chair, huddling with redemption.

The call for boarding, with all its excitement and frustration over the long delay, woke Carmen, but according to plan, she stayed well behind Caitlin until they were on the plane. Once they were seated, they watched the passengers, trying to determine if any of these strangers was hunting them down. When their plane rolled to the head of the runway, they held hands until it was high in the air, levelling off. If their friendship remained a body of unfinished business, for the moment, they had mutual trust, not a bad thing to work with.

Within the first half hour, Carmen crawled over Caitlin to the aisle to check the passport she had just stored in the overhead compartment. 'I want to see the money that isn't there,' she laughed. With almost one full day of sleep to her credit, she was stoked with energy. Dragging her bag down from overhead, she remarked, 'Geez, this thing is falling apart. I'll have to buy a new one when I get home.'

Caitlin tried hard not to comment, but she failed. 'Any colour but yellow!'

'You're back! Don't fall asleep now – stay with me. I did a lot of thinking at the airport.'

'Thinking! You were asleep before you hit the chair.'

'Don't be mean now. I woke up a few times. Anyway, I was thinking I'll find a part-time job when I get back home, use that money to pay off my credit cards and begin to save for next year's vacation from my regular salary.' She motioned for Caitlin to let her finish. 'I know Miami is off limits for us. I've been thinking that we didn't have a real vacation this year, due to unforeseen circumstances.'

'Unforeseen circumstances?'

'In a way, right? Doesn't change the fact that next year we'll need a break. Hell, I could use a break right now! What about Cuba?'

'Cuba?'

'What kind of trouble can we get into there?'

338

EPILOGUE

IAN, FORMERLY KNOWN as Nipples, had taken his reprieve seriously. Stepping into Bobby's position on the consignment account, he had supervised the new college mules and collected the drug money owed to the boss. Ian had packaged the cash and handed it over to Pedro himself. The episode of the lost two million was a closed chapter. Retribution had been made. The mushroom cloud of suspicion never hung above his head because the only two gang members who could have linked him to the long-ago police call that began the downward spiral had moved out of harm's way. Ian's father was transferred to Atlanta, and greedy, reckless, young collegians stepped into Ian's vacated position on campus, continuing the chain of risk and waste. Ian was free! At Georgia State University, his grades greatly improved. Unfortunately, while channel surfing one night, Ian came across the new television series, *Nip/Tuck*. Temptation is a cruel master.

Bobby Wells spent his first of these eight months in great demand. On the one hand, his parents and the police searched far and wide for him. Ian gave what help he could. Bobby was sick with food poisoning, and he had spoken with him both days before his disappearance. On the other hand, beneath the surface of things, the fish of the lake had Bobby for dinner every night for weeks. When their invitations dried up, without his beloved gel and most of his flesh, like a mammoth spider, Bobby floated from the lake to the ocean edges. Once he was scooped from the water, identification had not been an easy task. Only dental records saved Bobby from the crash and burn of oblivion. Not the loose brackets of opinion, but hard, cold facts had put a name to the bones on the gurney. Bobby would have been pleased.

Club One had not been sold as all feared it would be. The gang, without the C's, had already booked for next year.

For months, The Sands Motel withstood the burden of tragedy. Steve's ashes mingled with the sand around the old deck. The boards and nails and hammer that Larry had planned to use for renovation on their 'motel' were returned to Club One in the first few days after his disappearance. The sandy bed under the deck remained empty. Still, there were flowers left for Steve by tourists who didn't even know him. The place was quiet until Monday morning of the third month. It took twelve days to raze The Desert Inn beside Club One – it took only a few minutes to level the deck, better remembered as The Sands Motel. Maybe that was for the best, everything considered.

Larry had not gone back to dumpster diving in the lanes of South Beach, nor was he holed up across a picnic table on Haulover Beach. Larry had gone to work with Toothbrush at The Bar. The cooled-down section between 70th Street and 68th Street on Collins that had fizzled for the last twelve years was suddenly *hot* again. *Cool* started making its real comeback a few months after Larry's return. Toothbrush and he had stood across the street as The Bar went under the ball and hammers. Old regulars stumbled after them, cursing and slapping poor Toothbrush on the back to say 'thanks for the good times'. The old dive, handcuffed by the trendiest new restos, fruit bars, designer duds shops, art boutiques, even a *Nip/Tuck* facsimile, was the last wisdom tooth to be painfully extracted from the history of the street. The simple sign, grimy, rusted, beaten up, a sign that had never grumbled about its humble setting, crumbled when it was pulled from the wall.

The next day, Larry and Toothbrush sat on old bar stools they'd carried from the tavern to the sidewalk and watched its resurgence. Construction material arrived daily. The black hole was hammered and stretched and painted and bricked. The floor was tiled and sanded down. An apartment was set up in the back and Toothbrush and Larry moved in together. Bar counters, tables, chairs, booze, glassware, murals, everything but a doorman for this A-grade club, began to take up space with careful execution and deft planning. The social network of the Miami scene is as deep as the ocean, so this place didn't need promoters. The super-confident young crowd of Cubans who now swarmed the area every weekend discovered the new drinking hole. They quickly added it to their web of nightclub connections and gave the place a certain *frisson*. The guys' new place was edgy, impossible, but it worked!

Larry was glad Toothbrush had decided against retiring, happier he had kept one of the old stools. The 'Brush' did not forget his regulars – Monday was 'crony night'. Drinks were fifty cents a pop. During the rest of the week, money rolled in like the Atlantic tide. Toothbrush grew a handlebar moustache. He perched on his old stool, regaling the hip-hop brats, the new kings of the dot-com world, the beautiful people with buff bodies and tight clothes, even celebs who elbowed their way into the place, with a history lesson of the 'block'. The gangstas, the drugs, the rum running, the murders... A new page opened in the lives of both men.

Around four-thirty each morning, Larry closed up and walked across Collins to have a good look at the place. Carrying a crystal champagne flute, he tossed back a little of the bubbly and toasted miracles. Some nights, he thought about The Sands Motel, but less often with each passing week. Mostly, he stood alone, admiring the new bright yellow neon marquee flashing the name he had chosen for the christening – *Money Bags!*

ACKNOWLEDGEMENTS

MUCH GRATITUDE TO my publishers Michael and David Price for their warm welcome, punctual feedback, good two-way exchange, diligence and enthusiasm.

I owe a huge debt of thanks to my friends, the proofers and editors. Thanks to Gina Pingitore for her support from the outset, extending herself even at times when her own work was piled high on her desk, to Sandy Jarymowycz for her technical skill and professional work and Judith Isherwood for her edits and time.

Thank you, Glen and Ted, for a great cover and detailed maps. A big hug for my sister Mary, always my first reader and my powerhouse sales rep.

I feel an enduring appreciation for Sunny Isles, Florida that for many years has shared its sand and sun and stretch of ocean with me. I carry your memory, etched on my heart, back to Canada.

ABOUT THE AUTHOR

SHEILA KINDELLAN-SHEEHAN is a Quebec-born writer who winters in Miami. Her memoir, *Sheila's Take*, was published by Shoreline Press in 2003 to critical and popular acclaim. *The Sands Motel* is her first novel.